RUSSELL B. FARR is the founding editor of Ticonderoga Publications and has published over sixty titles since 1996. His anthology, *Belong*, explored the concepts of home and migration. Previous works as editor include award-winning anthologies *Fantastic Wonder Stories* and *Dead Red Heart*, award-winning collections by Sean Williams, Angela Slatter, Lisa L. Hannett, and Kate Forsyth and Kim Wilkins, and Australia's first work-themed anthology *The Workers' Paradise*. In 2013 he was the recipient of the A. Bertram Chandler Award for 'outstanding achievement in Australian science fiction'.

Russell lives in Greenwood, Western Australia, with his wonderful wife Liz Grzyb, an unimpressed, sociopathic cat and an enthusiastic puppy. He also likes whisky.

AURUM

A GOLDEN ANTHOLOGY OF ORIGINAL AUSTRALIAN FANTASY

A GOLDEN ANTHOLOGY OF ORIGINAL AUSTRALIAN FANTASY

EDITED BY

RUSSELL B. FARR

I'm blaming this one on the original Eidolon *crew: Jeremy G. Byrne, Jonathan Strahan, Richard Scriven, Robin Pen, Chris Stronach, and Keira McKenzie; who threw a rock in a pond almost 30 years ago that is still making ripples.*

Aurum edited by Russell B. Farr

Published by Ticonderoga Publications

All stories are original to this collection.

Designed and edited by Russell B. Farr
Typeset in Sabon and Cheltenham

A Cataloging-in-Publications entry for this title is available from The National Library of Australia.

ISBN 978-1-925212-32-7 (limited hardcover)
978-1-925212-33-4 (trade hardcover)
978-1-925212-34-1 (trade paperback)
978-1-925212-35-8 (ebook)

Ticonderoga Publications
PO Box 29 Greenwood
Western Australia 6924

www.ticonderogapublications.com

10 9 8 7 6 5 4 3 2 1

#61

The editor would like to thank Jo Anderton, Stephanie Gunn, Juliet Marillier, Angie Rega, Cat Sparks, Lucy Sussex, and Susan Wardle for their incredible words and extraordinary patience; all of our fabulous crowdfunders; Janeen Webb and Jack Dann, who've had faith in me for over 20 years; Angela Slatter, Kaaron Warren, and Anna Tambour for always pushing me to do better; Anthony Phillips for his everlasting enthusiasm; and the incredible Liz Grzyb for everything, always.

CONTENTS

WORTH ITS WAIT . . .

$23219.17

WENTY-THREE THOUSAND, TWO hundred and nineteen dollars and seventeen cents. That's what this book would be worth if it was solid 24 carat gold (if you've bought the limited hardcover you're looking at a cool $31,682.67).

You're holding a bargain, because I sincerely doubt you paid that much for this book (or any book, but if you are in the habit of paying $20K for a single book, call me).

There's a lot of gold in this book, over 250 pages of it. I'll try not to keep you away from it for too long, but with *Aurum* being so close to my heart, bear with me. I might even be able to give you a paragraph or two that don't have numbers.

Gold is gold, valuable, pretty, and shiny. When it is put in the hands of a skilled artist, its value is increased, and true treasure is made. Sometimes treasure is made, then lost, and only discovered years later.

This should have been the 50th Ticonderoga book, that was the plan hatched at convention in Canberra when I realised that there was a milestone looming. I'm not a big one for celebrating my own achievements, but even 50 seemed to be A Big Deal. It's a tough gig, there aren't too many small press editors in Australia who've made it that far. I flipped a mental coin, do I make something of a best of, puling together some favourites of the hundreds of stories I've published, or could I make something new, something original. No points for guessing the result, as the "o" word is on the cover.

For maybe the next six months to a year, I enthused, and asked a whole bunch of writers whose work I admire to consider writing something for me. Along the way I also got the idea to ask for longer works, novellas 10,000 to 20,000 words, stories that gave the writer some space to tell a full tale. And then I faltered, and a bunch of things happened.

While I started putting this intro together in my head, one of my big early influences, Harlan Ellison, passed away. Love him, hate him, be confused or perplexed by him, it doesn't matter, but now I've got him in my head, his incredible introduction to Tom Reamy's *San Diego Lightfoot Sue and Other Stories*, and his equally moving intro to his own collection *Angry Candy*, and this isn't exactly going to be the introduction I was planning a week ago.

It's not going to be a brutal and honest Ellisonesque evisceration of anything, I stopped trying to write like Harlan at least 20 years ago. It will be honest, and tinged with sadness, and will hopefully touch you, the reader, in some way, like good writing should.

In between conceiving this book and me throwing these final thoughts out there, the sf field has lost a lot of unique and powerful talents. Just this year we've said goodbye to Kate Wilhelm, Ursula K. LeGuin, Australia's own Peter Nicholls, Mary Rosenblum, and Gardner Dozois. No one lives forever, and no one is irreplaceable, these incredible writers and editors were once young turks ready to show their own elders and betters just what they were made of, only to become the establishment for new young voices to love and hate, challenge and admire.

Between starting and finishing this book I had the chance to briefly meet Tanith Lee, Kit Reed, Susan Casper, and Brian Aldiss, including hearing Mr Aldiss accept a lifetime achievement award with the rousing words, "I'm not done yet!" The world is without their voices now. We don't get to choose when we are born or when we die, only how we live the time in between. And the words we leave behind.

For everyone who has waited the years to hold this book in their hands, including the incredibly generous crowd funding backers, I'll ask for a little more time and indulgence, as there are a handful of people who have been waiting even longer. Back to Mr Ellison, for perhaps the last time, as there have been moments when *Aurum* was looking like *The Last Dangerous Visions*, a millstone to forever weight me down, an anthology of unseen gems destined never to shine together in sunlight. During this time, the writers you'll soon be reading, Stephanie Gunn, Susan Wardle, Juliet Marillier, Lucy Sussex, Cat Sparks, Angela Rega, and Joanne Anderton, have had the greatest patience with me. They've let me hold on to their incredible stories, and kept the faith, believing that the day would come and this book would be thrust into the world. Thank you.

I first started reading Jo Anderton about ten years ago, and she was kind enough to write me a wonderful vampire story the last time my name graced the cover of a book. Her stories are as dark as she is light, she is one of those wonderful people who fools us all, she doesn't look like the person who would write the deep dark tales that are published in her name. In "I Almost Went to the Library Last Night" she gives us an excellently gritty dystopia wrapped around a good look at ourselves. Streetwise and clever, much like the writer, who I should add is an excellent companion should you need to take a train through Melbourne's less glamorous south-eastern suburbs.

It gives me great pleasure to have Stephanie Gunn in this anthology. I first met Ms Gunn in the slushpile maybe 15 years ago, and I flagged her as a writer to watch. The early stories she sent were delicate, ethereal, atmospheric. I longed for the day when she would give the reader more: incredible worlds, strong characters, the whole package. She's exceeded all expectations, and has become an incredible voice with her tales of strength, compassion, heart and soul. "Pinion" gives us an incredible glimpse into a world of haves and have-nots.

Juliet Marillier needs no introduction, certainly not from someone like me. It's hard to believe I've been fortunate enough to publish a book of her short stories, as well as the simply stunning "Beautiful" at the end of this book. Most readers will know her from her longer works and series, yet she can still create incredibly moving tales in the space of a few thousand words. "Beautiful" is all that and more, bringing an overlooked character to the front and centre in this retelling of a Danish fairy tale.

Where do I start to talk about the wonderful Angie Rega? One of the most positive people I've ever met, caring, dedicated, and full of Mediterranean generosity—I have never left her company with an empty stomach or a sad face. I think we met after she sent me a wonderful story for *Belong*, a touching tale of old world customs in the new world, and cooking. In "With this Needle I Thee Thread" she stitches love and hope together in a moving, magical tale.

No one writes dystopian futures like Cat Sparks, tales where humanity confidently races headlong into the looming abyss, full of dogged determination to make the best of a rapidly disintegrating situation. I feel this is a theme dear to Cat's heart: she started Agog Press after I wrote an article outline exactly why going into small press was absolute folly. She faultlessly explores this theme further in the sublime "And the Ship Sails On".

Lucy Sussex intimidates the absolute bejeezus out of me, I don't know how else to put it. Quietly spoken with a tremendous intellect, I first encountered her through her transcendent collection *My Lady Tongue and Other Tales*, whose title story alone is well worth the price of admission and I will be forever in awe of the mind that conceived it. "Lady Brilliana" is another amazing piece of writing, blinding us with science, history, and a cat.

Time to state the obvious: Susan Wardle doesn't write enough. I've been a huge fan of her work since "Iron Shirt" leapt out of the slushpile at me in around 2005, but due to a bunch of perfectly reasonable reasons her output over the years has added up to maybe a dozen published pieces. I was going to say that the reasons for this are understandable, but there's just a small part of me that doesn't understand how the world allows such a unique voice to be so muffled. If the haunting tale "Shatterglass" doesn't stay with you long after you've finished reading it, I mourn your cold lifeless heart. And if it does continue to resonate once Isobel's last notes fade, tell Susan to write more.

Seven damn awesome writers. Anderton, Gunn, Marillier, Rega, Sparks, Sussex, and Wardle can write just about anyone under the table. This is as good a dream team as any editor could hope to put together, whether for a superb table of contents, or as back up in a bar fight.

I'm not going to bore you or feed you any lines about why it has taken so long for these seven magnificent tales to see the light of day: as understandable as my excuses are, what is more important is that you have these stories now, to read, savour, share. These may be the last stories I have the pleasure of revealing to an uncertain world, they may be the last stories you read, or we may both be around sharing inspirational tales of awe for many years to come.

Far from being the golden fiftieth, *Aurum* is the sixty-first book from Ticonderoga. Sixty-one books in twenty-two years is a fair achievement for a small press, the product of my own dogged determination to keep publishing fantastic and amazing stories like these seven. I'm struck by the image of a lone prospector panning in a gold rush, hunched over a stream sifting and scrubbing, digging and agitating; when truthfully I'm the last one awake in the house with a laptop on my legs and a snoring dog at my feet.

There is gold in these pages, 24 carat solid gold. While this gold does glister, you won't just find nuggets lying around, you'll be captivated by what these artisans have made from the gold: threads as fine as any spider web, designs that capture the imagination, rings that bind any heart that beats, perfect orbs held in intricate patterns that catch the light just so. Which might all just be a fancy way of telling you that this book will be very hard to put down.

Now it's your turn to bravely enter these seven amazing, dangerous, and thrilling worlds, where you'll be surrounded by characters driven by love and determined to do the best they can no matter what they've been dealt.

There is gold in this book, all you have to do to discover it is turn the page.

Russell B. Farr
June 2018

SHATTERGLASS

SUSAN WARDLE

ATHER FOUND US IN THE GARDEN—Tommaso with his breeches around his ankles and me with my skirts in disarray. I wasn't fearful—we were destined to be together and not all the rage of my Father could stop the singing in my soul.

Locked in my room, I spent the quiet hours in a haze of daydream and memory. I was sixteen when Tommaso first came for dinner. At twenty he and my brother, Alberto were so grown up *and* handsome in their evening attire. Flustered by their presence, I fumbled my wine glass. It fell, throwing red wine across the damask tablecloth. Alberto leapt up—his face red. Dark spots marked his new fawn vest.

"Isobel!" he spat the word at me.

My chest ached as if a stone had lodged between the wings of my ribcage.

Then Tommaso smiled gently across the table, his brown hair half hiding his eyes. "It's just a spot Alberto. Besides, that colour never suited you."

Alberto glared at me before his features relaxed into a half smile. "Waste of good wine," he said more mildly.

I smiled at Tommaso and my heart thumped when his lips curved in response.

A few months later, Tommaso caught me practicing my music while visiting Alberto. "You play well." He sat beside me on the narrow clavicord bench. "Do you know Maria's Song?"

I nodded, fingers finding the keys. Self consciously I sang the first few words and he joined me—his voice merging with mine. Until that moment ours had not been a joyful house.

The steady replay of happy moments slowly faded as I waited in my room. I watched from the window day and night until the clock stopped ticking and I knew that what I believed never existed.

A tap on the door dragged me from my fugue.

"Sister? Isobel?" Alberto put his head around the corner. I stared at him listlessly. "Father wants to talk to you."

I shook my head. "I can't."

"You must. Edda is bringing you some food. Eat it, wash, dress and brush your hair."

Edda bustled in behind him, a tray in her hands. The smell of chicken broth came with her and my traitorous stomach growled.

"Why hasn't he come?" I whispered to Alberto as Edda laid the tray on my side table.

"His family won't allow it."

"Money?"

Alberto nodded. I exhaled a long trembling breath and forced away the tears that threatened.

He gripped my hand. "I will see you downstairs. Don't take too long." With a curt instruction to Edda to see to my toilet he left, his steps echoing on the bare floorboards. We may have a direct blood link to the Duke—but our fortunes didn't match our nobility.

After the first few mouthfuls I lost my appetite and pushed the bowl to one side.

"Your water is ready," said Edda gently.

It was both a relief and a sadness to wash away the salt and the staleness of two days and nights of vigil. In doing so I also erased the last touch of Tommaso from my skin. My eyes prickled .

"Come child. Get dressed." Edda put a soft towel into my hands.

I dried myself quickly and let her help me into a fresh chemise.

"I've laid out a blouse and skirt my lady." It was the black velveteen skirt that I'd worn after our mother passed. The blouse cut down from a dress of hers made of finest linen with a lace collar and cuffs. A sombre outfit.

Thus armed against my father's wrath, I left my room and walked down the stairs, not rushing, not riding the bannister and wailing like a Demoni as I had done as a child.

Father was in his study. Since Mother died it was the room he lived in during his waking hours. The curtains were threadbare and there were gaps on the shelves where the first editions and collectors items had been sold off.

"Isobel." He steepled his fingers.

"Father." I sat and brushed some imaginary dust from my skirt.

He sighed. New lines had gouged their way into his forehead. He looked weary. His rages I could cope with, but not this.

"I'm sorry Papa," I said softly.

He reached across the table to me and I let him take my hand.

"The city is aware of your disgrace. Tommaso has not been discreet."

I felt cold all over. "No! He would not do that. Someone else must have seen us."

Papa shook his head. "There is no-one else. Who other than you, your brother and your woman know of this business?"

I shook my head unable accept the betrayal. Father was still speaking—mouth moving, grey eyes serious. I forced myself to listen.

"Do you understand? The Duke will not forgive this. You will not be allowed back into society. Our families are too close. He will not recognize you—not without the promise of a marriage."

I gripped his hand. "Talk to Tommaso's father. Tommaso loves me—I know he does."

"What do you think I have been doing the past two days? Tommaso's father will not receive me or your brother. He will not marry you." Papa sighed. "There is only one option. I have written to the Council and put your name forward as a Shatterglass bride."

A chill engulfed my scalp. "No! Papa. I cannot go. Let me stay here. I will live in seclusion and look after you and Alberto." Sharp-eyed Signora Costa was a returned Shatterglass bride. She lived up our street and never appeared without a veil. She was apparently as hideously disfigured by the Shatterglass sickness as she was wealthy.

Papa continued as if I had not spoken. "Council met today and it has been agreed. An airship leaves tomorrow morning. You will be on it. You will be treated with all the respect of your position as a member of the royal family and as an affianced woman. There will be no more talk of your disgrace."

I threw myself at his feet. "Please, Papa. Anything else. I will get the sickness. Is that what you want?"

"Not all get the sickness. You are of good bloodline and healthy. You may return after ten years, earlier if you bear them three children. You will still be a young woman with your life in front of you and all smear on your name removed."

"No!" The tears I had denied myself over the last night and day as I realised Tommaso was not coming started to fall. I sat at my Father's feet, my head in his lap and wept as I had after Mother coughed her last.

He hadn't promised me then that it would be alright. He didn't promise me now.

* * *

It was a beautiful dawn, the sun rising in a purple and pink sky over the red sands of the Great Inland Sea. The airship bobbed lightly against its ropes, its green silk balloon hovering above it, ready to lift it into place in that palatte of gold tinted hues.

Alberto stood beside me, the shadows on his chin matching the dark lines under his eyes. He'd met me at the front door, coming in as I went out for the last time. His lips and teeth stained with red wine. I was grateful for his company. Papa had said his farewells last night.

Even while I watched the airship being loaded my eyes flickered around the dock, looking for that familiar fall of brown hair, the shy smile that was no reflection of the man. If yearning could have made him appear—then Tommaso should have been on that dock.

My trunks were already loaded, Edda wept silently to one side. I kissed her cheek and tasted her tears. "Go home, Edda. You must look after Papa and Alberto for me. Make sure they write."

Beside me Alberto grunted. He'd ever been a poor correspondent. His compulsory military service had been punctuated with two line letters—usually requesting money.

"I'll visit," he said abruptly.

"You will?" My heart leapt.

"Once your dowry comes in there will be money."

I hugged him. He stood stiffly in my arms. "Go on, they're calling for you." He pointed to the gangway where a veiled servant waited. I shuddered.

"Head up," said Alberto, as if he could read my hesitation—and I went—putting one foot in front of the other until I was on the deck and they were casting off behind me.

The burners roared, lifting the ship up and away from the familiar city streets of my home and the green countryside to the east that arced around it like a mother's embrace. The half dozen crew leapt into action, tidying ropes and adjusting the sails that sat either side of the balloon like giant paddles. In moments we were far above the ground, leaving Paloma behind, a grey speck in the distance. The burners were turned down and our gentle movement became silent, bar for the creaking of the wicker deck and occasional command from the Captain.

Far below the sand rose and fell in static waves beneath us.

"It's beautiful, isn't it?" The voice was female and well spoken.

I turned—it was the veiled servant who was my companion to Shatterglass Isle. "Yes, I've never seen anything like it."

"I am Alessia Morelli." The veiled head turned to mine—as if expecting a response.

"Isobel di Sangro."

She laughed, the tinkling laughter of a young woman. "I know who you are. Today I think all of Paloma knows your name and by nightfall all of Shatterglass will know it also."

My face heated. "Is Alessia Morelli a name I should know?"

"You've had no reason to know it before today—but I hope you will come to know it. I am to be your new sister. I have come to bring my brother, Lucio Morelli's, bride home."

Coldness radiated from my spine out. I tightened my grip on the rail to stop my knees from collapsing. I wanted to scream. Instead I kissed her on her cheek with my frozen lips—grateful for the sheer veil between us. "Sister."

She touched my shoulder gently. "Enjoy the view. I'm going below—join me when you wish to rest. The stateroom is for our use."

I nodded. She drifted away leaving me a small circle of personal space to look blindly across the sands of the Great Inland Sea and conjure up the memory of Tommaso. If, as I turned to come in, my eyes stung and my cheeks were washed clean, then surely it was caused by nothing more than the scrub of sand blown on the breeze.

A cabin boy, seeing my hesitation at the stairs—directed me to the stateroom—a large surprisingly light cabin towards the back of the boat. Alessia was sprawled on a pile of cushions, veil removed and a desert fig raised to her perfect pink lips. I stood in the doorway a moment examining her olive skin for any obvious flaw, for any sign that the glass had begun to possess her. Nothing.

"I am without the glass mark." She beckoned me in. "Do you want me to tell you about your husband to be?"

"Of course." I forced my lips into a smile. "Is he as handsome as you are beautiful?"

She laughed. "He's a God amongst men."

She said it in jest—but an undercurrent in her voice betrayed her high opinion.

"I look forward to meeting him," I said primly, as if Tommaso had never had my legs up around my ears.

She held out a silk wrapped item tied with a bow. "A gift for you from Lucio."

I took it reluctantly and pulled the ribbon. The silk fell away revealing a large glass bowl. It looked clear until I lifted it to the window, then the gold pattern inside the glass shone. It slipped in my hands and, for a heart stopping instant, I thought I'd drop it.

Laughter filled the room. Alessia touched my hand lightly. "It won't break. Not that easily. Or chip. It's Shatterglass. There's no glass stronger."

I clutched the bowl to my chest. "Why is it called Shatterglass then?"

"Look at it again."

I carefully held it up again and inspected it. The gold pattern inside looked like glass that had been broken, in that instant before it collapses, when it's shattered but still in one piece. It sparkled, like millions of small diamonds.

"It's the pattern. Not all Shatterglass has it. In fact some of Lucio's best works are in clear Shatterglass. But it's the traditional pattern that it's named for."

"It's beautiful." I set the bowl down on the table and rewrapped it. "What of yourself?"

"I am to be married too in a few months. My Nico is a journeyman glass maker—he works in the old glass—not Shatterglass." She smiled at me. "So you do not need to worry that I will live with you forever and disturb your peace."

"And your parents?" I asked.

"They are both gone. Father to the wall and Mother in childbirth. There was to have been another son after me but . . . " Alessia shrugged. "The Morellis of Shatterglass do not make old bones." She stood abruptly. "I'm going up on deck. We should almost be able to see Shatterglass. Do you want to come?"

I smiled. "I'll join you shortly."

She left in a swirl of silk skirts. Once the door had banged closed behind her, I fell back onto the soft cushions. I closed my eyes and tried to empty my mind.

Tommaso's face came into focus, as if the image were burnt onto the inside of my eyelids. I pulled myself back up to sitting and rose. That dream was over.

On deck, Alessia was gripping the rail, her veil back in place. I joined her.

"Why do you wear a veil?" I asked.

"It's better than the constant taste of sand. Look!"

I followed the line of her finger and saw my new home for the first time. It protruded from the desert, lit by the sun, shining glass towers topped high rose tinged sandstone walls. All of it in light pink tints, unlike the grey smear of Paloma left behind this morning. Behind the city the sky roiled with great pink clouds that darkened to black as they rose into the sky. I shivered.

"We should get there just in time. It's looks like there's a sandstorm moving in," said Alessia.

The airship floated closer to the city.

"There he is." Alessia waved at a black clad figure standing outside the city gates on what looked like a short road, the dock no doubt.

"How can you tell from this distance?"

She laughed. "Who else would it be? He's come to welcome his bride." She grabbed my hands and danced us in a circle. Through her fine veil her eyes sparkled. "Don't be afraid. It will be wonderful. I've always wanted a sister."

I managed a smile before turning back to the rail to study my new home. Glittering figures stood at attention along the wall. "What are they?"

"They are the Grand Masters, turned to glass. Should threat come to the city it is said they will come to life in its defence."

"Really?"

She frowned. "Plenty in the city believe it."

We sank closer to the ground. Finally, with a round of shouts and the peeping of a whistle, ropes were thrown overboard and caught by a team of men on the ground. We were pulled back to earth, gently bumping onto the sand next to the dock.

The gangway was laid out and Alessia led me towards her brother, Lucio.

My heart pounded and, despite my intent, my fingers tightened in Alessia's grip.

He turned, and with a surge of disappointment I realized he, like Alessia, was veiled.

She introduced us and he bent over my hand. He was taller than I. Taller than Tomasso. The faint glitter of his eyes through muslin his only distinguishing feature.

"Welcome." His voice was deep. "How was the trip?"

"Good. Thank you."

He clicked his fingers. A white and gold palanquin with six bearers came forward. "There is a storm coming. We will meet properly once we are safely home."

"Come on." Alessia pulled me towards it. As I climbed in I looked back at the airship. Already the balloon was deflated, lying over the ship like a silk sheet as men hurried to pack it away and secure the ship.

Lucio handed us into the palanquin and then stepped back. "I'll see you at home." He slapped the side of it. The muslin curtains dropped and we were off, the palanquin bouncing as the bearers ran. We passed through the main gates to the city. I gained an impression of paved stone roads surrounded by graceful buildings that rose up around us, with decorated windows and overhead walkways and then the storm hit with a howl. The curtains whipped around us and sand peppered my face, filling my eyes. We jerked left and the wind eased for a moment before an opening into a piazza gave the storm another opportunity to attack us. Its roar was deafening. Terror beat in my chest like a bird trying to escape and tears filled my eyes.

The wind eased a fraction and we passed through a sandstone passage. The palanquin jolted to halt.

Alessia pulled my hand. Half blind and deafened by the noise of the wind, I let her lead me where she would. An instant later the wind dropped completely. Doors slammed behind us. We were inside. Alessia released my hand with a gentle squeeze. I stood were I was, blinking frantically, trying to clear the sand from my watering eyes.

* * *

My future bride stood, shivering like a dog after a beating, a pool of pink sand forming at the tips of her kid leather boots. Sand covered her, smoothing away the fine features I'd seen as she came ashore. She was beautiful, more beautiful that most of the brides Paloma sent us, and well bred.

"You need a veil," I said. The first words that entered my head. She needed more than that. I eyed her sand encrusted velvet bodice and long skirts.

She lifted her head and looked directly at me, her eyes blue seeking mine through my veil. "I did not expect to arrive on the wings of a storm."

Her voice was even, musical as it lilted over the words.

"Alessia will show you to your room. You will wish to bathe. Come down when you are ready. It will just be cold platters tonight."

She nodded and let herself be led away by my chattering sister.

I watched her go, measuring the sway of her hips with my eyes.

After I had seen to my own comfort and changed into clean robes, I went to the dining room to await the women.

Alessia was down almost at once, her slippers dancing lightly over the tiles. Veil removed. "Is she not beautiful?"

"She is."

"And of the royal family too. Of the Duke's bloodline."

"It's convenient isn't it? That just as we approach the renegotiation of the treaty and lease, a woman of the Duke's bloodline disgraces herself and is sent to us as a bride."

"Is that why you're still veiled? You don't trust her?" Alessia looked at me, her bright eyes piercing.

"I don't know what I think yet." And until I did I would hold myself at a distance.

Clicking heels made their way across the paved floor. My bride—dressed as if for a slightly crumpled dinner with the Duke himself.

I rang the bell to alert the servants and went to greet her.

* * *

I felt as if I were eating shards of glass. Lucio sat, in full veil, barely speaking.

"What do you like to do? Do you sew or draw?" Alessia asked.

"I used to sing." I had sung for Tomasso.

Alessia smiled. "That's wonderful. Lucio loves music. Will you sing for us after dinner?"

I shook my head. "I couldn't." Not now. Not in this strange place and in front of the anonymous veil of the man I was to marry.

Alessia's smile drooped. "But you must . . . "

Lucio interrupted with a gesture. "You must be tired. Perhaps you will sing for us another evening."

I nodded, grateful for the reprieve.

After the meal I made my apologies. All I wanted was to find my room and my bed.

"Might you spare me a moment?" Lucio asked. I nodded.

Alessia squeezed my hand. "I'll see you upstairs." She slipped quietly away.

"I wish to speak of our wedding. Is there any reason for delay?"

I felt my face warm.

"I am informed of the circumstances in which you come to me. If there is a child, it will be accepted as a Shatterglass child. It is no reason to delay the ceremony."

"Then there is no reason for delay." It hurt to speak.

"Good. I shall request the priestess to attend us tomorrow afternoon. It will be a private ceremony here at home. Alessia will attend you. Good night." He bent in a stiff bow and left the room.

I stared at the silk canopy above my bed. Tomorrow I would marry a stranger, not just that but a man whose face I had yet to see. What was Tomasso doing?

I didn't think I could sleep—but at some point I did for it was morning and the maid was throwing open the shutters with a bang and rearranging the drapes.

The wind had ceased overnight and golden light fell into the room.

I pulled on my wrap and walked over to the window. The house looked out over a small piazza. Below, two figures swept red dust from last night's storm into piles. I was three storeys up and could see across to the rooftops on the other side of the piazza and beyond that some higher towers gleaming with glass windows. The city looked clean and bright as if it floated, unlike home with its dark wood and grime encrusted buildings. To my left the city walls rose up, blocking out the view to the Inland Sea and to the right, a few streets away a viaduct bounded a profusion of greenery. Gardens or a park perhaps, something to explore later.

Alessia arrived minutes later. "There is no need to dress. Lucio is at the workshop. Come down in your robe. I've asked the dressmaker to wait on us this morning—so you would just need to undress again."

* * *

Isobel wore a gold drape for our wedding that revealed one white shoulder and the swell of her breasts. Her hair was piled in a mass of pale curls atop her head, its colour a paler tone to the dress itself. She was in every way more than I had expected in a bride.

Afterwards, Alessia toasted us with chilled sparkle-berry wine served in Shatterglass goblets that I had fashioned myself. Once the glasses were drained she disappeared leaving my new wife and I to an awkward silence.

"I bid you goodnight," I bowed stiffly and left her. I walked quickly, large strides to take me away from her temptation. I might be suspicious of her presence here, but it did not stop me wanting her. Outside the city was in the twilight hour, golden light filtering between the towers and high points of the city. I hastened to the the underground vault that housed my workshop—saving me from the heat of the day and the city from the risk of fire.

There I laboured into the night, calling for the furnace to be stoked until sweat rolled from every limb. I tried to lose myself in the glass. Despite it all, the curve of her body under gold silk stayed with me, that night and the next.

* * *

I was sick a sennight after our marriage. By then I had ceased to expect my veiled husband to warm my bed. I was both glad and guilty—knowing the contract unfulfilled on my part. I dreamed of Tommaso—not my hidden husband.

He was always courteous and ever veiled but still I grew to know him. The sound of his step on the marble floor, the width of his shoulders, how much space remained above his head when he stood in the doorway, the slight stiffness in every movement he made.

I stopped him one night as he made to leave the room after dinner. "What do you wish me to do with my days, Sir?"

His head tilted and I saw the movement of his eyes through the sheer black muslin. "Whatever it is that wives do. Shop, call upon each other . . . " He shrugged as if he couldn't begin to imagine the world of women.

"I wish to be of some use. I had the running of my father's house for some years. I can count, write in a clear hand, I am not a woman who can do nothing."

"I shall instruct the housekeeper to wait on you tomorrow and defer to you in all matters relating to the house."

I nodded. Strangely deflated, I had prepared myself for an argument not this comfortable agreement.

"Perhaps when the child comes you will be more content?" he suggested.

"Perhaps," I agreed, knowing then that he had heard of both my sickness and long walks through the city and hours spent on the city walls looking out across the desert ocean towards Paloma and home.

* * *

The letter arrived on my eighteenth birthday a few months after my arrival. "Alberto is coming to visit." I smiled across the dinner table to my still veiled husband and sister-in-law.

"When does he arrive?" asked Lucio.

"On the next airship." I smiled—pleased despite the constant roll of my stomach.

Alessia's eyes widened. "So soon. We must have a party."

"Does he have business to attend to?"

I looked at Lucio's veil, trying to assess his mood. "He has recently joined the Duke's staff. He says he has some papers to deliver."

Lucio inclined his head. "I look forward to greeting him."

The city bell tolled a day later to mark the airship's approach. I hurried down to the dock to greet my brother.

"You have a new outfit," I said after he'd kissed my cheeks.

"As do you." He stood back looking at me until I felt my face heat.

"It is the style here." I ran my hands over the silk dress. Lighter than the heavy fabrics and figured tailoring of home.

"But tell me, how did you come to be on the Duke's staff?" I tucked my arm through his and walked him to the city gates past the Grand Masters of the wall.

"It is not so surprising. We are family after all. Tell me of your husband. Will I like him?"

"Of course you will," I said lightly. "We are having a party in your honour. Tomorrow—Lucio has invited some of the other Masters and their wives."

"What is Lucio like?"

My face warmed. "I do not know."

Alberto looked at me, surprise written all over his face. "What do you mean?"

"He is veiled."

Alberto laughed. "What? Even when you bed him?"

I shook my head.

"You don't bed him?" Alberto looked at the swell of my stomach. "It's Tomasso's child?"

"It will be a Shatterglass child."

Alberto gripped my arm. "Your husband is an important man. You must try to get along with him, to please him. Not just for your own sake—but for the relationship between our two cities."

"I am doing my best."

"Are you?" He glared at me.

"How is Tomasso?" I asked softly.

"You must forget Tomasso. Lucio is your future. Lucio will probably be the next Grandmaster—the most powerful man in the city."

"Lucio is my present. Once our contract is over . . . " I shrugged, not willing to put into words the dreams I had.

"Lucio's happiness is important to Paloma. If Lucio is happy, the Duke is happy. If you have any dream of returning to Paloma once your contract is done then you must keep the Duke happy."

I nodded, nausea filled my throat. "How is Edda?" I asked. "And Papa?"

* * *

I called my son Matteo, and he filled my life. I sang as I hadn't done for almost a year. The memory of Tommaso was still an unhealed wound—but no longer one that ached and bled with every day that passed.

Matteo filled the gap left by Alessia when she married Nico. We welcomed the pair of them to the house once or twice a week—but it was different. The space between Lucio and I more apparent.

Lucio continued to hide behind his veil. I watched him more closely, trying to see through the fine muslin to the man beneath.

A servant brought a smiling round little man to me one morning while Matteo was sleeping.

"The Master said to admit him." She bowed and left us.

I flushed. "I'm afraid you have the advantage of me, Sir?"

He bowed low over my hand. "I am Signor Ferro, your new singing instructor." He looked at me his head tilted to one side. "Your husband tells me you have a beautiful voice—perhaps we can practice together?"

I smiled. "Thank you." I felt embarrassed. Lucio was kinder than I deserved. He delighted in Matteo and I found him at odd moments in the nursery, watching the baby sleep or leaving the nurse with strict instructions as to his health and upbringing.

Alberto visited again and, having admired his nephew, chastised me. "Is Lucio a bad husband? Does he beat you? Publically abuse you? Does he treat your bastard child with anything but love?"

"Matteo is not a bastard!"

"And who do you have to thank for that, Sister? After your lover abandoned you; who convinced father that the one thing that could save your name and your position would be a Shatterglass wedding?"

The truth of his words reopened the wound I had thought begun to knit.

"You must bed him. Now; tonight. He has waited for you to have the babe; to move on from your childish dreams. He has given you time to heal. For your sake you must or the next ten years will leave you nothing but sorrow. Matteo is a Shatterglass child. They will not let you leave with him."

"Bastard!" I lashed out at him, hating him for the truth of his words. My hand printed itself across his cheek and I felt the sting in my fingers. "I love Tommaso."

"Tommaso is married to a di Trabia. He has a baby only weeks younger than Matteo. You have a husband who buys you anything you wish and treats you well. Are you a fool?"

I ran. Out the front door and through the city streets to the stairs that lead up the wall. I stood—where I had stood a hundred times before as Matteo grew inside me and looked out across the desert sea to Paloma. I had no reason to grieve. My marriage was better than most. Tears blinded me, reducing the view to a blur of red.

* * *

Since Isobel arrived, I have lost myself in the glass. She sings for the child and it warms the glass in my veins and sets my blood buzzing as only working the glass can do. I do not ask her to sing for me—lest the request show a weakness. Her brother is an important man now, an envoy on behalf of the Duke. What complicity is she involved in?

Tonight, as I did last night, I ordered the furnace built up and work out my demons in sweat and glass. Small spikes of pain punctuate my body. The glass growing inside me. That is the price of working the Shatterglass. The glass becomes part of you and eventually all of you.

If I leave her long enough, I hope she will come willingly to me. I will not go to her while she dreams of another, until I have worked out if she is a pawn or a player.

I swung the blowpipe to my lips and puffed into it. The molten oval of glass at the end grew. Keeping the oval rotating I touched it with my knife, shaping the glass to produce four legs. A small breeze briefly washed across the back of my neck. Someone coming into the workshop. I continued to play with the glass, teasing out a head and neck with a free flowing mane.

It took time. Time enough for me to catch the scent of her perfume, to imagine her in exacting detail so that the final touches on the mane reflected the curl of her hair loosened by a breeze.

Finally, satisfied, I placed the piece in the final furnace to cool.

"You are very talented," she said softly. I turned then and so my bare glass scarred face looked into hers.

Her eyes widened a little; but she didn't recoil. "Husband."

"Wife."

I stepped towards her and, bent until my lips pressed against hers. "Are you sure?"

Her arms wrapped around my neck, drawing me in, until I felt I would drown in her. I'd like to say we spoke words of love and treated each other well. It was not the case. We came together like a storm breaking. If I was neither gentle or considerate—then nor was she. I had no complaints.

Afterwards she traced the line of glass that ran from my right eye down my cheek. "Does it hurt?"

I looked into her eyes and wondered if she were here because she wanted to be, or because her brother had told her to be. "Everything hurts sooner or later."

The next morning I advised the guild of Alberto di Sangro's visit and the letters he carried. They called a special meeting for him to present his missives from the Duke.

"Your city is beautiful," Alberto said as we wound our way through the city streets. I watched him taking in the sights. No doubt cataloguing the width of the streets, the gold leaf on the statue of the Goddess and the height of the city walls. It would all be reported back to the Duke.

We parted at the door. "I will see you inside." I nodded at him and moved onto my chambers.

There were no secrets when the guild met. I unveiled and left both my outer wrap and veil behind to enter the meeting hall.

Grand Master Caito was already in his seat. Glassification had overtaken a large portion of his emaciated face. Crystals twinkled around his mouth and nose. It would not be long before he could not eat.

I felt eyes on me, noting the slow increase of crystals across my own face. Beneath my clothes I felt the bite of glass on my arm. My hours at the furnace had hastened the spread of the disease across my own body. It was best they did not see the spread or like Caito, they would deny me access to the furnaces and the glass.

I bowed my head in greeting to Caito and took my place at his side.

When all had taken their seats, Grand Master Caito rapped his gavel on the table. Silence fell and the Grand Master gestured. I interpreted the meaning and, as the second most highly ranked glassworker, I spoke. "Alberto di Sangro, you have the ears of the guild. Speak."

My wife's brother stood to read out the letter. A light sheen of perspiration marked his forehead. I sat straighter.

"To the Grand Master Caito and the Masters of Shatterglass, and the people of Shatterglass Isle, we bid you warm greetings.

We have followed the achievements of our Shatterglass cousins and congratulate you on the success you have achieved in building an oasis of economic prosperity and beauty in the middle of the desert . . . "

Fulsome words washed over the room. A number of the Masters relaxed in their seats.

"We have considered the lease renewal and believe that it is to the benefit of all that our two people not just maintain our strong relations but look to build and grow our relationship. To this end we propose that the people of Shatterglass become citizens of Paloma. Therefore the lease will be allowed to lapse and instead we will work on a treaty joining our peoples for all time."

He had our attention by then.

There was more, assurances that we wouldn't lose our independence but gain administrative and military support. As Alberto continued to read murmuring rippled around the room.

Renaldo Bertoli was the first to rise. "What insult is this? Has the Council forgotten that the lease has an option for another fifty years?" Renaldo's wife had come to him from Paloma scarred from a house fire when she was a child. That was what Paloma usually sent; its cripples and misfits. If a bride was beautiful—then like my lovely wife she usually carried another man's child. It was the way the aristocracy of Paloma got rid of its unwanted daughters and sisters—each bride intended as an insult to the lease and the payments we made.

"Outrageous!"

Caito banged his gavel and a sullen silence was found. "Di Sangro—does the Duke attempt to deny the option provided to us in the lease to allow a fifty-year extension?" he grated. A line of blood trickled down his chin.

Di Sangro, for his faults, did not hesitate. "Grand Master, the Duke and his Council deny nothing. They simply propose a way to work together for a better more peaceful future."

I stood, "Are you suggesting that if we do not work to the Council's wishes our future will be less peaceful?"

Di Sangro paused. "Of course not." Sweat poured off him.

I let him stand a moment before nodding. "You may go. You have given us much to think on."

The second the doors closed behind Di Sangro the room erupted into noise. Caito let them go for a moment before banging his gavel. When he had their attention he waved a hand at me to carry on.

* * *

"How was the Guild Meeting?" I asked my husband over dinner. Lucio looked at me, his eyes searching my face.

"You were late home," said Alberto. "Long meeting?"

"You gave us much to discuss," said Lucio.

The air thickened with unspoken words. "Will someone explain to me what happened today?" I asked, my eyes fixed on Lucio.

He gestured to Alberto. "Let our guest speak first."

"Alberto?"

Alberto smiled. "I delivered a letter from the Council which proposed our two states merging harmoniously to form a greater whole."

"Our two cities merging? Or Paloma taking over?" I asked.

Lucio smiled, a fierce smile that set the crystals in his cheek to glittering in the gaslight. "That is the question, brother-in-law."

Alberto flushed. "A merger. The details would need to be worked through. There are many benefits . . . "

"Really? Name one benefit that you can see for Shatterglass?" Lucio asked.

"Greater protection."

"Before they can conquer us, a country must conquer the desert. We've not faced any threat in our last fifty years. What new threat do you see emerging?"

"Paloma has a well organized political and administrative system. There is much we could share—giving you more time to work the glass. And trade, we have a strong farming base . . . "

Lucio turned his attention on me. "What do you think of this idea, wife? Do you relish the opportunity of once again being a part of Paloma? Did you perhaps already know of the Duke's offer?"

I didn't understand the thread of anger I heard in his voice. "Would it be a bad thing?"

"Not for Paloma. Would the taxes we'd be expected to pay be more or less than the rent and bride prices we currently offer up?"

Alberto shrugged, a nervous smile on his face. "There is time to work out the detail."

Lucio rose abruptly. "Forgive me. I have work to do tonight. I will leave you to enjoy each other's company. I'm sure you have much to discuss. Old acquaintances perhaps? Alberto, there will be a response for the Duke tomorrow. You will be able to catch the airship that leaves with the afternoon southerly."

As he went I felt his absence like an amputation. Alberto watched him until he was out of sight then leaned forward, his hand gripping my wrist. "You must talk to him. You must make him see the sense of this."

His grip tightened painfully, his fingers dug painfully into my bones. I gasped from the pressure of it. "You're hurting me."

He released me immediately, looking abashed. "I'm sorry, sister. It has been a long day. Forgive me. I would never hurt you." He brushed a finger down the side of my cheek and then left.

I looked after him sadly remembering the night he first brought Tommasso home. Life was simpler then.

The night air was cool, and served to ease the heat inside me as I walked through the streets to Lucio's workshop. A servant dogged my heels. I waited, as I had done the first evening I came to him, watching the play of yellow light on the muscles of his back. The glint of glass in his arms as he swung the blowpipe in circles.

When he was done he stood, his shoulders slumped.

"Husband?" I said tentatively.

"What do you want?" He did not turn.

I walked to him and touched his shoulder. "I want you." I held his hand over my stomach. "I want your child. Is it so wrong to want that?"

His eyes brightened. "Are you sure?"

I nodded.

He buried his head in my neck. "What the Duke wants is not a merger but a complete takeover. We would become slaves to the glass, rather than masters of it. There would be taxes to be paid and quotas and the art we do would be lost. They would work us until the glass solidified in our veins."

I traced the length of his arm and then across onto his chest where already a line of glittering glass tears had appeared. "This spread of the glass, it is not usually this quick, is it?"

He shook his head. "If the guild knew they would force me to rest for a month, maybe more."

"What happens when it covers all of you?"

"Most likely I will go to guard the wall," he said softly.

For a moment I didn't understand, then the image of the life-size glass statues that lined the city walls came back tome. "No!" Nausea bubbled in my throat. "That's not real people?"

"It is the eighteen Grand Masters. They guard the city. It is said they are . . . sleeping, not dead. Should something threaten the city it is said they will rise in its defence."

"Do you believe that?"

He smiled sadly. "I would sleep better at night if I did."

"You must stop working the glass. For me. For our children."

He touched my face, a feather-light touch on the cheek and I leaned towards him, unable to deny the pull he had on me.

"I will rest for a month, more perhaps. But the glass is part of me. I can't stop—not forever."

"Love me." I pulled him close.

* * *

A grim-faced Alberto left on the next afternoon.

"What is in the Guild's letter?" I asked Lucio as we watched the airship from our bedroom window.

"We thanked them for their generous offer and formally invoked the option to extend the lease."

"They won't be happy with that, will they?" I rubbed my wrist where Alberto had held me.

"It doesn't matter if they aren't happy—so long as they honour the agreement."

"Of course they will!"

Lucio smiled. "I wish I had your confidence." He reached for my hand. "Will you sing for me?"

* * *

The city bell tolled.

"What is it?" I looked at Lucio. His face was sombre.

"Grand Master Caito is going to the wall. Come."

We went down through the city and out to the dock. The other Masters had gathered, and many of their wives. Alessia met us there, her eyes glittering with tears beneath her veil.

"Where is he?" I whispered to her.

"He will come. He retired to his workshop last night after the meeting to finish his mask. When it has cooled he will come."

We waited in silence, bar the bell tolling, calling the city to attention. The sun was slipping over the horizon when a ripple moved through the crowd. "He is coming," said Alessia.

Lucio squeezed my hand and then dropped it. "I must wait with the other Masters," he said.

A smattering of applause sounded from within the city, a noise which moved and swelled as it came towards us. As if carried on its wave, the Grand Master appeared in the gateway.

His face was covered in a glass mask that reflected the pinks and purples of the sunset. He was clad in a gold robe. He moved slowly, shoulders back, his step a slightly hesitant long paced march.

As he drew nearer, the full detail of the mask become visible. Diamond like cut glass twinkled in a circlet across the forehead. Around the eyes, filigreed glass sat like a lace veil. Below the veil was a perfectly proportioned nose and mouth all covered in a sheen of gold.

"It's beautiful," I whispered to Alessia.

"They always are. Their final masterpiece."

The Grand Master's robe brushed my arm and then he was past us and at the wall where the Masters waited.

My Lucio stepped forward and helped the Grand Master up onto one of the remaining empty pedestals on the wall.

As the sun slipped behind the horizon the Grand Master seemed to stiffen. Beside me Alessia sobbed.

"The sadness will pass." I touched her arm to comfort her.

She pushed me away. "In twelve months or two years, that will be Lucio. Do you think that sadness will pass?"

She picked up her skirts and ran into the city, pushing people out of her way.

"What's wrong?" Lucio asked.

"She's upset. She thinks of you."

He nodded. "What of you? Do you think of me?"

"Of course! But you will rest—you promised you would. And this will not happen. Not for a long time?"

He took my arm. "I will walk with you. The guild will not meet until tomorrow."

He was silent on the walk home. I wanted to talk to him, to find a way to comfort him, but something held my tongue. An echo perhaps of my love of Tomasso which had cost me so dear.

* * *

I wanted to ask Isobel to sing for me, but did not want her to guess the depth of my grief. Caito had been as a father to me after my own had gone to take his place on the wall.

I did not sleep for thinking of Caito and Paloma's demands. I joined Isobel for breakfast. A cough interrupted us. One of the outdoor servants. "What is it, Gino?"

"A message for you, Master."

He handed over a crumpled piece of paper.

"What is it?" asked Isobel.

"A new communication from Paloma, brought overnight by dove."

I dropped a kiss on her forehead and left for the Guildhall.

I banged the gavel to call the meeting to order and stood.

"I declare the seat of Grand Master vacant. All those who wish to compete for the position are to present their Masterpiece in seven days. All in favour?"

Twelve hands rose.

"As Caito's deputy, I will chair until then. Does anyone disagree?"

Silence.

"Very well. We have received new correspondence from Paloma. This time they don't even have the grace to send a messenger with their letter. It appears the Council has decided, after due consideration, that the original treaty is flawed in law and the option to extend the lease is not valid. They renewed their proposal to merge our two city states into one country."

Bertoli slammed his fist on the table. "Bastards! The only problem with that original treaty is that we became wealthier than they ever expected."

Agreement ran around the room.

It took some hours to fashion our response. We would proceed to fill the terms of the original lease and treaty.

I feared the Paloman response—their weapons of war had grown more sophisticated in recent years. The desert would no longer protect us as it once had.

I broke my promise to Isobel that night. Instead of going home to our bed—I went to my workshop and ordered the furnace lit. I could not afford a month off—not with a Masterpiece to craft and only a sennenight to do it.

It would not be the kind of masterpiece traditionally submitted, but these were not traditional times.

* * *

Lucio lied. I smelled the furnace and the glass on his clothes. He held me tight as I railed against him. Lashing out with my tongue and fists.

"Your child will need a father, not a glass statue outside the city gates." It was only now that I risked losing him that I realized how much I wanted him to stay. Now that I carried our child.

"Caito is dead. Once my piece is complete, I will rest. I promise." He held me tightly, so I couldn't hit him again.

When I had finished sobbing he started to talk. His voice low.

"I am creating something to help safeguard you and our children. A masterpiece like none created before. Something to protect us, A weapon. Your safety, the safety of the city, that is all that is important. All that I now live for."

I shook my head. "All that is important is that you live for us. A child must know their father."

"A child must be proud of their father," he said. Stroking my hair as if I were a child myself. I let him soothe me.

Alessia returned to our house that morning. "What is Lucio up to? He has asked Nico to help him."

I shrugged. I did not know the detail and in my pain did not want to know.

"He should not be working the glass," I whispered. My voice was hoarse from crying.

Alessia looked at me.

"The glassification is more advanced that you think. He told me he would rest. But now Grand Master Caito has died and he must make his masterpiece."

Alessia paled. "He is right. He must make his masterpiece. It is expected. No-one else competes against him. If he does not complete it, we will have no leader."

"You may end up with a leader but for how long? This masterpiece might kill him."

"No, he only has a little on his face."

"It reaches the length of his arm and across his chest."

Alessia's mouth gaped.

"We must stop him. You must talk to Nico."

"No. He can rest once it's done. If he keeps away from the glass after his Masterpiece it will still be years before he must go to the wall. He knows what is needed. We cannot stop him."

I turned from her, tears burning behind my eyes. "He is your brother."

"He is a Master of the Shatterglass and at this moment that must come first."

"I don't understand you." I walked away before she could witness my tears. Before I said something that I couldn't take back. It was different for her. Nico didn't have to fear the glassificiation.

* * *

The thought of Isobel, Matteo and our unborn child pushed me. They were the ever-present reason for what I now created. I set my sister's husband, Nico, to labouring on the mirrors. They were important too, but it was the construction of a lens that obsessed me. I covered slate after slate with calculations to work out the radius and curvature of the lens before I started work on creating two flawless disks of convex glass that I would bring together.

After a day of cooling, my initial effort failed, chewing into my already to scarce time. A subsequent effort had to be ground down to create the unmarked surface I required. Once it was complete I started work on its twin, casting multiples at the same time as insurance against failure. I lived with the fear that on dawn of the seventh day I would have nothing to show the Guild. I laboured day and night until I could feel the glass crackling in my blood and new encrustations sawed through the skin of my chest.

Just before dusk on the seventh day, I took the Guild Masters to the city walls, leading them up the narrow staircases, all of them huffing and puffing behind me.

It looked fine, with its brass fittings and simple lines. It was not greeted with cries of wonder. Instead the Masters walked around it, studying it from different angles. Bertoli finally asked, "What is it?"

"It is a fire-maker. A giant lens that catches the sun and concentrates it. We will make more of them and mount them on the walls. When the Palomans come, as they certainly will, we will burn their airships and set fire to their supply wagons."

"They cannot cross the Great Inland Sea. The sand will stop them."

"The sand will make it harder—but they will come. The airships can provide support for them, so they need not carry the water they will need. Perhaps not a great force—but some will cross the desert and come to our gates."

Finally Bertoli nodded. "Show us how it works, Lucio."

I turned the great wheel to angle the mirrors that captured the sun's rays. "Watch that tree." I pointed to a lone palm that stood on its own a few hundred feet from the city walls. Another wheel lifted tilted the machine so that the sun's rays bounced off the mirrors and through the great magnifying glass. A concentrated disc of light appeared on the sand not far from the tree. "Track left," I commanded Nico and the machine slid slightly to the left. The circle of light fell on the tree. I held it steady. A small stream of smoke lifted up from the tree, then it burst into flame.

A spattering of applause rang out.

"That is how we will bring their airships down."

Antonio shook his head. "It's a fine thing. But unnecessary. The Grand Masters of the wall will protect us."

"Doubtless—and with this weapon and other ones like it—we will help them."

A crowd had gathered below us. "Come. Let us return to the Guildhall. You must decide if the Masterpiece is sufficient."

* * *

A letter arrived for me this morning, addressed to Isobel di Sangro. It was a shock to see my maiden name and in a hand that was still familiar to me.

I was alone when it arrived, as I had been while Lucio worked on his masterpiece and his own death at the same time. My heart beat a little faster as I studied the missive. I should burn it unopened. Instead, I broke the seal on it.

Tomasso's fluid script filled the page. He wrote of his wife's death in childbirth and his realisation that he still loved me. The words, each one on its own insignificant, set my emotions churning. I should not have cared for what Tommaso thought. Guilt stirred in my already queasy stomach.

The second half of his letter expressed his fear that war would separate our two cities and he would never see me again.

I screwed the letter into a ball and hurled it across the room. Did they think that I would betray my husband and my new home for a man who had not stood by me when that was all I desired?

"Isobel?" Lucio stood in the doorway, his face grey with fatigue.

"Lucio. The Guild has met?"

He smiled. "I am the new Grand Master." He held out his arms and I went to him, desperate for the comfort of his touch. I felt his body stiffen as I pressed mine against him.

"What's wrong?"

"Nothing. I am tired."

"It's the glass, isn't it?" I moved away lest my body was pushing against new protrusions and causing him pain. The nausea that had been hovering since I opened the letter returned.

He nodded. "I cannot stop. We must make more giant lenses. We cannot trust the Grand Masters to rise and war comes, I am sure of it."

Sadness settled on me like a heavy blanket, stifling and thick. "I will order some food. Bathe and then we can talk." I turned before he could see my tears. What was there to say?

* * *

The guild accepted me as Grand Master but they doubted the need for my fire machine.

"The desert will defeat them. They cannot come en masse."

"They can come by air and by land."

Bertoli shrugged this off. "What can an airship take? Twenty? Maybe thirty souls if there is no cargo. If they find a way to cross the desert, the Grand Masters of the wall will protect us."

"They will come and we would be wise to think to our defences. We can make shields. Glass lances. Arrow tips."

Bertoli laughed. I could only hope they took my words home with them and thought on them.

I went back to my workshop and single handedly set to manufacturing more of the lenses. My skin burned with the furnace as more glass forced its way to the surface, cutting through my skin. Night after night.

Isobel learned not to speak of it.

I lay back in my copper bath and relaxed, letting the warm water soften my skin and ease the pain.

"Lucio!"

I opened my eyes. Isobel stood in front of me, her face blanched of all colour.

"It is not so bad," I said.

"It is worse than bad." She came over to me and perched on the edge of the tub. With a finger she touched a new eruption of glass on my shoulder. It was a spontaneous gesture of care and it almost brought me undone.

"You should not touch it. The condition is hereditary and inflamed by proximity to the glass, but in its later stages it can be passed on from one to another. I wouldn't risk you or the baby."

She held a finger to my lips and I let her silence me. With gentle touches she traced the path of glass, across my chest and down both sides of my body. In return I placed a hand on her belly and felt a small movement through the muslin of her dress.

"I cannot stop. What I make is a last resort—but if they come then the fire machines may give us a chance. I would give that chance to you and the children. Matteo and this one."

"You will die before your son arrives."

I didn't lie to her. "Will you sing to me?"

She nodded. I sank back into the tub and let my eyes close as her voice rose in song. A lullaby. As her voice fluted up the scales the vibrato gently resonated against the glass inside me, filling my body with a warm hum that eased the pain of the day.

It took me only two weeks to build three more of the lenses. It was easier now. I had the feel for shaping the glass to the convex and knew the thickness and width I needed.

Nico worked beside me—making the smaller parts, and organizing the brass fittings to hold them together.

Once I had four of the lenses I set to making shields and lances and arrow tips. As the months slipped by the glass encased my legs in glittering stockings that scored my flesh beneath the loose robes I wore.

"How are the teams going on with the lenses?" I asked Nico. "They must practice everyday."

He nodded. "You know the airship has not come this week?"

I shook my head. "They will come soon."

"You must rest." Other than Isobel, he was the only one who suspected how far my sickness had progressed.

"I have one more job to complete—then I will rest."

I went home. Walking stiffly through the paved streets, enjoying the fall of afternoon light on the pink sandstone walls and overbridges of the city. At home I went up to the nursery. Matteo was on a rug, playing with a rag ball with a bell hidden in it. When he saw me, his face stretched into a gap-toothed grin and he crawled over to me and used my robes to pull himself to standing.

Isobel came into the room. She was slower now, her belly prominent under her dress. "You look beautiful."

She blushed. "I'm not."

She was.

I picked Matteo up and stood, ignoring the rasp of glass against my inner thigh. I tossed him in the air and caught him, balancing the pain of each movement against the joy of his laughter.

"It's almost his bedtime," said Isobel sternly and beckoned the nurse to take him.

"Dine with me," I held out my hand and together we left nursery.

We drank wine and Isobel sang. Finally I drew her to me, holding her gently so as not to cut her body on my own sad sharp flesh. "I must go to the workshop."

She knew then, perhaps she'd known since I came home a Grand Master. "So soon?"

I nodded. She stood on tiptoe and pressed her lips against my right cheek. There, at least, it was still skin, as opposed to my left which was now tightly crusted with glass.

"I will be at the wall," she said, her voice husky.

"You are my joy," I reached a finger out and caught a tear from the edge of her eye and then left before I weakened.

* * *

Lucio went to his workshop for the last time this evening. Although he did not say it, he has gone to craft a mask of glass, his final work before taking his place on the wall.

I thought about sending a note to Alessia, but stopped myself. There would be time to share the hurt. Instead, I went up to the rooftop garden and looked out across the dark desert ocean. My heart felt as if it were growing shards of glass that sawed and ached deep inside me. As dawn's grey and pink tendrils made their way across the sky, I rang for a servant.

Alessia arrived in a swirl of robes, her tears hidden by a veil. "Why didn't you tell me it was so close?" she demanded.

"He didn't want anyone to know."

Her anger did not affect me, caught in a cocoon of my own grief. "Will you wait with me for the bell?" I asked.

"Of course." She wrapped her arms around me. "He's my brother and you are my sister."

The day passed in a haze. Outside the sun shone and the street vendors still sold their wares. Nico joined us in the evening. The servants brought food, which tasted of clay and the minutes and hours slowly ground by.

It wasn't until around the middle of the next day that the city bells tolled. Nico had returned to his workshop so Alessia, Matteo and I walked hand in hand to the city gate.

I wore a veil, to hide my reddened eyes but as the applause marked Lucio's appearance I pushed it back. I wanted him to see my face. To understand that I loved him. A different love to that I felt for Tommaso—a more powerful one in the end. Matteo clapped his chubby hands as Lucio approached,

My eyes glazed with tears so it was not until Lucio passed by me that I saw his mask. Like the giant lens, it was simple unadorned clean lines. His greater work had gone into a Shatterglass sword that hung at his hip sheathed in a golden scabbard. Its pommel was made of swirls of glass, perfectly formed.

Alessia turned to me. "He breaks the treaty—we are not allowed to bear arms."

"It is a piece of art. Something he carries to his grave. If it comes to war then it would have done so anyway." I kept my voice calm. Around me all were talking about the sword.

The guild surrounded him and I went forward. Pushing between them until I stood in front of him. He kissed my fingers. I reached up to caress his glass mask. It was warm to the touch, Lucio's flesh hidden beneath it. His eyes closed for a moment in a long slow blink and then re-opened.

"Mistress Morelli?" Bertoli gestured for me to step away and I returned to Alessia, trembling with pain.

I watched while they helped him up onto the dais that would become his resting place and waited as the crowd slowly dispersed.

"Will you take Matteo?" I asked Alessia.

She held out her arms. "Come Matteo."

In front of me a woman in a blue veil shook her head. "The second Grand Master gone in as many months."

"Such a young man. So sad."

I let their comments and the others I heard wash over me. When they were all gone I sat at Lucio's glass encrusted feet and sang a lullaby, one of Matteo's favourites.

"I'm sorry," I said. Sorry for not loving him when I should have. Sorry for not thanking him for his kindnesses. His love. "I would do it differently." I was angry too. Angry that he had worked the glass so constantly, shortening his life.

I wept then, ugly juddering sobs that, when they faded, left me hollow. I stood to leave. The last light of the day had shot the sky with hints of crimson. I thought he inclined his head to me as I left. In the failing light and with eyes swollen with grief, I couldn't be sure.

* * *

My second child was not so much born, as ripped from my pain addled body. While it was tearing its way into this world I wished nothing more than to die.

They laid him on my chest and I looked at his squashed unfamiliar face and waited for the wave of love that had engulfed me after Matteo's birth. He gummed my breast painfully. "Take him away." I dissolved into tears, matched moments later by my new son's.

The midwife took him and came back to prod my stomach until, with another lurch, the afterbirth exited my body.

I tried. Every day I tried. And every day Luciano scrunched up his red face and repudiated me with screams.

Alessia dragged me out of the house to try and lift my spirits. We bumped into Master Bertoli's wife, who, with a blush turned away from my greeting.

"How dare she!" Alessia said.

I touched a hand to her wrist. "It is nothing. I am nothing. Not without Lucio. It does not matter."

When the letter arrived, three weeks after Lucio had gone to the wall and I had given birth, it seemed a lifeline.

It was written more than a week prior to my receiving it. The airships were not as regular as they used to be.

Word of Lucio going to the wall had reached them. Alberto bade me come home.

I was torn. I longed for Edda's comfort and to see Papa. It would give me an excuse to escape the babe briefly. Guilt wracked me.

Alberto's letter urged me to come immediately—before the problems between Paloma and Shatterglass separated us all for a short time.

Alessia looked at me, her face pale. "You cannot go. Your home is here now. With your sons. With us."

I held my hands out to her. "I miss them. I need to see my Father and Edda. I will return for Matteo and for the baby."

"The baby has a name. Luciano."

Tears filled my eyes. They were never far these days and my voice was permanently husky from crying. "I must go, Alessia. I must."

She hesitated a moment and then pulled me into an embrace, my face mashed into her shoulder and her tears mingled with mine. "I wish you would stay."

I sent a letter to Alberto and told him that I would come with the next airship, whenever that might be. I ordered the servants to pack and Lucio's agent arranged for the final payment of my dowry to be ready. Three chests of coins and gems. The price of my youth and the two sons I would leave behind.

It took ten days from when I placed my letter in the hand of an airship captain to when the next airship arrived. Ten days between airships when we had been used to a service every two to three days. When the bell rang signalling the sighting of a ship, I rushed to the nursery to kiss my boys goodbye. Matteo clung to me, bringing me close to tears. Luciano was asleep, his chubby face beautiful in repose.

"Isobel?" Alessia stood in the doorway. "They will miss you."

"It won't be for long," I promised. "A week, perhaps two . . . "

With a last kiss for Matteo I left, my servants following me through the winding streets laden with my dowry.

Alessia caught up with me on the dock. "I'll see you onboard."

I smiled, my cheeks wet again.

I looked out across the red sands, trying to compose myself. The airship loomed close and behind it a large pink cloud. I blinked, clearing the last of the tears from my eyes. There was something strange about the cloud, it lay low, close to the ground and had none of the dark hues that a storm cloud usually held.

The first ropes came over the side of the airship and Alberto's voice called out. The ground crew swarmed to pull the ship down.

"Hurry Isobel, we must get aloft before the storm hits. Quick men, load her baggage."

The gangplank slapped down on the dock and Alessia drew me into a hug.

"It's not a storm," I whispered into the silk of her veil. "It's Paloma. They have come." My heart thudded in the cage of my chest. She pulled away and twitched her veil down. "What will you do?"

"Sound the alert. Get to the walls, go as if you are farewelling me, they will not want us to raise a warning. I will delay."

"Good-bye, Sister." She kissed my cheek and then went, calling the servants to follow her.

I looked to the Grand Masters lining the wall. Would they rise in defence? They looked no different to yesterday, or the day before.

"Isobel?" Alberto had come down the gangway.

"Brother." I turned to greet him.

"This is everything?" His eyes roamed over the chests lined up behind me. A smile lightened his features.

"It is my dowry." I said. "I am thinking to leave it behind. After all, this trip is just a visit. The children and I will need the money to live on once I return."

"You can bank it in Paloma—and arrange for a line of credit. The banks know no boundaries. But come, we must hurry." Sweat beaded on his forehead.

"It's not a storm, is it?" I asked as the bell started to toll from inside the city.

"What do you mean?" Alberto gestured for one of the crew to pick up my baggage. I moved in front of him and laid a hand on his arm to stop him.

Another figure appeared on the gangway, Tommaso. He held out a hand to me. "Isobel."

I looked at him, his hair looker darker than I remembered and there were lines around his eyes. He was a weak man. "Did you ever love me?" I asked. I felt I was nibbling at the edge of truth. "Or was it all just a plan to ruin me so that I could be sent to Shatterglass for my dowry and connections?"

Colour rose in Tommaso's cheeks. "You know I love you."

"Do you?" I asked. It suddenly all made sense. What I fool I was. "Then why did you abandon me when my father came to demand you marry me?"

He flushed.

"And now you are here, arriving in front of an army." I turned to Alberto. "Did you come for me? Or the rest of my dowry?"

"Don't be foolish, sister. You know my only thought is for you."

I laughed bitterly. "Is it? Or is your only thought about what I can bring you? Was it your plan, or Father's?"

Tommaso stepped forward. "Please come with us, Isobel. I will spend the rest of my life proving my love."

I shook my head. Certain now of the betrayal. "No. You were all in this together weren't you? What was your share Tommaso? How much of my dowry did you get?"

"It wasn't like that. I love you." He held out his hand to me, inviting me to come.

"If you love me, I am sorry for it." Above them, a red dot appeared on the balloon. The giant lenses marking their target. Alessia had reached the wall. I stepped back. "I'm sorry Alberto. What have I to go back to in Paloma? More lies?" Tears were coursing down my cheeks again. "I trusted you. I trusted you all." On top of the grief was rage. Unstoppable anger. I backed away from the ship, and the red dot on its balloon. Around me the ground crew were responding to the alarm sounding from the city. One by one, dropping ropes and running.

"Come Isobel!" Alberto looked bewildered.

"No!" I turned from him and Tomasso and I ran. My slippered feet pounded over the uneven rock length of the dock.

As we approached the gates a cry went up from the ground crew ahead of me. The great steel doors were closed!

"To the Grand Masters!" I cried. I turned right and threw myself into the niche in the wall with Lucio. A blast of hot air washed over my back. Behind me I heard screams as the balloon exploded in a ball of fire. I looked back, shading my eyes to see through the heat haze that hovered between myself and where the ship had been.

It was gone. Nothing but a couple of broken scraps of wood and burning pieces of cloth. Alberto. Tommaso. Gone. The breath left me and I doubled over gasping. What had I done? Guilt rose like bile in my throat.

A shout from near by drew my attention to the desert in front of me. The army had drawn closer, clearly visible beneath the dust cloud that hovered above them. It was an enormous. Half a dozen airships hung in front of the clouds.

This was not a small army that would break on the walls. It was a horde that would likely overwhelm the walls.

"Do something," I said to Lucio. "Rise up, defend the city." I punched his armoured form and blood welled from my knuckles. The Masters stood paralysed in the face of the approaching destruction.

I looked back at the army. In the distance I could see more airships lowering crates and boxes over the side. Weapons. The ships hadn't carried troops—but the supplies to get them here and arm them.

As I watched a third airship sailed towards us. I saw a red dot fix on its balloon and, as it gently floated towards us, the balloon exploded, scattering burning debris over the army below.

Confusion reigned for a moment. The people on the ground were clearly unsure as to what had happened. They had seen the airship with Tommaso and Alberto disintegrate—but they hadn't seen why. Now this. The remaining airships slowly backed away until they were out of range.

"Mistress?" One of the airship ground crew stood by my side. "We must move—we'll be caught in the crossfire once they get closer."

"No." I shook my head. "We must wake the Grand Masters. What good will hiding do if the city is overwhelmed?"

He was young, little more than a youth, the first sproutings of hair apparent on his chin. As I watched his stance straightened. "What must I do?" he asked.

I cast another look at the approaching army.

An advance party had drawn closer. They were constructing a cannon, no doubt its parts lowered from one of the airships. We had no cannons of our own. The terms of our lease removed the power to defend ourselves. We had muskets—bought in secret and hidden until now. But they had not the range or power of a cannon.

The cannon fired with a deafening explosion. An instant later the ball hit the city walls with a thump that reverberated through the wall at my back. The youth jumped, fear blanching his face of colour.

I screamed. Tears poured down my cheeks. This was the end. What would happen to my sons?

I screamed again, a wordless shout which held all my grief and anger. I would die out here with Lucio. Locked outside the city that was my home.

As my cry faded, a piece of glass dropped onto my arm, and then another. I looked up. "Lucio?"

Sing. His voice spoke in my head and I understood.

I cast a look out to the Paloman army, its cannon fired again and another ball thumped into the wall above the gate. Musket shots retorted uselessly from the walls.

I turned to the youth. "We must sing to them." I raised my voice. "All of you. Stand in front of a Grand Master and sing." I didn't wait to see if they obeyed. I took a deep breath and opened my mouth and let sound flow out. I sang songs of war and rage and as my voice fluted up the scales I found the tones and notes that resonated in the glass.

"Sing!" I yelled at the ground crew from the airship.

More, Lucio's voice echoed inside my head. I put all of myself into the next run of notes. Holding the vibrato until my skull buzzed with it. A pain formed inside my throat, like a small pebble trying to force its way out. I drove myself to keep singing and felt something sharp explode out of my skin. As the pain clawed my throat, Lucio cracked then moved, stepping stiffly down from his pedestal. I still sang, but more softly now, nursing my throat. Around me the ground crew were trying to harmonise.

Lucio, touched my shoulder. His glass gauntleted hand was surprisingly warm through the cloth of my robe. Then he was gone, marching with a stiff-legged stride across the sand, Grand Master Caito shifted from the niche next to Lucio's. I kept singing and half a dozen other Grand Masters slowly shifted into action, following stiffly behind Lucio.

I sang and sang, working out harmonies with the ground crew and waking the remaining Masters one by one and sending them out to battle. The rest of the ground crew had worked out what mixture of notes and vibrato seemed to work and laboured alongside me in discordant harmony.

When the last Grand Master rose my voice was hoarse, and I could sing no more. It was only then that I was able to turn and look at what we had created.

Lucio led the Grand Masters, the sun reflecting off his sword. Muskets fired and hit his chest creating small puffs of crystal.

Behind him, the Masters waded into the army, knocking down men in swathes. One bent and then straightened, a lance in its grasp. They seemed bigger than normal men, as if their time as statues on the wall had stretched them, made them more god and less man.

They shone with unnatural light, as if channelling the same powers as the giant lens. Small fires erupted around them.

Flashes of gunpowder marked the Paloman defence. I cried out as Lucio was hit again and again. He didn't fall. The glass resisted the shots like armour.

I heard the rattle of chains. Our own city gates opened and the people of Shatterglass came out, some bearing Shatterglass shields and lances, others with muskets to support their glass warriors. They came out in a wave; men and women. Unstoppable.

I had no weapon and so trailed behind. Greedily following Lucio's progress from afar, flinching as soldier after soldier tried to bring him down.

A small group managed to trip one of the Glass Masters up and, using ropes, pinned him to the ground.

Two other Grand Masters, I think Caito was one of them, overturned the cannon in a puff of sand and gunpowder.

It seemed a lifetime of heart beats paused, until a ripple ran through the Palomans. Their lines seemed to sag and then they broke. Running away, trying to scatter into the blood red sand.

A white flag unfurled over the side of an airship and a roar erupted from a thousand Shatterglass mouths.

"Mistress?" It was the youth who had sung with me to wake the Grand Masters. I motioned him to silence, my throat too sore for words. I waited until, his steps still stiff, Lucio returned.

The light had faded from him and his glass tunic was covered in a myriad of tiny chips and miniscule cracks. The Shatterglass can resist much it seemed, but not all.

"Lucio?" For a moment I thought he would pass me by, but he stopped. I reached out my hand to him and he lifted it to his heart. Behind his mask his eyes glittered. No longer truly human.

He released my hand and stiffly marched away towards the wall.

"Take this." A scrap of cloth was pushed into my hand. Councillor Bertoli stood beside me. His face covered in sweat, blood stains on his sleeve. He carried a glass shield in one hand.

I wiped my eyes.

"I saw what you did. If you had not woken the Masters . . . " He shook his head.

* * *

I accepted the invitation to join the Guild. I was Shatterglass by marriage and choice, but my history and ancestry was Paloman. I stood over the Duke as he signed the new treaty.

I do not sing anymore. Each vocalisation is formed with pain from the glass crystal that burst from my throat the day I sang the Grand Masters to life.

I do not know if the glassification will grow, if I will end up like Lucio, a glass prison for a long dead human soul.

One day Matteo will want to know of his past, of his Paloman inheritance. With a generation of Paloman men lost in the red sand outside Shatterglass, Matteo stands closer in line to the Duke than I would wish. It is too early to tell if Luciano will follow his father in the glass—but it is likely.

I dream of Lucio and sometimes of my brother and Tommaso. Always surrounded by flames. If I wake with tears on my face then they are for Lucio and the love I found too late. Love that lives in Matteo and Luciano now.

They are the faces of my love.

❋

PINION

STEPHANIE GUNN

1.

WAS BORN TO THE SHADOW OF THE Angel.

This is the first truth the Mothers teach us: we workers were brought forth from the Angel's Shadow by Her Divine Will so that we may serve Her and the City. We are the City's blood, and She is its heart.

The Angel stands at the centre of the City: a gold figure who looks down upon us from atop a tall column. Around her lies the inner City: four Towers, each one flanked by a low dormitory. In the Towers live the Chosen, and we, the workers, occupy the dormitories. Around the inner City is the Wall, which keeps us all safe from the outer City.

My first memory is of standing at the base of the Angel's column, craning to look up at Her. I bore only three scars on my arm, the newest still not fully healed. As I stood there, the light in the City seemed to shift, and for one glorious moment, She appeared to be looking directly at me, Her gaze Blessing me.

That night, in the darkness of West Dormitory, I dreamed that She flew down from Her column, cupped me in Her wings and lifted me up.

I woke before the dream was finished, and lay awake, wondering how it would have ended.

Maybe She would have lifted me up into the Towers to live with the Chosen.

Maybe She would have touched the twisted bones of my spine, given me wings. Together we would have risen into the sky, past the clouds and into whatever it was that lay beyond.

For the first eleven scars of my life, I held onto that moment where I felt Her Blessing, onto those maybes. Every morning, on the way to training, I knelt at the base of the Angel's column and looked up, waiting to be Blessed again.

Waiting for Her to lift me up.

2.

The twelfth scar hurt more than any others I remembered.

A Mother woke me before dawn, her grey-cowled face swimming out of the darkness of the dormitory. She led me in silence past the ranks of beds lining the walls of the long, thin building. Each bed held a sleeping Boy or Girl from the day shift, a few ringed with iron bars for the younger ones, each sunk deep in the unmoving slumber of the bone-weary.

At the end of the dormitory were the beds the Mothers slept in, and beyond them, the Blessing chapel, a small round room lined with dark tiles. At the beginning of each day, the Mothers stood there together and Blessed us, chanting the litany of the Angel. The only other use of the chapel occurred at night, when workers were summoned for the bestowment of a scar that indicated the completion of a cycle of training or work.

The Mother bade me kneel, then began chanting the litany in a low whisper: *You were born to the Shadow of the Angel. You were brought forth from Her Divine Shadow by Her Divine Will. To serve the Angel, to serve the City.*

I repeated the litany, and she spoke it again. Eleven times, one for each of the scars I wore. I ran my thumb over each band of scarring as I spoke, moving from the most recent back to my very first scar. This one was said to be given by the Angel herself. Mine was thin, barely there at all, the ends not quite meeting to form a circle.

After the twelfth repeat of the litany, I held my breath, expectant. The twelfth scar indicated that I had completed my training and was now a full worker of the City. I would be allowed to climb alone.

The Mother unhooked her sickle knife from her belt and held it up, then sliced around my arm with a quick, practiced movement. I held out my arm, blood dripping onto the tiles, as the Mother dug into the pouch on her belt for a palmful of ash. It stung when she rubbed it into the fresh cut, but I didn't flinch, just held steady as she wrapped my arm with a bandage. The soft fabric had once been a gown such as the one I wore, the garment worn to threads and holes before it was repurposed. Nothing was wasted in the City.

An hour remained before morning bell. The Mother went directly to her bed and was asleep instantly, her breath synchronising with that of the other Mothers.

The previous eleven times I had been through this ceremony, I had returned to bed as well, but this time I found myself walking past my bed, out through the door. There was no lock on the dormitory: no one to keep out, and we workers needed no locks to keep us in.

The first light of the sun was just beginning to rise over the Wall, staining the clouds red. Something lifted in me, seeing that light. It felt as though the City itself was acknowledging my twelfth scar.

I sank down onto the stairs, watching the light crawl across the inner City, climb the steel-and-brass cages surrounding the Towers. Beneath the cages, each of the Towers was clad in black non-reflective glass. Only the cages catch the light.

Attached to those cages were the networks of pipes and pumps which serviced the Chosen in their Towers: pipes which fed clean water, others which removed wastes. In shafts which ran up the centres of the Towers were gas and hydraulic systems which regulated air temperature and purity. All workers were taught basic recognition of all systems, but were given training in only one of them. Mine was water, specifically the maintenance of the pumps which send clean water in to the Tower.

The light slid across the bare dust of the central square, then slowly climbed towards the Angel. She was made from bronze, with her wings stretched behind Her, one foot raised as though She was springing into flight.

Morning bell sounded from within the dormitory, indicating that it was time for everyone to rise and make ablutions before

Blessing. Time for me to go inside, and yet I found myself crossing the square, kneeling at the base of the Angel's column.

"I will serve you, Angel," I said. I squeezed hard at the bandage on my arm. Gritty ash rubbed into the fresh cut, pain flaring white hot. "Whatever it is that you brought me forth for, I will do it. I will serve the City."

The light thinned as I knelt there, face turned up to the Angel. On the Towers, I could see the small figures of Boys and Girls descending the cages, the light on the Angel signalling the end of night shift. Though there was enough light to see by, many still had their cramp lamps glowing. Many of them would keep them burning throughout the day while they slept, too, rousing every few hours to rewind them.

Water was my system, and so it was the water workers I picked out. Apart from the half hour given over every morning to Blessing, there was always a minimum of four workers maintaining the pumps of each Tower's water systems, with at least two more standing by with manual divert tubing and pumps. The water workers of West Tower gathered at the lowest level of the cage, just above the clouds of steam that rose from the great engines at the base of the Tower. There were two Boys with divert tubing slung over their wide shoulders, and three wiry Girls wearing the pocketed belt of the pump maintenance worker. Only three, which meant that someone had fallen during the night shift. At least they had managed to fall clear of the great engines. A half cycle ago, a Boy had fallen directly onto them. There had been minimal damage to the engine itself, thank the Angel, but for days the steam had been filled with the stench of cooking flesh.

After Blessing, it would be my turn to climb as a full worker for the first time. I flexed my twelve fingers, longed to feel the pumps beneath my hands.

The workers descended, and then, one by one, began to emerge from the clouds of steam around the great engines. All of them were naked, their worksuits and gear in arms, skin and hair dripping water. Two scars ago, the Girl who had been training me had whispered that the Chosen actually cleaned themselves by submerging their bodies in pure water, rather than steaming and rubbing down as we did. I'd wondered where she had heard such a thing. The Towers were sealed: no one went in or out. I'd gone to the next shift determined to ask her, but she was not there, fallen or sickened or sent belowground.

Every time I walked through the steam since, I had wondered that it would feel like to be submerged in water. Would you feel heavy? Light? Would it be like falling? Like flying?

"Day shift, bed thirty-six?"

The voice pulled me away from my thoughts. One of the Boys from the night shift stood next to me. He smelled like scorched metal, and there was a fresh burn on his stomach. He'd put his divert tubing away, but still cradled a divert pump close to his chest.

I nodded warily. "Yes?"

"They said you're good with words." He held out the pump, the muscles in his arms quivering and his breath coming fast and shallow. I wondered how he had found the strength to descend the Tower safely, even as I envied him that deep fatigue. "This one, should it be recycled?"

Part of our training is the recognition of words. Some of the pumps have symbols on their dials, but many have words as well. Some workers are better than others at remembering the shapes of words. I was better than most. I collected new words, hoarded them the way some of the younger Boys and Girls collected broken bolts. I leaned over the pump eagerly, scrubbing at the dials with the hem of my gown to clear them of char. Nothing new, much to my disappointment.

"Flush the lines, change the oil completely and it should be fine," I said. "No need for recycling yet."

He nodded and headed away to the workroom at the back of the dormitory. While he slept, other workers would service the pump, and it would be ready for his next shift. Silence fell, and in the quiet, I could hear the beating of the subterranean pumps. Right now, there were small crouched Girls and Boys working at the bellows of pumps that sent sewerage to the treatment centres, or brought water from the reclaimers. Those workers were either those unable to continue working aboveground, or those brought forth from the Angel's Shadow with something that marked them as intended for belowground work. Either way, once you went belowground, you never again returned to the surface. It was the Angel's Will.

All at once, the pumps went silent. It was time for Blessing. In the Dormitories, the Mothers would be starting to chant the litany. Belowground, I imagined the Boys and Girls whispering the words as well. Time for me to return.

Just as I started up the steps to the dormitory, movement across the square caught my eye. There was a woman emerging from behind East Tower, her steps hesitant and uneven. A ragged earth-coloured robe hung around her skinny body, and she cradled a bundle of the same fabric in her arms.

She was not dressed like a Mother or worker. The Towers were sealed, and no one went in or came out. There was only one place she could have come from. The outer City.

Outside the Wall was chaos, the Mothers taught us. War, tortures, sicknesses that could flay the flesh from your bones, turn your body liquid. People more animal than human. The Wall kept all of that out. Kept us safe.

My heart hammering, I stood there and watched as the woman limped towards the Angel and knelt down. When she looked up at the Angel, I saw that the woman had no eyes, just bare bone where they should have been. She laid her bundle down in the Angel's Shadow, something like dull metal glinting along the inside of her arm. She paused, turning towards East Tower as though glancing back, then leaned down to press her cheek against the bundle.

When the woman straightened again, she seemed to look directly at me. I froze, told myself that there was no way she could see anything at all.

The woman turned and limped away. The first strains of Blessing came from within the dormitory.

And the bundle left beneath the Angel moved, a small arm reaching out.

The Angel looked down at me. I took a step, my eyes on Her, waiting for some kind of sign. There was nothing but the Mothers' voices coming from inside. I crossed the square, knelt down beneath the Angel again.

Inside the bundle was a baby, its face covered by a fold of fabric. The child made a soft sound, its hand reaching up to me. A ragged, shallow cut curved around its wrist, the ends of the wound not quite meeting.

An emissary of the Angel, I thought, that's who the woman must have been. Or else some aspect of the Angel made flesh. Warmth expanded within me, and I reached out, pressed my six fingers against the baby's five. Maybe this was what the Angel had brought me forth to witness. This was what I had been brought forth for.

I glanced up, saw that there were words painted on the Angel's column. They had been splashed on with red paint, and the shapes of most of them were unfamiliar to me. I recognised *you* and *angle*, nothing else.

At the same time as I noticed the words, the baby's hand closed painfully tight on my sixth finger, pulled hard. I yanked my hand away, and as I did, the fabric fell away from the baby's face. Like the woman who had laid it here, the baby had no eyes. But unlike her, its eye pits were not empty. In each was an assembly of brass cogs and gears, all intricately meshed together. The teeth of the outermost gears were pressed so deep that they have to have bitten into bone. There was no blood, just metal flowing smoothly into skin, as though the mechanisms had grown there. All of the brass and steel was untarnished, unscratched, gleaming brighter even that the bronze of the Angel above us.

There was a soft click, and the mechanisms shifted. In the centre of each mechanism was an annular gear, with a small pinion within. These both spun, then steadied, as though the pinion and annular gear were eyes focusing upon me. *Seeing* me.

The last strains of Blessing were sounding from the dormitory. Blessed by the Angel or not, I had to be inside before it finished. I walked back to the dormitory, that warmth expanding afresh within me, every step as light as though I had grown wings.

* * *

I entered the dormitory to find everything in chaos.

Most of the Girls and Boys were pressed back against the walls, the hems of their gowns held to their faces. The Mothers were clustered in front of the Blessing chapel, all of them bent over the figures of two Girls. Both of the Girls were twisted up into themselves, wracked by convulsions.

All of that warmth drained away instantly. I knew the flux when I saw it. The sickness came from time to time through the dormitories: a burning from within, joints winding tight enough that they could break bones. The Mothers said that it happened to those who had not served the City to the best of their abilities, those who the Angel had cursed.

As I watched, the smallest of the Girls shuddered, then fell still. Quickly, the other followed. They lay curled together on the floor, arms and legs intertwined like some strange machinery, both of them grey. Both of them dead.

I had never seen the flux take anyone so quickly. I shuddered, thinking of the baby, of the woman. What if seeing them had been no Blessing at all, but a curse?

The Mothers worked quickly, wrapping the Girls up and removing them from the dormitory. One Mother remained behind, her barked orders quickly returning order to everything. Night shift workers changed into their gowns and took to their bunks, cramp lamps glowing bright above every one of them. The day shift workers, myself included, filed into the antechamber to prepare for our work shift.

As a new worker, I was assigned a new worksuit, the pale leather creaking as I pulled it on. It was too snug around the back, the standard fit not allowing for the way my spine twisted, but it would do for a shift. My new belt cut into my hips as I loaded up my pouches with tools and parts, compressed coal and water flasks. All the time I worked, I touched my fingers to my cheeks over and over, gauging my temperature, looking for signs of flux.

I was the last worker to leave the antechamber, to move through the beds to the exit of the dormitory, where a Mother waited with a bowl of nutrient wafers. I took one, popped the whole of the dark, moist wafer into my mouth. It was one of the Angel's Blessings, these wafers, a single one of which was enough to sustain us for an entire shift.

I touched my cheek again before I left the dormitory. My skin was cool, no sign of flux. When I passed the Angel, I saw that both baby and words were gone.

Maybe they had been a test, I thought as I climbed the Tower. Maybe everyone new out of training saw something similar, and the Angel waited to see what we would do.

I knew what I would do. I would work, maintaining West Tower's water systems the way I had been brought forth to do.

Around me, the systems of the Tower hummed placidly. For once, all of the pumps and pipes were working flawlessly, no work for the divert Boys at all. I occupied myself topping up engines with water and compressed coal, feeling a flicker of that warmth begin to spread within me again. Whatever test the Angel had given me, I must have passed.

The sun was beginning the downward slide towards the Wall when I stopped to assess the supplies in my pouches. I was running low on compressed coal, but it should suffice, so long as none of the engines suffered catastrophic failure. I was about to move onto the next pump when something flashed behind one of the struts of the cage. Bright metal, catching the lowering light. A lost tool or forgotten flask, I assumed, going to retrieve it.

It was neither tool nor flask, but a machine no larger than the palm of my hand. It was fixed to the cage with looped wire, its gears working in a complicated pattern. A small key unwound slowly on one side, dials flickering on the other. The metal of both machine and wire were bright and untarnished. As bright as the mechanisms in the baby's eyes.

Bitter acid rose in my throat as I stared at the small machine. I could feel the Angel behind me, watching. Was this another test?

I started to reach out to the machine, intending just to turn it enough so I could properly see the dials, see if there were new words on them. My fingers were close enough to feel the heat rising from the machine when I remembered those two Girls, dead from the flux.

Swallowing hard, I pulled my hand back. Whatever the machine was, it had nothing to do with the water systems, and therefore nothing to do with me. I moved on to the next pump and did not look back.

I lost myself in the work of topping up engines, and it was only when I saw a Boy climbing past me with a glowing cramp lamp at his shoulder that I realised that I had worked on through the end of day shift and into the night. I descended alone, careful to skirt around the place where that bright machine had been, stripped and walked alone through the steam of the great engines.

Every part of me ached, and the steam stung the places on my back and hips where my suit and belt had rubbed my skin raw. I welcomed both the pain and the fatigue, for they showed that I had served the City well.

Everyone in the dormitory was asleep when I entered. I grabbed a cramp lamp and wound it just bright enough to illuminate my path to the antechamber to stow my gear, then back to my bed. I hung the lamp there, still glowing faintly, telling myself that I'd return it in the morning.

The raw patches of skin on my back and hips stung, and I turned from side to side, trying to find a position that would ease the aches in my body.

I turned over and opened my eyes just as the last light of the cramp lamp was fading. And noticed what I had missed before. The bed next to mine was empty, the sheets stripped away.

Mattresses were only left empty when the previous occupant was dead or had been sent belowground. I stared into the darkness, trying to remember who it had been who had slept there. Was it a fellow climber who had fallen? One of the Girls who'd died from the flux?

There was nothing, no memory at all of who had slept there in bed thirty-five. Nothing but for the fact that they had been there, and now were gone.

* * *

The next morning, I woke from a restless sleep to find that metal bars had been erected around bed thirty-five, fresh sheets stretched across the mattress. A Mother approached, a cramp lamp half-wound held in one hand. Her other arm was cradled around a baby, its face pressed into her shoulder, limbs hanging limp.

"Another one brought forth from the Shadow," the Mother said, seeing me awake. "We are Blessed."

"To serve the City, to serve the Angel," I whispered.

The baby made no attempt to hold onto the Mother as she laid it down. It lay there limp, long body wrapped in a gown, face turned away from me. Only the slight rise and fall of its chest told me that it lived.

The Mother started to turn away. I remembered the empty bed the previous night, the lack of memory of who had lain there before. "Boy or Girl?" I asked.

The Mother looked back at me, her eyes narrowed, but she didn't reprimand me for the question. "Girl." She reached over the bars and lifted one of the baby's arms. The baby Girl had long fingers, and her nails were broken, black driven beneath the ragged edges. "She would have been a good climber." The Mother released the baby's arm. It fell to the mattress with a dull thud. "But for the eyes."

I knew what I would see before the Mother turned the baby's face towards me, yet still I looked. Someone had tried to pry the mechanisms from her eye pits. In her left eye, the annular gear and pinion were gone entirely, all that remained a series of broken gears and springs pressed into her skin. All of the parts remained in her right eye, but the annular gear was bent, the pinion unmoving. The baby's face was bruised black, blood viscous as oil oozing from the places where metal met flesh.

"What will happen to her?" I asked.

The Mother's eyes narrowed again, but again she did not reprimand me. "Belowground, I should think." She must have seen something in my face, because her expression softened. "She would not have been brought forth if there were not a place for her. All kinds are needed for the City. It is the Angel's Will."

For all of that softening, the Mother's eyes were still sharp. I lay down, closed my eyes, pretended to sleep. I listened to the sound of the Mother returning to her bed. In the silence that followed, I could hear the mechanism in the baby's right eye vibrating, gears trying to mesh together.

When I opened my eyes, I found that I could just see the baby by the light of the cramp lamp the Mother had used, now hanging at the end of her bed. I thought again of that brown-robed woman, the bare bone where her eyes should have been. She had come from somewhere, and someone had placed those mechanisms in the baby's eyes. Had it been the Angel? Had it been something—or someone—else?

I ran my fingers along my scars, let them rest on the first one, the one that was given to me by the Angel herself. "Angel," I whispered. "Give me a sign. Show me what it is you brought me forth to do."

The baby's eye mechanism vibrated harder, a dissonant chime sounding as gears finally managed to mesh. Metal scraped against metal, and then came the unmistakable sound of a spring breaking.

I don't know why I reached out. Maybe it was an instinct, my cycles of training making me reach towards a breaking machine without thought. But when I slid my hand in through the bars, the baby also reached out her hand to mine. Pressed her palm against my palm.

Between our hands was a gear. A tiny one, one which I knew was the pinion, broken free from her eye mechanism. The mechanism itself was still and silent now.

For a moment, we were both still, our breaths synchronising as the Mothers' breaths did. Then the baby turned away, leaving the pinion in my hand. The metal was sticky, warm as blood.

I pulled my hand back from the baby's bed, turned the pinion over between my fingers. There was a broken tooth along its edge; this gear was fit for nothing but recycling now.

3.

The baby occupied the bed next to mine for less than half a cycle.

She rejected most of the feed the Mothers gave her, and grew only slowly. Some nights she barely moved at all, just lay there, eye pits constantly leaking black blood.

I kept that pinion, though it was against all rules of the City. At first, I'd thought that perhaps I'd be able to replace it, repair the eye mechanism. I smuggled the pinion into the antechamber, even went into the workshop itself, though it was not somewhere my work required me to be, in search of a suitable replacement. There was nothing, all of the gears we made too large and unwieldy.

Once, I even went in search of the strange machine I'd seen wired to the cage of West Tower, thinking that perhaps it had some parts I could use. It was gone, only light scratches on the cage showing where it had been.

Even then, when I knew repair was impossible, I didn't take the pinion to recycling. During the day, I kept it tucked in the bottom of one of my pouches, and at night, I slipped it into a tear in my mattress.

One morning, I woke to find the baby gone, the bars dismantled and mattress stripped of its sheets. Down the end of the dormitory, the Mothers were turning Boys and Girls out of their beds, tearing sheets from mattresses, gowns from backs. There must have been an outbreak of flux during the night, large enough that all of the linens would be burned.

When they stripped my sheets, they would find the tear in the mattress, would find the pinion. Suddenly nothing else mattered but keeping that gear. I quickly leapt out of bed, tore off the sheets and scrabbled to retrieve the pinion.

The Mothers were approaching. I couldn't think of anything to do but swallow it.

Against my tongue, the metal was warm, and the mingled tastes of blood and oil bloomed in my mouth. It should have made me gag, but instead it felt almost familiar. Like I was tasting home.

I swallowed the pinion. I could feel it moving down my throat, lodging somewhere deep in my guts. There was a sharp stab of pain, and then I felt a deep vibration emanating from it, as though it had meshed with my flesh the way it had with the baby's eye pits.

The vibration flickered, and I felt another pain, this one sharp enough to bend me double. It was gone as soon as it came, and when the Mothers reached my bed I was standing there naked, my gown and sheets ready to be collected for burning, the pinion pulsing steadily within me like a second heart.

4.

The steam pump shuddered beneath my hands, coughed once and then died.

There was a Boy clinging to the cage nearby, divert tubing and pump at the ready. He'd appeared from around the corner as I'd started work on the pump. Like most workers with many cycles of experience, he'd learned to listen to the sounds of the Tower, hear when a pump or pipe was beginning to fail. He knew his place, and he wouldn't divert water unless he was asked by a pump worker like me. I nodded to him, and he moved into place.

It took only moments for him to set up the divert tubing. The heavy muscles of his arms and shoulders flexed as he worked the manual pump, his eyes on its dials. I watched the flow of water until I was certain there were no leaks, then turned to the failed pump.

There were thirteen scars on my arm now. A full cycle of work completed, and I was only just beginning to develop the knack for listening to the Tower as a whole. My body had adapted over the last cycle, the long muscles of my thighs grown lean and strong, my palms thickly scarred, burned over and over by steam and hot metal. The callous that formed was tough enough now that I could plunge my hands into steam and not burn, and yet the skin there was still sensitive enough for me to do my work. My fingers were naturally long to begin with, but they had become more nimble, the flesh paring down almost to bone. The extra finger I bore on each hand had changed even more, becoming longer and thinner again, the nail flattened and turned harder than steel.

I lifted the lid of the pump, slid my fingers into its guts. I located a gear with broken teeth and a worn spring, replaced them both, storing the broken ones in a pouch to take for recycling. I could feel the pinion within me vibrating as I worked, as though it longed to become part of the machine in my hands. Over the last cycle, I had felt it shift several times in my guts; each time those bright pains eased, I felt it lying slightly higher within me.

I went over the pump again, tightening all of the screws with my nails. The mainspring was wearing, but it would do for a while before it needed to be replaced. Finally, I added fresh compressed coal and topped up the water chamber from a flask. When I switched the pump back on, it hummed smoothly into life.

The divert Boy switched everything back over, waited to see that everything was working, then hoisted his gear onto his back and vanished around the corner of the Tower again.

My muscles were cramping, and so I hooked my knees over the cage and let myself fall back, hanging there upside down. It was a trick I'd learned from other workers, hanging like this to stretch out the muscles of your shoulders and arms. I swung slowly from side to side, closed my eyes and listened to the Tower. In my guts, the pinion hummed, and when I swallowed, I tasted oil in the back of my throat.

The sound of the Tower changed.

I hauled myself back up, listening closely. It wasn't the dissonance of a breaking pipe, or the wheeze of gears about to shear. It was something that I had never heard before. I waited for a moment, to see if any other workers were coming to investigate, but there was no one on the face but me. I climbed towards the place where the sound had changed, the pinion pulsing hard and fast within me.

There was a hole in the Tower.

A square of the black had been opened, swung open like a window, its outer edge propped against the cage. I climbed higher, positioned myself behind a strut of the cage and peered around it to see.

There was a Boy standing just inside the opening, looking up at the sky. He was wearing something like one of the gowns we wore at night, the fabric brighter than anything I'd ever seen. His gown was shorter, the hem of it half-tucked into a lower garment like a worksuit cut off at the waist. Both garments looked soft, much softer than the leather of my worksuit or the robes of the Mothers. Around his neck the Boy wore a strange brass contraption, the metal shining and unmarked. His hair was dark, the curls clean of grease, his skin almost as colourless as his half-gown. His eyes were a colour I had never seen before, a colour I had no name for. He looked soft, untouched, cleaner than any baby newly brought forth from the Shadow.

He lifted the brass contraption to his eyes, fingers moving across dials set into the sides of the thing. I heard the smooth whine of oiled gears shifting inside it, and the pinion inside of me pulsed hard, as if in response. There were no callouses on the Boy's hands, and when he paused in his adjustments to push his sleeve back, I saw that he wore no scars.

I had never before seen someone unmarked by scars. Anyone so soft.

He was a Chosen, of that I was certain. And I was just as certain that I should not be here. I started to climb away, and the spare parts in my belt rattled as I moved. The Boy's eyes instantly moved to me, and I froze in place, mid-swing.

"Shadow," he said. His voice was as smooth as his skin, a strange melody in the word.

Words bubbled up in me, dozens of questions crowding my throat. I should leave, should climb away and pretend that I hadn't seen this Boy or the opening in the Tower. But the pinion was moving within me again, small spikes of pain coming every time it shifted. I swallowed, tasted oil and blood.

"What colour are your eyes?" I asked.

The corners of the Boy's mouth turned up. "They're blue. My mother says that they're the colour the sky used to be."

I stared at his eyes. Impossible to think of the sky being so bright, so clear.

"You can come closer," he said. "There's no one else here. It's safe."

The pinion vibrated harder as I moved towards the opening in the Tower. The space beyond the Boy was as white as his half-gown, and as painfully clean as he was. As best as I could see, the room was empty.

"I saw your shadow," he said. "Outside the shielding. I wanted to see what the shielding was made from, how it worked." He touched the contraption around his neck. "My binoculars let me see through with the right lenses, but everything is flat, no definition." He reached out and touched the closest strut, careful to keep everything but his arm inside the Tower. "I thought these were part of the shielding, but then I saw you. What are you doing, climbing out there?"

I shifted my weight, the twisted bones of my spine rubbing against my worksuit. I'd adjusted the suit over and over during the last cycle, but no matter how many patches I added, my bones kept twisting, my skin rubbing raw as I climbed. Even now, I could feel fresh blood trickling between my skin and suit. When I breathed in, I could feel the cool air from within the Tower filling my lungs. The air had no scent, and I was suddenly aware of the thick musk that rose from my own skin.

"I'm a water worker," I said, touching my belt. "I maintain the pumps."

His brows drew together. "Pumps? Out there?"

"There's a pump right below you." I pointed, but he didn't lean out to look. "Weren't you taught about the Tower's systems? How you get water? How your wastes are taken away?"

"I turn on the tap and there's water. I flush and . . . *it* goes." His cheeks reddened at the last. "There are wires in the walls," he added quickly. "No one can tell me what they're for. Red and yellow, brown and green. Is that what you mean?"

I shook my head, even as I wondered what *yellow* was. I knew the others. Red was the colour of fresh blood, brown the colour it went when it dried. Green was the shade that copper and bronze went in the weather.

"There's a pump right below you," I said, balancing my weight on one knee and pointing again. "If you lean out you'll be able to see it. It's just below your . . . " I shrugged, not knowing what to call the opening.

"Window," he said. His face was tight, and he braced his hands against the sides of the *window*, leaned out. He moved back inside so quickly that I wondered if he'd seen anything at all. He kept his eyes closed for a moment, breathing hard.

"The great engines are beneath the Towers," I said. "More systems are in the shafts in the centre of the Tower. I only know how to work water, though." I moved closer to the window again, worry blooming in me when he didn't open his eyes. "Are you well? Is it the flux?"

He opened his eyes, and the bright *blue* of them startled me all over again. "I don't do well with heights." He took a deep, dragging breath, focused on me again. "You don't have a harness, or any ropes. Nothing holding you onto the building. What if you fell?"

I shrugged. "If I fall, the Angel brings forth another to take my place. It is Her Will." The pinion shifted within me, sending a stab of pain through my belly.

"The Angel?" he asked.

I gestured to the Angel. "She watches over the City. It is by Her Will that it runs, that we all live."

"That statue?"

"Is the physical embodiment of Her Divine Self." I smiled, imitating as best as I could the serene expression of the Mothers when they gave Blessing. "I was born to the Shadow of the Angel. To serve her, to serve the City."

The boy's eyes lingered on the Angel for a long time before he turned back to me. "My name is Luis Antonio. What's yours?"

"Name? What's that?"

"It's what my father called me when I was born. What did your father call you?"

Father. Another new word, one that felt as though it would cut my tongue if I spoke it. "I'm a Girl. West Dormitory, day shift, bed thirty-six." I shifted my weight against the cage, standing as straight and proud as my spine allowed.

Luis Antonio's eyes went to my wrist, to where the sleeve of my worksuit had pulled up as I moved. "Those scars. Did someone do that to you?"

I held my wrist out. "The Angel made the first one, but the rest were made by a Mother."

He recoiled. "Your *mother* did that?" Before I could answer, a soft chime sounded from deeper in the Tower. "That will be my father, come to take me to my lessons." He reached out, grasped the edge of his window, careful not to look down as he did. "I have to seal this now. Will you . . . will you come back?"

"I climb the Tower every day. It is my work."

"I'm in contemplation every day right now." Luis Antonio made a face. "If I asked, Father would probably double the time in my schedule. He'd be proud of his pious son." His lips twisted on the word *pious*. "Tomorrow, then, Shadow."

Moisture from the engine below us had condensed on the inner surface of the window, transforming the usually flat black into a reflective surface. As Luis Antonio swung the window inwards, I caught a glimpse of a scrawny figure in that surface. She wore pale leather darkened by grease and soot, her ragged hair the colour of rust. It was only after the Tower had sealed again that I realised that the figure had been me.

When I breathed in, I was aware anew of the smell of my own skin, the metallic tang that hung in the air of the inner City. New words tumbled through my mind: *blue, yellow, window, binoculars, father, name.* I hadn't imagined there would be so many more to collect.

My muscles were cramping again, and I hung upside down, swung slowly from side to side. The pinion rocked with me, rolling in my belly as though around an annular gear. I didn't look at the Angel, but up at the copper clouds, trying to imagine the sky *blue.* All I could see were Luis Antonio's eyes.

* * *

The next day, Luis Antonio was waiting for me with scraps of wire, and he showed me *yellow.* He told me that the names for his clothing were *shirt* and *trousers.*

He gave me the yellow wire to keep. After he had closed the window, I turned it over in my hands. The yellow coating crumbled, revealing bright copper beneath. I wound it into the next pump I tended, hidden away beneath the mainspring where no one would see it.

* * *

I held the nutrient wafer out on my palm. It was pliable and warm, one corner bent in from being squashed in my pouch as I worked, waiting for the face of the Tower to clear so I could climb up to Luis Antonio.

He had given me the yellow wire, and I wanted to give him something in return. At first, I'd thought of some of the spare parts I carried with me, but the metal of those was pitted and corroded, nothing like the bright metal of his binoculars. The only other thing I had to give was a nutrient wafer, and so I'd pretended to eat mine that morning, slipping it into my pouch as I'd gone out to work for the day.

Luis Antonio lifted the wafer from my palm. Even against the scarring on my hand, I could feel that his skin was cool and impossibly soft. He turned the wafer over, rubbed it between finger and thumb, then bit it in half.

Something in me cringed, seeing the wafer consumed with no Mother in sight. I started to whisper the litany of the Angel, but the words trailed off as the pinion in my belly vibrated.

"Protein, I think," Luis Antonio said after he swallowed. "A full load of vitamins, probably synthetic. Some fat, and other chemicals

I can't recognise." He turned the remains of the wafer over, rubbing at the surface of it with his thumb. "It would be interesting to have it tested. Perhaps I could take it to one of the labs."

More new words, so many of them that they made my head ache. "They are the Angel's blessing. That is all that anyone needs to know. All of it must be consumed. Nothing is wasted in the City."

He looked at the remains of the wafer, then popped the rest into his mouth. "Pity they don't do more about the taste, though. The iron makes it taste like blood." He rummaged beneath the window—I assumed there was a shelf there, or some kind of storage—and withdrew a glass bottle with a metal cap. It was filled with clear liquid. He unscrewed the cap and took a swallow, then held the bottle out to me.

My stomach was curled tight, and I wished that I'd only given him a portion of the wafer. There would be no chance for another until the next morning. "What is it?"

"It's just water."

I lifted one of my flasks from my belt, shook the murky stuff within. "*This* is water. Water is only for the engines."

"You don't drink water?"

Another new word. My head was aching in earnest now. "We only consume nutrient wafers. One per day is enough to sustain us."

He touched his fingers to his lips. "Fascinating. There must be something in them that compensates for the body's need for water."

When I swallowed, my throat was dry. My teeth were beginning to ache. I touched my hand to my cheek, wondering if it was the flux. I was cool enough, though.

"Try some," Luis Antonio said. "It won't hurt you. People are supposed to drink water."

I hooked my knees around the cage, took the bottle. The glass was so perfectly smooth that it almost slid from my hands, and I curled my fingers hard around it, lifted it to my mouth. Took a small sip.

The water tasted like everything and nothing, all at once. It was cold, too, the sip uncurling in my stomach. When Luis Antonio nodded, I took a bigger swallow. The aches receded, and fell away completely with another mouthful. The pinion made that odd vibration in my stomach again. I wished that I could curl it in my hand, hold it close to my cheek. Show it yellow, and water, and shirts and trousers and windows and blue.

In the dormitory that night, I slept deeper than I ever had. And in the morning, when I consumed my nutrient wafer, all I could taste was blood.

* * *

That day, I worked with the taste of blood in my mouth. From time to time, the pinion rocked within me. I'd seen one of the Mothers sometimes pick up a fussy baby new from the Shadow, rock the Boy or Girl in their arms until they slept. It felt like that, like being comforted.

That night, I dreamed that I was kneeling at the base of the Angel's column, my forehead pressed against the dust. Beneath me I could hear the beating of a subterranean pump; within me, the pinion matched the beat. The Angel flew down from Her pedestal, lifted me up. In the dream, Her arms were both whole, the bronze of them pliable and warm as flesh. She rocked me as She lifted me up, and when I looked into Her eyes, I saw that they were the same blue as Luis Antonio's.

Up and up we flew, up through the copper clouds—sticky to the touch, and clinging to me until the Angel waved them away—and through, up into the blue that lay beyond. The Angel smiled at me, and the blue faded, light dimming to a black darker than the dormitory at night. One by one, small lights pressed out of that darkness. I felt something expand within me, looking at them. It felt like looking upon the face of someone I had known long ago, their features forgotten until this moment.

The Angel exhaled, and the clouds below us parted. I saw the City: the Towers, the dormitories, the Wall which surrounded it all. All of the buildings were webbed with lights, and I knew somehow that each of those lights was a person: a Boy or Girl, a Mother or Chosen. I could even see the Boys and Girls working belowground, their lights dimmed only slightly by the earth. So many of them there, more than I had ever thought. The Angel passed a hand over my eyes, and all of the lights flickered, took on colours: red and gold and bronze and green and yellow and blue.

Another breath from the Angel, and the Wall came into clearer focus. There were lights there, too, somehow inside the structure of the Wall, two at each of the cardinal directions. They were not dimmed, as the other underground workers, but somehow within the Wall itself.

One more breath, and darkness rolled back from the outer City. When I saw what was revealed there, all thought of the rest of the City fled. There were lights there, a multitude of them. More than in the inner City, far more. Many of them were dim, some flickering out even as I watched, but they were *there*, all of those people living outside of the Wall. They stretched out and out, a web of lights that seemed to stretch on forever.

Slowly, the Angel descended, laid me down again at the foot of Her column. When she pressed her lips to my forehead, the bronze was cold now. "When the Angel flies, you will all be free."

Her voice was like the clear water that Luis Antonio had given me, bright and true. She pressed a hand against my spine, fingers seeking for the places where my bones twisted the most. A bright pain flared there, and I felt the pinion shift in my guts, moving higher.

The Angel smiled. "You can be free."

* * *

I woke the next morning kneeling on the ground at the foot of the Angel's column.

Morning light was just beginning to creep over the Wall, the lights from cramp lamps still moving over the Towers. As I pulled myself to my feet, that pain clutched again at my spine. The pinion shifted, and it was in the same place in my stomach as it had moved to in my dream.

Above, the Angel was shadowed, indistinct against the clouds. *Had* it been a dream?

Moving quietly, I slipped between West Tower and its dormitory. Everything was silent, but for the faint sounds of pumps belowground. I kept walking, my heart hammering, until I reached the Wall.

I had never before stood so close to the Wall. None of us workers had any need to go to it, though it had never been expressly forbidden. From a distance, it looked solid, but as I stood there now, I could see that there was something like a door there, the Wall on either side of it slightly thicker than the rest. I thought of the lights I had seen from above in my dream.

The Wall was cold to the touch. I laid my hand on it, leaned close. "Hello? Is anyone there?"

For a long moment, nothing. Then a faint sound came from within, like something shifting. Like *someone* shifting. There was no answer, but I knew that there was someone there. A worker, somehow within the Wall.

Bile rose in my throat, and I backed away, returning to the Angel's column. Words were painted there in powdery yellow, words which had not been there when I woke, though the square around me was empty.

I knew the shape of them from my dream. *When the Angel flies, you will all be free.*

5.

I gained my fourteenth and fifteenth scars.

The words on the Angel's column appeared again and again. Some mornings, they would still be there when we filed out to day shift, a Boy or Girl scrubbing at them with a wet cloth. They began to spread over the inner City, appearing on low pipes and pumps, even along the long wall of West Dormitory. A watch was set, but still the words appeared.

Every day that I could, I visited with Luis Antonio. He always remained inside the Tower, never reaching out, just as I always remained outside. Even when he passed me his binoculars to try, both of us were careful to meet precisely half way. We both knew our places. No one ever caught us. Luis Antonio was locked in contemplation, and a chime would warn him of anyone arriving. I grew better and better at listening to the Tower, could hear an approaching Boy or Girl long before they'd see us.

I taught Luis Antonio what I knew of the inner City: the rhythms of my shifts, the workings of the Towers' systems. In return, he showed me his work. Tiny intricate machines made from bright brass, machines which could be wound up with keys. Clockwork, he called it. That machine I'd found on the Tower so long ago had been his work, constructed to assess the air quality outside. Others he made could tick off slices of time, stir water in a flask.

One day he brought out a machine smaller than the ones he had shown me before. This one, Luis Antonio said, was made in the likeness of a now-extinct animal called a cat. This machine was more finely made than the others he had shown me, the gears and springs more delicate. It had been made by Luis Antonio's tutor, a man named Nataneal. When Luis Antonio wound up the cat and placed it in my palm, the pinion within me vibrated hard, small pains coming as it climbed higher within me. The cat turned a small circle and then lay down, vibrating rhythmically against my skin. When I asked Luis Antonio what the purpose of the machine was, he told me that it had no purpose beyond that of memory, an idea of what once had been.

Nataneal had taught Luis Antonio that the world had been different, before. There had been no Towers, no dormitories. No Chosen. The Angel herself had stood in a different city, stairs spiralling up the centre of her pedestal so people could climb up to Her, could touch Her.

The thought of anyone being able to touch the Angel was abhorrent, sacrilege. I thrust the cat back at Luis Antonio, who fumbled the small machine. It fell to the floor with the sound of breaking gears.

I descended the Tower, not looking back, and plunged myself into the steam of the great engines, standing close enough to them that I felt the hot metal scald my flesh. I did not move away, but stood there, repeating the litany of the Angel over and over until my voice was gone.

* * *

For the span of ten shifts, I did not return to Luis Antonio.

I heard the sound of his window standing open, and deliberately I climbed in the other direction, did not look his way. At night, I could not sleep, but lay awake thinking of what he had said.

In the mornings, I knelt beneath the Angel again, as I had when I was still training, and looked up at her. Wanting her to tell me if what Luis Antonio had said was real. Wanting some sign that She was real.

When I finally climbed up to meet Luis Antonio again, I found him pale, with dark smudges beneath his eyes. In his hands, he held a flat object.

He opened up the object, revealing many layers inside. "This is a book, Shadow," he said. "I smuggled it out of my parents' quarters. Only adults are allowed to possess them."

Everything else forgotten, I leaned over the book, greedy for new words. There were so many of them: hundreds or thousands, with only one or two here and there that I recognised the shape of. A faint ache started in my chest as I looked at the book, the pinion rising higher, vibrating just beneath my ribs.

There were pictures in the book, too. People as clean and soft as Luis Antonio, cities filled with buildings like the Towers, but made of glass that reflected the light. More things that I could not name or recognise.

It was a war which changed everything, Luis Antonio said. The last war or the first, no one could tell him. There had been bombs which had created massive waves of heat and wind, an invisible force called radiation following which had sickened the world. Some people had retreated into the Towers and had hidden there, safe behind the shielding. They had been taught that everything outside was poisoned with radiation, everyone dead or twisted by invisible sicknesses. That the world would never recover.

"I was afraid that you weren't going to come back," Luis Antonio said.

His breath moved against my cheek as he spoke. I had been so entranced by the book and the worlds that I had leaned further into the Tower than ever before. I could feel the warmth of his skin, smell the clean scent that rose from his shirt. This close, the colour of his eyes was so bright that I had to look away.

"I don't know what to do," I said. "What do I do, knowing this?"

"I wish I knew. Nataneal would know, but I can't find him anywhere. My father says that he's probably in extended seclusion, but I'm not sure." He set the book aside and withdrew a small, red object from his pocket. He set it in my hand. It was round, warm from contact with his body.

I turned it over. "What is it?"

"It's an apple. Food." At my perplexed look, he smiled. "Like the nutrient wafers. Take a bite."

The outside of the apple was tougher than I had expected, and it took some work to get my teeth through it. As soon as I broke through, something like water filled my mouth. It tasted like nothing I had ever known.

"What you're tasting is called sweet," Luis Antonio said. "The hydroponics lab is working on cleaning up some of the old seed stocks, making new hybrids. My father is most impressed at my sudden interest in the project, needless to say, and it was easy enough to smuggle one out for you."

Luis Antonio had explained the concept of father to me on one of our previous visits. It still seemed strange to me, that a man and a woman could produce another person. I'd told Luis Antonio about the baby with the mechanical eyes, then, of course, and he had theorised that the woman laying her beneath the Angel might have been her mother.

Thoughts tumbled through me, too many of them to grasp onto. I took another bite of apple, breaking through the flesh to something small and brown within.

Luis Antonio reached over and pulled the object free. "This is the seed. You plant it in fertile soil, give it light and nutrients, and if you're lucky, it will grow into a whole new tree, give you new apples."

The pinion rolled within me. "It's so small."

"Small things grow, Shadow."

Movement in the corner of my eye caught my attention. The words on the Angel's column had been painted high enough that a scaffold had needed to be constructed in order for them to be reached. A Boy had climbed to the top of the small cage, and was reaching out to scrub at the lowest letters. He was so young that he had to be half trained at best, and didn't know how to balance his weight yet. As I watched, he slipped and plunged to the ground. He did not get up.

"When the Angel flies, you will all be free," Luis Antonio said.

I turned to him. "What did you say?"

"Those words are being painted inside the Tower, too, Shadow," he said. "Whatever's happening, it's in here as well as out there."

I looked down at the unmoving boy. Another Boy approached him, but didn't aid him, just climbed up the scaffold, his weight as ill-balanced as the first. "What do you think it means?"

"I think it's a promise," he said.

"What's a promise?" I asked.

He smiled, reached out and cupped my hand in his. Curled into my palm, the small seed warmed. "Something like this."

He leaned in close, and pressed his lips to mine.

6.

And so it went.

I climbed the Tower. I repaired and serviced the water pumps. The words were painted in the square over and over, and I started to hear them whispered in the still of the dormitory at night, in the billowing steam of the great engines.

I kept the apple seed tucked into the bottom of one of my pouches during the day, and placed it beneath my tongue at night. Sometimes

I woke with a start, afraid that I'd swallowed it, that somehow the seed would grow into an apple tree inside of me, that I would begin to sprout fruit and so betray my contact with Luis Antonio. I never did, my body somehow knowing how to keep it safe.

In my belly, the pinion rolled and rolled, moving higher and higher until it felt as though it had lodged in the muscle of my heart, beating there with the rhythm of my pulse.

7.

In the year of my eighteenth scar, the fever came.

At first we thought it was merely the flux, but the wave of sickness rolled over the inner City, emptying beds in the dormitories one by one. As I lay awake at night, I could hear Boys and Girls moaning as their blood boiled. As each of them died, they whispered the promise, and every time, I whispered it too, the pinion shivering against my heart.

During the days, those who were well enough climbed to service the Towers. We worked on other Towers, other systems, those of us who were well enough trying to keep everything running as best we could. For the first time, I worked a night shift, a cramp lamp glowing at my shoulder.

The Mothers told us that the Angel was displeased with us, that we had not served the City as we had been brought forth to do. We worked harder and harder, and still workers grew sick, still they died. The fever moved belowground, the subterranean pumps falling silent one by one.

The Mothers, too, began to fall ill.

I caught the fever in the last wave of it. A mild case, but still I shivered and sweated in my bed. I turned over once to see the last Mother in our dormitory standing in the chapel, propping her weight against the wall as she tried to deliver Blessing. Midway through, she slid to the floor and lay there unmoving.

Though I was still burning, I knew that I did not want to die there. I dragged myself out of bed, donned my worksuit and climbed West Tower to Luis Antonio's window. The window was sealed, but somehow I knew that he was there on the other side. I tied myself to the cage, leaned my face against the glass and waited to die.

For the span of two shifts, I stayed there, barely conscious. No one else climbed the Towers, and no one moved below. The City was completely silent.

On the third night, my fever broke. I stayed there for a long time, just staring down at the Angel. The pinion had risen into my throat: I could feel it beneath my skin, pulsing like a second heart, one much steadier and stronger than my own thready pulse.

My muscles much weakened by the fever, it took me the better part of a shift to descend the Tower, clinging tightly the whole time to keep myself from falling.

8.

The column of the Angel was covered with layers of paint, the promise layered over and over, no one able to be spared to clean them away.

I wore twenty scars now, more than the Mother who had been newly assigned to West Dormitory. My worksuit was more patch than original leather now, black stitches crawling all over me. The fever had burned much of the muscle from me, and when I stood for too long, I shook, black eating at the edges of my vision. I ached constantly, and the skin on my back was always raw and bleeding.

Before the fever, I would certainly have been sent belowground. Now, there was no one else, and so still I climbed.

The morning had dawned unseasonably cold, and blood was freezing beneath my worksuit as I made my way across the square. There was a bundle lying in the Shadow of the Angel. A Mother came flying out of a dormitory and snatched the bundle up. Her hands shook, much as mine did, and she fumbled the bundle, dropping it. As it hit the ground, the fabric fell open, revealing what lay within.

Not a baby, but grey ash moulded in the shape of an infant. It held its shape for a moment, then came apart, ash billowing everywhere. From within the grey cloud came a hundred tiny clockwork machines, something like a spider I had seen in one of Luis Antonio's books, each blaring in unison the promise: "When the Angel flies, you will all be free!"

The Mother flew into action, stamping machine after machine beneath her feet. The metal sliced through the thin soles of her shoes, and soon the dust was running thick with her blood. She managed to stop perhaps a dozen, but the rest scampered past her, scuttling away into the inner City. One crawled over my foot, one of its legs bent from being crushed by the Mother. The pinion in my throat vibrated, and before I could think, I pinched the spider shut and slid it into one of my pouches. It stilled and went silent.

Luis Antonio's window was already open. The muscles in my legs trembled as I propped myself on the cage outside. Before the fever, it had taken no effort to balance myself on the cage. Now, it seemed to take all of my concentration.

He smiled. "Today is my birthday," he said. "In all of these years, you've never been here on my birthday before."

"Birthday?"

"Like the scars on your arm. We celebrate every year on the day we were born. Without the pain."

We'd talked about this: how we measured time in cycles, while in the Tower things were measured in years. As best as Luis Antonio had been able to figure, the length of both was about the same.

"How many scars would you wear today?" I asked.

"Thirty," he said.

I stared at him. His hair was free of white, his skin unlined. Our new Mother bore sixteen scars, and her hair was white, her spine bent almost double.

"I found a new book in the library," Luis Antonio continued. "I wasn't able to smuggle it out, but it had a story in it about a woman like you."

"A worker?"

He shook his head. "She had an extra finger on each hand, just like you. They called it the mark of a witch."

"What's that?"

"The book didn't say exactly. It said that she flew, so I figure she must have been something like the Angel." He reached into the shelves below the window and withdrew a small bundle of white fabric. "It's tradition to receive presents on your birthday, but I wanted to give you something instead."

Since that first apple, Luis Antonio had brought me food many times: apples of different colours, oranges, tomatoes, soybeans, an avocado.

I expected food again, and my mouth watered as I unfolded the fabric, my fingers leaving black smears on the cloth.

Inside was a clockwork angel.

She was no taller than my thumb, her body made of gears and springs, her wings of loops of wire. A tiny turnkey rested between her shoulders. Luis Antonio turned the key and a humming came from the belly of the angel, the pinion in my throat vibrating in response. The tiny angel's wings began to beat, and she lifted off, hovering above my palm for the span of three breaths before she fell down again, her metal warmer than my skin.

"Nataneal would have known how to make her fly higher," Luis Antonio said. "This is the best I could do."

"She's amazing," I said, touching her wings lightly. "When the Angel flies, we will all be free."

In my pouch, the spider machine stirred, whispering the promise back to me. I set the clockwork angel down carefully, then slid the spider from my pouch. "These were released into the square."

Luis Antonio took the spider from me. It shivered against his hand, spoke the promise once more, and then went silent. "It doesn't even need to be wound up," he said. "How is that possible?" He pressed against a spring, and the voice came clear again. Luis Antonio's eyes went wide. "That's Nataneal's voice. He made this, Shadow. He must have gotten *out*. He's out there, and he's trying to free everyone. Don't you see—"

Whatever he had been about to say was lost in the sound of an explosion down in the square.

I whipped around, half falling from my perch as I did. Scrambling to catch myself, I was too slow to catch anything but a flash of light beneath the Angel's column, then black smoke billowing up. Almost on top of the first came a second explosion. This one was louder, the light so bright that it seared my eyes. There was a wave of heat, and then the Tower itself was shaking, the cage shuddering as though it wanted to break free. I tipped backwards, my hands slipping from the struts and I was starting to fall-

And then hands were closing around my wrists, pulling me up, pulling me inside the Tower.

Into Luis Antonio's arms.

He reached past me and pulled the window closed, and then sank to the floor, still holding me in his arms. Panic rose immediately in me when I looked around at the room. The space was too small, the walls too close. Luis Antonio pulled me near, pressed my face against his chest. His body was warm, and I could hear the beating of his heart.

The Tower shook again, and again.

"They wanted to make the Angel fly," Luis Antonio said. I heard his voice both through the air and resonating through his sternum.

"It was a symbol, to try to incite the people to revolution. It's so much like Nataneal. He always emphasised choice, not coercing people into doing something.

I blinked, seeing the afterimage of the explosion. "Do you think they will?"

He was silent for a long time. "They need to. There aren't enough people in the Towers. We need the people outside as well." His arms tightened around me. "You almost fell. You're not strong enough to climb anymore, are you? You have to ask them for other work."

"There's nothing else. Just belowground. And if I go there, I don't ever come back." *I don't ever visit you again*, I added silently.

"I wish I could keep you here," he said. "I know the way they work, though. After this, they'll be on alert, and they'll search everywhere."

"You could come out," I said. "Find Nataneal."

He went still, and I knew that I had no answer. He wouldn't—or couldn't—come out, and I couldn't come in. "What do we do? What if no one rises up?"

"I don't know, Shadow. I don't know."

9.

After the explosion, the Mothers ushered all of the workers into the one dormitory and barred the door with lengths of steel. Both day and night shift workers were there, all of the night workers with their cramp lamps glowing. Before the fever, we would have been four to a bed, but now, even with all dormitories here in one room, there were empty beds between all of us.

The doors were kept barred for a night, then a day and a night again.

The first night, I lay awake, listening. Occasionally, I heard one of Nataneal's spiders scuttle across the roof. From time to time, someone shouted the promise. Each time their words were followed by a short, sharp bark, then silence.

On the second night, I slept, and dreamed of the Angel falling. Her wings were torn, the bronze leaking thick black blood, like the eyes of the baby, so long ago. Her hands clutched at me, and she pulled me down beneath the ground, down to where I would never again see Luis Antonio. The earth fell in on me, black and heavy, filling my mouth and nose, smothering me in fetid darkness.

When I woke, I was choking. I coughed, and the pinion fell from my lips. The edges were smoothed, but the metal was still bright. It lay still in my palm as the Mothers worked to open the doors and start Blessing.

I tucked the pinion into my pouch as I went out to work, nestling it next to the apple seed still there. Beneath the Angel's column, I stopped and stared.

The Angel was back up on her column. Her left arm was gone altogether now, and one of her wings hung at an odd angle. Her column leaned to one side, and it looked as though any moment she would slip and fall. One side of her face was flattened, the metal deformed. She hadn't flown at all, but fallen, as any lump of metal would. There was nothing divine about her, nothing that would save any of us.

Angel no more, but only an angel, a statue and nothing else.

Turning my back on her, I made my way up West Tower. The sound of the Tower was cacophony, many pumps failing. I ignored them all, just climbed straight to Luis Antonio's window.

It was closed, the black glass smooth and without break.

I stayed as long as I could, but it did not open.

* * *

Luis Antonio was not there the next day.

Or the next, or the next or the next.

Soon, I stopped climbing to him at all.

10.

Slowly, everything fell back into a kind of rhythm. I worked my shifts, and at night, I fell into a sleep so deep that waking was like digging my way out from belowground.

After the explosion, no more words appeared within the inner City. But for the Angel's missing arm and the tilting of her column, it would be easy to believe that none of it had happened at all. Sometimes, my hands in an engine, I forgot about Luis Antonio as well, and it was only when I encountered the apple seed or the pinion at the bottom of a pouch that I remembered that he had been real.

At the end of one shift, I slipped from the cage as I was descending. It wasn't a fall, not quite, but I jarred my ankle so that I was limping heavily by the time I returned to the dormitory. The Mother watched me closely as I tended it, and I knew that she saw everything: the twisting of my spine that made it hard to breathe if I turned in the wrong way, the way the muscles of my legs and arms had wasted away after the fever. I knew than that my days aboveground were numbered, and I couldn't find it in myself to care. Let them bury me. What difference would it make?

As I made my way to my bed, I looked around the dormitory and realised that, for the first time in my memory, there were no bars around any of the beds, no younger Girls or Boys anywhere to be seen. That bundle of ashes and clockwork spiders had been the last thing born to the shadow of the angel.

A Mother's cowled face swam out of the darkness above me, her touch on my arm jarring me out of deep sleep. I dragged myself up and followed her to the Blessing chapel, knelt at her feet. When she recited the litany, I did not speak it, just stared at the black of the tiles beneath us.

The sickle knife cut lightly, the Mother's hand pressing only a light scattering of ash against my arm. The scar, when it healed, would be as faint as my first.

The Mother smiled at me. I think, perhaps, it was the first time I had seen any of the Mothers smile. "This shift will be your last. See me when you return."

I didn't return to my bed, didn't even care if she saw me leave. I went out into the square and knelt beneath the Angel. Pressed my hands to the ground and listened to the stuttering sound of the subterranean pump. After this last shift, it would be me down there working those bellows.

Air moved against my skin, and I thought, for the first time in many cycles, of the dream I'd had of the angel, how she had lifted me up to see all of the lights of the people in the City.

I lifted my hands from the ground, dusted them off. I didn't have to go belowground. The Mother had done me a kindness in giving me one last shift. Had given me a choice.

I could fall.

11.

My muscles cramped yet again, forcing me to rest in the crook of two struts of the cage. I was only a third of the way up the Tower, and the sun was already crawling high in the sky. I had passed several failing pumps, but I didn't stop to service them. Today, I had brought nothing with me but the apple seed and the pinion.

I had planned on climbing to the very top of the Tower, but the way my body was failing me told me that I was probably going to have to settle for falling from lower. That risked a lesser injury, of course, and if I survived that, I could still be sent belowground.

Behind me, the angel watched me, her face impassive as always. I knew now that there was nothing divine about her, and yet when I started climbing again, I found myself chanting the litany of the Angel beneath my breath, over and over.

And then, a voice, rising in counterpoint to mine, "When the Angel flies, you will all be free."

Luis Antonio stood inside a window, this one in a different part of the Tower to his usual white room. Behind him, the space was shadowed, and his clothes were stained, the collar of his shirt torn. A purple bruise bloomed on one cheek.

He said nothing, just reached out, grasped my hands and pulled me inside.

I fell into the Tower, fell into his arms.

The thudding of his heart was as irregular as the failing engines on the Tower. He had dropped weight, and beneath his clothes, his skin was dry and hot.

"Where have you been?" I asked.

"I'm sorry, Shadow," he said. "I had no way to find you, no way to tell you what was happening. After the attack, the Towers went on lockdown. No more seclusion or contemplation, everyone watched all the time."

From deeper in the Tower came a heavy thud. "What was that?" I asked.

Luis Antonio smiled. "That is my father trying to get through the barricades on these quarters."

My heart skipped. "He'll find us!"

"Nataneal made those barricades," Luis Antonio said. "My father will get through them eventually, but we have time."

I swallowed, tasted blood and oil. "Time for what?"

Luis Antonio pulled the window closed with one hand, keeping the other entwined with mine. I blinked rapidly in the sudden darkness, objects pressing out of the shadows as my eyes adjusted. There was a bed, shelves holding books, more items of furniture that I couldn't name.

"Where are we?" I asked. "Is this where you live?"

"These are Nataneal's quarters. He came back, Shadow. Back from the outer City. They thought that the explosion would be enough for people to make people see that they had a choice, that they could rise up. Make them see that they were more than slaves."

"Is he here?"

He shook his head. "He was . . . injured in the explosion. He was able to stay here for a while and help me, but he needed care. I don't know where he is now. Maybe back in the outer City." He paused. "Out there, beyond the Wall, women and men exist only to create children. The babies which are placed in the Angel's Shadow. Nataneal confirmed it. You have parents, Shadow. A mother and a father, people who mourned your loss."

I pulled away from him. "No one would mourn me."

"I would."

Another shuddering crash, this one strong enough that the floor shook. "What will happen when your father breaks through the barricades?"

Luis Antonio touched the bruise on his cheek. "No doubt he will make an example of me. But it doesn't matter. All that matters is the revolution. The first symbol they tried didn't work completely, but they're ready to try again. *We're* ready to try again."

"Another explosion?"

"Something else. Something more."

Luis Antonio still had his hand in mine. He pulled gently on our linked hands, drawing me through into another room. This one was more immediately familiar to me: a workroom lined with benches, the surfaces scattered with tools and clockwork parts. Scattered amidst small piles of new gears and wire were fragments of other machines: the air quality machine stripped to a skeleton, the cat missing all of its paws. Only the clockwork angel stood still whole, watching over everything.

One corner of the room had been curtained off with white fabric. Still holding my hand, Luis Antonio pulled the fabric aside.

Standing there was the figure of a woman made from a flat grey material. She was thin, her body bent in an almost graceful wave. A leather harness wrapped her waist and shoulders, slender straps reaching out to encircle her upper arms and thighs. All of the leather was carved with scrolling lines, a small gear caught here and there in the loops. From the harness hung wings.

They were like the wings of the small clockwork angel, but made to be lighter, wires forming a cage which enclosed the working machinery. The wings were not symmetrical, but flowed with the shape of the harness, so cleverly made that they were still perfectly balanced. A series of keys ran down the length of the spine of the wings, each of the keys ornately tooled with more curves and scrolls.

I started to reach out for the edge of one of the bright wings, but stopped before I touched it, knowing that my fingers would only mar the surface.

"When the Angel flies, we will all be free," I said. "They're beautiful."

"Nataneal and I wanted to attach an engine, but all of our designs ended up being too heavy." Luis Antonio ran his fingers down the keys, and a shiver went down my own spine. "She flies. Not as long as we would have liked her to, but she will fly." He moved around to stand behind me, and pressed his fingers against my back, fingers splayed over my ribs. "This is what made me start to think of the wings. The muscles here are what twist your spine, and probably what make you such a good climber. Too heavy for human bones. But strong enough for wings."

I glanced back at him. "What?"

He moved back towards the wings, reached beneath the harness and brought a handful of wires out. Yellow and red, the ends stripped of the coating and gleaming bright copper. "It was the baby with the clockwork eyes that made me think of this. Clockwork and human muscle, working together."

"Me? You want me to fly?"

Another crash came, this one closer, but I hardly noticed it as Luis Antonio turned me around. "The wings were made for you, Shadow."

He took my hand and guided my fingers towards the wings. As my fingers brushed the wires, the metal warmed and vibrated against my skin.

"See? This was what you were made for, Shadow," Luis Antonio said. "We need to test them, see if I need to make any adjustments. I don't have Nataneal's skill, but I should be able to manage."

Another crash, followed by a sound of falling glass. Closer again.

Luis Antonio paled. "Those barricades should have held longer. My father must have found . . . " He trailed off, shaking his head.

"There's no more time, Shadow. It has to be now."

I reached up, cupped my hand around his cheek, for once uncaring of the marks I would leave behind. "They don't need to be tested. If you made them, they will work. The revolution will have their symbol. I will fly, and they will all be free."

He breathed in, exhaled shakily. "I'll need clean connections between the wires and your skin. Have you ever had a bath?"

* * *

It was like falling and flying, all at once.

I lay in the bath, clean water up to my chin. Luis Antonio had already changed the water twice, and this was the first time it hadn't turned murky with dirt from my skin. He had lathered my hair with something that smelled like apples, applied lotion to the scarred skin covering my spine to soften the callouses there. The whole time, his cheeks had been pink.

The crashes came from time to time, but neither of us paid them any attention now. There was only us, and the waiting wings.

Clean, I rose, and Luis Antonio dried me off with a soft towel, rubbed more lotion over my back. He dressed me in a white gown, the back cut away, then cinched the harness around me. The leather hugged me, moulding perfectly to my shape.

He ran a hand over the harness. "It took me forever to get enough leather from the synth-vats to make this. How do they find enough leather for all of your worksuits?"

"Nothing is wasted in the City," I said.

Luis Antonio paled, and looked away from where my worksuit was crumpled in the corner. "*Oh.*" He swallowed hard, then turned back to the wings. "This may hurt," he said as he pulled out the wires from beneath the harness one by one. "The wires have to go into your spinal nerves. I looked up the places I need to put the wires, but seeing nerves on a page isn't the same as pushing wires into someone's spine."

In truth, the pain wasn't so bad. There was a slow burn as he pressed the wire through the scar tissue, then a heat, as though the metal was melting into my muscles. He pushed the wire deeper, and something sparked inside me. I flexed my shoulder, and gears moved in the wings.

"It works," Luis Antonio said. "It really works."

"Of course it does," I said. "You made it."

He inserted the rest of the wires, each of them finding their mark almost without needing guidance from him. When he was done, he leaned in and kissed the nape of my neck, then wound up the keys along the spine. I felt the potential gathered there, a spring waiting to be released.

"Try moving the wings," Luis Antonio said.

I flexed the muscles along my spine, and the wings moved. At first the movement was jerky, uncontrolled, but soon I was able to move the wings smoothly. As easily as though I had been born with them.

One beat, two, and then I was rising from the ground. I was flying.

The keys wound down one by one, and I slowly lowered back to the floor. Luis Antonio grasped my waist and helped me balance.

"I don't know how much time you'll have," he said. "If you fly back to me, I can wind the keys up again."

I shifted my weight. "Could the wings hold us both?"

He shook his head.

Another crash came, this one close enough that cracks appeared on the wall next to us.

"Don't worry about me," Luis Antonio said. "I'll be perfectly safe. I promise." He picked up the small clockwork angel. "Take her with you."

I shook my head. "Hold her. When I come back, I'll take her." Another crash came, the cracks in the wall widening. "You could climb out, close the window behind you."

Both of us smiled, both of us pretending that it would be okay. Pretending that I would have time to fly back, that he would find the courage to step out of the Tower.

We crossed to the window. There, Luis Antonio frowned.

"I didn't think of that," he said. "The width of the opening between the struts is too narrow for the wings. We'll have to take them off, take them apart, and reassemble them somehow out there. Dammit, why didn't I think of that?"

He started to reach for the wings, but I leaned out, closed my eyes. Thought of the dream of flying with the Angel, of the baby with clockwork eyes. A thought, and the wings folded back close to my spine, narrow enough now to pass through the opening.

Luis Antonio stared. "I didn't make them to do that. How did you know how to do that?"

"I was born for it," I said.

Sliding my hand into his, I looked out over the City. The angel stood on her crooked column, her shadow extending across the square. On the opposite Tower, I could see a Girl working on a pump, a divert Boy waiting nearby. I thought of all of those lights I had seen, so many of them in the outer City. Out there, I told myself, thousands of rebels were massed, waiting to enter the inner City, to free everyone. Once everyone saw me, they would rise up.

The floor shuddered, a chunk of the opposite wall falling away. I caught a glimpse of something black and gleaming out there, heard voices raised in unintelligible shouts.

I turned to Luis Antonio, kissed him. "You'll come outside, and you'll be safe."

"And you'll fly back to me."

"When the angel flies, will we all be free."

"We are free."

I moved out onto the cage, let my wings extend out again. Luis Antonio's hands moved down the keys, twisting them up as tight as they would go.

And then I stepped out into the air.

For a heartbeat, I fell, and then the wings began to move almost without conscious thought, lifting me back up to Luis Antonio's window. He was still standing behind the open window, his eyes fixed upon me, the clockwork angel in his hands. There was another crash, and the wall behind him crumbled completely, fire and smoke pluming into the room. I had one last glimpse of him before someone reached out with a black-gloved hand and dragged him into the smoke.

He would be okay, I told myself. The rebels will make sure that he's okay.

I turned mid-air, the movement coming as naturally as breathing, and flew across to the statue of the angel. Close enough to touch her face, to feel that she was only cold metal, nothing else. Voices came from below, and I looked down to see a handful of Boys and Girls standing beneath the angel, all of them looking up.

"When the angel flies, you will all be free!" I shouted, spreading arms and wings wide. Below me, the Boys and Girls all spoke the same phrase. The Boy and Girl on the opposite Tower did, too. "You have all been lied to! You are all slaves! Rise up and be free!"

As one, they roared back, and I flew up, up, up.

The keys began to wind down, and still I kept going up. Up past the highest part of the cage surrounding West Tower, high enough that I could look down on the Tower itself. There was a flat platform there, and on it stood a girl, watching me. She was wearing white trousers and a close-fitting shirt, her copper hair pulled back from her face. I hovered next to her, and her eyes fixed on me, their surfaces oddly flat.

She reached up, and pulled those flat eyes from her sockets, revealing intricate clockwork behind. It was the baby with the clockwork eyes, somehow still alive, somehow here.

"When the angel flies, you will all be free," she said.

I reached into my pouch and withdrew the pinion and the apple seed, held them out to her. "Help Luis Antonio, if you can."

She took them from me, clasping them between our palms for a moment as my wings beat the air around us. "My name is Lucia."

"He called me Shadow."

Her hand slid from mine, fingers curled around the pinion and seed. "You are free, sister."

I flew higher still, and even when the keys had all wound down, I kept the wings beating, even as I felt blood begin to run from the places where the wires pierced my flesh. Higher and higher, up through the copper clouds, and just for a moment, I caught a glimpse of blue beyond, sky the colour of Luis Antonio's eyes.

When I began to fall, I did not fight it, but let the wings cup me, let Luis Antonio's creation hold me.

I was flying.

I was falling.

I was free.

❊

LADY BRILLIANA

LUCY SUSSEX

FACT ONE: *cats have nine lives, everybody knows that. But these lives are not all necessarily feline.*
FACT TWO: *old proverbs, admonitions, are coined for good reason, for they contain certain basic truths.*

—*De Mortuis Nil Nisi Bonum*

N THE YEAR OF OUR LORD 1632, LADY Brilliana Harley, English country gentlewoman, sat busy at her castle's accounts. She got interrupted: young Ned, her son, ran sobbing into her skirts. She let him snuffle into her apron, smoothing his long hair, while his personal storm subsided.

"Well Master Ned, what now?"

He knew better than to lie, for Lady Harley had a mother's sixth sense.

"*De Mortuis nil nisi bonum*," he got out, before one last sob constricted his throat.

"I know my Latin."

"I told Kitty"—

"Master Pyne, since he is your tutor!"

— "I told him it meant the dead are nothing but bones."

"Fy!" She pulled his ear, not too hard, for underneath his tears he was beginning to smile. "When you knew perfectly well its true meaning: speak nothing but good of the dead."

"When K—Master Pyne gets angry," he said, lolling across her lap, "his face goes beet-blood-red."

"True, but was ungodly to provoke him. You deserved his thrashing."

He stood up suddenly. "Ow, your baby kicked me."

"Quickened babes do not know any better. But you did, Ned. Go and beg Master Pyne's forgiveness. And, in your prayers tonight, remember your Harley and Conway ancestors, who are assuredly more than bones, being holy spirits in the sight of God."

"Even the Papists, from over a century ago?"

"Ned!"

He ran down the stairs three at a time, knowing she was too great-bellied to give chase. She sat, vexed, half-minded to summon Pyne and order him not to spare the rod on her young heir, lest he become a limb of Satan. Then she repented, thinking of the family monuments in the parish church, the marble husbands and wives, the serried ranks of offspring, those who died young with little skulls chiseled over their heads. In the Harley vault are too many children, including what would have been her stepchildren, had they lived, along with their mothers, her husband's two previous wives. Should things go badly with her next lying-in, she, the baby, or the both of them, could join the company of Harley family dead. And then Master Ned, his younger brothers and sisters, would be motherless.

Were she a Papist, like that pretty but accursed Queen Henrietta of England, she would cross herself at the thought. Instead she bent over the accounts again, turning her moment of fear into worthy industry. But in the letter she wrote to her husband, Sir Robert, that night, she besought his prayers.

De mortuis nil nisi bonum. There is another reason why the dead should have nothing but good spoken about them. That is, like the living, they are vain: spectral ears burn to hear their names, even after centuries. In other lands, far from the Harley's

England, the admonition is not to mention the dead at all, lest they be involuntarily summoned. That too has its truth.

And thus, centuries later, the ghost of Lady Brilliana, not dead in childbed, but of exhaustion, and courage stubbornly maintained, assisted by a chill, stirs in the spirit world, rousing to consciousness. Someone speaks of her, and so her shade rushes to hear the report. In her haste a rare conjunction occurs: she collides with a spirit heading in the same direction, not towards the same source, but very close. It little matters that this soul is animal, not human: the spirit world makes no great distinction. They conjoin, coming to rest in a small body lying in the gutter, on a cold, rainy night.

A Cat has Nine Lives

"It *is* a thesis topic that has been done before, Lady Brilliana and her times—oh SHIT!"

A brake, a skid, a coming to a stop. The moment of calm, with just the drumbeat of rain on the car roof.

"I don't want to see what happened."

A long pause. "We've gotta."

They turn away, open their respective doors, step out.

"I don't see anything."

"In the gutter."

Lady Brilliana, lying still and in pain, thinks herself back in Brampton Bryan castle, the rain coming through the roof, as penetrating as the enemy bombardment. "You will die in a ditch!" a Royalist soldier had shouted at her. Had he been a foreteller, speaking her doom? Here she lay, draggled with mud, feeling as if her life was indeed ebbing out of her. Strange accents spoke in her ears, English but not as she knew it, foreign mercenaries, then?

"So we didn't run over it after all."

"But did some damage . . . oh, poor thing!"

"It's breathing. We can't leave it here."

Hands lift her gently. She cannot understand more than the tone, which is kindly. She must offer thanks, but though she opens her mouth, only a faint cry emerges, before the darkness of unconsciousness sweeps over her. From it, she only fitfully wakes: to pain, and the smell of the foullest physick a chirugeon could ever concoct, she thinks. She vomits, and sinks down into blackness once more. Much later, she opens her eyes, sees bars. Oh, the castle is taken, and she is surely imprisoned! She tries to rise, but is confined too close to do more than kneel. She remembers, acutely: poor Lady Colburn, who lost an eye in the bombardment! Lady Brilliana can see, but what else might she have lost?

Those voices again.

"I thought she was a goner—bruised, concussed. But no broken bones."

"She's tough."

"Well you did need a subject."

A sigh. "An expensive subject, with all the vet bills. But she's pretty, without the mud."

"We couldn't leave her in the gutter."

Lady Brilliana has the sensation of movement, being carried, and slips into memory again. Milord her father, Viscount Conway, on his grey charger, taking her for a ride along a North Sea beach, outside the port of Brill, her nameplace, in Holland. High waves, spume on the lead-coloured sea, skeins of seaweed under the horse's hooves. He had been asking her about her lessons, and she, to please him, replied in Latin.

He laughed, and she turned to face him, raising an inquisitory eyebrow.

"Mistress Brill, King James whom I loyally serve, says to teach women is to make them cunning. But is their cunning so bad a thing in this wicked world? A lady needs her wits as much as a lord."

She pondered. "Yes." Then: "Gallop?"

And so the great horse pounded down the seashore, the mane in her face, and sand flying up from the scooping hooves. Her father's fox-lined cloak had been wrapped around her, against the sea-breeze. Some kind person has done the same for her now. In the warmth of the memory, where speed, and soft fur, and affection mix, she basks, drifting into sleep, and flickering dream. A jolt, and she opens her eyes briefly. She must be in a carriage, moving at a gallop, for trees and roofs pass at dizzying speed. It is too much for her, and once more she closes her eyes.

Another fond memory, of her dear husband, carrying her over the threshold of Brampton Bryan Castle. Of lifting her head, hooded with her travelling cloak, and seeing the portcullis pass above her. The two gatehouses, stout, of stone. A fine place, and she to be its chatelaine, to guard as strongly as her virtue.

"How like the Antient Romans, sir," she said, as he set her two feet on the flagstones of what was her new home.

"You know that?"

"I am learned, and have cunning," she said. This older man to whom she had been united by the usual arrangement, between their families—who was not a complete stranger, but still an unknown, as a husband—he smiled, with real pleasure.

"You will need that, to be a Parliamentary wife."

She is being carried again now, a door opening, and closing, seen through her slitted eyes. Then bright light, and someone lifting her bodily, lying her on a floor. Strange smells, that disturbing physick again, intense, and overwhelming, but now it seems to come from her body, under the furred cloak.

She kneels, on hands and feet, suddenly desperately, ravenously hungry. Those voices again.

"Oh, no, we forgot to get her nosh."

"Anything in the fridge?"

"Apart from frozen pizza? . . . Oh this should do, for the moment."

"They can't digest lactose!"

"It fills her belly for now, ok?"

She smells milk, not her own. A deep platter is set down in front of her, and forsaking the last remains of her dignity, she lowers her head, drinks.

"Well that's the weirdest thing. Like someone slurping soup."

"Is she brain-damaged?"

"Oh I hope not!"

Lady Brilliana, her wits and strength a little restored, sits back on her haunches. Her eyesight had worsened with the privations of the siege, but she wonders what is further wrong with it now: the colours seem extraordinarily intense, the proportions of the room around her oddly distorted, the light blazing. Staring down at her are two worried faces, absurdly large. She tries to focus on her outstretched hand, gloved in white, and clenched, then on the sleeve above it, a puritan dark grey, near sable in hue, but cuffed with rich fur. The cuff extends up . . . into a jacket, it seems. And where in God's name are her skirts?

One of the faces, a giant's it seems to her, wears spectacles, which slip to the end of the button nose, and fall to the floor. With the clatter, her nerves, strained by the siege, give way—she leaps sideways, only to find herself facing a great cat, big as a tiger, it seems, mostly sooty grey, with touches of white, its eyes wide and staring. A giant hand reaches down towards her, she shrinks from it and so does the . . . the reflection in the mirror. She screams, her mouth opening to reveal pointed teeth, but out comes an animal's howl. And her hand in that white glove, is but a paw and her fur jacket extends all over her nakedness, a beast's pelt! What witch has she vexed, to gain the semblance of a devilish familiar?

"Has she never seen herself in a mirror before?"

"I don't know. Normally they try and go around the back, to find the other cat. They fail the self-recognition test, just like gorillas, and human babies. And unlike dolphins and chimps, who do recognise themselves."

At this point, the basic instinct of the body she inhabits, a skerrick of its animal soul, takes over, a panic reaction. She dodges the reaching hand with a scramble up a chair leg, a scuttle down the rectangular length of a table, a wild leap onto a lecturn, on which a great book rests, open.

"Oh no, not the King James Bible."

The rational part of her mind registers those three words, the first she has understood in these outlandish accents. She gazes down, and sees she is perched on a page, an elephant folio, it seems in her new, diminutive guise. She bends closer, reads:

"If I say, peradventure, the darkness will cover me."

Familiar words, from a book she reads every day. No darkness will cover me, she thinks, even though I may walk in a cat's array. For though this household is beyond her comprehension, it possesses a Bible, the Protestant Bible of the Church of England. And therefore, no devils can abide here, she knows that. She is, as ever she believed she was, safe in God's hands. Should she walk through the valley of the shadow of death, He will be with her. Thus she submits herself to His will—even if it should be to wear a beast's guise, for whatever unknowable but divine reason.

It is strange to be a cat, without also being in an equally strange household. From watching her two rescuers, and listening intently to their talk, she learns some details. A young couple, that is clear, so newly wed they have not had time to increase yet. He is Will, a good old English name, and he calls her Yei-ling, a name she knows not. Perhaps she is a Tartar, from the Muscovies. While he is fair, she is sallow, so much that Lady Brilliana would have mixed her up a decoction from the still-room, for the liver. But she has a fine head of black hair, long as a horse's tail, and otherwise seems in good health, apart from poor sight, as her thick spectacles show. How sad for such a young woman!

How they live, though, quite confounds her. Yei-Ling departs each morning, carrying a white cloth long jacket over one arm. Will, once she is gone, tidies up the breakfast dishes like a serving wench, and then spends his time pouring over books—which suggests the scholar. He is not a daydreamer, though he seems to spend much time staring out a window. Or is it a painter's screen? —something that she saw once, in Holland, when her parents were having their portraits done. A camera obscura, that was the name. Yet Will never grinds paints, far less applies brush to canvas. Or is he a musician, since he plays the keys of what could be a spinet, except that it makes no sound?

Their voices sound above her head, in the cadences of conversation.

"Professor Prda never said anything about pets in the houseminding interview." That was Will.

"He never said *no* pets, either."

"He did say he hoped you never took your work home with you."

"After he cracked those terrible jokes about rats."

"At which, as I recall, I dutifully laughed. On your behalf."

"I was trying hard not to barf, actually."

"Look, I'm just worried about his art collection."

"Relax. She's not a sprayer, even if she acts feral. And anyway she can't aim that high."

"She climbs"—with a nod at Lady Brilliana, at her perch on the Bible.

"So, all the drawings and prints have glass frames, and we can hang cloths over the oils."

"What a good idea. They're hideous."

"Even if they are Abstract Impressionist and worth a mint."

Lady Brilliana, for her part, can comprehend about one word in ten. The sentences have the form of English, but most of the words are alien. But she understands that they are not unkindly disposed to her. Food is put down, good fish and meat, which her cat-body devours daintily, in pawfuls. She has a privy to herself, a luxury she never had at the castle, and absolutely nothing to do, unless they should desire her to catch rats. If that was what they were talking about, which she rather doubts. Mostly she sleeps—a blessed relief, after the endless nights of worry over the months of the siege.

She was never a vain woman—paint me as I am! she had commanded the portraitist. And so he had, her fine wispy hair, mousy-brown before she greyed, her pointed, prominent nose, her gown cut low, as was the fashion. When, Will being deep in his work, she inspects herself in the hallway's full-length mirror again, it is to see a domino mask across her face, and underneath her chin a falling ruff of fur, as white and goffered as if fresh from the laundress. Her eyes had been hazel, wide-set—these cat-eyes are larger, yellower in tint. They have perfect, acute vision: not only fine to the sight, but fine *in* their sight. She can see clearly that her fur is something that might adorn Queen Henrietta, and the cat's tail is as plumy as the most expensive ostrich feather. She walks in handsome array, she knows, permitting herself briefly the sin of pride, since this body is not actually hers.

At the edge of her consciousness, though, she can discern the soul of the cat whose body it *is*. Just as its instinct is to creep up to a mouse, so it creeps up on her, unexpectedly, so that she finds herself behaving cat-correctly, without any sense of volition. She takes these acts as a blessing, or benison: it knows about these things best, after all. Thus she avoids alerting Will and Yei-ling that their cat is even more uncanny than they think. Would they drown her in a mill-pond, like a witch's malkin, if they knew her nature, or rather unnature? She cannot take the chance. Odd though it seems, she lets the cat-body take care of its raiment, discovering how her tongue can act as both comb and a washrag. Cleanliness and godliness meet, even in a cat.

The care of her immortal soul is another matter. She was a woman of the world, running the castle and her domain in her husband's frequent absences, reading the Corantoes for political news—with increasing concern as the war neared—and relaying its contents to her family, like Ned at Oxford. But she was also a woman mindful of her life in the next world, who scrutinised her soul as closely as she did her household linen. Ill in bed, she read and translated into English a life of Martin Luther. Theology for her was an abiding passion, of both the heart and mind.

As a consequence she gives continual thought to her predicament. Had she access to Milord her father's library, she would search through his volumes, for a precedent. This house has many books, as she has found during her explorations, from the kitchen to the attic. But she cannot make head nor tail of the titles: by Yei-ling's side of the bed, *Studies in Comparative Cognition: from Nim Chimpski to Alex the African Gray*; *The Neuropsychology of Play*; by Will's *The Alchemy of Revolution*; *Cromwell and Communism*. Upstairs, in a library which neither Will nor Yei-Ling enter, books line the walls from floor to ceiling, and they are worst of all: *Abstract Expressionism: Theory and Praxis*; *The Abject and the Abstruse*; *Jackson Pollock: Psychoanalytic Drawings*.

She considers Classical precedent: the enchantress Circe turning Ulysses' men into swine. That would be a hard fate, transformed into a beast of the field, whose purpose in life is but to be eaten! Then Old Testament: Nebuchadnezzar being given the mind of an animal until he acknowledged God's sovereignty. It seems the opposite of her case; and was she not besieged for putting her Divine Ruler above her Earthly one, Charles Stuart? New Testament then: Christ driving the possessing demons into the Gadarene swine, who immediately ran off a cliff. She has possession of this cat form, but is very definitely not a demon. Her mind, like a lathe, turns other possibilities. Did the Royalist attackers include a witch, or enchanter?—she would not put it past them. But God has a purpose for her, she believes, He would not treat her with malevolence.

At times, worst of all is the lack of an opposable thumb. In cat-form she lacks her long fingers, agile with a needle or a pen, and even pastry-making. All she has is stubby little toes on all four feet. Yet she has a tool in her claws, sharp, as she discovers when Will tries to pet her, too much of a familiarity for a lady to bear. She responds with a slap, that draws blood. He sucks his hand, looking sad. "Sorry, puss."

Dusk and dawn are when she finds sleep deserting even her cat-body, and so she prowls. They do not let her outside, not that she minds that—the Bible is her anchor to sanity as well to sanctity, she will not stray too far from that. As the light changes from black to grey, she sits on a sill and watches the world wake up, the birds stirring, then soaring across her vision. She is glad of the sight of sparrows, and starlings, but what of those squawking parroquets, they are not surely flying free in her England? As she watches, the cat-soul within her takes brief charge. Her jaw drops, and she makes, quite involuntarily, a chittering sound: come hither, sweet bird, to me!

"Well that's one time when she behaves like a normal cat."

"Instead of like a feline psycho."

Lady Brilliana, for her part, is disconcerted to find herself feeling blood-lust, and worse, actually drooling. To calm herself she returns to the Bible, which she is pleased to see Will consults frequently. But to her annoyance he has it open at a section comprising interminable lists of who begat who. She retreats onto a nearby shelf, considers the matter. A claw can hook a page, but would tear it—an iconoclasm. But what if she licks her paw, as she has seen some people do, when reading, would that mean she could turn the page?

When Will is out that day she hops up onto the table, where Yei-ling has left a volume open. The content makes no sense to her—some treatise about parrots, but she persists. Yes, if she licks her paw and presses firmly onto the paper, she can turn a page, if she is careful.

Several evenings later the couple busy themselves in the kitchen, their cooking elaborate and unfamiliar in smell mostly, though she recognises some pungent, expensive spices. They are moneyed, it seems, but unable to afford a cook! She thinks back on the pigeon pies she sent dear Ned at Oxford. Where are they, her husband and all her pretty . . . kittens? Oh, that was not what she meant at all! Surely her little family have not been transformed into beasts too? At that the longing, all the love she has carefully stowed at the back of her mind, threatens to overwhelm her. She runs upstairs and hides in the darkest corner under their bed, to be unobserved in her misery. But a cat cannot weep.

In the end her cat curiosity rouses her from that dusty exile, at the sounds of a new voice downstairs. She pads down to the dining room, to the long table where Will usually sits at his work. Tonight it has been laid for dinner, cutlery, plates, crystal, napkins. A stranger is here, a sparse tall man, hair and neat beard white, engaged in opening a bottle. He eyes Lady Brilliana.

"Hi kitty, kitty, cutie-pie."

Lady Brilliana and her cat-host are united in feeling here: no endearments from a complete stranger. She stalks past him, leaps up onto her perch.

Someone comes noisily to the front door. Yei-ling opens it, pinny and all, to reveal another older person: a woman all in black, with a white collar.

"Jack, I don't think you know Will's supervisor. Dr Ruth Dallmore. From History, Philosophy and Religious Studies."

"Our new portmanteau department, in the ever-shrinking Humanities."

"I know Ruth by sight. We *are* at opposite ends of the Campus."

"Likewise," says the woman. "But Professor Jack Raphael and his grant money are famous."

"Wine, Dr Ruth, or are you teetotal?" (Jack)

"I'm a Uniting Church Minister, not a Rechabite."

Lady Brilliana is puzzled. The woman has announced herself a Churchwoman, but in all of Lady Brilliana's extensive Protestant knowledge, she has never heard of petticoated Ministers. Perhaps the Uniting is a schism of the Anabaptists. They are righteous allies of the Puritans, if a bit odd . . .

Dr Ruth turns, glass in hand, and nearly drops it at the sight of Lady Brilliana's intense stare.

"Oh this is the puss you rescued?"

Yei-ling sighs: "Who seems completely weird."

Dr Ruth arches one brow.

"No purring. Hardly any mews, and when she does, they're bizarre."

Lady Brilliana understands *that.* She frowns underneath her fur. Clearly she is not a completely convincing cat, despite her cunning.

"And speaking of bizarre . . . " Will starts, but the attention of the gathering has shifted, with the arrival of the first course. Lady Brilliana sniffs: unleavened bread, oysters, pickles, their scents more intense than ever she remembered in her human guise. She discerns the ash in the bread, the seaweed in the oysters, dill and pepper in the preserves.

Ruth to Jack: "You mind if I say grace? Don't worry, I do it silently. In deference to all the other religions on campus."

"I'm hardly Orthodox. I eat oysters, and worse. Go ahead."

She bows her head, they sit silently, waiting. It seems a funny kind of grace to Lady Brilliana, but better than the heathen nothing.

"That cat is staring at me again. Does she want an oyster?"

"Don't try and feed her one, she'll claw you. We can't get near her, far less bundle her into a carrycage and take her into the lab for the experiments."

"Feral?"

"Abandoned, the vet said."

Lady Brilliana pricks up her furry ears. Abandoned, indeed, though not by God.

"But spayed, microchipped . . . "

"Linked to an address, a house now demolished."

Demolition, Lady Brilliana thinks. What the Royalists would do to Brampton Bryan, should she let them.

They have emptied their plates, and Yei-ling returns to the kitchen, making great clatters and stirrings.

Jack to Ruth: "It is a sad fact on campus that of the two cultures—science and humanities—never the twain shall meet. Except in our hosts."

Ruth: "So how did you two meet?"

"Sharehouse."

"That still happens? Despite the rent-hikes?"

"Yes. But it's rare you find a kindred soul that way."

Yei-ling, in the kitchen grins; the pair briefly lock gaze happily.

"How do you find minding Professor Prda's house during his study leave?"

"Swell. If you ignore the art collection."

"I did hear in the tea-room that was an issue."

Will: "He more or less said he didn't trust his grad students. A historian and a cognitive scientist at least had the virtue of ignorance. That he did say."

"As if we'd flog his precious collection on Ebay," Yei-ling shouted from the kitchen.

"It is insanely valuable, I hear," says Ruth.

"State of the art—if you like that sort of thing."

Ruth eyes it, her gaze moving around the room, and coming to rest at Lady Brilliana. "Oh! That cat is sitting on the Bible."

"She seems to like it, that's all I can say. And that's not all she does," says Will. "Take a look at this. Yei-ling asked me to leave my webcam on, just to see what happens when we're not around."

Their three heads bend over the screen. Yei-ling wipes her hands, flits from the kitchen, gazing over their shoulders.

"Oh," says Ruth. "What is she doing?"

She swivels around to gaze at Lady Brilliana again. As she does, Lady Brilliana catches a snatch of what they view, a window with blurred movement, showing a small dark shape, bent over a book. The image licks her paw, applies it to the corner of the page, and turns it.

"Playing with Irene Pepperberg's book on Alex the parrot, but so gently I'd never have known it."

"She does the same with her food, more than most cats. But I wasn't expecting her to do the same with a book."

"That's very dextrous, for a feline," says Jack.

"If I'd had better quality of image I'd have uploaded it on Youtube. The Reading Cat!"

Lady Brilliana on the lecturn, feels her hair rise—all over her body, a disturbing sensation. What devilry is this, to spy upon her?

"See her reaction?"

"Self-consciousness?" Jack to Yei-Ling.

"I doubt it. More like recognising the threat of another cat, on her territory."

"Maybe she might be a suitable subject, after all."

"Why a cat?" says Ruth. "I mean I know about rats and experiments—but wouldn't a cat be a totally contrary subject?"

"Of course," says Jack, as Yei-ling retreats to the kitchen. "But very widely owned. And with a need, given city dwellers and small apartments, to be entertained, lest they shred their owners' curtains and furniture from sheer boredom. And thus we have all this lovely money from the pet companies."

Ruth snorts: "Catch them funding the Humanities."

"Applied arts, possibly," says Will. "Games, apps."

Jack: "But enough of the sciences. We're monopolising the conversation. Will, tell me about your subject."

"It keeps changing."

Yei-ling places a heaped bowl on the table. "Help yourself. Stir fried tea-smoked tofu, with broccoli and baby corn. Our last sharehouse was vegan: their recipe."

"Were those the ones who threw you out when they discovered your supervisor was Jack?"

"Not threw. Asked politely."

"They weren't so bad. It was their friends who were the problem."

"Nonetheless, to make up they helpfully passed our names to Prof. Prda."

"Shame you couldn't stay and spy," growled Jack. "Could have had advance warning of those pesky demos."

Ruth: "Freedom of speech!"

"If only it stopped at that! We've had attempted break-ins, a security guard clobbered."

Ruth: "So *do* you torture animals?"

Jack: "The University has an Ethics committee."

"Which I'm sure makes exception for large corporate donations."

Yei-ling quickly intervenes: "No torture in my case. Unless you consider video games torture."

"I would, personally, but then I'm a bit of a Luddite."

Yei-ling: "My position is, from increased knowledge comes empathy."

Ruth nods. "How unlike Descartes. He once dropped a pregnant cat out of a window, because he said it didn't have a soul."

Lady Brilliana is recalling various small acts of unkindness to cats in her life, including dressing in babyclothes—and feeling something akin to penitence.

"Automata without self-awareness, he said, or even feeling."

"Do I get the idea that even the family dog disliked him?"

"Certainly the cat . . . "

Lady Brilliana, from her perch, agrees.

Will: "He never saw a chimp with a mirror. Come to think of it, he probably never saw a chimp at all. Small pet monkeys at the most."

"These days the LOL-cat lovers would lynch him." Yei-ling.

Jack sighs. "I believe in the scientific method, and not in anthropomorphic vandalism. I said so to the media, in simpler words. And became a bogeyman."

Ruth: "Two extreme positions, with no possibility of reconciliation. Will, you see the resemblance?"

"To the lead-up to the English Civil War? Paranoia about Catholics vs paranoia about Calvinists? Each party sure they defended the True Religion? Of course."

Jack has been addressing himself to his meal. "Wow. You can tell your PETA pals, this really is delicious."

Lady Brilliana, though not much of the conversation is comprehensible, is beginning to sense certain things. The two young people, they defer to the older ones, like a scholar and his University tutor. But a woman, at Oxford, either as student or don? And also some sort of Protestant Minister? It perplexes her.

"But enough of my problems. We were talking about Will's diss."

"And he was avoiding the subject," says Yei-ling.

"Because I'm having real troubles narrowing down to a suitable research question."

Yei-ling: "Will says it's like being on opposite sides of a divide."

"My subject is from beyond the intellectual rift called the Enlightenment. It's a doozy. Even with an online course in seventeenth-century Calvinist theology."

Jack: "Oh, the Bible is not only a cat-perch, I see."

Will: "Let me show you—call up my subject onscreen."

He taps again, and revealed is a scrap of paper, with handwriting. On her perch, Lady Brilliana cranes her head, staring: it seems very familiar.

"The broad scope of the thesis is a cache of English Civil War letters. Nearly 500 of them, by a devoted wife, mother and Puritan war-heroine. And also contemporary of Descartes."

Lady Brilliana focusses with her acute cat eyes, as she could not have done in life, at this distance. How can it be, that a letter she had dashed off to Ned at Oxford, full of admonitions for his physical and spiritual health, should be displayed for all these strangers to see? Then another thought, following hard upon: my dearest boy, preserving his mother's words! She hopes. Surely her letters have not fallen into the hands of the Royalists?

"She happens to be a distant ancestress of mine."

Ruth: "When Will told me that he was descended from Lady Brilliana Harley, I felt we had a thesis topic made in heaven."

From the lectern comes a shriek.

"Yes, her mews are weird, I agree. Is she hungry?"

"I doubt for tofu," says Yei-ling.

Lady Brilliana gazes at Will. His hair is red, he has blue eyes, but could it be . . . that he is a Harley? Has her line prospered, begetting and bearing like the Biblical genealogies? Then something else strikes her, with such emotional force that she almost falls off the lectern. Ancestress, was what Will had said. That means, the war has been fought and decided, that her beloved husband, and her children, and their children and children's children, all are dead. And so must she be, as well. But what afterlife is this? How can a good Puritan woman be a cat, on earth, and not in the heaven predestined for the Righteous?

She digs her claws into the wood of the lectern, praying for the Bible to protect her.

"Your puss has put her ears back, again," observes Ruth. "Now I'm not an expert in inter-species psychology, but I do know when a cat is unhappy."

They all stare at Lady Brilliana; and she in utter misery stares back.

"She might have post-traumatic stress syndrome," Will volunteers. "From the accident when we nearly ran her over."

Jack: "But as Will just showed, she *is* unusually dextrous. I think you should try her as a subject, Yei-ling. If necessary, take equipment home. I'll approve it."

"Dessert?" says Will. "Apple pie, I made it. Because reading Lady Brilliana's letters was making me hungry for old-fashioned English nosh."

That night Lady Brilliana wanders the house, up and down the stairs, from kitchen to bedroom, unable to sleep. She pokes her head into the bedroom, where Will lies, one arm around Yei-ling, the other trailing nearly to the floor. She walks up to it, would kiss his hand, but she fears to wake him. He does anyway, opening one eye.

"Hey, looky-there! Almost touching."

Yei-ling rouses too, briefly. "Amazing."

Lady Brilliana retreats to the bedroom door, eyeing Will like a fond grandmother, though she hates to think how many generations they are removed. Even if, to judge from a scrap of pie, fallen on the floor, he has not inherited her skills at pastry.

There is a word at the back of her mind, a possibility barely able to be considered, because it is pagan: metempsychosis. Otherwise known as the transmigration of souls. An Ancient Greek belief, something she thought quaint when explained by her family tutor. But now, as an explanation for what has happened to her, it is something that sits most uncomfortably with her beliefs. Another pagan, Hippocrates, is equally disturbing: "The soul is the same in all living creatures, although the body of each is different." What she needs is a theological library, such as Ned described to her at Magdalen College, to investigate further. But as she leaps up Professor Prda's library steps, to read in the dark the quite incomprehensible titles, it seems she is completely out of luck.

She is staring out the window in despair, when from the top of the neighbour's low wall a shape moves, gazing at her. Another cat, from his head and bulk a tom. Her ears fold like a fan, her mouth opens in a silent snarl. Come any closer and I will rip you to pieces. The last time she had got so angry, it was with the Royalists, and with the thought comes a realisation of what she can do, and well. She will defend this castle, strange though it is, and her kitten, her many-times grandson Will.

The tomcat jumps down, on the other side of the wall. But she remains watching, a furious sentinel, as darkness turns grey, and a rosy dawn sun rises. Only then does she sleep, long and dreamless, into the hours of the new day. When she finally wakes, she is hungry—and the house is empty. Will! He is all she has left of her kin, and she misses him. But when someone comes to the door, it is Yei-ling, carrying bags and her long white coat.

"Oh there you are! Not on that blessed Bible, for once."

She sits on the kitchen floor. Lady Brilliana, also sits, beside her food bowls, wondering if Yei-ling has suddenly lost her wits. An empty bowl, a cat waiting: surely that is message enough?

From her bag Yei-ling brings a flat board, which she taps—an artifact similar to Will's. She also brings out a bag of cat kibble, open.

"Here, puss."

She puts a single kibble on the board, sits back. Lady Brilliana would prefer not to get too close, but the lure of food is too much, she having slept through breakfast. She reaches for the biscuit, and as she lifts it in her scooped paw, the board lights up like a lantern.

"Yes, that's how it goes." Yei-ling puts another kibble on the board, in a different spot, but closer. "C'mon, be a good cat."

I am NOT your good cat, thinks Lady Brilliana, but applies herself to the board again. She misses, slightly, and a line of flat alphabet blocks appears, paw-sized.

"Er, that's the keyboard, from before I got the new Tablet."

Tablet? thinks Lady Brilliana. Surely nothing to do with Moses . . .

"Not your thing at all, puss. Try again."

Curious despite herself, Lady Brilliana pats, retrieving the kibble.

"Great. Now you've activated the browser. See, I've linked it to sites of interest to cats. Such as the tennis."

The board comes alive with a dot, which moves rapidly across the screen. Lady Brilliana stares at it perplexedly, then the cat in her reacts, batting at the screen. Stop it, stop it! she thinks!

Yei-ling smiles, then taps again at the board. Now a mouse appears, darting from side to side rapidly. Lady Brilliana regards it with contempt, her paws twitching. Imperiously, she swats at it, to hear squeaks. Underneath her paw appears a swathe of colour, as if some artist has set to work. Again and again, she swipes, but then she glances up, and sees Yei-ling staring at her—almost hungrily. She retreats to the food bowl, almost but not quite ready to spit.

"I know," says Yei-ling. "It's not real. It's an app that holds a cat's attention, but only briefly. You've probably set a record, getting bored with it in zero time. Now I have to find something else to entertain you. Make Jack and the pet food corp happy, and get me a diss. So let's run through the trial apps."

But when Will comes home, with the shopping, he finds Lady Brilliana baleful on her perch again, and Yei-ling in the bathroom awkwardly and left-handedly bandaging a deep scratch, running from fingertip to wrist.

"Let me do it," he says, taking over the dressing.

"She seems to like you better. Slightly. Maybe I should let you do the experiment."

"Yes, I think she does like me."

Ancestress and unwitting scion, they settle into a domestic routine. Will works, with Lady Brilliana watching. She re-reads her letters, over his shoulder, and also letters written to her.

" . . . we think fit to acquaint you that Sir William Vavasour by His Majesty's command hath drawn his forces before your castle, with resolution to reduce it before he stirs from thence, your ladyship may do well to take into consideration the position you are in. Bristol is taken by Prince Rupert . . . "

She remembers that. A summons, from three Royalist Commissioners, gentlemen awkward because they knew her of old as a good, dutiful wife, but now, as defendrix, she perplexed them quite. She reads on, savouring then as now, their embarrassment.

"His Majesty's forces are successful everywhere, so that your ladyship cannot hope for any relief, and upon these terms if your ladyship should be obstinate we cannot promise those conditions and expect those conditions for you that are fit for your quality . . . "

She bares her teeth, a sight rather more fearful when two at the front are long fangs. My quality is higher than yours, for was my father not a Viscount, and Secretary of State? To say nothing of my immortal soul's quality. But that was not to be said to these gentlemen, whom she rightly suspected to be a little afraid of her, behind their weighty politeness. What she wrote in response had been logical, perfectly conventional and with an air of injured innocence to boot. What, they would take and despoil her castle?

"I must endeavour to keep what is mine as well as I can, in which I have the law of nature, of reason, and of the land on my side, and you none to take it from me."

There! She had actually implied they were lawless, something to make her smile into her brocade sleeve.

The commissioners had known her, as Herefordshire landed gentlemen. Sir William Vavasour did not, and thus he was ordered to besiege Brampton Bryan, despite his protests (so she had heard) that it was utterly beneath him to attack a petticoat. He wrote to her, courtly but threatening:

"I am your servant and to one so noble and virtuous am desirous to keep off all insolencies that the liberty of the soldiers, provoked to it by your obstinacies, may throw upon you; yet if you remain still wilful, what you suffer is brought upon by yourself."

What insolence! even if he addressed her as Madame. Since when was obstinacy provoking, in a lady? And to call her wilful, as if she was a giddy young maid! Well, to give him as good as he gave, her next argument would be that since she did not know her husband's current mind on this matter (well, not since his last letter, which had given her a coded carte blanche) she could do nothing against Sir Robert's will—except be a good wife and defend his property. So there!

Will taps, and the words disappear from the screen.

"Time to move, puss. I need to consult your holy seat again."

He reaches out to the Bible, and she obligingly leaps off. Since she is on the table, once his reference is checked, he takes the opportunity, as he does periodically during the day, to activate Yei-ling's customised Tablet. He watches her feline reactions, recording via web-cam, making quick notes.

From: *WillH@lmfu.au*
To: *Yei-ling@lmfu.au*

This morning's report, as promised. No interest in the big cat pictures, the zoo-cam footage. Nor for Sunil's antechinus breeding program. But when I called up a contemporary map of Brampton Bryan castle, she practically sat in my lap to watch. See? XXXXXXXXXXXXXX

From: *Yei-ling@lmfu.au*
To: *WillH@lmfu.au*

Yes, you're right. That's very weird. I'm going to be late tonight, any requests for takeaway? Or should I bring home Abdi's prototype cat-scratcher? XXXXXXXXXX

From: *WillH@lmfu.au*
To: *Yei-ling@lmfu.au*

The pole-thing thing that pulsates? I thought it was the office joke. XXXXXX

From: *Yei-ling@lmfu.au*
To: *WillH@lmfu.au*

No, he's put in for a grant to develop it further. XXXXXXXXXXXXXXXXX

From: *WillH@lmfu.au*
To: *Yei-ling@lmfu.au*

Abdi is a very sick boy. Thai, since you asked. XXXXXXXXXXXXX

Game and match: while Will and Yei-ling are not learning very much about their cat, nor getting results from the experimental apps they try on her, Lady Brilliana is being a very acute pupil. She now understands a good deal of how people in this far and future land communicate. Though the words appearing on the bright window-screen in front of Will are an unfamiliar sight, what Will and Yei-ling are doing is perfectly clear to Lady Brilliana. Left to right, the words progress, with no pen visible—yet they are writing letters to each other, by touching the little alphabet blocks.

A memory arises, of her sitting in her garden, under a quince tree, similarly busy with ink and paper. She summarised the latest Coranto, with the threats of conflict like dark, cawing birds flying towards her, not visible yet, but certain to arrive soon. That missive was for Ned, still at Oxford, though he talked of joining the

Parliamentary troops, once the standard was raised, and Charles Stuart declared war on his subjects. She must investigate a code, soon.

Hostile eyes were turning towards Brampton Bryan. The Harley's neighbours, and the great county families being devout Royalists, former cordial relations were turning to vinegar, if not actual vitriol. Reports came to her from friends, fellows in religion: Parliamentary sympathisers being driven out of home; or having to turn covert in their opinions. They wrote to Lady Brilliana, in the absence of her husband the highest-ranked Puritan in Herefordshire, seeking the promise of sanctuary. Or else they slyly helped by passing on news: of troops sent here, fortifications built there, cannons being transported by ox-cart up the country laneways.

Such information she knew was beyond price. Thus on another sheet, she again neatly summarised it, for not only her husband, but others like-minded, in the neighbouring counties, the secret networks of Puritans preparing for war. Was she then becoming a Sir Francis Walsingham, whom her parents knew, he who defended his Queen from the Papists? Walsingham they called spy-master, and gladly would she turn spymistress to help the cause.

Now she must attend to housekeeping. Her steward stood before her, to approve a list of supplies to be ordered. She added, to the bottom, with a quick scrawl of her pen: muskets, shot, bandoliers, gunpowder. Better to be prepared than sorrily unprepared. Then a PS, instructing that the weaponry be well-concealed, transported at the bottom of the carrier carts. She had a legal right to bear arms, she knew, if the worst happened, and the conflict came to Brampton Bryan. How many arms she had not the slightest intention of letting her neighbours know.

Finally she wrote to Sir Robert Harley, in London, busy at his Parliamentary duties: My dear husband . . . and paused, flicking the end of the pen-plume against her cheek, like a caress. What to say? What the men expected of her, a missive from a good wife who would not vex the recipient by showing she was so very, very worried. "I very much long to hear from you . . . ." and paused again. Should she stay, and defend what is hers, or should she flee, leaving the castle to be despoiled by the unrighteous? She knew what her husband expected of her: sense and sound judgement. She would cope, as usual, with God's help.

These men, her Royalist neighbours, now her foes, knew her to be a dutiful wife. But if they expected womanly submission from her, they would be surely disappointed. The only earthly man to whom she owed that was her husband. And in his absence, over her dying body only. She bared her teeth, a snarl-smile

—and returns from memory across a great distance, to her cat-life, with her scion. Will has summoned another letter of hers, and so she reads, over his checked-cloth shoulder. He wears an ill-made shirt, she sewed much better, in her human life. The letter is to Sir William Croft. Despite her precautions, word had got out about her collection of defensive arms, and Croft had written to her in remonstrance. He had once told her that he admired her spirit, he knew she was not his meek mouse of a wife. Very carefully, she had chosen her words of response, part defiance, part politeness, and part, who, little me?

"Sir, it is a mystery to me that the arms I have, which are not the hundred part so many as those you have at Croft, should be looked at with an ill eye and yours to be there of right and mine not. I understand it not."

Will has gone to the kitchen, to brew another cup of his habitual drink. She supposes it is the kaffee Ned wrote was the latest rage in Oxford, imbibed by dons and students alike, to enhance the wits. Well, better that than alcohol, which dazes, dulls, and in excess leads to sin. Back again, Will opens a window on his screen, in which Yei-ling appears, not a portrait, but her living self, though oddly, slightly, slowed . . . just like the image shown at the dinner party, of a cat licking her paws, trying to turn pages.

He is talking now, not to himself, for Yei-ling is answering, though as if from a great distance.

"Yes, they do want me at the presentation."

"Short notice."

"When funding calls, we all come running, I guess."

"Flying."

"And that means I can catch the last days of the conference. And do that panel after all." She sighs. "I'll pack my bag tonight."

He glances up at Lady Brilliana.

"It usually freaks cats out. Packing."

"With Miss Contrary, I doubt it."

"Hey, is that a name for her at last?"

"No. When a cat gets a name it just fits, and with her . . . "

"Nothing does."

A name, thinks Lady Brilliana. Of late, her memories have taken to flying up from her past like migrating birds, forming a dense cloud, or occlusion of this present. They claim her attention, and so she sinks into them. A strange name . . .

"Priam Davies, at your service, Milady. Captain and musketeer."

She had looked up from the table in the great hall, a place that was now part-pantry, now part site of Brampton Bryan's personal Council of War, surrounded with supplies, muskets, bags of wheatgrain, casks of gunpowder, and a worried group of people, all deferring to her in the face of the Royalist threat. A plain and raw-boned man, young and old at the same time, with the hard look of soldiery upon him.

"From your name and accent you are Welsh."

"From over the border." He bowed deeply. "I have come to join your company, lest the Puritan fire in Herefordshire be extinguished."

"We are but few. Two score and ten men of arms only. That same number of women, children, and the elderly to guard. Against 600 Royalists, I am informed, coming hard upon."

"With two cannon. I have seen them."

If he thought to test her mettle with this news, then she would show him no surprise, since her network of informants had already appraised her of the threat. Defiance was a weapon, a stance she found suited her well.

"I am not afraid of their cannon," she said. "But, Mr Priam, who bears the name of a King besieged, are you prepared to endure the same? With a Lady as Commander?"

He knelt. "I will follow you into the cannon's mouth."

"Brave man! We welcome you, then. And your musket."

The very next day, Yei-ling trundles a bag on wheels down the garden path, with a cheery wave and hug from Will. "Have fun!" he shouts. "Bag a big fat grant."

He works as usual, diligently under his cat-ancestress' gaze, but as the day wears on, comes under the burden of a gradually increasing cold.

"A pox on this virus," he mutters, blowing his nose. It is a sentence Lady Brilliana mostly understands, though the last word is new to her. She comes from an age when the smallest sniffle threatened a death-bed, and so she watches with maternal frustration. Had she her still-room, or understood this kitchen, she could make him posset, or a poultice of healing herbs. When he finishes for the day, he cooks himself hot soup, and plays his own versions of the games that Yei-ling tried to inflict on her. It could be worse, she considers—he could play cards, the devil's picture books.

That night, lying alone in his bed, he wheezes and splutters, waking fitfully. If he were her Ned, she would smooth his fevered brow. But lacking that, she sits on his pillow, and when he finally sinks into the rhythms of deep sleep, protectively wraps her little form around his head, to keep it warm. She puts her mouth to his cheek, kissing not like a cat, with a touch of the nose, but as a human does, with pursed lips. He stirs in his sleep, whispers a name: "Yei-ling." When dawn comes, she prudently retreats to the end of the bed. He wakes, smiles:

"Well that's an improvement."

He spends the day in bed, reading or snoozing, she coiled neatly at his feet. Next morning, he seems a little better, he gets up and dressed. Throughout the day he manages to work, but with increasing distraction. As evening approaches, he takes to staring out the window, beyond the garden and down the street. Then, from a small box, into which he now and then talks, as if beseeching God in vocal prayer, although what is said seems to be exclusively mundane, comes a tune, played tinnily. He lifts it to his ear:

"Hey, Darien. (pause) Long time no see, since I left the sharehouse (pause) Thesis, y'know (pause) Thought you were off with *Sea Shepherd* (pause) Yep, I too wouldn't have wanted to meet Putin's droogs (pause) Trivia night at the Wheatsheaf? (pause) Ooh, temptation! (pause) Look I've got a cold, but the missus is away (pause) All right, you're on."

From the Bible, Lady Brilliana listens in concern. Temptations are to be avoided, at all costs—and up until this time Will has seemed a well-behaved lad. He puts the box away in his pants pocket, dons a clean shirt. Then out the door he goes into the twilight, whistling as he walks. At the gate he turns and waves at her, as she watches from the window ledge, then behind the high box hedge is lost to sight.

She is annoyed; and worried, but in her cat form is learning even more the virtues of patience.

—also a weapon, against the Royalist commanders. She wrote: "You must be patient with me, Sir William, I am only a weak woman," which as the days of parley and stalemate continued, had become an increasing lie. But until Sir William Vavasour lost his temper and his chivalry completely with an English gentlewoman, she could play the waiting game, and hope for a troop of Parliamentarians, to come and relieve the siege—

So she merely returns to the Bible, reads some good holy martial words from the book of Judith, then settles herself down to sleep. It is deep, and long, until a noise at the front door rouses her. Will with his key! but he trips on the steps, and falls headlong onto the hearthrug, half in and half out of the dark, moonless night.

She leaps down, and rushes up to him. Drunk! She could box his ears, though not with the force she had as a woman. Yet, underneath the stink of hops, she discerns something else: a physick. This drunkenness is not entirely natural; something else has stupefied her Will.

From behind the hedge comes voices. She leaps off him, and runs down the path, crouching low to hide her white markings, and to be in this darkness no more than a scrap of shadow, even if moving. In the hedge, among the strong scents of box, unfamiliar plants, and even the faint and old muskiness of mouse, she smells more hops, and gazing between leaves sees several young men behind the open gate, gazing up the path to where Will lies sprawled. They speak, and she knows the tone: unfriendly.

"OK, Rowies really do work."

"I only gave him half. Wasn't expecting him to make a break for it, far less stagger nearly home."

"Tough bugger."

"Always was. Before Yei-ling he could match me drink for drink."

"Well, at least we don't have to pick his pockets for the key."

"You want to leave him there?"

"It's dark, and a quiet street."

"So no nosy passers-by."

"I reckon we can go get the van."

"And the others."

"Hey, we're art thieves now!" They pat hands, high, a gesture incomprehensible to Lady Brilliana, though the expression on their faces is triumphant.

"Prda always gave me the shits. And 51%."

"It's for the cause, Darien."

"And if we get access to old Prof Raphael's labs as well . . . "

"I couldn't believe it! Dude was always a chatty drunk, but with the Rowies indiscreet as well."

"I nearly cracked it when he volunteered that Yei-ling left her lab pass at home."

"And then you fished: 'Chick-passwords are all pets and astrology'."

"And so he says, No, and actually tells us: Will, plus his birthdate. Which I knew already."

"We just have to find the card, though."

"Plenty of time to search."

Their voices and footsteps retreat down the street. Lady Brilliana, her hair on end, scuttles up the path to the doped-out form of Will. Oh, my dear, my dear, wake-up! wake-up! She bats at his face, and he stirs slightly. The enemy are here, she tries to say, though the words she forms in her mind emerge as raw sound, mews. What enemy, though? They have long hair, like Cavaliers, but the shabbiness suggests plain outlaws, or beggars. She remembers the Sea-Beggars, privateers who captured her nameplace of Brill from the Spaniards. She is not going to let these beggars harm her Will, take any castle she inhabits.

In pure rage, she swipes at his face, caterwauls in his ear, and finally despairing, bites him, hard.

"Ouch!" He lifts his head, revealing a grazed, raw, forehead, then jolts half upright. "What the . . . puss!" He gazes around muzzily, and on hands and knees, crawls over the threshold, no bridegroom carrying his bride he, just Lady Brilliana riding on his back, chivvying him along with paw and claw.

"Oh Christ I feel sick," he slurs.

Do not take the name of your Lord in vain! she thinks, but as his trailing foot clears the door, she leaps down, and with all her small strength and mass pushes it shut. Oh, for a portcullis!

— Priam Davies at her door again, as she stared, pen in hand, at a sheet of paper, wondering how to delay Sir William Vavasour's attack, now he had lost his temper with her. Oh well, the 'I am only defending my husband's interests, I must as a helpmeet' line could only last so far.

"Well, Captain Davies, what are they doing now?"

Having already razed her orchard and garden for firewood, demolished the village and the mill, poisoned the mill-stream, and killed every kine she could not fit into the castle already, to feed the besieged.

"Milady, they have raised a cannon into the church tower, on a winch."

"Such impiety," she tutted, and then both their eyes widened, at the implications: the church tower of Brampton Bryan was the highest for miles, and gave vantage over the castle.

Not impiety, but strategy . . .

A deafening crash, sending both Davies and she, paper and ink bottle and all to the floor. Wails sounded, from the defenders, and thinner, from somebody's baby . . .

"Lady, are you hit?"

A spreading stain across her dress. She touched it, and her fingertip came away black.

"No, 'tis only ink."

He stood, offered his hand; she pulled herself from the floor. Ink would not stain her old black woolen mourning dress. She released his hand, stood rocking a little, in thought.

"Let us check the damage. Then, assign a marksman to church tower duty. If we cannot harm the cannon, then we can pick off those who fire it."

He bowed. "A tactician's notion, Milady."

She laughed. "My brothers learnt Martial, and Tacitus. And I listened, and remembered."

—Will, of his own volition, has actually managed to stand, take staggering steps into the hallway and the dining room/his study. "Yei-ling!" he murmurs. But then he falls face down, half across the table, luckily breaking most of his fall on the soft, padded wheeled chair he uses when working. In doing so, he knocks Yei-ling's screen-thing onto the floor, it lighting up on impact.

She climbs up him again. But all he does is whisper: "Yei-ling! Help!" before falling into a deep drugged sleep.

She stares at him. They are coming back, she understood that, and that buys her time, but how much? And what can she do in her cat-form, to thwart them? An idea surfaces in her mind.

Earlier than expected she hears the voices from outside:

"Shit, where is he?"

"Can't have gone far."

"That's his moby, by the doormat."

"Darien, get the torch!"

A face at the window, followed by a beam of light. A dark lantern, but more powerful.

"Actually made it inside."

"But conked out completely."

"How do we get in, then.?"

The light moves, then sweeps across the garden. She leaps up onto a shelf, the highest vantage she can manage. Her night sight is perfect, and she can see the attackers grappling with the stone sculpture in the front garden, which since it has no particular shape, cannot possibly be a graven image. They roll it up the steps, then position it against the window.

—the crash of the cannon had become almost habitual now, several weeks into the siege. She glanced up, but saw no further damage to the roof, just the hole created last week, with a view of puffy clouds. Rain, later, she supposed. Again. Vavasour had decreed a slow campaign of misery for her, in which every room of her home gained, if not a gaping hole, then a leak.

Priam Davies at her side, for the first time since the siege began looking shaken: "The Cook is dead, Milady. Dr Wright says the bullet must have been poisoned, the wound was not otherwise mortal."

"Our first casualty," she said dully. Around, her fellow besieged clumped, as if looking for succour. Among them were her three youngest children, Tom, Doll and little Meg, weeping and clinging to her skirts, the privilege of family. What can I give them? she wondered. How to rally them? And then she had it.

Gently disentangling herself from her children, she stepped up onto the table, and shouted: "And how many of them have we killed?"

A ragged cheer, from the defenders. They had counted the enemy bodies as the snipers shot them down, with their musketfire. Over a score, and more . . . with only one casualty within the castle. God was surely on their side.

"I swear to you, even if they kill me next, we will not surrender."

As the words left her mouth, she felt a moment of chill, as if, as the saying was, somebody had walked on her grave. For a moment, she trembled, then she set her jaw, hard, stilling her teeth lest they chatter. If God has willed, then so be her fate!

—A crack, in the glass, then a further tap, and crash. A substantial chunk of the window-glass falls into the room and onto the Persian carpet. A hand reaches through the gap, seeking the windowcatch. From the concealment of the curtain, she darts her paw at lightning speed, and pricks the intruding hand.

"Ouch! What was that?"

"Spider—watch out!"

The hand has jerked involuntarily away, and in doing so scrapes against the broken glass. The smell of human blood, thick and rich, fills the air.

"Stop snivelling, and wrap it up."

"A bandaid won't do. Need more!"

"Use your bandanna, wimp."

"Stop pussyfootin'!" This time the sculpture is lifted, smashing the glass completely. She dodges the flying shards, then retreats underneath Will's chair.

—Lady Colburn, devout and genteel, was screaming, one hand to her eye. From between her fingers, blood seeped.

"What the—!" Lady Brilliana knelt before her. "Oh my dear, let me look."

A bloody mess of one eye, the other staring at her beseechingly. Dr Wright, rushing past with a poleaxe, and more supplies of shot, stopped, bent to inspect. He turned towards Lady Brilliana, pursed his lips grimly. I know that, she thought, I can see when an eye is lost.

Very gently, Wright removed the offending long sliver of glass from Lady Colburn's eye, palming it in his hand.

"The maids can tear up another sheet for bandages. You'll soon be fine again," Lady Brilliana lied.

—now they are coming through the window, and she is gauging the threat, what she can do, within the considerable limitations of her cat form. If they bother Will, she will rip them to shreds, well as much as she can. She leaps up, onto the table, then the bookcase. A very ugly ungraven image, clay, is at the top. With a little judicious pressure, she sends it crashing onto the knotty head below. Opportunity and occasion, and also the luck of war!

—As happened at Brampton Bryan, after six weeks of siege. A major battle loomed at Gloucester, to which Vavasour, and his subordinate Colonel Lingen were diverted to attend. The Royalist troops took their arms and retreated, their numbers significantly diminished; inside the castle, with no further lives lost, up rose prayers in jubilation, to the highest heaven.

"They will be back." Priam Davies.

"We need supplies, replenishment, afore they return."

Unspoken: otherwise, we will starve.

"Lady, what will you have us do?" That was Dr Wright, physician first, but increasingly a soldier.

Her slow smile, at the license to misbehave again.

"Plunder!"

An answering smile from Davies. "Milady, you are Bellatrix indeed!"

"And while we are at it, let us level the earthworks they raised against us."

"That is not soldiers' work." Wright again

"The tenants!" Those false Harley servants, giving succour to the enemy! "They can do it."

"And if they refuse?"

"Not with a musket at their heads."

She might be a woman, but she has gained the hardness of a warrior, like armour, perfectly fitting her slight form.

— "Hey, there's a cat."

The dark lantern shining on her, blinding.

"Experimental subject, Will said."

"Hey puss, puss, we'll rescue you."

Over this dead cat body, thinks Lady Brilliana, but while you try to catch me, I gain more time. And so she leads a dance, around the room, the clutching hands repelled with scratches. She leaps, from the shelf onto a painting, which since Prda's house is old, and the artwork dependent from rails, swings wildly with the extra weight. As she leaps off, her thrust sends it swinging into a fall, the glass crashing out on impact. Onto the next picture, then the next. More glass shatters, a frame cracks on the head of an intruder, but she has leapt down via the table, to the floor and up the stairs, to the Professorial library.

— "What else, Milady?"

They called her Commander in Chief now, something she will only admit to herself that she enjoyed. A letter had come from Sir Robert Harley, advising her to leave her home to the Royalists. "I am not afraid to die," she told him. She also wrote like a good fearful wife to her distant children. Ned was now a Colonel in the Parliamentary army, her eldest daughter, also Brilliana, was of marriageable age, and safe with an aunt in London. She told them that she longed to depart Brampton Bryan. Yet, if truth be told she was more afraid to lose this strange, exhausting but exhilarating time, in which all her life, marriage, seven times the travail of labour, the curse of Eve, seemed but a pale preparation.

"We attack, less they think us weak."

Her gaze fell upon a map, on which the enemy positions have been marked.

"Raid Knighton, where Colonel Lingen left a troop! Take what you can, horses, arms, even prisoners!"

Captain Priam Davies would later write:

"She commanded in chief, I may truly say with such a masculine bravery, both for religion, resolution, wisdom and warlike policy, that her equal I never yet saw . . . "

Lady Brilliana never knew his opinion, though the admiration in his eyes was clear, nor that he wrote her epitaph. As autumn descended towards bitter winter, the Royalists gone, the castle and its defenders undefeated, a chill carried her off.

"The last period of her mortal abode in this vale of tears drawing upon apace she with an undaunted faith and resolution looked death in the face without dread, and the Lord Jesus with joy and comfort, to whom she resigned her soul."

He had been more than a little in love with her, decorously and platonically. And gritting his teeth at the thought of the Cavalicrs, and the waste they had created at Brampton Bryan, he added:

"She has received an immortal, an incorruptible inheritance and crown, which none of her enemies can reach to rob and despoil her of."

Lady Brilliana can remember from her deathbed only the candle lit beside her, of the sudden sensation of falling towards that light. As she did, the hymns sung during the vigil, raggedly, in voices hoarse and cracked from weeping, they changed, became angelically pure, like a bell rung for Evensong, summoning her to hear His holy word.

—in the library she scarpers up the ladder, and from the upper shelves sends a succession of heavy books, art theory, object theory, even Prda's discreetly bound collection of S&M (the illustrations of which, as they topple and open, merely suggest to her manuals of torture) down onto the attackers. Until, that shelf denuded, and overreaching herself, she essays a leap to the shelf in the facing corner. Darien on the ladder launches a footy tackle at her furry legs, in the process toppling backwards with a yell. She falls too, and in that moment, the cat self, who had been patiently waiting, as cats do, launches a fierce attack upon the intruder. It drives her out of its body, and into the memory, her last as a human, which envelops her, as she floats free. A little grey and white cat, now nothing more, hits the floor of the library, awkwardly, beside the groaning Darien, just as another light and a hellish siren din intrudes: help at last.

Later, Will and Yei-ling would wonder how it was that Will, groggy from the drug, had managed to use the Tablet and send Yei-ling an email, strangely spelt (all that seventeeth-century reading getting to me, he ruefully said) and full of typos, but nonetheless, an SOS. The notion that it might have been anyone else never enters their minds. Lady Brilliana is no longer present, to smile behind her whiskers at how, fear and protectiveness bringing out the best in her again, she performed the sequence of strange new actions that wrote and sent a message into the ether.

Yei-ling receiving it on her iphone, and activating remotely the web-cam, saw the dim figures in the dining room, Will's unconscious and bloodied face. So, from far away, she called the police, and also University Security. They found a wasteland: broken glass, books and pictures knocked off the wall, and several dazed, concussed activists, the rest having fled.

The cat was hiding underneath the bed, and was only found by Yei-ling, who having caught the soonest flight home, arrived late the next day. The cat was very hungry and sorry for herself, limping on three legs. At the sight of Yei-ling, she purred—the first they had ever heard from her.

"It's like she's a completely different cat."

The stray, delighted to be in complete charge of her body again, was docile and grateful in the way of cats: rubbing against legs, even occupying laps. Suddenly they have no trouble in affixing a name to her: Irene, after Dr Pepperberg. Yei-ling gets out the laptop games, at which the feline Irene, who is not particularly dextrous, particularly after the sprain in her front paw, proves a dunce, in test terms.

With all the upsets, and sudden dashes across country, and the re-location from Professor Prda's place, when the insurers descended, an accident is waiting to happen. Thus it is that Will and Yei-ling find themselves going over lists of baby names, with the prospect of being gradschool parents.

"By Christmas! Which Sir Robert Harley got banned, in Cromwell's reign."

"The things you know!" Yei-Ling says fondly. "I suppose you want to choose Brilliana."

"If it's a girl."

"I'd have chosen Irene, but it's been taken already."

Deep in the spirit world, a spectral ear turns, to hear the better . . . and then determinedly goes to sleep again.

⁕

AND THE SHIP SAILS ON

CAT SPARKS

HE GUIDE, KNOWN TO THE OTHER men only as Doc, was the only man not brandishing a gun. He swung a machete from side to side, casually lopping off random, jutting fronds. Shafts of light stabbed through breaks in the jungle canopy. No sound but the crunch of deep-tread boots through leaves.

Behind him, five sweaty men in lightweight, baggy trousers, wide-brimmed hats pinning down mosquito head-nets. Grubby rags wrapped around thick necks, shirt pockets bulging with insect repellent sprays. Doc himself wore little in the way of protective garments: green combat pants and a long sleeved shirt, a pale and rumpled linen jacket topped off with a Panama hat. A wilted hibiscus pinned to his lapel.

"Big game. That's what the purser promised," said Everington, loudest, stoutest and richest of the passengers. "We don't see something big, then I want a refund."

"Biggest game you'll find for a hundred miles. In all directions," answered Doc, laughing at his own stupid joke.

None of the others found the joke amusing. They kept on walking, sweating and complaining, slapping at clouds of invisible mites and midges. Somewhere beyond the thick green leaves, unseen animals squawked and screeched and hollered. Birds or monkeys was the general consensus. Doc refused to answer when they quizzed him on specifics. The five had never believed his big game bullshit. They'd signed up for the safari out of desperate boredom. The superliner *Frederico Fellini* had been at sea for years and was running low on entertainment options.

One member of the expedition let out an involuntary squeal as a startled tapir scurried across their path. Doc laughed as the lower bushes shook out a tumbling guinea fowl. He raised his blade but paused it, mid air. Turned back to the others, shot them a lopsided grin. Pointed upwards with the weapon. Above their heads, a clutch of curious spider monkeys hung on drooping branches, wide eyed and watching every move.

The man who'd squealed flushed red with embarrassment. "Where's these ruins you've been spouting on about then?"

"All around us," said the Doc, swinging the machete in a wide and languid arc. "Used to be the major shopping concourse . . . "

"We know what it *used* to be," said a stern-faced man called Hargrave. "Everybody knows what everything used to be."

"Well here's something the Company doesn't want its passengers to know," said Doc leaning in conspiratorially. "In 2025, when they added the Atlantis Dream Casino to level Six, they trashed part of the dining area and stuck on another sound stage. Circuses and magic shows came back in favour right after the Six Week War—if you remember."

Hargrave sniffed, unimpressed by the potted history lesson, the other four nodding in concurrence.

Doc continued. "I'm talking about old fashioned circuses—the kind with animals. Nothing too big, mind you. There wasn't anything too big left by then. Could never have gotten an elephant onboard even if they'd managed to find one." He paused the blade, turned and leaned in closer, dropped his voice down to a harsh whisper. "Atlantis Dream bought clowns and acrobats, tarts in skimpy holo-lycra, feather headdresses and all that razzle-dazzle. They caged some of the animals down here, below, started advertising the jungle zoo as a separate cruise ship attraction."

Eerie silence resonated after he'd said his piece. Jungle walls pressing in—only minutes earlier there'd been monkeys but now there was nothing, not even a couple of high-up squawking parrots.

"Animals," piped up one of the men, "what kind of *animals* you talking about?"

Doc nodded knowingly. "The shooting kind, of course."

Everington snorted. "Pigs and fancy-looking chickens. A few feral dogs and cats is all you mean—admit it, man!"

"If you say so."

"Top Deck passengers don't fool so easy," Everington continued. "We paid good money for this expedition. Whatever there is to shoot had better be worth it."

Doc Corduroy smiled, revealing crooked teeth stained brown with nicotine. He balanced the blade across his shoulder. "Tell you what, fellas. If you're not satisfied—truly one hundred percent—then I'll give you all your money back, no questions."

Everington unknotted the sweat rag from his neck, mopped his brow and looked from face to face. Each man nodded in agreement, mumbling things like *can't get fairer than that.* When the last of them had made a comment, he stuffed the damp rag into his pants pocket. Was about to have another go at Doc when something peculiar caught his eye.

"Dear god, what is that thing supposed to be?"

Not far ahead through a veil of hanging greenery sat the ruins of a plaza strewn with chunks of toppled marble column, pink and white, half buried under debris and entwined with thick liana vines. Light bled through in ragged patches. All five gasped when they crowded close enough to behold the massive moss-and-lichen-encrusted statue standing at the centre of a clearing. A ring of offerings had been placed around its base: fruit and flowers in varying stages of decay. Personal items: watches, jewellery, vases. Paper rolled in cylinders tied with string. A plate bearing a delicate pyramid of small round sugar cookies, the kind routinely doled out at Madame Lucinda's Top Deck Chiffon Tearooms.

Doc waited patiently for one of them to speak. For the group of men to string the clues together.

Hargrave frowned. "I don't recall that thing in any brochure. Was this ever part of . . . "

Doc cut in quickly. "Nope, see, that's the curious factor. That there statue . . . nobody knows who built it. Where the stone came from or how long it's been guarding the ship's interior."

The statue's face—if it had one—was obscured by growing things. They stared in silence at the great stone god holding court in a shaft of garish sunlight.

"Don't believe a word of it," said Everington, more stern-faced than ever. "Must have been one of the original attractions—and you're just making a big deal out of nothing. Trying to rip us off, the same as always. We came here to shoot—and we can't shoot that."

Doc didn't bother with a comeback. He removed the limp hibiscus from the lapel of his linen jacket, sauntered over and placed it gently at the faceless god's stone feet. Sheathed his machete, tipped his hat, leaned against the stone god's bulk as a cloud of midges swarmed across his skin.

Nothing happened. Not straight away. The five stared at him stupidly. Only one man fumbled for his gun, while another glanced up at the canopy treetops as if an explanation was going to fall down from the sky—or the upper decks.

"Well come on, man," barked Everington—"what are you waiting for?"

"For Fangaloka," said Doc, picking at his teeth with his pinky fingernail. "Seem to spend half my life waiting for that guy."

"What the devil—"

A blur of blade and gleam and tooth, a terrifying scream. Shots fired, random and useless. Fat men scattering, running for their lives.

Doc pulled back into the shadows as a group of thinner men, bare chested, with khaki tatters barely covering their thighs darted into view, machetes raised. Two expedition members floundered flat on their backs, gored and bleeding amongst the leaf litter. Doc sneered as the thin men rifled through the pockets of the dying. No sign of the shifty warlord himself, of course. The men Fangaloka sent to do his slashing and stealing always lied about the bounty they took back. Fangaloka always claimed Doc Corduroy owed him.

The khaki killers left as soon as they'd gotten what they came for. Doc stepped over the twitching bodies, swinging his machete two and fro, walking back the way they'd come, deep in troubled thought. The time had come to make a stand—all he needed was the opportunity. To hack and slash a passage into the root-infested I09, a corridor running the entire length of the ship. To get to Fangaloka when his guard was down and liberate portions of his secret stash.

He eased himself down onto a tumbled stone, cleared a square of ground with the machete. Etched a rough diagram of the ship's lower level into the dirt. The problem was important enough for the devotion of serious thought. He wasn't due on top deck for at least an hour or two and more than anything else on ship he loved to keep those wrinkled bitches waiting.

* * *

Amber's Wednesday had begun like every other, daybreak in the Humphrey Bogart lounge, staring up to watch pixel numbers march across the big flat screens like ants. A tight-lipped gathering with few emotions shared—best not to arm your neighbours with unnecessary ammunition, not to let them second-guess your true predicament. Telltale signs were always present, you could read them if you had the skill, or time or inclination and who amongst the Top Deck folks did not possess ridiculous amounts of time? A hint of a fellow passenger going under could provide a whole week's entertainment. Or grief, if it was somebody well-liked. Stock market flutters and fluctuations took place in the cloud, the unseen realm of algorithms, intangibles and hedges.

Nothing on the morning screens to cause Amber concern. No huddled groups of twos and threes, plaid blankets wrapped around crumpled pyjamas, ashen faces tilted upwards in rigid, sleepless disbelief. Not today.

Relieved, she took her customary stroll amongst the sunbathers, nodding and smiling, doling out selective grace. Winking at the occasional handsome swabbie. After all, politeness didn't cost a cent and in a world like this, it was the *little things* that mattered. Politeness could get you many little things, from contraband tobacco through to an extra white bread roll at the dinner table.

Sadly, Amber's tobacco stash had dwindled down to crumbs and she could not bring herself to touch the bitter tasting seaweed beadies rolled by the swabbies and netters and haulers, the stink of which clung and lingered around certain regions of the ship, generally no-go zones for wealthy lady passengers.

She watched three young men on their hands and knees scraping green-grey lichen from the deck. Dressed in patched, torn cargo pants, the faded logos on their t-shirts indecipherable.

Above the deck, two Black Hawk helicopters hovered like giant robotic gnats. Amber ignored the noisy contraptions, made her way to her customary lounge situated close to the bar and the Top Deck clock; the one they all set their own watches by as the ship breezed in and out of different time zones. She picked up a well-thumbed magazine and settled. No hellos for the other women already stretched and sunning. Greetings amongst Amber's friends were considered gauche.

Lindsay dipped her own magazine, then her sunglasses for a clearer look at the choppers. Amber took note of the familiar gesture. The wooden lounge creaked beneath her weight as she nestled herself. "Anything?"

Lindsay's exposed, steel-grey roots were badly in need of touching up. She sniffed. "Manoeuvres. Just the usual. Nothing to get excited about." By which she meant not pirates, or another change of course. The *Federico Fellini* had been encounter-free for fifty-five days running. The last attempt at a raiding party had turned out laughable; a pathetic flotilla of fishing junks weighed down by heavy guns. Thin brown women waving battered AK-47s, firepower aplenty but all they could do was shoot. They couldn't board—the *Fellini's* sides were far too sleek and high. First security turned on the water hose, then the Black Hawks made short work of the leftovers.

Afterwards there'd been bodies in the water, bobbing up and down like driftwood. No survivors—ship's drones made sure of that. They'd all watched the footage on the big screens in the Frank Sinatra lounge to the rousing accompaniment of *you get 'em boys and that'll teach 'em!* Fists air pumping, an elderly couple linking arms in a celebratory jig. The ship had never been in danger, the Company assured, all bullet holes in the side were plugged by sunset.

"They wouldn't be wasting fuel for nothing," added Lindsay, still staring at the wide blue sky, resplendent with its tissuey wisps of cirrus. Lindsay, being the oldest of the friends, remembered the ship when it was almost new, when the ice rink was still skatable and the golf course not ploughed up and used for crops. When the *Fellini* boasted twenty-one freshwater swimming pools, a surf simulator and thirty-seven bars. The desalination plant was still kicking on, thank god, even if fresh water could not be spared for the blistering sculpture garden. The ship had once had seven 'distinct neighbourhoods'—there were plenty more than seven now and *distinct* meant friends like Lindsay, Amber and Katelyn were not safe within them unless accompanied by well-fed bodyguards.

"We can ask Doc what's going on—if he ever gets here," said Amber, pretending to focus on her magazine, a dull affair filled with recycled articles photocopied onto greying recycled paper. 'Game Changing Skincare Treatments' had been run last year and 'Ten Ways to Turn Yourself into a Morning Workout Person' twice. With different accompanying photographs so that at least was something, but standards had been slipping—without doubt. She could see it in so many subtle ways, from surly wait-staff to never ending shortages. Meals where you couldn't be sure what you were eating. It wasn't Wagyu or Cervena venison—*that* you could be sure of. Most of what they ate came from the sea and they dumped their trash straight back in there without concern for the brown stain trailing in the vessel's wake like diarrhoea.

Lindsay was doing her best to hide her twitching irritation. Doc was late—that man was always late, a trait the women begrudgingly endured. But not today. Today both Lindsay and Amber needed Doc. "Oh god, doesn't Raymond look awful?"

Amber put her magazine back down and made a disapproving face. Said nothing as the older man walked by at a distance, head down, ignoring everyone—even Mr Travis and his corgi. One hand gripping the visor of his cap, even though there was no wind to speak of. No danger of him losing it overboard, which is what, rumour had it, had happened to Gerry Hargrave, Mr Travis's brother-in-law. Nobody had seen the ruddy-cheeked man in well over a fortnight. Not the done thing to mention missing persons, not if a whole two weeks had passed, not if there were rumours of late payments.

Amber sniffed and scanned the crowd in search of Doc's trademark crumpled linen and stupid hat. Instead of Doc, she found her daughter, a nut-brown girl of seventeen, dark hair falling free down to her waist. Standing by one of the outer railings, staring hard and admiringly at the lichen-scrapers' bulging, muscled arms.

Amber pursed her lips into the cat's bum expression denoting her very severest disapproval. She sat up straight and craned her neck, the magazine abandoned. "Olivia, darling, yoohoo—come on over!"

The girl's head turned at the mention of her name. She pushed a strand of long dark hair behind her ear and angled her body in the direction of couple of older men decked out handsomely in shining

Company whites, appropriately maritime, so long as you didn't look too closely at the fraying cuffs and mismatched buttons. Details her mother couldn't see without her glasses.

The lichen patches blooming across the deck were easy to make out. The abundant weed grew back relentlessly regardless of weather or applied corrosive chemicals. The purser said it wasn't lichen but more like a form of moss and its spores got into everything, especially wood. Bryophyte was the proper word but lichen was the term that stuck. The boys tasked with removing it wore cowboy bandanas to protect their faces, but their arms and lower legs were exposed as was everyone breathing downwind of them. The spores were said to cause fever dreams, nightmares and hallucinations, yet another reason why Amber and her friends fought so hard to defend high turf beside the Top Deck pool bar.

"Such a shy little slip of a thing," said Katelyn from the next lounge over, her long arms clattering with bangles.

Amber waved her hand with a flourish. Olivia hesitated, as if considering her options, then crossed the crowded, open deck to join the familiar clique on their wooden lounges, the cushions of which had once been brightly striped but were now bleached and faded by the sun. There was nowhere for the girl to sit. Amber sat up—properly this time—shielded her eyes and waved until she had the attention of one of the pool boys. One of the Joses, Alfredos or Alonzos. She felt exhausted trying to keep track of their names.

"My Olivia requires a seat," she shouted sharply. The boy flicked a glance across at the girl, nodded, then busied himself about the task.

"I don't like that young man's attitude," Amber added, not waiting until he'd moved out of earshot. "Some of those pool boys have forgotten where they came from."

"Most of us have forgotten where we came from, dear," said Lindsay, patting her arm.

Amber ignored Lindsay's customary snark. She was always tetchy when she was waiting for Doc.

Being responsible for Olivia meant Amber had to keep her eye on everyone. One handsome, savvy pool boy and everything might be ruined. The girl had reached that *certain age* and was developing bad habits, such as wandering off on her own, exploring areas of the ship best kept well clear of, sometimes being unaccountable for hours.

"So how's that Deb dress coming along, Olivia?" said Amber loudly, squinting in the harsh glare. "Tell me you've at least chosen the fabric."

"Ooh yes," chimed in both Lindsay and Katelyn, leaning forward. Everybody loved a Debutante Ball. The ship had held one every year since Sydney, tradition being so good for morale.

Olivia's eyes were wide and brown. She stared at Amber, then down at her own hands, then out across the pattern of interlaced semicircular decks after the pool boy, who was wrestling with chain looped between a stack of wooden lounge chairs. He needed a key but apparently didn't have one. She said something to this effect, how he was going to have to find a porter.

"For god's sake, Livie, stop your mumbling," Amber snapped. "Speak clearly when you're spoken to. You never know who's listening. It's always best to make a good impression."

When Amber looked back to the pool boy, he was gone. She shivered as a Black Hawk's shadow swept across the deck, the machine dipping low enough to make a messy chaos of their towels and magazines. Close enough to see the comforting logo emblazoned on its side: two blades crossed.

"See. Just routine, like I said. Nothing we need to be worrying about," offered Lindsay smugly as the chopper swooped in a wide arc across the water. She returned her attention to scanning the crowd for Doc.

Olivia kept both eyes on the noisy machine as the older women debated what kind of dress she ought to be wearing and the fact that the current Captain—not so long since he inherited the job—had decreed the Ball would be held in the Zsa Zsa ballroom. But surely the Zsa Zsa was too small, and the Sophia Loren more suitable? Not to mention that it was *three floors down*, a precedent none of the women could ever approve of. Because who knew where things might go from there? Three floors to Zsa Zsa was a slippery slope.

"Captain Grecko never would have stood for such an outrage. We pay good money for Top Deck privilege. It's the little things that matter—don't you agree?"

The other women all agreed with Amber. Little things—or the lack thereof—had indeed become more irritating of late. Amber missed chocolate more than she ever would have believed possible. The stuff on the menu *supposed* to be chocolate was nothing of the kind. Just coconut oil, boiled, compressed and flavoured. The young ones liked it, but they had never known Lindt or even lowly Cadburys, which had come in blocks of a family size, available at Coles and Woolworths for a few dollars.

"They say Sophia Loren's got broken lighting fixtures," said Katelyn, leaning in conspiratorially, "but I don't believe a word of it. Reckon there's something they don't want us to see."

Amber rolled her eyes theatrically. She fanned herself with her magazine—at least it was good for something. "You think everything's a conspiracy, Katelyn. That everything is secret for a reason."

Lindsay gave them both a knowing look. She'd been convinced for months that something large was following the ship. She was not alone in this belief. Everyone had seen *something* at one time or another while staring out beyond the rails at an ocean vast and deep and strong that changed from minute to minute, that drove emotions with its thrust and swell and held them captive as completely as a sturdy prison cell.

Amber was certain it didn't help that, inch by inch, the jungle that had begun life as a tame, miniature park, a fancy concourse at the centre of the ship, was taking over. A feature grown into a nightmare, climbing up the inner balconies, pushing through cracks and rents and splits, forcing its way along the rails and pipes. A park metamorphosed into a jungle filled—so it was claimed—with dangerous beasts. Animals that were not supposed to be there. However had monkeys and wild pigs and deadly snakes made their way on board? Such a thing was patently ridiculous, yet they had all glimpsed monkeys and other hideous things—like the time Consuela Dalton had discovered an actual python in her bath. *A python!* She had screamed and screamed but absolutely no one came so she'd grabbed a towel and run along the corridor. That was when they'd learned the truth, that the intercom system was no longer functional. That they could scream as much as they liked but no one could hear them.

Amber got up suddenly to brush imaginary crumbs from her lap and legs. "Where *has* that lazy doctor gotten to? How come that man is never around when you need him?"

Katelyn and Lindsay raised their eyebrows but neither offered an opinion. Doc Corduroy was rumoured to favour one or two of the lower deck casinos despite the rules and regulations—and other dangers. He stayed up late and slept in later. Kept odd hours and company, not the kind of man you'd choose to associate with, if you had a choice but when it came down to it, choice was pretty thin on the deck. Doc Corduroy had his finger on the *Fellini's* pulse. If ever you needed something, he could get it—and who did not need a little something now and then in this terrible, omnipresent heat? Providing it was an item that could be bought, bartered or sourced. If it was on the ship, Doc Corduroy could get it.

When Doc eventually made his appearance, both Amber and Lindsay busied themselves flipping through magazines they could practically recite by heart.

He slumped down in the lounge the boy had dragged across for Olivia, repositioned the Panama hat to cover his face. Stayed that way for twenty minutes while Katelyn did her best to flag down the drinks trolley which, Amber swore, was getting later every day, not to even mention the fact that the girl last week hadn't had the *first clue* how to mix a proper pink gin. And the stuff coming out of the Bombay Sapphire bottles was anything but. It wasn't even *Gordon's*, just some nameless swill being boiled up in the *Fellini's* jungle-stricken bowels.

Doc did not stir until the whumping helicopter blades drowned out the chatter. Black Hawks returning from their never ending search for solid ground.

When at last he sat up and removed his hat, all eyes fell upon him, hungry.

"Did you bring it?" asked Lindsay sharply.

Doc sniffed, fumbled inside his jacket pocket, removed a small tatty envelope, passed it across without so much as a word. Lindsay snatched it from his fleshy fingers.

"You're welcome," he said with the feigned casual demeanour he'd been perfecting across the past few years. Amber tried to catch his eye, but he'd become distracted by the chopper setting down on the landing pad, high above deck in the no go zone beside the capsule of bullet proof blue glass.

Top Deck was crowded—more than usual—bustling with animated folks, all stirred up by the noisy choppers, fretting that perhaps another change of course was imminent. That one of the Black Hawk pilots had seen *something*. That land might be waiting over the horizon.

Doc Corduroy clambered to his feet, tipped his Panama hat. "You ladies all have a wonderful day now, won't you?"

Amber stared at the back of his head as he dodged and shoved his way out through the throng, *en route* to wherever a man of his kind spent his daytimes.

Neither Lindsay nor Katelyn commented as Amber sprung off her lounge and headed after him, battering her way through the languid, irritating crowd.

Lindsay stared after her absently, clutching the Doc's envelope in a balled up fist. "I'll be in my cabin if anyone wants me."

* * *

The lower decks weren't safe at night but Liv had her own special place. One of the abandoned inner rim balconies not yet entirely claimed by creeping jungle. Not too difficult to scale, hand over foot. Enough space to stand without brushing against lianas or the fur-like moss thickly coating the walls.

Liv usually wore gloves and occasionally a surgical mask. But not tonight, with a fresh breeze blowing heady scents up from the decks below. Mango and papaya easily discernible amidst a delicious floral mulch.

She closed her eyes and let the smells wash over her, the taint of jungle lingering on her skin. She had to be careful not to stay too long. If Amber found out about her special place then she'd make one of the swabbies board it up. Lately everything made her mother furious. Too much of this, not enough of that; things that could be shrugged off, explained and blamed mixed in with more resilient kinds of disappointment.

Amber's tight-knit circle of friends could be extremely unforgiving. They complained about everything, even things that couldn't be considered anyone's fault.

Those women had the best of everything. Free run of the deluxe Top Deck sections, servants to fetch them chairs and bring them drinks. Lives untroubled by the world and its great sorrows—the countless millions who had already lost their lives, their residue lingering across the sea and sky, in dreams and nightmares shared across the globe. The shame of a world in which three billion souls had starved to death. Probably another billion since the lucky ones stopped caring enough to count.

Three billion was too big a number to hold inside her head. Three billion meant the world was filled with ghosts.

Liv had seen so very many ghosts. Impossible not to encounter strangeness trapped on a ship stuck out on the open ocean. Phantom waves and waterspouts. Dark shapes moving just beneath the surface. Swell so clogged with jellies and plastic, the ship had to clear a passage through with lasers. A sky so wide it threatened to swallow them whole.

If the *Fellini* were to vanish in a fog, who left behind would even know they'd gone? The last real 'earth' she'd glimpsed had been an inhospitable craggy protrusion, the cause of much momentary excitement, that moment passing swiftly once they'd lost sight of the *Fellini's* small scout vessel. The Captain had dispatched it choked with flags of hope and peace and friendship. The barometer fell and the mist rolled in, then nothing for five excruciating hours. Two choppers scrambled to determine the little scout boat's fate. Liv's mind filled with splinters of shattered driftwood mixed with sodden, tangled colours. They'd heard the shots but could see nothing through the mist.

The open sea was deadly, as was the jungle blooming up and out of the *Fellini's* troubled heart. She'd never set foot inside that jungle but she knew people who had. People who'd entered the verdant fold and never come out again to speak of it.

A monkey screeched in the darkness down below, disrupting Liv's concentration. The worst-kept secret on Top Deck was how her mother planned to marry her off to a man more than twice her age. An officer in frayed-cuff whites who spent his days sequestered behind blue bulletproof glass. His nights in lower deck gambling dens if the rumours turned out to be half true.

Liv curled her fists in barely suppressed rage. She would not do it. She would find another way, far from Amber and Top Deck's alcoholic haze.

Liv pictured herself clambering down the crumbling inner balconies, throwing herself down, down and deep into the jungle's heart. Some place where Amber and her awful friends would never find her.

Not just a dream. She had a plan. She would make her move during the latter stages of the stupid Debutante Ball, when the lights were dimmed and everyone was drunk. She knew a girl who knew another who shacked up with a couple of swabbie boys from third. The jungle's mouth lay down below on six, but there were rumours of secret passages. Safe ways of tunnelling through roots if you had a guide, if you knew what you were doing. She didn't know what she was doing, but she figured she could learn. Whatever it took, whatever the risk, she'd do it.

A single tear rolled down her cheek. Despite the bitter promises and all the hurt between them, Olivia knew she did owe Amber something. Despite the bullshit and the lies. Despite the things she wasn't supposed to know.

Liv knew she had not been born upon this ship. Her earliest memories were of thirst and blinding white. Endless sun, blistered skin and savaged bone, wasted muscle and emaciated hope. Watching the big white shiny superliners push on through layers of roiling plastic sludge amidst the squall of filthy, desperate children.

Bony hands passing her up through a porthole, exchanged for food or drink or medicine, her painful, limited world turned inside out. Bright light replaced by dark and stifling heat. The repetitious pound of hammering engines.

Eight years old as close as she could reckon, put to work in a giant greasy kitchen, scrubbing on her hands and knees, in filth from hard-to-get-at places, fighting with feral rats for scraps, sleeping in a scratchy plastic basket, curled up like a dog—only dogs got better treatment than the paid-for children on the *Fellini's* bottommost decks. Dogs were cherished, trained and prized. Down below, every two-bit druglord kept a dog and treated it with respect.

But somehow Liv had made it out and through and up, passed along by the hands of women who'd seen in her the potential for something brighter. And she paid them back, every single set of hands, stealing from the wealthy ones who'd dress her like a doll, paint her cheeks and comb her hair, tell her how she was such a *lucky* girl, how all that had gone before must be forgotten.

Her dreams were steeped in kaleidoscope, deep green streaked with hibiscus pinks and yellows. Palm fronds waving casually in gentle breeze, warm sunlight on her face. Darkness: deep, impenetrable. Pure fantasy, according to Amber—the woman who had bought her with hard currency. Fantasy generated by her deeply troubled mind. Olivia—not the name she had been born with—dragged free of a barely floating pontoon hellhole, rescued from starvation and disease, all memories from which she had been clinically disentangled. Just as well—because nobody needed burdens as grim as those. Just as well . . . but Olivia remembered.

"I will not marry him," she said out loud. But how was she to escape her future when trapped on a ship in the middle of the ocean?

* * *

"Hey Doc—wait up," screeched Amber across the backs of passengers sunning themselves like porpoises, the deck divided into different camps along diplomatic lines. Some religious, others according to class and cash: the haves, have-mores and the have-more-than-they-ought-tos, gradings she found thoroughly appropriate. A quarter of the Top Deck sunbathers had no real right to be there but so long as they kept their distance from the upper pool bar and Amber's turf, she was willing to pretend they didn't exist.

Doc paused the third time Amber called his name. Turned to face the woman he'd been successfully snubbing for days.

Amber got straight down to business. "Have you given any more thought to my *personal proposal*?"

Doc tilted his hat to reveal more of his face. Eyes swivelled upwards in the direction of the blue tinged glass encasing the bridge and its privileged officer class. He cleared his throat. "I presume you're referring to that young officer? Remind me—what was his name again?"

"Luciano. As you well know. Thirty-five and used to be married but I don't suppose that matters anymore."

"Don't suppose it does," the Doc agreed. What happened when the tsunami obliterated Sydney three years past was not something people liked to talk about.

"Luciano," Amber repeated, eyes glittering with malice. "And don't try any of your bullshit tricks on me. I've paid you good money up front and I expect results."

Doc splayed fingers through thinning hair before placing the Panama hat back on his head. "Don't I always get you ladies what you pay for?"

"You do," she said, "which is why we all come back and never report you—or poison other customers against you. Which we could do very easily," she added.

If he took the half-threat seriously, he wasn't going to show it. "Luciano," he enunciated in a serious tone, "Yeah, I know the guy. Frequents the level Four gambling suite off hours. Owes a motza to some big guy with a Polynesian name."

Amber's lips thinned as she pressed them tightly together. "I don't give two shits about some Polynesian arsehole. Is Luciano currently married or isn't he?"

Doc paused. "No. He isn't married."

"Gay? Bisexual? Prone to violent fits or temper tantrums?"

Doc snorted. "It's a bit late in the day to be getting picky." Doc could have affirmed the man's hetero status by offering up tales of young girl prostitutes scaling ropes to squeeze through portholes as the ship pushed through drifting arrays of rag tag settlements built up on plastic strong enough to stand on, but he decided to keep such details to himself. For the time being.

"His filthy gambling will have to stop, but otherwise he'll do," said Amber. "My daughter's developing an unhealthy obsession with that godforsaken interior jungle. Time has come for her to settle down, to start thinking about the future."

Doc Corduroy smiled a greasy smile. "Mother always knows best." The future she was talking about was entirely her own. He'd watched how long and hard she stared at the exalted senior crew, their shadows protected by the blue glass of the bridge. Aiming those binoculars as if she was peering up past clouds straight into heaven.

Olivia. He licked his lips involuntarily whenever he heard her name. His dick got hard and his throat went dry as he thought about taking her off Top Deck forever, only not in the direction envisioned by her ghastly wrinkled mother. She wanted up but he wanted down, *down down down* into the secret jungle's heart. Deep places where even shafts of light couldn't penetrate. Where they'd have plenty of marijuana, opium and each other. That case of beluga caviar and crate of Moet he'd souvenired during last year's ill-fated mutiny attempt. He'd clear out one of the looted jewellery stores off the old mall strip, sweep away the broken glass and rubbish, make it all nice and cosy, like a little house—all for Olivia.

Amber's mouth was flapping up and down but he hadn't heard a word. He tuned back in and made an effort to pick up all the threads.

"And a decent stateroom for the Mother-of-the-Bride thrown in as part of the deal. Somewhere the plumbing's still functioning like intended."

Doc pulled the face he always pulled when wheeling and dealing with women. The one meaning *sure, hell, right—but it's gonna cost you.*"

"Don't give me any of your two-bit bullshit," Amber added savagely, her voice dropping an entire octave. "If I'm giving *that man* my only daughter, it better wind up worth it—for me *and* the girl."

Doc's eyes travelled from Amber's garish turquoise eyeshadow, across the tops of the deck sunbathers and all the way to where Olivia stood in one fell, admiring swoop. "That daughter of yours sure is a pretty little thing," he said.

"Precisely," Amber said drily. "I can count on your discretion in this matter." Her words were a statement, not a question.

Doc reached for his hat and made as though to tip it, signifying their business was concluded. Amber turned and picked her way back across the deck, kicking aside other people's possessions, not caring if she stomped or tripped on the legs of lazing sunbathers, more than half of them drunk or stoned on weed grown deep in the *Fellini's* rusted belly. In that creepy, overgrown jungle, where rumour had it Doc Corduroy could come and go as he pleased, just like he had means and ways of insinuating himself amongst the officer class. A fact Amber would milk to her advantage. With all the world shot up and gone to Hell, one had to use one's skills and breeding to enforce civilisation at every opportunity, because who knew what the next sunrise might bring? The screens in the Humphrey Bogart lounge were never far from her mind. The scrolling tide of numbers rising and falling.

Meanwhile, Doc was dreaming up a sunrise of his own, a deal that did not involve some pot-bellied, glorified wop-swabbie who went by the name of Luciano—known as 'Lucky' to his mates—for reasons which would render him unsuitable for *anybody's* daughter if the old bag ever caught a whiff of any of it. But marriage brokering, shit, that was easy, something Doc could do with his eyes closed, in his sleep, something he'd done a few times already across the years on this ill-appointed voyage.

His gaze lingered longer on Olivia's lithe form. Even barefoot in a faded stonewashed t-shirt and floral sarong, she was a rare catch, no doubt about it, no, no doubt at all, and if not-so-Lucky Luciano thought he was getting it all for nothing, that arsehole had another think coming.

* * *

Amber aimed her binoculars at the flat expanse of blue that stood between the bridge crew and the rest of them. She'd invested so much time and effort into researching Luciano, yet had barely glimpsed the man this fortnight past. A troubling development, with the night of the Debutante Ball approaching fast. Doc assured her everything was shipshape, but when did he ever not sprout such consolatory bullshit?

White uniforms were becoming a lot less prevalent on Top Deck than they ought. In place of them, an endless seep of former Russians and nouveau-riche subcontinentals, working their way up, deck by deck. No one was doing anything to stem the tide.

She lowered the binoculars. Not much to see up there on the bridge. Whatever took place behind blue glass was a mystery.

She was preparing to scope the helipad when somebody shrieked out "Land Ho! Land Ho!"

All at once Top Deck became a frenzied hive, with everyone shoving and fighting their way portside, whooping and chittering like monkeys.

Amber's concentration held fast, despite the jostling and irritation. She didn't notice Lindsay approach, not until her friend lit one of those dreadful beadie cigarettes, releasing an acrid puff of scented smoke.

As usual, Lindsay was overdressed, tottering around in heels not made for promenading slippery decks. She never tripped—she'd been a catwalk model back in the *days before* and she was doing that thing they all did sometimes, dressing up in the best of everything she owned. Rings and jewels and pinned-up hair. *Just trying to make myself feel human, darling. Those little things one does to feel alive.*

Amber flapped at the plume with her free hand.

"Something's following this ship," said Lindsay, taking a deep drag. "I can feel it—and I'm not the only one."

"Rubbish," snapped Amber, her patience pushed to the limit by a toxic mix of Doc Corduroy and the heat. "And anyway, what if it were it true? No pirates have ever been able to—"

"Not pirates." Lindsay sniffed, wiped her cheek on the back of her hand. "Something else."

"Something else? Amber lowered the binoculars. "What kind of *something else?*"

Lindsay shook her artificial curls. Stared blankly at the smear of black mascara on her wrist. "The creature doesn't like the helicopters. They keep it scared away."

"You talk such nonsense when you're stoned—and when are you not stoned? You didn't see *anything*. You couldn't have *because there's nothing there to see.*" Amber returned to her binoculars. Rumours something large was following the *Fellini* had intensified since the ship pulled out of Papeete, never realising back in those days how much their world had utterly transformed. That the land they'd left behind was gone for good—in some cases literally sunk beneath the sea. In others, reduced to resonance politics and commerce, events beyond all influence and control.

The shoving and swearing amped up as the portside upper deck got crammed. Any glimpse of land, even rumours or mirages, anything at all reminiscent of *terra firma* brought all those with upper access flocking, no matter the weather or the time of day.

Today's ocean was calm and dull, same as it had been for weeks. Flat sea. Flat sky. No birds. But rumours of something unseen and following dragged like undercurrent; so much easier to ignite than gasoline.

"There's nothing out there," said Amber, reconfirming, gripping the binoculars, trying not to sound as bitter as she felt. "Go back to your room and sleep it off."

Lindsay didn't move. She stared at the horizon with glazed eyes. Sooner or later everyone glimpsed something weird: flirtatious phantom lights in the far-off distance, promising a future that never seemed to arrive. Land that turned out to be another junk flotilla filled with human detritus.

Lindsay had seen more peculiar things than her fair share: water tumbling from the sky in thick cascades like the waterfalls of old. Bright lights dancing through the stratosphere. Voices calling on the wind, the names of the dead or soon-to-be. On board ghosts ranged from the recently disappeared or dear departed to phantom images of people from long lost times. Long lost places, cities drowned beneath the waves, workers clutching suitcases and take-away cappuccinos, faces frozen in disbelief, at whatever it was they could see that the corporeal could not.

"I know it's close," continued Lindsay to no one in particular. "Something dark and vast and deep, bigger than a whale. Big enough to crush the ship if it—"

"For god's sake, will you shut it!"

Lindsay flicked her beadie and wandered over in the direction of starboard rails, away from all the shoving and excitement.

Amber sniffed with deep contempt. No wonder Lindsay smoked so much skunk. She'd pinned her hopes upon Central

Otago, a bit of New Zealand still advertised as high ground with infrastructure, clean water and a functioning transport system. Even an airfield—supposedly. Amber wondered often about the claim of aeroplanes. In early days planes had flown above the ship with comforting regularity. Big ones, air buses and the like as well as short-range DC threes and other Black Hawks belonging to other ships.

The last aeroplane anyone had seen had seemed so lost in the sky's vast expanse, like a lonely dove in search of a place to land. At least a year ago, quite possibly much longer. So hard to keep track of seasons when there was nothing to mark them by. It was always hot except when it was too cold, too windy or the rain came down as sleet—sometimes hail; dangerous and unpredictable. And as for the storms, well so far their luck had held, although it wasn't luck. Not really. The ship's high-tech equipment had been holding its own against the worst of entropy incrementally and inevitably consuming the *Fellini* like a cancer. Eating away at them from the inside out. Sooner or later the day would come and they'd have to dodge the storms without technology.

Amber clutched the binoculars against her chest. She fancied herself a realist. Not like poor doomed fragile stupid Lindsay, blathering on about the life they'd lead 'when they arrived'. Babbling about real estate, refurbishment and grounds keeping. The cost of maintaining an adequate count of gardeners. About where Blue Moon and Amoretto Roses might be acquired in such a difficult agricultural climate. About water licensing and how you should be allowed to have as much of anything you could pay for.

The others let her run off at the mouth, not because they didn't have the heart but because to shatter or even challenge her illusions might be the final cascading straw for each of them. Women who had lost enough to frighten them into silence—the kind of silence that stretched across generations. There was no old money anymore. There wasn't even money. Merely the investments none of them could control or even access. They lived in the shadow of the cloud, of people who were no longer on the ship. People who vanished in the middle of the night with no explanation sought nor offered. Sooner or later those algorithm clouds would darken and turn against them. Until that day, well, there was always Doc Corduroy and the temporary solace his pharmaceuticals had to offer.

When they could get hold of him.

The Doc's sources remained mysterious. The wily old bastard had his secrets, ways and means. Alliances with drug lords embedded so deep within the ship that some had never been exposed to natural light. *Rumour had it . . .* Amber could not bring herself to believe such flagrant bullshit. They had simply not been at sea long enough for such barbarous tales to be true. The ship was awash with ridiculous stories. Everyone was bored to death. They made up lies to pass the time, spread rumours without thinking about the consequences. Amber liked to keep one foot on solid ground, so to speak, even if it was deck not ground, perpetually rocking and roiling through storms and squalls and random course changes, designed to swerve around the worst of world events. Remains and ruins of other ships and, sometimes, entire cities swept out to sea by the kind of storms the *Fellini* and its crew lived in terror of. Avoiding super cell encounters was the captain's main responsibility. Hopefully. It was always hard to tell what the Captain might be thinking.

The Black Hawk was taking a long time to come back. Amber trained her binoculars on the patch of sea where it had disappeared. She had a plan and she was going to stick to it. She could not save all of the world's helpless creatures but she could save one—Olivia—find the girl a husband amongst the Top Deck crew, someone whose future did not rely on algorithms calculated in cloud bank arrays by heartless, formless artificial minds. Someone who could provide them both with a solid, believable future.

The far-glimpsed land turned out to be a mirage—to nobody's surprise. The Top Deck chatter moved on to other things. Lindsay sniffed away the last of her tears as Mr Travis came into view, his fat old corgi Patch waddling alongside. Mr Travis was one of those passengers everybody liked. Always addressed them with a cheery wave, looked after that sweet old dog no matter what. "False alarm," he said, "but not to worry. We'll reach the land of the long white cloud before too long, mark my—"

Somebody let out a blood-curdling shriek.

"Oh my god, what is that?"

Lindsay, menacing in those ridiculous shoes, clung to the rail, face twisted into a hideous grimace, exacerbated by badly-run mascara. "Down there in the water," she wailed miserably.

Everybody rushed to the rail and raised their own binoculars in unison, those that had them, and started combing the sea's flat, glassy surface.

"I can't see anything . . . "

"There's nothing there, what's she on about . . . "

"Quickly, there—check out the rising wave!"

"Dark patches, but I'd hardly consider . . . "

"Christ on a flaming—"

The dark mass quivering just below the surface was impossibly huge and difficult to make out. Not until it breached and bobbed, raising what appeared to be a gelatinous appendage, which it slapped down quick and fast, too quick to see.

"What the fuck—it's bigger than . . . " The voice trailed off. The thing below the surface of the water was bigger than the superliner. No creature on earth had ever been so large. Not in the days of dinosaurs—or ever.

* * *

Calm seas stretched from bow to infinity. Top Deck emptied quickly following the confirmed sea monster sighting. An empty Top Deck had been inconceivable in the months before. Unnerving silence without the fling and smash of clay pigeons being blasted off to starboard. No shuffleboard. Not even Mr Travis—fat little Patch was terrified of whatever kept nudging the vessel and refused to leave the safety of his cabin.

Lindsay and Katelyn dragged their wooden lounges closer together. They huddled, wrapped in faded floral towels, sunglasses obscuring grim expressions. Neither spoke. Neither had anything to say after the sighting of the creature. All attention was focused on the bar.

An hour passed before Amber joined them. She made her way across the deck then sat down stiffly. The lounge creaked as she swung her legs around. Lindsay opened her mouth but Katelyn shushed her with a sharp shake of her head. *Not now. Not today. Possibly not ever.*

The handsome waiter who eventually brought their drinks had an unfamiliar face. Not one of their comforting Joses or Alonzos. He mumbled something inaudible as he placed each drink on a coaster atop the low glass-topped table. His hand spasmed as he reached for the last glass, a mai tai. Liquid spilled.

Amber jerked up suddenly. "You stupid, useless clumsy fuck, why don't you watch what the fuck you're doing—"

Katelyn lunged, moved quickly to Amber's side, gripped her shoulders with both hands. "It's ok, honey, there's no need—"

Amber slapped blindly at her friend as the insults kept flowing, thick and incoherent.

"I'm going to call him Jose, same as the other guys. No way I'm learning a whole new name, not after what—"

"Shhh, honey, it's alright. Everything is going to be alright."

The waiter backed off to a safe distance. He stood there blinking in the harsh light and confusion, shielded his eyes with the hand not pressing the circular drinks tray hard against his chest.

Amber perched on the edge of her lounge, lighting up one of Lindsay's foul and stinking seaweed beadies.

Katelyn kept up a steady stream of comforting sounds and motions.

"Now come on. You don't know what you think you saw. None of us do—"

"We didn't *see* anything. There's nothing there to *see*. Just a mirage, like all those islands turning out to be nothing more than floating garbage."

"I liked the old captain better," said Lindsay, dabbing at her watering eyes with a well-worn lacy handkerchief. She sniffed repeatedly but didn't blow her nose. "That man always knew what he was doing. He never would have permitted . . . "

Nobody had anything to say to that, but they'd all been thinking it. If Captain Grecko had been so smart, how come he disappeared? Captains weren't supposed to vanish, only passengers occasionally when their cloud-bound investments failed, or when they crossed someone who oughtn't get crossed or when bad things happened which couldn't be prevented with necessary and strategic foresight.

What use was a captain who couldn't keep a grip on his own future? None, as it had turned out, which is how the ship had wound up in the hands of Captain Floris.

Amber regarded Lindsay with bloodless, thin-pressed lips. Half an hour back the former model had managed to look half regal in all that catwalk getup, but in the harsh light of afternoon sun, now she just looked old. Old and broken by whatever the hell that *thing* was, swimming alongside the ship. Nudging the hull as easily as if it was a beach ball. The *Fellini* was a superliner, the biggest of its class. The thing in the water was big enough to swallow the ship whole, was what everyone was muttering, which couldn't be true. Not likely. Surely not.

Lindsay's endless sobbing was ragging on everyone's nerves. If that useless fuck of a doctor ever showed his face again, Amber would force him to give her something potent. To pick her up or calm her down. Either way, so long as she went quiet.

"We have to pull ourselves together," Amber enunciated loudly. "We've got the Ball to think about—the laundry's running at least a week behind. You know what *those women* down below are like. You have to shout to get anything done half right."

And where exactly were the officers throughout the ship's biggest crisis in months? Cowering in relative safety behind blue glass, that's where. Amber kept those particular bitter thoughts to herself.

But Lindsay's whimpering was starting to drive her crazy. "Snap out of it, sister—or I swear I'll take the rest of your stash and throw it overboard."

Lindsay wasn't listening. Lindsay was sinking into a world of her own and it didn't look like she was ever coming back.

The ship changed course abruptly within the hour and the Black Hawks swept the seas, back and forth, back and forth for hours with hurricane spotlights, just in case.

* * *

Doc stood in the tiny room he'd come to think of as his office. The narrow cot he occasionally slept on was covered entirely in guns ranging from a Yarygin PYa semi-automatic pistol through a Chinese Type 56 Kalashnikov AKM clone—to his good old Saiga 12 with removed buttstock, 10 inch barrel, and 20-round drum magazine.

He settled on a Ruger P345 and stuffed it through his belt. Thuds and shouts echoed down the corridor outside. The past hour had been rife with rumours of rats preparing to jack a couple of 'Hawks and jump the ship. Doc Corduroy would be making sure that he was one of those rats, but not before putting a bullet through Fangaloka's skull.

Shoot the warlord, nab his stash, grab Olivia and hit the open skies. He chopped and snorted a line of coke off the back of a broken dinner plate. Braced himself as the bulkheads shuddered from what was either explosive charges detonated somewhere on the deck below, or the resonance of something large hitting the ship. Either way, he had not much time. The *Fellini's* hours appeared to be numbered and his options becoming fewer by the minute.

He hoovered up the rest of the cocaine, waiting until the slap of running boots on metal no longer echoed down the corridor. Shouldered the assault rifle and aimed a parting glance back at the guns he regrettably would have to leave behind.

* * *

The sea was lumpy and gunmetal grey the night of the Debutante Ball.

"It's chilly for this time of year, don't you think?" said a stranger done up in flamingo pink, encroaching on Amber's turf, staggering towards the pool bar as if she had a right to stand wherever the hell she wanted.

Amber was far too stressed for requisite reinforcement of protocol. She agreed with the flamingo horror that indeed the nights were getting chilly, even though the temperature was the last thing on her mind since the ship had started zigzagging on a daily basis. The *Fellini* was lost, that much was certain, lost and far from the trusty pontoon refuelling stations bobbing near Nuku'alofa and Vanua Levu.

The Debutante Ball was the only adhesive holding Top Deck together. The lowest decks, however, were an entirely different story, one involving rapid machine gun fire and more than one explosion in the past twelve hours. The hoot and holler of animals perpetually unseen.

Unable to sleep, Amber had paced Top Deck alone despite the danger and uncertainty, hating how she was forced to care about what those savages below were getting up to. Belowdecks used to be where *manufacturing* took place—what little there had been of it—and the engines, lowest down, of course. Somebody had to keep the *Fellini* on the move. A whole great chain of somebodies keeping reliable at their stations. The jungle occupied the middle like the lettuce in a sandwich—only now the lettuce was taking over the ship. The once-clean decks were slick with lichen, with roots and tendrils pushing up through cracks not evident mere days earlier.

Tonight, if Corduroy had done his work, would be the night everything changed. No more flamingoes and pushy, social climbing subcontinentals. Amber and Olivia would ascend the private stairwell, with Amber scoring a stateroom all of her own. So high, the roots and lichen couldn't reach. Amber wasn't greedy—she had every intention of sharing her good fortune. Inviting the others over for tea on her own private balcony. Popping the corks on her top-shelf booze whenever there was something to celebrate.

Somewhere close, an orchestra grinded out Pachelbel's Canon. Real live music rather than tinned. Mothers and daughters promenaded the circular decks arm-in-arm. Waiters stepped up, proffering trays of brightly coloured drinks. Bathtub gin, but nobody was complaining. The *thing* slamming into the ship's side at random intervals had given up its game in the early hours. No longer to be spoken of, by general consensus. Onwards and upwards, stiff upper lip and all that.

A cloud of commotion cut across the music; all gosh and wow and tittering and coo. Amber turned in time to see her Olivia illuminated in a shaft of orange sunset. All the girls were dolled up pretty but none of them looked half as good as her Olivia.

Amber managed a watery smile. They could still frock up like a million bucks despite persistent shortages. Amber and her friends hailed from a particular segment of society. The right kind of people with the right connections, even when forced to shape them on the fly. Even when they had to make concessions. Trade away things they had never thought they'd part with. Such had become the way of the world and there was no point in moping about small details.

"I want my daughter dressed in white," she'd told that dreadful dressmaker, the one who'd argued the remaining ivory fabric should be saved up for the brides, but who was *he* to be telling *her* what she could or couldn't have? Amber won in the end, she always did, and here was proof, Olivia, princess of the seas, veritably glowing like a treasured pearl.

Amber gently nudged a passage through the sequins, lace and taffeta as sunset orange faded from the sky. Relieved the girl was wearing the dress and taking their future seriously—for once.

"Darling—what are you looking at?" Amber tugged Olivia roughly away from the rail. Why did those dirty lower decks so often attract the girl's attention? Doc Corduroy insisted she couldn't possibly remember the cramped and stinking horrors of her childhood.

But Amber was wrong. Olivia had not been peering down the ship's gargantuan side, but staring out across the ocean, past the engines' ever-churning whitewater filled with dirty, floating things that did not bear close up examination.

"That creature's still following the ship," Olivia stated, eyes transfixed on the far off distance. "I can feel it. Lindsay feels it too."

"No it isn't, and no you can't," answered Amber decisively, grabbing Olivia's arm and yanking her further from the rail. "You can't feel anything because there's nothing out there. It's nearly time to go in." She smoothed the girl's hair and patted it in place. "Focus, darling. You only get to be a debutante once."

Olivia nodded and permitted herself to be led toward the warm spill of coloured party lights, the buzz of chatter, the clink of gin-filled champagne flutes, the laughter of the other young girls, each one in borrowed jewellery and the finest dresses their mothers could afford.

But before they'd made it halfway to the central staircase, she suddenly stopped and pulled Amber around. "I'm not going to marry that horrible man," said Olivia defiantly. "Even if the ship wasn't under attack, we weren't in danger and Lucky Luciano was the last man left on Earth."

"The ship is *not* under attack," snapped Amber, lowering her voice the instant she realised others were taking an interest. She snatched a drink off the nearest tray and pressed it into the girl's hands. "Sip this—it will help to calm your nerves."

Olivia raised her palms and stepped back as the glass smashed on the deck. "You can't manipulate your way out of this one, *mother.* There'll be no more marriages. No more debutantes. The creature hunts us. It smells our blood. It seeks vengeance for the sins of the world. The jungle is the only safe place."

Amber stared in horror at the shards of broken glass as Olivia's crazy words started sinking in. Olivia turned and forced her way out through the murmuring, disapproving throng.

Amber skirted the glass and chased on after her. "Wait!"

Olivia crouched down to unstrap her high heeled shoes. Once barefoot, she ran full pelt for the central staircase, the *Grande Descent* they would all be filing down to the Zsa Zsa lounge. Bounding along plush velvet carpet two steps at a time, avoiding the startled guards with her duck-and-weave. Long gone before Amber pushed her way to the ivory enamelled rails and started shrieking her name at the top of her lungs.

* * *

The I09's flaking grey paint corridor ran the entire length of the lower levels. It stank of salt, of rotting leaves and fermented, curdled sap. Of piss and shit and other gruesome elements on the days the septic system backed up too hard.

I09 had once been the crew's easiest route from stern to tail, back in the days before the jungle pushed its way through staterooms and corridors alike, roots and creepers that could grow three feet across a week—or faster. The plants loved the humidity of the lower decks, tolerated the briny ocean seep, sucking out the life sustaining liquid, leaving thick encrustation of salt crystals glued to doorways, hatchways and portholes.

The night had not been going the way Doc Corduroy had planned. Seemed he wasn't the only one hoping for last minute business dealings with the warlord before they were all forced to abandon ship. Amongst so many other valuable items, Fangaloka was rumoured to have a map of the Pacific Ocean's Bunkering pontoons—floating fuel stations carrying diesel oil and benzine.

With one hand in his crumpled linen jacket, Doc ducked a hail of bullets, fingers curled around his reliable Ruger P345, an older weapon with a comfortable grip, a gun that had seen him through the rougher patches.

He could recognise Fangaloka's lieutenants by their khaki and dark smears of jungle paint. But the man himself was nowhere to be found. The warlord's staterooms had been decimated long before Doc's arrival, the blood on the carpet, walls and ceiling testament to the fact that Doc was, unfortunately, too late.

Too late to the party, too late to the escape. Doc had flown UH-60 Black Hawks in Iraq back in the day, which he'd figured might make him a useful asset, under the current, particular predicament. But a chopper would be useless if he didn't know where to take it. The *Fellini* had twisted and turned around so many times, they literally could be anywhere in the Pacific.

Doc was thinking maybe this was it, the day his old school smarts and cunning finally failed to sail him through the straits, when the entire corridor lurched, then shuddered, so violently that two of Fangaloka's machine gun-wielding thugs along the corridor got slammed up hard against the bulkheads. One of them let out a torrent of mangled curses in Torres Strait Creole. His offsider, a thick-lipped, pale-faced man, had had his M4 Carbine raised and ready when whatever-the-fuck-that-was had hit the ship. Hit it like a hurtling meteor—or perhaps they'd been rammed by another superliner? Because what else could set the Io9 to shuddering?

The men had quit their haggling over the price of poppy oil, over who had let the wild pigs in to savage whose marijuana crops. When whatever-the fuck rammed the side again, a torrent of filthy, stinking water surged between the thickened twisting roots. Next came foetid compost stench and screaming.

Then, more screaming and scrambling over tangles. Belching smoke from deep below and enough salt water bleeding through the cracks to make the men abandon all business concerns.

Gunfire, rapid, in the distance. Doc bolted for the nearest stairwell, the fastest he had ever moved in his life. And what a shitty life it had been, the one now strobing before his eyes in jagged pieces. The man he'd knifed for his identity—and passage on this stinking tub. The women he'd . . . no, Doc did not have time to waste on women. There was only one girl still in his mind, only one pure enough to make him care. Thoughts of Olivia propelled him up the crumbling stairwell, two steps at a time, guided him to a safer corridor. One the rising waters had yet to reach.

* * *

Charcoal storm clouds coagulated in a bruise centred directly above the *Frederico Fellini*. Passengers squealed and clung on to each other as unsecured items hurtled across the deck.

"We're not moving—why aren't we moving?"

"Get back down—who's blocking the goddamn staircase?"

None of the regulars were truly terrified until they comprehended that the unthinkable had happened. The Top Deck clock had stopped—for good this time, stuck fast on 11:11, as eerie an omen as there had ever been. As if the choppy seas were not enough. And the light, a pallid, sickly cast that might have been appropriate at sunrise. Only sunrise wasn't due for several hours.

Katelyn took up position on the tier above the lounges, a rifle balanced across her knobbly knees. Nobody asked where she'd gotten the gun. Things were changing hour-to-hour and it didn't hurt to be prepared for the worst.

Lindsay fought her way across the deck, those years of catwalks in precarious heels finally standing her in a decent stead. Shoving the wayward and clumsy aside, passage hindered by lounges not tied down.

"That captain oughta drag his carcass down here off that bridge," she shouted, wide-eyed and chemically alert, back to her old self again—to Amber's relief. Shouting had become necessary with so many competing sounds. The terraced, circular decks around the pool bar were filled with gawkers checking on the stopped clock themselves, even those whose staterooms still featured working screens. The Top Deck clock was the only one that mattered, its consensual time the glue that bound them all. They could handle the jungle, the lichen and the weather but timelessness was another matter entirely.

When Katelyn slammed a pink gin into Lindsay's hands she drained it in one gulp. "Propellers are fouled with plastic," she reported grimly. "Surrounding seas choked thick with those filthy jellies." She nodded in the direction of the blue-tinged capsule bridge. "Consuela Dalton says the crew have barricaded themselves inside."

Amber's eyes blazed. "Connie—how the hell would she know that?"

Lindsay threw her an exasperated look, then jiggled her glass, empty but for a couple of tiny melted cubes. A glance in the direction of the bar confirmed the worst. A crush had gathered. Voices were raised and getting higher. The two Joses on duty didn't stand a chance of fending off the thirsty, frightened crowd.

"Here," said Katelyn shouting from behind. Passing a hip flask, one hand resting firmly on the rifle, just in case.

Lindsay mouthed a relieved *thank you* as something large and hard slammed into the ship. The hip flask clattered to the deck. Everyone began to wail and scream.

Amber scrambled to her feet, grabbed the nearest railing for support just in time as the creature struck again. The air filled with the wrench and creak of grinding, tearing metal. People shrieking, falling over their own feet.

Amber flung her gaze towards the bridge in search of answers and got one soon enough. Those familiar Black Hawks swinging into view. Behind them, a grey and boiling bank of cloud that seemed to have spewed up from the angry ocean.

"Look—those bastards—they're leaving us!" shrieked Amber. She snatched the rifle out of Katelyn's hands. Aimed and fired, the force of the bullet flinging her backwards to slam hard against the rail. Her bullet bounced harmlessly off the tinted glass.

Both fists and voices were raised in anger as one of the hovering Black Hawks dropped a ladder from its underbelly. Amber took squinting aim again as one by one, the bridge crew climbed on up.

"Come back you cowards—take me and my daughter with you," she screamed, shrill voice snatched and obliterated by a mix of wind, wave, storm and brute hysteria.

The bridge crew ascended as charcoal silhouettes, individuals indistinguishable, none of Amber's bullets hitting home.

The only one on the upper deck not screaming was Doc Corduroy. He kept a firm grip on the railing as he scanned the crowd from face to face, knowing Olivia had to be there somewhere, comprehending that this was it, his chance had finally come. The stuck-up bitches were going to have to hand her over because they wouldn't last the night without his help.

He cupped his hands and yelled "Olivia!" as rain soaked through his precious linen, plastered thinning hair against his scalp. Clutching his Panama hat for fear of losing it. "Olivia!"

His voice obliterated amidst the thunder and confusion, rain sleeting down with angular precision. Passengers and crew alike slipping and sliding all over the listing deck as pungent stenches swirled and belched and wafted. Rotting vegetation, the kind you'd find at the bottom of a swamp, seeping from great cracks in the vessel's structure. Doc blinked streaming water from his eyes as he watched cracks widening in the deck and walls, thick-coiled roots pushing up and through, wooden lounge chairs hurtling like tumbleweeds.

"Olivia!"

A shadow blotted out the lightning, cleaved straight through Top Deck like it was butter.

"Olivia!" Her name dispersed by shrieking winds as Doc and hundreds of other passengers tumbled headfirst into the churning, foaming void.

* * *

Women's arms and women's faces, soaked and dripping with stunned disbelief. Arms strong enough to haul him up and over the boat's fibre-reinforced plastic sides. Women. Doc Corduroy's heart flooded with palpable relief. If this had been Fangaloka's boat, he wouldn't stand a chance. Too many debts; too many altercations. But women . . . he could always find a way into a woman's heart. Manipulate them into supplying whatever he needed.

Olivia did not appear to be amongst the damp, bedraggled throng, although some were wrapped up tight, their faces covered. No matter, he would find her some day, somehow, either Olivia or another girl just like her. Someone young and soft and pure. A girl the world hadn't soiled with its corruption and despair.

He coughed and then some pinch-faced crone was leaning over, wiping his salt-drench face clean with her hands. "Thank you, my dear," he said as kindly as he had learned was best. Her teeth were crooked and non too white. He didn't like crooked teeth. He would close his eyes until she went away and the worst of the storm had fled the sky. Rest his head and dream of better times and better days. The sea was choppy but the squalling rain had all but stopped and that, at least, was something.

Doc Corduroy fell into a fitful slumber through which he hacked and slashed with a dull blade through thick, impenetrable jungles, which morphed into thrashing killer waves and dark skies etched with diagrams, red line and black scrawl defacing off-white paper charts spread across a table depicting instructions for the Williamson turn, an ideal method in reduced visibility, with rescue throw and heaving lines. Man overboard was a tricky business. Sometimes it was impossible to turn a ship the size of this around.

Churning water interrupted by the songs of angels dragging him back into his skin. Above him spewed a wicked spill of brittle constellations: Magellanic silver-white star clusters, Carina, Centaurus and the Crux: once visible in ancient Athens, a thousand years before the Earth had shifted on its axis. The skinny boy who had shared his meagre astronomical penchant had lost his life in a knife fight over nothing. Such had always been the way of things.

Something in the boat had changed. Hunkered down a few metres ahead sat a big man wrapped in a damp, polyester blanket patterned with black and purple tiger stripes. Not enough light to catch his features, but there wasn't any need to see his face. Fangaloka, curse his filthy rotten luck. Fangaloka; perpetual survivor. Last man standing and the first to find a boat and get away while everyone else stood screaming and distracted by monstrosities, either real ones or imagined, apparently. Doc was no longer certain about any of the things he thought he'd seen during the *Fellini's* final disintegrating moments. All those toxic spores and pollens; lichen scrapings distorting vision and clouding up men's minds. A storm had sliced the Fellini into ribbons —- the only conclusion that made sense. The ship had been lucky to keep sailing on for as many years as it had done.

Fangaloka: Prince of Darkness. Tattooed shadow swirls across dry skin. With effort, Doc Corduroy managed to haul himself to standing, shuffling his feet to keep his balance. Damn, but every gun he owned lay ruined at the bottom of the sea. He couldn't win a one-on-one with this overmuscled human mountain. He would have to think of something clever.

The lifeboat was bigger than he'd first presumed. Perhaps all was not lost?

"Friend," said Corduroy, grinning fiercely, wiping his salty palm down a damp trouser leg and stepping forward. "To new beginnings. To new opportunities."

Bedraggled women shuffled themselves and children out of the way as the mountain rose, shrugging off his tiger skin, a Ka-Bar USMC glinting in each outstretched hand. Corduroy raised both palms in mock surrender. "Relax, my friend, there's no need to fight. Plenty of everything to go around." He smiled and raised an eyebrow in the direction of one of the women. Not the crone with the crooked teeth. A younger one whose hair might well be blonde if only there had been more light to make out subtle differences and details. No matter. Doc was not a fussy man, and first things first, which meant the mountain would have to come to Mohammed and the two of them work out how to split the spoils. How to forge a better future from the splinters—to find dry land and claim it for themselves.

"My boat," said Fangaloka.

"Of course it is, good man. Of course it is—and a very fine crew you've assembled for yourself, I might add. In very difficult circumstances, too . . . I've always admired that kind of ingenuity, especially in a crisis . . . "

Fangaloka lunged, both blades glinting silvery with starlight.

Doc flung himself backwards, barrelling into a cluster of women. Flailing his arms to prevent himself from falling.

Doc Corduroy didn't fall. His bulk was gathered and pushed along; shoved and prodded until it reached the starboard rail. Nobody said anything. No signal had been issued. No words spoken. No consensus reached.

"Wait . . . no . . . what? . . . stop! Help!"

So many nameless, faceless women with sinewy arms and tight-gripping hands. And then, finally a face he recognised.

"Amber! Amber! My pockets are full! I have everything you need. Everything!"

Amber pursed her lips and watched as Doc Corduroy's bloated, wriggling form was launched over the side, slamming hard into waves thickened with coils of writhing, jellied plastic. Corduroy went down and under, his head rattling with cold shock response statistics, his vision dimming and faint bells ringing in his ears. Too cold to breathe, swallowing more water than air. Kicking to keep his head above the surface. Kicking hard until the very last.

* * *

Flat sea the colour of dirty snow. Sunlight slicing through the low cloud scatter. A sudden, rough lurch of the lifeboat nudged Amber wide awake. Huddled down under drenched tarpaulin, warm bodies pressed all around, at first she couldn't remember where she was. Flooding panic as she punched and pushed at the heavy, dripping canvas overhead. One by one the survivors sardined beneath tarpaulin stirred, engaged in their own brief rituals of panic before helping to shift the sodden, weighty mass enough to let in welcome, salty air.

A wave of bright and dazzling light amidst excited cries.

"Land! Land Ho!"

"An island, Mama—it's an island!"

"Jesus Mother Maria, we are saved!"

Sobs and whimpers evaporated as one by one survivors glimpsed the yellowed slick of sand, comprehending *en masse* that their lifeboat had beached itself on a shallow spit. At the very least, they were safe from drowning. The last thing anyone remembered was the storm, the shattering ship and the Black Hawks fleeing. All belonged to yesterday or maybe a week ago. It was hard to remember.

"But where are we?"

Amber rubbed her pounding head and stared. The island looked like every other island from a pastiche of memory and glossy brochure: a stretch of fine sand fringed with dark green foliage, palm trees jutting at irregular angles, the kinds of trees that took many years to grow.

Amber tried to conjure images of New Zealand, north and south from sites she'd frequented before the web went dark—back then, she'd only been half interested at best, depending on her mood.

In her heart of hearts she'd hoped the *Fellini* might have found a passage to Hawaii and onwards to whatever remained of the Americas. Tahiti was more probable, but the truth was they could be *anywhere*, blown off course in all directions, if that wretched captain had ever been telling the truth.

The captain. Intrusive flashes of evacuating Black Hawks, the bridge crew—Luciano included—abandoning the rest of the passengers to their fate. Two big men fighting in the centre of the lifeboat, slashing blades and swinging punches, both tipped unceremoniously over the side and swallowed by a monster from the deep.

Good riddance to bad rubbish, as Katelyn used to say.

Poor Katelyn.

Memories struggled to cohere and set, but a final yank of sodden canvas followed by a flurry of arms and legs rescattered them. Women, girls and a handful of children spilled over the lifeboat's side in clumps of twos and threes, leaping and tumbling and wading through shallow streams up the beach, some on all fours, some of them praying, others laughing, clutching at handfuls of dry sand when they reached it, tossing it into the air in joyous arcs.

And there she was, Olivia, standing on the warm and welcome sand, barefoot in a ruined debutante dress.

"Be careful!" cried out Amber through cupped hands, her words scrambled and scattered on the breeze unheard. Olivia was the only one not rolling in the sand, her attention fully taken by the wall of green and a couple of peculiar jutting structures. Too far away for Amber to see clearly—her glasses were probably at the bottom of the ocean. Taking great care, she jumped down into the shallow, lapping waves, unsteady on land after so many years at sea. Throwing a nervous glance over her shoulder to the boat responsible for their lives, relieved to note it was wedged deep in wet sand.

The long, curved beach was littered with dark streaks. Seaweed she presumed until she poked at one of the dark streaks with her foot, stubbing her toe on metal entangled with slime. Charred helicopter fragments in a variety of shapes and sizes. She sniffed. That cowardly captain and his bridge crew brought their fate upon themselves. She'd gone a fair way along the stretch before pausing to consider the possibility of mangled body parts.

Olivia struggled through heavy sand ahead, adjusting to the gravity and drag. Distracted by the enormity and splendour of the towering jungle wall.

"Be careful, Olivia—you don't know what lurks within," Amber shouted, louder this time, her voice dissolving uselessly in the wind. The girl had never seen a genuine jungle. Or a sandy beach, or so many of the ordinary things that Amber still took for granted because they lived on in her memory and some part of her still believed that they were out there somewhere waiting to be rediscovered. But the girl . . . how much of any of this could possibly be real to her?

Ahead, Olivia, wind-whipped hair out of control, tentatively approached the jungle's edge. She stopped and pointed upwards at a pale pink, protruding shape.

Amber sloughed through thick, coarse-grained sand. "Don't touch anything. Wait for me."

"A column from the promenade!" said Olivia.

"Don't be silly, dear . . . " The words were out of Amber's mouth before her eyes could properly focus on the thing, the shape with its fluted edges and soft pink tinge. "But how . . . "

Cries of exclamation repeated up and down the beach. Amber turned to watch smashed segments of helicopter dragged free and identified, piece-by-piece, the lifeboat survivors bending to tug at them, assembling the narrative of what might have taken place the night before.

"I can't feel sorry for those pathetic cowards. Not one little bit—no decent man, let alone a decent captain . . . " But when Amber turned back, Olivia was gone.

She panicked. "Olivia!"

A clear trail of footprints scuffed the sand right up to the jungle wall. Amber followed and plunged straight through the green. She would not be left behind, no matter where that silly girl thought she was headed.

The undergrowth was not as thick as it had appeared from the beach. With dismay, she wondered what had happened to her shoes—not to mention Katelyn and poor darling Lindsay. Those two had driven her half crazy across the years but dear god, they had deserved much better than to go down with the *Frederico Fellini*.

Thick, humid air echoed with birdcall: whoops and caws and high-pitched screeching—parrots or monkeys or other kinds of unseen, exotic beasts.

"Olivia!"

The foliage seemed to absorb Amber's cries. The louder she called, the weaker the effect. At last she stumbled into a clearing scattered with chunks of stone the colour of Himalayan rock salt. Another column jutted at an angle of roughly thirty degrees; pocked and weathered, looking like it had stood for centuries but of course that couldn't possibly be so. Most definitely one of the supporting columns from the *Fellini's* promenade, she would know it anywhere. They would all have known that column anywhere.

Pushing on beyond the column, she was relieved to find Olivia standing in a ragged clearing, frozen still, both hands covering her mouth. Staring up at the clearly identifiable helicopter blade embedded in a palm tree's trunk. Transfixed by the sight of the bruised and bloodied body lashed to the palm's thick base below. Doc Corduroy, those grubby, sodden linens unmistakable, the front of his shirt drenched thick with blood. Head lolling forward, face obscured by a battered and sodden Panama hat.

"Don't look," instructed Amber. Useless words too late. She strode forward matter-of-factly, intending to check the body for a pulse because she had to be sure the Doc had finally gotten what was coming to him. Trust *him* to somehow have escaped the raging sea.

Doc Corduroy's flesh was rubbery and cold. A leather knife hilt protruded from his heart. Fangaloka's weapon—she pictured the two locked in a death grip below the roiling waves, then debated whether or not to pull it free, to cut him down or just leave him up there for the birds. Still thinking about it when Olivia took off again.

"Olivia—no—wait!"

Amber abandoned dead Doc Corduroy to chase after her daughter. "Olivia—be careful, there might be anything in there—"

She watched as Olivia's torn, white dress became obscured by foliage mere feet beyond the rage of her grasp.

Fronds slapped at Amber's face as she hurried onwards past another chunk of marble, this one lying on its side, half covered in the same pale clingy lichen that had permeated the ship in recent months, despite the relentless scratching and scraping performed by those bare chested pool boys in bandanas.

"Olivia—wait for me!"

Further on, the trees grew higher, trunks entangled with thick liana vines. When she pushed through a wall of draping green,

Amber got the surprise of her life. Beyond lay another clearing, this one flooded with soft light. No sign of Olivia or anyone else. Instead, an enormous statue carved from gleaming obsidian. A goddess, her features regal and sublime; her face identical to Olivia's—no mistake about it whatsoever. *Identical.* The goddess stared at the encompassing jungle, peaceful and serene. Colourful fruit and flowers ringed her feet.

Amber tried to speak her daughter's name. Her lips parted but no sound came out. All around, the jungle burst alive with shrieking creatures: cockatoos, macaques and tarsiers, sloths and flying foxes, elephants and tigers crashing through the undergrowth. Chattering gibbons, cobras and crocodiles and other things she did not know the names of.

Amber swore obsidian Olivia's carved face cracked into a smile as she stared across the jungle, her domain.

⁕

WITH THIS NEEDLE I THEE THREAD

ANGELA REGA

"Cosi gentile il profumo d'un fiore! Ma i fior ch'io faccio ahime, non hanno odore."
"How sweet is the perfume of a flower. Alas! The flowers I make don't smell."

—Mimi's Aria. La Boheme

ISS EZRA WAS A DRIED BEANPOLE of a woman with a starched face, her lips so thin they seemed folded up inside her gums. Without waiting for an invitation, she marched into our workroom. A gust of wind followed that slammed the door shut behind her. She took off her navy felt hat and put it on the stand.

I unravelled the roll of grey fabric on the workbench to conceal the hair bracelet I had been working on and cast a look at my sister, Poppy to hide what she stitched on her sleeve Then, I stood behind my chair the way Ma had taught me when greeting distinguished guests.

"Good morning." I bobbed my head and sat down again. Miss Ezra bobbed her head back in acknowledgement and stared at my elder sister, waiting for a polite greeting. I cleared my throat and kicked my sister's chair leg, hoping it would jog her memory about social decorum. Miss Ezra often came to collect Poppy's embroidery and my accurate stitch work for display in her gallery. Being the sister of the Post Master, she sometimes even brought Ma's much anticipated mail. We were told to always be on our best behaviour in her company.

Poppy didn't stand up. She let out a large sigh and slumped across the table, arms outstretched, as if in the throes of a consumptive fever.

Miss Ezra clicked her tongue in a way that could only mean stern disapproval. Poppy's exhibition had revealed what I had wanted her to hide: a series of velvet red hearts my sister had stitched all the way up her own sleeves. Only women who sold love wore such things.

My mother's light footsteps came down the stairwell. Just in time. I smiled sweetly at Miss Ezra. She didn't smile back. Instead, Miss Ezra reached out and grabbed my mother's arm and lowered her voice to a whisper, pointing at Poppy.

"Eudora, she shows signs of it, already."

Tension straightened my mother's back, like a starched dress bodice too tight to wear.

"Signs of what?" I asked and Miss Ezra sliced my question clean with a sharp change of subject. She picked up the cross-stitch purse Poppy had embroidered with intricate stitched flowers in purples, creams and yellows and cooed in admiration.

"This will do nicely for the gallery display. "

She yanked the fabric near me to expose the half-hidden bracelet and smiled like a magician revealing a trick.

"A fine bracelet. Whose hair is it?" Miss Erza fondled the soft auburn hair I had plaited into a wristband.

My face reddened. It was meant to be a surprise for my mother.

"Violet, it's rude not to answer when spoken to," my mother scolded.

"My father's," I muttered. I avoided eye contact with my mother; her expression would have pained me. He had been away at war for so long, our only contact now sporadic letters.

"Poppy! It is rude to slouch in company!" My mother snapped and Poppy sighed. I looked at the auburn hair of the bracelet and then at the matching crown of glory my sister possessed.

When I was a wee thing, I dreamed of a day when I, too, would have those luxurious locks, but my hair hung long and black with a purplish sheen—hence my name, Violet.

Miss Ezra picked up my stitch samples and smiled.

"These two examples in my gallery should guarantee you some work for the next couple of months." Miss Ezra put the cross-stitch purse in her handbag and then turned her gaze towards Poppy. Her eyes narrowed to a fine slit and her voice lowered to a whisper.

"Seamstresses and embroiderers are born to make pretty dresses for ladies and handsome suits for gentleman. They are born to embellish with embroidery pretty purses and borders, doilies and pillow cases."

She turned to look at me and said louder, her eyes wider, "All with accurate stitches and perfect line." She moved closer to Poppy, bringing her pointy nose next to my sister's round tipped one. "I think you are getting the Gift. A little too early, perhaps. Be careful."

I watched my mother's upper lip twitch a little. "Was there any mail for me today at the Post Office?"

Then Miss Ezra unfolded those thin lips to a smile, clearing any evidence of her warning.

"Not today. The queues at the post were so long today. How about a nice cup of tea, Eudora?"

"Of course." My mother wiped her hands on her apron and moved to the stove to fetch the teapot and china.

Poppy returned Miss Ezra's threat with her liquid brown-eyed stare and a lazy smile. Recently, my sister has started to ooze an aura of love that took one's breath away. It wafted out from her pores and the curve of her breasts, from the radiant glow of her skin. Perhaps this was the Gift?

Two nights ago, I had seen with my own eyes the effect my sister had on the tenor that sang Rodolfo in *La Boheme*. It was the last performance of the Spare Penny Opera outside the Bellusini Theatre. One look at my red-haired sister seemed to steal his very breath away. His chest heaved as he reached for those tenor high Cs.

But her beauty made Miss Ezra squirm with discomfort. I saw the way her mouth contorted and twisted, the way she looked at her with distaste. It made me uncomfortable, scared, even. No, this couldn't be the Gift.

Ma handed a saucer that balanced our best fine bone china cup to Miss Ezra. Her fingers were long like spiders' legs as she picked up the cup and sipped at the hot tea. "I can guarantee you, if Poppy uses the Gift the way I think she will," Miss Ezra put her cup down as if for dramatic effect and whispered, "*Gnanera will come.*" At the utterance of that name, both Ms Ezra and my mother turned to look at the iron door in the salon. The iron door had been in the salon ever since I could remember, covered by a large red velvet curtain so long it puddled onto the floor. I could have sworn I saw the curtain undulate but before I could comment Ma answered. "Too soon. I'm sure my daughter will use The Gift for good."

Miss Ezra paced past our workbench and over to my mother's table; she fondled the long skirt my mother had been stitching with those long spider-leg fingers. "A fine skirt. Is it for Permelia?"

"How did you know?"

"I know everything, Eudora."

Miss Ezra took her leave, with Poppy's purse and my stitch samples. She nodded without saying goodbye, letting the door slam behind her.

"Poppy, when Miss Ezra comes, you should behave in a manner that is proper for a young seamstress of your age," Ma scolded.

"Brrr! She's such a cold, dried up, miserable creature!" my sister feigned a shiver. "Thank goodness she's gone! I have a surprise." She stood up and clapped her hands together like an excited child and dragged a box from underneath the table to the floor between our workbench and Ma's.

Ma broke into a smile; it was hard being angry at Poppy, even for a minute.

Like a magician's assistant, Poppy paced around the box, her arms outstretched covered in those velvet red hearts. She pulled the lid off and shouted, "Voila!"

I gasped.

Inside was a gramophone, ebony and shining, with white floral etchings bordering the horn.

She pulled it out of the box and beckoned for me to look further inside.

"What else is in there? " I hopped on one foot in excitement.

"How much did this cost?" Ma fretted.

Poppy ignored Ma's question and beckoned me to look inside the box.

"Help yourself," she said.

I kneeled down and pulled the slim package out. It was a record cover of the opera we had seen performed by the Spare Penny Opera, *La Boheme.* A woman with long red hair and pale skin swooned in the arms of a swarthy man. They were surrounded by snow and a starry sky. It could have been Poppy on the cover.

"Let's play it," I said.

"Can I play my favourite first?" Poppy asked but she needn't have. She already had the gramophone needle ready to play the tune she wanted to hear.

"Go ahead," Ma said.

"It's Mimi's aria," she said.

Ma closed the window so that nobody could hear the music from the street.

"Poppy, how did you pay for this?

"The Grand Abbess. I stitched these same velvet hearts up my sleeve on her bloomers."

I stifled a giggle. "Madame Velvetina?"

Velvetina was the local lady that sold love to sailors, young boys looking for experience, and old men looking for release.

"She services a need just like we do," Ma said in the matter-of-fact tone she used when she made us take castor oil before bedtime.

"She pays much better than the ladies with too much money in their pockets," Poppy added and then broke into song.

And the lyrics that Poppy sang the loudest were from Mimi's aria. Mimi too, stitched for a living. She sang of the gentle perfume of a flower and how sad she was that the flowers she stitched did not smell.

Ma smiled as Poppy waltzed around the room, her skirt billowing up as she and I danced. She grabbed my arm and we joined in.

We danced until the sky darkened to dusk and the raven call became lazy and tired. With the curtains drawn it was our little world. Still Ms Ezra's words haunted me. *Gnanera will come.* Would she come through that big iron door? Both Miss Ezra and Ma had looked over at it when her name was uttered. I had never seen the iron door open. I looked at the curtains on the wall that concealed the iron barred door. I could have sworn I saw them undulate but then hearing Poppy's shrieking laughter made me think I must have imagined it.

* * *

Later that evening, upstairs in our attic room, I watched Poppy brush her hair, one hundred even strokes. I wished I was as beautiful as my sister. Her pale skin, almond shaped dark eyes, and flaming red hair could have made anyone fall in love.

I was two years younger than Poppy and wondered if, and when, this Gift they talked about would come to me.

I curled up in our bed while Poppy hummed Mimi's aria and puckered her lips into a kiss in the mirror for an imaginary Rodolfo.

"*La Boheme* was so romantic. Rodolfo loved Mimi so much in the opera, didn't he?" I asked; it was a statement more than a question.

"*La Boheme* is *the* most romantic."

"You just love Rodolfo." I teased.

"I love Mimi, too." Poppy answered.

Poppy began to sing again and Ma shushed from her bedroom. Poppy leaned in close to me over the bed and whispered. "Do you want to know who loves you?" I nodded and sat up against the bed head.

"We need a candle, a hand mirror and an apple." Poppy picked the candle up from the bedside table and shone it under her chin. She kept her eyes wide, unblinking. It made her face emanate an eerie unworldly glow.

"Stop it!" I pushed the candle away from her face. "And where are we going to get an apple?" I asked, but she had already anticipated this question and pulled one out from the top drawer of her dresser.

I slid out of bed; the floorboards were cold under my bare feet. I stood next to my sister, shivering, but ready to listen to her instructions.

"Hold the hand mirror in front of me so I can see my reflection. In my right hand, I hold the lit candle, in my left, the apple. I take a bite of the apple, stare into the candle flame and then stare into the mirror. The shadow of my future love will appear behind me. We will see him in the mirror."

"What if he grabs you and steals you away?"

"Really, Violet, you can be such a child! It's only a shadow of your future love. If only he would come and take me away!"

"Okay." I held the hand mirror up to her face. My sister needed no encouragement. She placed the lit candle in her right hand. The flame flickered and shed light on her long locks so they looked like part of the flames. There was a crisp sound as her bite burst the apple flesh open. Poppy stared into the flame and then turned to look into the mirror.

I held my breath and the hairs on my arms prickled. From the back of the room, just in front of the wardrobe, a hazy shadow materialized. Head first, then torso and limbs. I held my breath and prepared myself to scream. He walked towards her, as if in slow motion. Poppy watched him through the mirror as he got closer and closer; her breaths were short and rapid. What if he snatched her away from me?

The shadow man stood just a hand's length away. He was taller than my sister by a foot. One step closer and he would have dissolved into her, but still Poppy didn't flinch. Her chest heaved. I opened my mouth, wanting to call out and frighten the shadow away but as quickly as he materialized, he vanished into the air, not leaving a trace of his presence.

The candle flame guttered out, leaving us alone and cold in the darkness.

I put the mirror down, my hands trembling and felt my way back to the bedside table to the box of matches and lit one. Poppy took the match out of my hands to light the candlewick.

"Did you see my love's shadow? Did you see?"

I nodded. Fear gripped my voice. It had worked. I thought back to the twitching curtain and the name: Gnanera.

"Now! Your turn!" She pushed me forward and picked up the hand mirror and the bitten apple from the bed.

"I'm scared."

"Don't be silly." She held the mirror up to my face.

I turned the apple to the uneaten side and took a small bite then stared into the candle flame. What if I summoned the same shadow as Poppy did? What if he was not Poppy's future love but a sinister ghoulish wraith ready to come and snatch us away?

I waited.

A draught came in via the windows lifting the bottom of the curtains but no shadowman came.

"Concentrate," Poppy whispered.

My legs shook. As much as I wanted to, I was not filled with love and did not understand the feelings Poppy had for Rodolfo.

Poppy watched the curtain move. "The spirit has been summoned but he will not appear."

I dropped the apple onto the bed and tears welled in my eyes. "Perhaps no one will love me."

"Don't cry, Violet. One day someone will love you. You're not creaturely like Miss Ezra. You're loveable."

She came over to hug me. Something warm and sticky from her chest pressed against mine in that embrace. I pushed her back. When I looked down in the candlelight at my chest, a drop of blood began to trickle from where our breastbones had met. Embroidered on her nightdress were three red hearts. One on the chest, one on her sleeve and one down low where her thighs met. Like little fists clenching and releasing they pumped and trickled blood. Droplets formed rivers that streamed down her white gown. My shaking legs now gave way beneath me.

"Poppy!" It was all I could say. But Poppy was not in shock or afraid. She looked triumphant.

"I've got the Gift. The things I stitch have come to life."

* * *

Poppy's gift made customers queue at the door. She stitched stars and moons on pillowcases and anyone who rested their weary heads on her embroidered pillows travelled to the Milky Way in their sleep: astral journeys were sold on Poppy's bed linen. For the ladies who sold love, Poppy embroidered roses on their dresses so they did not need to pay for perfume. She embroidered men's lips under lonely women's skirts and soft small hands in the seams of men's trousers: there was enough love in her embroidery for all.

When I wanted a kitten and Ma said no, Poppy stitched one with brindle thread out of the corner of my eiderdown. Pouncer came to life in my dream hour, tickling my face with his long whiskers and nudging his wet nose into my ear. His purr was like the three-wheeled motor that putted down the street every Sunday. Ma furrowed her brow but let me keep him: he would be able to survive on the blood of the many mice that lived in our pantry and scullery. He could earn his keep.

Today he sat on the ledge watching a moth fluttering its wings against the closed window, his tail swishing in frustration that the moth fluttered on the other side. We sat finishing our needlework in silence. Poppy wouldn't let me see what Miss Ezra had commissioned her to make.

"Tell us, what did she ask you to make?"

"I cannot say. It's a secret!"

"Oh please!" I begged.

"Come with me to drop off our work and I might tell you!"

"You won't."

"But I might."

I averted my gaze. Since Poppy had gotten the gift it was like she was part of a secret world I didn't belong to. I was eager to be a part of it. Eager to belong. After my shadow love didn't appear, I was convinced I would never get the gift. I put my coat on and headed out the door, trying to keep up with my sister.

Dusk cloaked the city like a heavy damp sheet as the lamplighters climbed up and down ladders to light Belgravia for the evening. At the sight of Poppy's flaming long red hair, loose across her shoulders, the shorter of the lamplighters froze on the lamppost, legs around the pole and let out a mighty whistle.

Poppy giggled.

"Poppy! Let's go!" I said.

I scurried forward and turned, beckoning for her to follow. Now that it was dark, Ma would be fretting. Miss Ezra left me to stand on the street but let Poppy in. Such a shroud of secrecy since she got the Gift! I picked up my pace to show her I was annoyed. Poppy blew a kiss to the lamplighter, caught up to me and grabbed my hand, holding it all they way home.

When we burst through the door and into the workroom, Ma was standing over the kettle warming her worn fingers over the steam vapours. I expected her to scold us, instead she gave us a smile and said, "Girls, it's my turn to have a surprise!"

I clapped my hands. I loved it when Ma gave us surprises. The last time was when she had bought us tickets for the Great Wheel in Rochester Square. It had forty carriages and large steam engines underneath that propelled it round and round. Poppy refused to get off until she became very dizzy and vomited up her afternoon tea.

"The ferris wheel?" Poppy asked.

"The Moxham Sisters are performing in the Bellusini Theatre. I've bought three tickets!"

"The women that see the future and talk to the dead?" I asked.

Ma nodded. "There has been so much about them in the newspapers. Some believe they are phoney, some believe they have a gift."

Poppy giggled.

Ma corrected herself. "Not your gift, Poppy. Only seamstresses and embroiderers can get that kind of gift when they come of age. No, their gifts are different to ours. Ready, girls?"

I grabbed my shawl and one for Poppy and threw it over her shoulders, making sure it covered the bleeding heart on her sleeve.

"How did you go at Miss Ezra's today, girls?"

My cheeks went red. I didn't want to say that Miss Ezra made me wait outside while she whispered to Poppy and shoved money into her hands. Poppy didn't say anything either, "Good."

I closed the heavy door behind us and we shuffled off, linking arms. Poppy stood in the middle of us, pulling us forward with her skips to reach the theatre; we giggled, letting her excitement propel us.

The Bellusini Theatre seated 1,000 people and its interior was a sea of red velvet chairs. They sat in gentle curved rows all facing centre stage. The gaslights glowed from every balcony and across the balustrades, giving the theatre a welcoming golden hue.

But tonight was not the opera—the only opera we could afford was the Spare Penny Opera and Poppy was excited because they were setting up performing for a penny or two or a bottle of gin out the front of the Bellusini Theatre.

"Rodolfo will be there!" Poppy said.

"You mean the tenor that plays Rodolfo will be there," I retorted.

"He is Rodolfo."

"Girls!"

We followed down the aisle to our seats. Three armchairs of plush black velour stood on a sparse stage with a gaslight circling each of them. We sat in our chairs as the theatre filled. The stage lights dimmed and the curtains screeched shut. Then the babble of the crowd ceased until all that was heard was the odd boiled lolly wrapper unravelling. The pianist tinkled a jangling tune while the curtains were drawn back to reveal the Moxham sisters.

I glanced at the program to see who was who and then up again to the stage. The two elder sisters Margaret and Clarisse sat on either side of Janice, the youngest. She wouldn't have been more than twelve, the same age as me. The two elder sisters had long nutmeg coloured hair was tied in tight braids wrapped like coils around their heads. Unlike her sisters, her hair hung long in two charcoal plaits down the sides of her sallow face.

All three wore severe long black dresses with cheap high ruffled lace collars and sat as still as stones, their eyes firmly shut.

The youngest sister opened her eyes and the people in the front row gasped. They had good reason. Even from where we were sitting I could see they were a magnificent colour: the pale grey of an overcast sky. The young psychic girl's gaze was heavy and seemed to pierce a hole through my forehead. The elders sisters' eyelids fluttered, their lips muttered messages and secrets of those whose lives were shortened and those who were gone from this dimension while the youngest, Janice, sat still, not blinking and staring.

Margaret called out the names of missing soldiers from the war against the Boers and with each name uttered, someone in the audience swooned or fell to their knees in grief. Confirmation of death. Now I knew why she had bought us here. She wanted to find out what happened to father. I put my hand in hers and squeezed it tight. Poppy was oblivious to Ma's hopes for this evening. She stood with her fingers crossed behind her back and eyes closed saying over and over: pick me, pick me, pick me, Rodolfo, Rodolfo, Rodolfo.

"They're not going to tell you who your true love is going to be."

"How do you know, Violet? You've become such a bore!" Poppy whispered back, indignant.

"Shhh!" Ma interrupted.

Ma clenched my hand. She was hopeful for a message from father but I knew this would never happen. Deep down, I knew that he was gone; his body buried in the dry sands of a country we had only seen in illustrations in books.

Janice listened to the mutterings of her older sister and repeated the names of young boys and men who had gone to fight in the wars. At the utterance of the last name all three sisters closed their eyes and the curtains closed abruptly. The pianist broke into a doleful tune.

"Well, that's intermission declared," Poppy said and cracked her neck from side to side.

"They didn't call out father's name," I said.

"He must be still alive, making his way home to us," Ma said, her eyes wet with tears.

I put my hand in my pocket; the hair bracelet was now finished and I had kept it there, waiting for the right moment to give it to Ma. I pulled it out and showed it to my mother.

"Perhaps this will bring our father's memory closer to you." I slipped the bracelet on Ma's slim wrist, noticing that really it was not much bigger than mine.

"You are a good daughter." Ma stroked my cheek. "Where's Poppy?"

Poppy stood in the foyer talking to Madame Velvetina. They stood apart from rest of the crowd. Women that sold love never had company in public although they had so much in private, Ma said.

"Poppy!" Ma called and Poppy skated back. Madame Velvetina winked at me and I smiled shyly at her. I was very fond of her and hoped that I would be able to stitch things that helped her sell love, too, one day.

When I got the Gift. *If* I got it.

The pianist started again, a signal to return to our seats. I glanced at the program, the second half was communicating with relatives, friends and loves in the afterlife.

The crowd went silent as Margaret got up and told a lady in the third row from the front that her mother watched over the daughter she had lost and the two were happy in the afterlife, playing Charades together. There was light applause and sighs of relief that the second half would be filled with news of those the audience knew were already dead and not of those they hoped were still alive.

Suddenly, Janice, the youngest, stood up from her seat, the chair toppling underneath her. The audience fell silent. "Death! Death!" She called out.

This was not in the program! The audience began to mutter but it did not fluster the youngest of the Moxham Sisters who now pointed her finger directly at Poppy.

"Death! Death! Death to the girl who wears her heart on her sleeve!"

The audience turned to look where Janice pointed. My sister stood radiant, almost triumphant, glowing brighter than any flame and the blood from another embroidered heart now bled openly down her sleeve.

Ma let out a little "oh!" and used her shawl to cover Poppy's heart that now stained her white long sleeves.

I grabbed at Ma and Poppy's sleeve and pushed forward through the crowd. Forceful hands fell on our shoulders trying to pull us back, strangers' fingers pried, clutching at tendrils of hair and bits of sleeve. They all wanted to see Poppy's bleeding heart and there were whispers of the words "Gift" and "dangerous" but I kept moving forward, clutching my mother and sister's arms so that my soft fingernails bent and pierced my mother's skin.

The eldest sisters called the audience to attention and began to shush the crowd. Margaret called them a gaggle of geese and threatened to end the evening. I dragged my mother and my sister behind me, brushing the strangers' hands off my shoulders as we pushed through the commotion.

Thud! A loud noise came from the stage behind us and a foppish young gentleman standing near the exit called out, "She's fainted!"

People lost interest in us and moved towards the stage. I took the cue to push the door wide open. The cold air slapped our cheeks. We were outside.

Ma hailed a barouche and we climbed in and the horses trotted off without hesitation.

"But I so want to see the Spare Penny Opera."

"We'll be going straight home. We've had enough attention for tonight, for tomorrow and for a good long time, I would say!" Ma scolded. "Poppy, you should not have let everyone see the pumping heart on your sleeve.. Now word will get out that you have the Gift. How many times do I have to tell you it's the kind of thing people seek out in private but condemn in public?"

"I don't understand!" Poppy folded her arms and pursed her lips, looking crossly at Ma. "I want to wear my heart on my sleeve!"

Ma grabbed Poppy's arm tightly as the rickety wheels of the barouche jostled us around. "Poppy, this is very serious. A woman may use the Gift for a short while but then, when it becomes too public, it is taken away. What you have done will summon Gnanera sooner than expected."

"I will tell Gnanera her services are not required—whatever they are!" Poppy pulled her arm out of Ma's clutch.

Ma just shook her head. "You do not understand what it means to be a woman. It's more than just wearing your heart on your sleeve. It's about having a uterine heart too."

Poppy laughed. "There is nothing wrong with being in love with love!"

I looked out the window of the carriage. I didn't understand. The Gift made things come to life, it made people queue at the door yet this had to be in secret. In public, people grabbed at Poppy—as if they were both hungry and hateful at the same time.

"Violet, are you okay?" Ma asked.

"Death. She pointed at us."

"She meant your father. He's not coming home." Ma tucked her shawl closer to her.

"What about what she said about hearts on sleeves? That was meant for me." Poppy sighed dramatically. "Death is for me—I shall die of a broken heart for my unrequited love for Rodolfo."

"Broken hearts won't kill you, daughter, but a bayonet will."

I put my head on Ma's shoulder and stroked her arm. My sister had chosen the wrong time to be selfish. Ma was grieving. I knew that father wasn't coming home.

The barouche came to a sudden halt outside the narrow lane way that led to the seamstress quarters. The alley was too small for the barouche to go through; we would have to walk the rest of the way home.

Ma jumped out first and pulled Poppy out, and me second, then paid a coin to the driver. When he was gone, she grabbed one of Poppy's long tendrils of flaming red and yanked it hard.

"Ouch!"

"Don't you ever sew a felt red heart on your sleeve for the whole world to see! That poor Janice girl probably saw it and went into shock. You are going to summon trouble before it's time!"

We walked in single file down the narrow way. Poppy strutted in front of us, showing us that she was annoyed with Ma for scolding her.

"Eudora?" Poppy called as she hung her shawl on the hat stand.

"Ma," I corrected.

"Ma, perhaps father's ghost did come after all to say he died in the war and it was just the shock of seeing my heart on my sleeve that made the poor wee girl get the hysterics." Poppy said and smiled at Ma. It was Poppy's way of apologising for her defiance.

But Ma didn't answer. She had retired to her room for the evening. I heard the lock fasten and the sound of the curtains being drawn shut.

"Poppy, I think that little girl sensed danger for you," I said.

"Oh what nonsense!" Poppy burst into her tinkly laughter that immediately warmed the room like the hearth fire. Then she parted her hair into two long braids and mimicked the solemn look the youngest Moxham had.

I stifled a giggle.

"Shall I tell you what Miss Ezra wants me to stitch into her undergarments?"

I remembered the scene of Miss Ezra ushering me outside, whispering secrets in Poppy's ear and smuggling money into her hands.

"Well, do you want to know what prim Miss Ezra wants in her undergarments?" Poppy asked insistently.

"Go on, then." I said.

"She wants me to embroider a pair of long fingered hands in her undergarments."

"Oh Poppy!"

* * *

We were sitting in the salon, Ma was hemming a mourning gown. Poppy was reclining on the chaise lounge reading a book of love sonnets and I was reading a copy of the *The Secret Seamstress Manual* with Pouncer curled up on my lap. Today I tried to ignore the iron door; the curtain had been looped up on either side with fine black cords revealing it and I found it unsettling. Poppy broke the silence.

"I want to embroider someone to love for me!" She took the largest needle from Ma's sewing box and pricked all her fingers and her lower belly. "I feel the love here," she said, stabbing her lower belly again "It aches."

"No, Poppy!" Ma snatched the needle from her. "If you use the Gift for your own love, you will lose it!"

Pouncer jumped off my lap at her sudden movement and began to wash his back in the corner. I closed my book and sat up. Ma got up and pulled loose the cords that fastened the curtain on either side, allowing it to hide the iron door.

"Poppy, the problem with the Gift is when you come of age, breathing life into embroidery for others is not enough. You want to create a love of your very own to satisfy the heart in your uterus."

"Mother! I am in love with love. It pulses right through me! I want to embroider a romance for my very own."

The sound of curtains drawing open silenced us. None of had moved the curtains. They had done this of their own accord. I remembered again the threat of Miss Ezra. Gnanera will come. Perhaps she was already here.

The door had a cast iron letter slot in it. I had never noticed this before, certain in fact it hadn't been there before. "Here puss!" I clicked my fingers for him to come but he skulked to the back of the sofa. Ma gently walked over to the door and put her thin hand through the slot. She took out a velvet roll. Ma unravelled it to reveal a shining silver needle, some pins, a dainty scissors and a spool of thread.

"Daughter, needles or pins? Your fate awaits." Ma handed her the roll.

Poppy pricked her fingers and lower belly again, letting the blood fall in droplets on her favourite skirt of velvet and damask. My sister pulled a long saffron strand of hair from her hair, licked, twirled and turned it through her blood, then threaded her hair through the needle and double knotted the end.

"Love stitches are best made in the night when musings of ardour are grander." The Secret Seamstress Manual had said. Poppy must have read it before me because she didn't start until the first sign of dusk when the lamplighters appeared to open the taps and light the jets.

Ma left the room, her eyes brimming. "My daughters are growing up."

I curled myself into the corner, mesmerised by Poppy's dreamlike state. Pouncer came and sat next to me, his ears pricked alert as if he, too, was intrigued. Poppy didn't tell me to go away. It was like she didn't even notice me in the room.

She pulled open the hatbox she had been collecting snippets of things from her visits to Rodolfo at the Three Penny Opera. A lock of hair, (I don't know how she managed to procure that), a cravat, a programme of La Bohème and the flower now dried that he thrown to her at the end of one of his performances.

She used running stitch to capture the whimsical nature of the love she dreamt up, blanket stitch to edge him and then blind stitch so that we couldn't see his stitches on the surface. And I suppose because love is blind—that's why too. He would love all the things she loved and know all the words to her favourite 'Mimi's Aria' from *La Bohème*. The song of a seamstress who sang that the flowers she embroidered didn't smell but sang of love.

And then, he needed stuffing. She hauled a large hessian sack from the storeroom into the salon. It was full of all red velvet hearts she had cut and embroidered. Full of her love for love, they pumped and covered her little palms with blood. She made his stuffing with these.

It was morning by the time she had finished. I watched the boy emerge from silk cravat and sock stitched together with the thread of Poppy's flame coloured hair and his, too, now added to the stitch. He stretched and yawned and sat up from the floor as if disorientated and very dizzy. Poppy laughed.

"Oh Violet! Can't you see?"

"See what? If you mean the foppish young man, I see him very well," I said and clung onto to Pouncer as if afraid the new young man would take him away.

"Well that's obvious, but I have championed our Mimi from *La Boheme*! Mimi could only manage to embroider flowers that didn't smell but mine have perfume. And now this! A love for my very own."

The young man blinked and looked around.

"Hello Rodolfo!" Poppy said and she flung herself into his arms.

* * *

On their third night of love, I woke to feathers tickling my face. I wiped the crusts from my eyes to see Ma pegging a mosquito net over my bed while trying to dodge gosling wings.

Pouncer skitted around the room, clawing the air and leaping the air to catch the tiny geese no bigger than moths.

"My goodness!" I giggled. "A room full of baby geese!"

Ma didn't share my humour. She rolled her eyes and pulled a peg out of her mouth to speak.

"Felix asked your sister how much she loved him and she told him that he made her feel that she had tiny geese fluttering their wings in her stomach. When he told her to prove it, she unpicked the love stitch that she sewed into her bellybutton, and all the tiny geese flew out."

"I like the way their wings flutter against the mosquito net."

"Poppy's gift will come to no good," Ma said.

I got out of bed, letting the goslings' wings brush against my skin. Pouncer had not managed to catch any, thank goodness. Like all things made with love they were almost transparent and intangible.

Still he persisted. I walked out into the corridor to peek through the keyhole of Poppy's room. I knew I shouldn't, but a burning curiosity had began in the pit of my stomach. It had overcome the jealousy, the feeling of not belonging, not understanding.

I watched Poppy prick her fingertips, her inner thigh, and her secret parts until she bled and let Felix put his lips onto the wounds and drink and suck until her eyes rolled back in her head. She looked as if she was weakened. Felix didn't care that she became weak. He just sucked and sucked. I pulled myself away from the keyhole; a strange sensation rushing through my body making my cheeks and private parts hot.

"When they die, I will make us a quilt with all the gosling feathers embroidered on it," I heard Poppy's voice through the door, punctuated with kisses. I walked back to my bedroom, crawled under the mosquito net and back into bed. Ma was still there, tickling Pouncer behind the ears, something she rarely did. I turned my back to her, ashamed at the feelings that had overtaken my body.

She stood in silence for a few minutes then I felt her hand on my shoulder. "Violet," she whispered. "I want you to see something."

I turned to face her. She unfastened her skirt to reveal a deep scar on her belly. It was aubergine coloured, fibrous tissue grown over what had once been very neat, accurate stitches, all of equal length. It made my stomach turn.

"It looks like it was painful."

"It is Gnanera's mark. The inevitable. What happens to every girl with the Gift in order to become a woman."

"Every girl born with the Gift gets cut like that?"

"For every girl who succumbs to it, once the time comes to have the needle passed. Only a few manage to avoid it. Only a few women manage to create a love that is not destructive."

"But I might not have it? The Gift?"

My mother bit her lip and didn't answer.

I put my hand out to touch my mother's scar. "Does it still hurt?"

Ma gently pushed my hand gently away. "No, darling, that's the good thing about Gnanera coming. It might hurt at first but once the wound heals, it is fine after that. You just don't feel that intensity anymore. The sensation to love wildly, passionately is gone."

* * *

Poppy and Roldolfo hadn't left the room for five days when a cold wind iced the salon like a storm of winters. I wrapped by shawl closer and Pouncer bolted under the sofa. The curtain framing the iron door blew as if tousled by torrents.

"Gnanera. She is here." Ma put her hands on my shoulders.

The door opened of its own accord and there she stood at the threshold of the door in-between.

Thorned white roses crowned her long white hair spattered with little drops of blood—but I knew she didn't feel pain anymore. She held her chin high like majesty, even though the chain around her neck was heavy with the weight of her scissors and seam ripper. The blades glinted but I couldn't take my eyes off them: they were curved not straight.

Ma ushered Gnanera in, closed the iron door, and the red curtains joined shut of their own accord, concealing the threshold again. Its hem now undulated like little waves.

Now the crowned woman was here. She gave me a thimbled hand to kiss.

"Is this the girl?"

My mother shook her head.

"This is Violet, my youngest. It is her older sister, Poppy."

"Naming them after flowers didn't help."

Slowly, I looked up. Gnanera's eyes met mine. They were colourless and made my head ache.

She stepped closer to me and grabbed my chin with her thimbled hand; the metal was cold against my skin.

I shut my eyes.

She released my chin. "Don't fret. You're still too young."

Gnanera took the scissors and seam ripper from her neck and placed them on the large dining table in our salon.

"Bring me the Blade Sharpener."

She clapped her hands twice and a small boy appeared at our salon door.

"How did he get in?"

But nobody answered.

"To sharpen my blades is the highest honour," she said and pursed her lips into a sly smile. "This is Ruben, my Blade Boy."

A screeching pierced my eardrums as Ruben pulled his little wagon into the salon. He curtsied to Gnanera and she offered him her hand. He kissed the tattoos on her palms: a cluster of spiralled pin pricks of blue ink. He took the curved scissors in his hands and pushed the edge of the blade against the sharpening rod until it squealed so loud I had to block my ears. Sparks flew into the air. Gnanera caught them in a glass lantern.

"A gift for the Violet." She handed me the lantern. "Well? Go on! Give it a shake."

I shook the lantern cage and the little glints grew into dazzling insects; their wings making a dull sound as they hit the glass.

"Violet . . . manners," Mother warned.

"Thank you." I bobbed, feigning a curtsey.

Gnanera slipped off the thimble and swiped her fingertip across the freshly sharpened blade. Ruben's beady eyes grew large as a burst of blood swelled from her digit. She plunged her bleeding finger into the boy's yearning little mouth, and just as quickly, pulled it out, leaving him to wipe his face clean with his sleeve.

"The blades are ready! Bring the girl!"

Head down, Ma bustled to the windows and pulled the drapes in the living room and kitchen closed.

The wheels of Ruben's cart scraped down our corridor. There was a skip in his gait and his mouth was puckered into a whistle. Ma touched my cheek.

"It's time to get Poppy."

Pouncer walked in figure eights between my legs. I pressed my nose against the window again. My heart raced and my breath became short.

I stared through the crack in the curtains at the front window and watched until Ruben disappeared into the distance; the sound of those scraping wheels remaining long after he was invisible. "Please, just a little more time."

"I'm afraid it's out of my hands. Poppy chose."

"I'm scared Ma," I whispered.

"There's nothing to be afraid of, it's a normal part of a woman's life—if she loves love.

"Will she hurt Poppy?"

"Everything worth doing in life hurts a little, darling." Ma closed the curtain of the window I was looking through.

I peered through a slit in the drapes. All the windows that opened onto the street had their curtains shut too. As if Gnanera's visit had drowned the world outside with silence. It was deafening.

"Why is it so quiet?"

"Because everyone knows these sacred things command silence."

"But Poppy is so happy."

"You're still too young. One day you'll understand." Ma put her hand gently through through my hair. "You must help me bring Poppy downstairs and make her ready for Gnanera."

Pouncer arched his back and rubbed his brindled fur against my calf. I took Ma's hand and climbed up the stairs with her, my feet like weights.

Poppy sat on her bed in the attic. She was naked except for the quilt over her knees. She stared out, her eyes glassy, while Felix sucked blood from her inner thigh.

"Darling," Ma said and wiped the sweat from her hands on her skirt. "It's time."

Poppy was humming Mimi's aria as she stitched the gosling feathers into the quilt, the tiny white feathers floated about the air to the romantic tune. "I can't leave Rodolfo."

"Gnanera is here." Ma's tone was gentle but her pull on Poppy's wrist was firm.

My sister was complacent, as are most girls who have the gift. She pushed Rodolfo's head away from her inner thigh and put a pillow under his head, wrapped a shawl over her shoulders and let Ma lead her out into the corridor to the kitchen where Gnanera was waiting.

Gnanera stood by the stove, stirring something in a saucepan. There were two small empty bottles, one marked Opium, the other Alcohol, standing on the bench top.

Our wooden table had been scrubbed clean with antiseptic and the pungent smell of bleach made my eyes burn and my nose trickle. To the left of the table, on a metal tray lay Gnanera's blade and a curved needle with a large eye for coarse thread.

There was silence for a moment when we all looked at Poppy. Except for her hair, Poppy stood naked, her long red tresses wrapped around her waist. Her beauty was starlight and buttermilk, her skin glowed; she was bright to look at, like a burning star in a dark sky.

"She is full of the gift, this one!" Gnanera said with disgust. "But we'll get rid of it! It will soon be all gone and you'll be able to go back to making fine bodices and gigot sleeves. You will be happy and you will be respectable." Gnanera pulled four thin cords out of her apron pockets.

Poppy's breathing made loud gulping sounds when she saw the blades. She tried to break free of Ma. And I let out a little squeak at Ma's force. Biting her bottom lip she pushed my sister hard down on the table. The back of Poppy's head made a dull thud against its wooden surface.

"Poppy, you know it's for the best. I've had to do it and now so do you."

Whimpering sounds choked from my sister's throat. For a moment, she almost resisted by lifting her arms, but relented when she saw our mother's silent tears. She let Ma and Gnanera tie her wrists and ankles to each of the table's wooden legs.

"Full of the gift—the girl named after flowers," Gnanera said as she poured the liquid into a cup. "Drink this."

Poppy took a sip and spat it out.

"Like that is it?" Gnanera pulled a dirty rag from her bodice and pressed it to Poppy's face. My sister lifted her head to resist and then thudded back to the table unconscious.

Everything seemed to be in slow motion even though Gnanera moved with swift, agile movements. I held onto the wooden table as my legs became weak beneath me. She opened her metal sewing box and pulled out heart shaped yellowed tracing paper and pattern weights and placed them on Poppy's naked lower belly. Her eyes rolled back in her head as she pressed the tracing paper down on Poppy's abdomen chanting harsh guttural words. Ma kept her hands on Poppy's wrists but they shook, making the uneven table leg rattle.

I covered my mouth. My sister's belly began to pulse, as if a heart lay inside her beating, the same shape as the tracing paper: Poppy's heart shaped womb.

"Yes . . . " Gnanera said. A moan came from the depths of her abdomen. The curved blade of the scissors slit into Poppy's pelvis and there it was—exactly the same shape as the tracing paper, beating rapidly.

Gnanera raised it up to her face and squeezed it tight with a victorious smile. When the little uterus beat its last she gave it a quick snip and cut the septum that made it heart shaped.

Poppy now had a pear shaped womb, perfect for normal child bearing, and void of gifts of love.

She plunged the uterus back into Poppy's abdomen and stitched her lower belly back together with the large curved needle and coarse thread. The room began to spin and I clutched the end of the table; the thread was so wiry and black against Poppy's milky skin.

For the next two hours, Poppy wavered in and out of consciousness, calling Rodolfo's name and vomiting up tiny dead goslings that smelt like bile and whiskey.

"How long will she be like this?" I whispered to my mother as I pulled at a pile of boiled sheets to clean Poppy's vomit off the table and floor.

"I need those sheets, Violet," Ma said, "Just use one."

Ma placed them between Poppy's blood soaked thighs. "She will suffer cramping and bleeding for a few days, but it is a normal part of the process. Soon Poppy will be a real woman and we will celebrate with a grand party and she will wear Gnanera's crown of roses and thorns for the day. Now she will never know love for any man that will be enough to stop her working and being productive. You should be happy for your sister."

I nodded my head and said nothing. I thought it was over but then Gnanera said, "Where is he?"

"Father? He's at war."

"No, not that one! Poppy's lover!"

"Upstairs."

She picked up the seam ripper and marched upstairs.

Gnanera could see the blind stitching that no one else could. Rodolfo screamed, begged and pleaded, but she didn't relent until she had unpicked all his stitches, until he was nothing but velvet and brocade and a little clots of Poppy's blood stuck to her hair strands.

I stood back in horror unable to speak. When Gnanera unpicked Rodolfo's last seam she clenched her teeth and sweat glistened on her brow. There was a final breath from Rodolfo that came out as a large sigh and I heard Poppy stir in her induced sleep.

Gnanera pointed at the scraps of fabric strewn and blood spattered on the floor. She pointed at me.

"Clean this mess."

Ma led her to the guest room and left me alone to clean up what was left of Rodolfo. The room had darkened, the gas light was nothing but a dim flicker.

I sat on the edge of the bed staring at the blood clots bled onto the sheets. Ma returned and sat next to me in silence. I could not look at her. I was angry.

"Why can't you keep the gift of creating love and still be a respectable woman?" I asked my mother. She pretended not to hear me.

"Ma?" I pleaded. I turned to look at her.

"That's the way it is, Violet. That's the way it is."

I left the room, leaving Ma to clean the remnants of Rodolfo. I could not face it.

"I'm going to bed."

Ma stripped the sheets off the bed. "Goodnight."

On entering my room I yowled like a wounded wolf so loud that Gnanera screamed out for Ma to silence me.

On the foot of my bed, I found a couple of whiskers, a drop of mouse blood and a little piece of eiderdown fabric that had once been Pouncer's brindled fur. With the gift of Poppy's love gone, my little cat, too, had come undone.

I put all his pieces into my special tin under my bed and cried silently. My little Pouncer was gone.

* * *

Three days later, a party was held to mark Poppy's maturity. Food was laid on the same table that had my sister was cut on, and the seamstresses from our street gathered to celebrate. Poppy received her very own sewing box. Even though Ma whispered that she was sad that the flowers Poppy embroidered didn't smell anymore and she felt sorry that Pouncer had come undone, she was glad to have a daughter who was now a proper woman. Poppy could focus on making dresses: sleeves had reached an enormous size and each one required eleven yards of fabric. Poppy could concentrate on her work without distraction.

Gnanera sat on my sister's right at the party table. I tried to stay away from her.

Feelings churned in my stomach like hunger, but I could not eat. It was a longing. I thought back to the images of love I'd seen through Poppy's keyhole and their memory stirred feelings inside me, as if I too had little geese fluttering inside. I had to do the test, to know if I also had the Gift. I slipped away unnoticed to my bedroom, pulled a needle out of Ma's spares box, threaded it with red thread and began to embroider a heart on my bodice. If it didn't beat, I wouldn't have to worry.

The red embroidered heart pulsed before I had even cast the last stitch. Gnanera would be sure to see: how could I have been so stupid to try finding out now? I covered it by wrapping a shawl over my shoulders and around my chest.

I walked back to the front parlour and watched Poppy. She sat at the head of the long table crowned in Gnanera's thorns. Her eyes were like hollows of emptiness, her cheeks sunken. My sister was no longer interested in Rodolfo, Mimi's aria, Pouncer or love.

My sister smiled a closed mouth smile. She stared blankly as if she sat alone. Under the table a small pool of blood puddled at her feet. If the seamstresses noticed the blood that lay in little puddles around her feet, they ignored it.

"I heard the septum that made her womb a heart had been a long one," an old seamstress whispered to another.

"She still suffers terrible cramping and bleeding even though it should have showed signs of slowing down," the other elder said.

"But that doesn't matter. Poppy is a woman now."

The other lady nodded and sipped her tea.

I leaned against the doorway trying to merge unobtrusively into the surroundings; I had the Gift. I was able to stitch things of love and bring life to them: flowers, hearts, hands and lips. I already felt a yearning for more: a love of my very own.

I watched Gnanera hold court with all the women in the room. There were many who told of their daughters born with the Gift who had taken the needle and, like Poppy, made a man and whiled their time away loving instead of sewing. Gnanera listened and nodded. Yes, she would come to perform the ritual. Yes, they should use the talent to embroider things that smelt and beat and hummed until that time for becoming a woman came around. A bit of extra income before they used the gift to create their own love happened only once in a seamstress's life. They always succumb to the their own selfish love creations. No good comes of that.

"Poppy?" I heard my mother call. Poppy didn't answer. She sat listless, rocking forwards and backwards with a gentle closed smile and those eyes like dark wells that once had water.

I avoided Gnanera's piercing eyes and cleared the plates off the table. I heard my mother say once that we cannot recognise light without having understood the darkness. In the same minute I experienced the joy of Pouncer's memory and the pain of losing him. In my recognition of the desire to love, I also understood the hatred I had for that woman that had cut the love out of Poppy.

* * *

I was the first to wake to Poppy's screams. I ran up the attic stairs and into her room. My sister lay entwined in blood soaked sheets. Her face trickled beads of sweat. She twitched involuntarily.

"Poppy!" Ma called and ran into the room and fell onto the bed, grabbing at my sister's hand and pressing it to her face. Poppy's breathing had slowed and she gurgled as if water filled her lungs.

My mother's cries warbled, caught in her throat like a distressed raven. She grabbed Poppy's other hand and squeezed. "Darling, please don't die."

"Poppy, please," I whispered in her ear and shook her shoulder gently but she could not hear me.

And then it seemed that the passage of time was iced and life stood still. It was that momentary silence that death brings punctuated by Ma's whimpers.

"Can you hear that?" I asked.

There was a sound like the gentle brush of gosling feathers fluttering.

I clutched my stomach. My sister's death felt like a strange pulling at my belly button. Like a sharp needle and thread tugged out my insides.

I picked up the quilt Poppy had stitched with all those gosling feathers. They, too, had dissolved into dust like all the things she had created from love when she had her uterine septum removed. I shook the quilt out to cover her limp body. The feathers materialised, glowing in new colour and feathered form. They floated off the quilt, and wafted about the room.

"How did you do that?" Ma asked me suspiciously.

I didn't answer. Instead I pulled open the bedroom window. We watched Poppy's filmy soul float out the window on the fluttering gosling feathers. Transparent, it made undulating movements as it took to the night sky.

"Violet, You've got the gift too."

"I do."

"How long have you known?"

Ma sobbed aloud when she turned to look at Poppy. Green fluid trickled from the corners of her mouth. I wiped her face clean with a corner of the bedsheet. When I lifted her lifeless body from the bed just to hold my sister one last time, there was a final exhalation of air from her lungs and a single white feather blew out of the corner of her mouth. I kissed her sour smelling lips.

We dressed Poppy into a pretty white nightgown and laid her on the bed with crisp clean white sheets. On the collar of her nightgown we pinned a needle and thread. Ma didn't let me stitch a heart.

My Mother and I didn't go to our bed for three nights. We lay with Poppy's cold body until her neck started to sag and her face began to swell and then we let the Undertakers come for her.

When Ma dozed at the foot of Poppy's bed, I cut back her fingernails and a lock of her long hair and put it in my box of special things under my bed.

* * *

A week after Poppy was buried, we started sewing again. We had a backlog of orders of dresses and overcoats but Ma did not let me do any embroidery.

"I don't want anyone to know that you have the Gift."

"What about this?" I said, showing the little heart that still beat on the bodice of my dress.

"Just keep it covered."

"Hopefully it will be a while before I have to pass the needle to you and Gnanera finds out. This is the life of a woman, Violet."

I continued cutting the fabric for the gown I needed to make by Friday. That night, I remembered the gift that Gnanera had given to me when she prepared for Poppy's ritual. The little light flies made from the sharpening of the blades, their wings still banging against the glass hoping for freedom. I released them into the night air and watched them flit away happily.

Sometimes, we don't use gifts in the spirit they are given.

* * *

Winter turned to spring and it looked like nature too had the Gift, breathing life into its creations. Birds remembered songs and branches grew leaves. The sun warmed our fingers making it easier to stitch. Winter hadn't been too brutal; thanks to the fire I embroidered on the rug in the back parlour. That fire was our little secret.

On the morning that I had embroidered the lyrics of Mimi's aria at the bottom of my skirt and the skirt began to sing in Poppy's voice, Ma realised it was time for the needle to be passed. Time for me to choose my fate. We hadn't listened to that aria since Poppy was alive and it made her memory strong. She put her hand through the letter slot of the iron door.

"Is this the same needle that was passed to you?" I asked.

"To Poppy, to me, to my mother and her mother before her."

I looked into my Ma's eyes. She stared straight back. I too, had been one of her love creations.

And then, I realised: the Gift was a lie.

All women have the gift, not just some—and I didn't want Gnanera to come and take mine away.

I wanted to stay in love with love.

I closed my eyes and jabbed the needle into my index finger's softest part and let the blood swell. Out of the spares sewing box I took the lock of Poppy's saffron hair and threaded it through the needle. Then, using her thread of hair, I stitched the music and her fingernails; I used overlocking stitch with my love to keep her together, to make her memory real.

"There is one more thing to do, Ma," I said.

Ma looked at me in that special way of understanding without having to use words, walked over to the red velvet curtain pulled it open to reveal the iron door, the threshold of in-between.

I threaded my needle with a thread made from Poppy's, Ma's and my own hair twined it in Ma's and my blood and used binding stitch to close the doorway to Gnanera. With the first needle puncture into the iron door, it started to undulate and become transparent, flowing as if water. The needle easily stitched through the door, sealing it shut.

Ma closed the red curtains and I stitched them closed too. The skirt singing Mimi's aria twirled like a ballerina and Poppy's voice hit that top C worthy of any soprano. We were content in our small world of memories that bound us all in its fabric of love.

And one day there was a knock at the front door. An unfamiliar nervous tat-tat-tat that made me wonder if Gnanera had other ways of entering. I straightened my back, covered my bleeding velvet heart and opened the door.

There stood Janice, the youngest of the Moxham psychic sisters, her solemn face framed by those two long plaits. For a moment I remembered Poppy's imitation and wanted to giggle but I contained myself.

"Yes?" I asked.

"Is Eudora here?," the girl said.

"Ma?" I called out but she was already there before I even finished saying her name.

"I have this." She raised a letter from her shaking hand.

I recognised my father's scrawling handwriting on the envelope. My mother's hand shook as she removed the letter.

"This is already open," Ma said. And then she began to read in silence. A single fat tear rolled down her cheek. "How did you get this? Miss Ezra usually collects my post," Ma asked.

"May I sit down?" Janice looked timid, almost curtseying in this request.

Ma nodded and motioned for her to take a seat.

"My sisters and I are fakes. We are not the psychic Moxham sisters but poor orphans that made a living out of the heartbreak of others. Miss Ezra used to intercept mail deliveries for us of the missing in action and news of the dead soldiers and we would use this information to call out the names of the soldiers missed here. This letter was one of the stolen letters. After I found out that your daughter died and then your husband, I couldn't retain the guilt of you not having the final letter he sent to you alive." Janice put her face in hands and sobbed so that her two long plaits swung forward.

"Despicable," my mother said. "What about the others? The other grieving families?

"We are returning as many letters as possible," Janice answered. "It will be in the papers tomorrow."

"You are a liar."

"But yet you foresaw Poppy's death?"

"Yes, you see, out of the three of us sisters, I do see things. I'm sorry about your daughter's death."

"Thank you."

"Good day." Ma opened the door prompting the girl to leave.

That night I didn't sleep as I stitched the letter into my mother's quilt. Now she would sleep with father's voice, declarations of his love and memories of the warmth of her body next to his.

I used my gift for love but not one that only satisfied my own yearnings.

And now grieving families come with the letters of their missing and deceased and I embroider their messages of love; the memory of their lover's voice whispering their heart's words in their ears as they fall asleep. I embroider their words into the eiderdowns so that they wrap themselves in the love of their deceased. Lonely people come to me to sew small hands in their trousers and full lips in their bodices. Ladies who sell love let me stitch roses that waft perfume and for dreamers I sew stars and moons on their pillowcases for their astral voyages.

I am the only seamstress of my age still with the Gift. The needle passed to me and I used the love to bring my dead sister's memory back to life, feeding her with a daily dose of blood from my very own stitched bleeding heart. And Pouncer, too, my little brindle cat, lies on the windowsill, eyes closed and purring, while the sound of Mimi's aria, the song about the lady who could only stitch flowers that couldn't smell is played on our gramophone every day.

⁕

I ALMOST WENT TO THE LIBRARY LAST NIGHT

JOANNE ANDERTON

ALMOST WENT TO THE LIBRARY LAST night," Eden says, and makes me drop the possum I'm skinning. He's leaning against the windowsill and grinning down at me. Probably thinks he looks all brave and shit standing there, the dawn light and the ever-fire from the burning tankers lighting the edges of him in red. He's just an idiot. They're all bloody idiots. Boys.

"Why would you do that?" I ask, between clenched teeth.

Little Georgie shows no such restraint. He's pretty well bouncing in his seat, stick-legs straight out in front of him, dirt on his feet and his pale face, hair already coming loose from the braid I just tied it in. "Serious, Edes? How close did you get? Was there lots of nutcases? Did they see you—?" he rattles on and on and Eden is grinning, nodding, but watching me, not the kid.

"None of them saw me," he says, when Georgie finally pauses to draw breath. "I was all careful, ya know."

"How can you be sure?" I ask. Suddenly I want to drag the tarp over the windows, and stuff the few things we own into our patchwork bags, just to be ready. Just in case.

"Aw come on Abi," Georgie prattles. "Don't be like that. Edes is the best. He's like a mouse in the shadows or an owl or, or . . ." He runs out of animals, and Eden says nothing.

In the silence, we all hear it. Footsteps on the stairs.

"Shit." Eden leaps to the door, two soft and graceful strides. I know what Georgie means, of all the boys Eden's a good one. He's not a violent arsehole like so many of them. That's why I'm with him. That's why Georgie tags along. But he's still a boy. And boys are idiots.

He peers around the corner. "One of the pricks followed me," he whispers, and something cold and heavy drops in my stomach. Not enough time to pack everything. Not enough time to take the food with us. Not enough warning. There never is.

"We have to go." I'm on my feet in an instant and pulling Georgie upright. Kid's not all that bright, and doesn't really understand the danger. He smiles at me, laughs too loudly, probably thinks it's a bloody game.

I hold his hand in as strong a grip as I can manage, and glance around the room. I have to take something. Tarp's too bulky, possum won't keep.

"Come on!" Eden hisses, and in the end I grab my best saucepan, the big one with the heavy bottom.

Eden counts us down at the door, "One. Two? Three!" and we're off, racing along the hallway. The nutcase is just stepping out of the stairwell, and I stumble at the sight of him. Why'd we have to get a nasty one? So many of them are starved and weak, lost in their pulse worlds too long. They're easy. But this guy is fresh. He's still got muscles on him. He notices us and screams, a terrible roar from deep in his chest. What's he seeing in that messed-up head of his? Not three kids running for their life, if the fear and the anger in his eyes as he lunges for us is anything to go by.

Eden's too quick, steps around him, but Georgie and me, we're not that fast. The nutcase grabs at me so I swing the saucepan, catch the side of his head and knock him back. Not enough. I get around but Georgie's hanging back, and the nutcase takes him down. Pins him to the floor. I try to loosen my grip but Georgie's the one holding me tight now, so I go down with him. He cries as the nutcase smacks him and punches and bites, over and over, rumbling out words about monsters and soldiers and not going back, never going back. Then Eden grabs the saucepan. Two blows to the side of the guy's head, and he falls. I take the pan back—bloodied now, will I ever want to cook in this?—Eden slings Georgie over his shoulder and we're running again. Down the stairs, out into the pink morning sunlight.

The trees are all broken, some flickering brightly, some darker than night. There's a huddle of nutcases slumped in an old bus stop, but they're regulars and harmless so we don't worry about them.

We take Georgie back to one of our old rooms, in a block that used to be shops with a few working suppressors still embedded in the ceiling. He's bleeding and purpling, groaning and crying. Eden helps me do what I can, even finds water we can boil in the saucepan to clean him up.

"We'll go back in a couple of days," Eden whispers. I tie strips from Georgie's shirt around the bitemarks in his arms. "The nutcase'll be gone by then. Get all our stuff back. You'll see."

I nod, and don't say it. That he shouldn't have gone to the library last night. That it's his fault. That all our stuff will probably be gone and Georgie, well, who knows how he'll fare. I don't say any of it, don't need to. I can read it plain and clear in Eden's eyes.

* * *

Mary applied her makeup in the library toilet. First that whitening cream she got from Chinatown, then the heaviest foundation and powder she could find. Purple eye shadow to blend in with the bruises. Deep red lipstick that stung in the cut but covered it up.

She leaned back from the mirror, and sighed. She had almost convinced herself that the makeup worked, when all the lights went out.

For a long moment she couldn't even breathe. Darkness wrapped around her, squeezing tight. Then Ollie started fussing in the stroller behind her. She turned, hands outstretched in the impenetrable black, and felt her way to him. "It's okay," she whispered, crouched by his side. She undid the straps that held him and balanced him on her hip. "Just a blackout," she breathed into his thin hair. "You're used to them by now, aren't you?"

Wasn't she?

The bathroom door swung open and torchlight flashed across the tiles. "Mary? Are you in here? Mary?"

Rescued by the librarian, Jane. That happened a lot.

They joined the remaining patrons in the foyer, where the desk and security gates had once been. Now there were rows of readers, dim and lifeless without power, VR glasses hanging from racks, and couches. More couches than books, Jane liked to say. She was an older woman, solid around the middle, sun-spotted, with a soft voice but a deep laugh. She remembered the way the library used to be. Only two shelves of books remained, hidden now in the gloom. All the long server stacks were silent and lifeless.

Mary swallowed loudly. The library was too quiet without the servers' perpetual hum. Her fingers dug into Ollie until he squirmed and wailed, and at least that did something to ease the silence.

"Here we go." Jane took Ollie from Mary's grip with practiced hands, and sat him down at a small wooden table. A hurricane lamp to see by, a piece of paper and a half-dozen crayons, and he settled quickly enough. Mary watched her with something like awe, something like envy, but always grateful.

"Now, dear." Jane by her elbow, guiding her away. "What can I get you?" Mary glanced over her shoulder. The other faces huddling near the hurricane lamp were familiar. A homeless old woman, and a shivering young bloke. Every evening Jane told them all this was a library, not a shelter. But she always kept the lights on long after closing, and never turned anyone away.

"Can't do tea, I'm sorry. Not without power. How about something cold, before the fridge starts to defrost? It'll get pretty hot in here without the aircon, and we're stuck until it passes. Doors don't open manually."

Mary nodded, feeling numb, as Jane pressed a glucose drink into her hands.

"But I suppose that doesn't bother you too much, does it?"

If they couldn't get out, then no one could get in either. Not even Jason. "Thank you," she breathed, straw pinned between her teeth. Gradually, the tension eased out of her shoulders. Even in the airless dark, like this, the library was her sanctuary. The only safe place.

* * *

Oliver steals napkins and a plastic spoon from the Chinese eatery while they're not looking. Three napkins, precisely three. He unfolds them and lines them up, one on top of the other. Then the spoon sits right in the middle. He cradles the package gently in his right hand. With his left, he fondles the fifty in his pocket.

The Chinese place is little more than a hole in the wall with a queue attached. The foodstuffs, and gas bottles, and a small biomass generator are safe behind security bars with a gap just big enough to hand money through. He cuts into the head of the queue, muttering to himself, stooped in his oversized jacket and thick-soled shoes. The other customers take pity and let him in. Most people do. He's only been abused once.

He pushes the fifty through the gap. "Sweet and sour pork fried rice," tumbles from his lips. Drool dots the counter. He's missing the nails from three fingers.

They take the fifty quickly—don't check it, hardly even look at it—before shoving change and a plate of steaming gloop into his hands. "Next!" they call as he shuffles slowly to the side.

He sits on the mouldy old tables and chairs in the food court and eats. His hands struggle. His teeth aren't so great anymore, and the pork has a rubbery texture that means it probably isn't meat at all. It's almost impossible to chew, so he swallows the pieces whole.

He leaves a single chunk of pork, a circle of carrot, a clear slice of onion and a small mound of rice. Carefully, he opens his package of napkins and balances the food on the spoon, before wrapping it up tight. Then he makes his slow way out of the court and down the darkened streets.

It'll take the Chinese place a while to notice the fifty's just a badly printed fake, and he'll be long gone.

Two security guards eye him as Oliver leaves the bright shopfronts behind. Bioluminescence has been bred into certain strains of gumtree to replace the inactive streetlamps, but it's not particularly effective. Faint traces of blue light trickle in the drying leaves at his feet. Pale branches reach over his head like ghostly arms.

It doesn't take long before little footsteps rustle behind him. Oliver pauses and crouches. He doesn't turn, doesn't make any sudden movements, just unwraps his parcel of food and extends his arm.

The creature that winds its way around his legs used to be a cat. There aren't many left nowadays. Cats are particularly susceptible to pulses, and most are now barren or mad. Either way, they end up eaten. But Oliver rescued this one from a cramped wicker cage before it could meet its fate. He bought it cheap: scrawny, wracked by mange and parasites, and not strictly safe for human consumption.

"Frankie," he whispers, barely louder than a sigh. "Come here Frankie, got something for you mate."

Frankie slinks out of shadows of his own making. The cat looks in no better condition than when he was rescued, but in place of mange are black pulse pieces, and rather than parasites he teems with wires. His eyes are cameras. They whirr as they focus on the parcel in Oliver's hand, and reflect the blue trees as they glance at Oliver's face. Frankie is a fussy eater. He counts the napkins and assesses the angle of the spoon before eating. A quirk of Oliver's poor neurological rewriting skills. Thankfully the cat doesn't require much to survive.

When Frankie's finished eating, Oliver straightens, and glances over his shoulder. The guards are gone. The lights from the shops feel unwelcoming, somehow, and he knows that means its time to go. He's survived this long by listening to his gut feelings. Frankie's disappeared, but that doesn't mean anything. That cat's been following him for thirty years and no one can stop him. Not Oliver's supervisors from pulse Repositioning, and not the thugs from Labour Resources. Oliver continues into the darkness, apparently alone. Time to get out of the eastern quarter, he's palmed off too much false currency to hang around any longer. He'll head back to the train lines, away from the glowing park ways and the major roads. From there, underground, down subway tunnels any sensible person would avoid, to cross the borders unnoticed. He'll head south, this time, and start again.

But even as he's crossing the road, something on the corner distracts him. He pauses. A building, wrapped in steel bars, all smoke-stained cement and shattered glass. There are other, stranger security measures too. A pulse suppressor pounded into the street at each corner. Warning signs stretch between them, dull words on the thin air. They must have been installed decades ago, and not well maintained. The corpse of an electronic emergency box lies on its side, the steel plating ripped off and most of its internal circuitry gutted. Cages and chains are piled up beside it, riddled with ancient cigarette butts.

But that isn't what catches Oliver's attention. It's the sign, fluorescent lights long dead, cracked and hanging loose above the door. Half is missing, but there's enough left that he can read—*library*. He stares up at it. He recognises it. He remembers it.

He's been here before.

* * *

"Do it make me one of them?" Georgie whimpers. "Being bitten. I a nutcase now?"

I'm peeling away the bandages over the worst bites, the ones around his neck. They're deep, they're messy, and they're not healing. I do my best, but I don't have much to work with. When we went back the room was empty, all our stuff gone. I miss the tarp the most. Nothing to keep the rain out or, more often, the afternoon sun.

"That's not how it works," Eden answers when I don't. "Everyone knows that. Pulses do it to you. Being a nutcase ain't contagious."

I don't think it matters. The bites are swollen, red and filled with puss. There're these raised pink lines running down from them, criss-crossing his skin. I've seen wounds like this before, and I know Georgie's in for it if we don't get help.

"Good." Georgie relaxes and I wipe sweat from his face. He's too hot. Doesn't eat but is never hungry. Been vomiting now too, mostly the water I force down his throat. "Don't wanna be like that. Wanna know what's real."

Technically, Georgie's not ours. Eden and me, we have an arrangement, but Georgie just dropped in on us from out of the blue. We don't owe him anything.

I wait until he's fallen asleep to draw Eden to the side. "We have to take him into town," I say.

He nods. "Tomorrow. Get him on his feet tomorrow."

Georgie's a survivor, he's got to be to have lasted in the suburbs this long. By dawn the next morning I've got tight strips of what used to be bedding wrapped around his neck, chest and arms, shoes on his feet and pills in his stomach. Our last ones, to stop the hurts and the fever. I wonder how we'll barter for more, now that we've lost so much.

Eden on one side, me on the other, we walk Georgie into town.

There's not much of the city left, but everywhere is a reminder of the way it used to be. Lots of houses and apartments. Some buildings towering into the sky, some dug into the ground. Most of that's ruined now, by bombs first, then riots, and finally pulses.

When you're a nutcase, you don't know your house is falling apart and you don't do anything to stop it.

We follow the safe streets, and there're other folks walking beside us. Most are poor like we are, nowhere safe to stay, willing to risk the suburbs rather than the council or the crims. Old people, a couple of kids, one or two families. There are also a couple of traders—adventurers and scum who risk life and sanity riffling through the rubbish in search of things worth bartering for. Eden considers himself a bit of a trader. It's why he takes such stupid risks.

Nutcases hover at the edges of the street, swaying in and out of the glowing suppressor lines. One foot in the real word, one in their own. Some of them must be trying to shake off the pulse, but it's harder than it sounds. Once a pulse drills into you it don't want to let go, and fighting it can scramble your brain even quicker. The scrawny ones are too far gone to notice the suppressor at all.

The lines don't keep the nutcases out. Patterns of light stretched in the thin air, suppressors are nothing you can touch. They beam out some kind of interference that makes it hard for the pulses to see people. And take them. Most of the suppressors in suburbia are old, and starting to fade, but they're better than none. We always make sure to stay close to one and we'll defend it, if we have to. Eden's done that, once or twice.

We don't head into town the official way. That'd do no good at all. The gates have got security guards and you need money and I.D., all the things we don't have. Instead, we slip past the suppressors at the last moment, and duck down lane ways until we come to one of the entrances to the underground.

Eden says it used to be a cinema. Big screens upstairs, moving stairs to a train station downstairs. He also says not to ask how he knows all this. He likes to say that a lot, so I'm never quite sure whether to believe him.

There's a crim guarding the suppressor at the entrance. Georgie and me hang back while Eden talks to him, and he lets us in. I wonder what he's given the bloke. Eden's allowed to do what he wants with the things he finds that we don't need to survive. All part of the arrangement.

The stairs are metal and wobble underfoot, the walls a dull silver covered in words and rude drawings. At the bottom the whole thing opens up to dirty tiles and dim lighting. It's busy here. Sawn-off tree branches crammed into trashcans provide the only light, giving the place a washed-out look. They fade over time, cut up like that. Booths line the walls with almost anything you could want to bargain for, even weapons, drugs, and old-fashioned internal suppressors. How desperate would you have to be to get one of them drilled into your brain, with no guarantee it'd actually work? And no idea, of course, of the brain it's been pulled from?

Further on, past the crowds, is the drop to the train tracks. The path into town.

"Let's be quick," I whisper to Eden across Georgie's head. I don't want to linger.

Eden nods. We might be able to get fever pills here, if we had something decent to trade and luck on our side. But we have neither. Even so, we try the booths. No one wants a saucepan, no matter how clean I've kept it. Or a skinning knife. There's one older guy who's kind of interested in Eden, but can't offer any decent drugs in return. No one wants me. Who'd have thought sixteen is getting too old for that shit. In the end, we take the drop to the train tracks. Georgie's getting wobbly, and I have to pass him down to Eden before taking the jump myself.

Invisible stones and god knows what else slip and rattle beneath us. Make me ache, feet first, then all over.

We come out at a ladder that's been slotted through a hole drilled in the floor of a fancy-looking building. A lot of the place has been stripped away, but the walls are still made of a shiny black stone and the floor all white and swirly. Another ladder up the shaft of a long-abandoned lift, then we push open a door of scrap-metal and wood.

There are too many people in town. They rush through the tight, dirty streets, all focused on the important business of keeping the place running. The streetlights still work here, because there're generators to power them. It stinks like smoke and gas and shit. Pigeons and seagulls argue over rubbish bins. Someone's cooking nearby, and the meaty smell makes me feel sick instead of hungry.

I hate coming back.

"How do we get there?" I whisper to Eden. The three of us hang back from the busy street. Some kids are loitering at a nearby corner—I want to get out of here before they notice us and report to whoever they work for. Council security ride by on squeaky-wheeled bikes. Great suppressor lines circle above us, all solid golden light.

It takes Eden a moment to get his bearings. He was always good at finding his way. Reckon he's climbed every inch of town, and now he's working his way through suburbia. "This way."

* * *

When Mary stepped out of the staffroom, the library was too quiet. The only sound was Ollie's crayons, scratching at the paper Jane had given him. It was difficult to see much around the hurricane lamp, and it was pitch black outside the windows too.

Walking softly, Mary approached her son. She was holding her breath—why? Where was everybody? All she could see was Ollie, scribbling away.

Mary knelt on the carpet beside him. "What are you drawing, sweetie?" She glanced around, then down at the paper. Could have been pointy ears and big, yellow eyes. "A nice kitty—?"

Something skittered across his paper, a bulbous rat-sized shadow with rustling legs. Mary leapt to her feet, spitting a, "shit!" as it disappeared off the corner of the table.

"Mary?" a low, drawn out whisper.

She turned towards the voice, shivering, keenly aware that *thing* was on the floor where Ollie was sitting. She hadn't picked him up, not like a good mum would, just flinched away instead. Thought about herself first, not her son.

"Something's wrong . . . Mary?" Jane, standing by the servers. The light from the lamp was uneasy, and Jane was standing in the shadow, but she seemed to be swaying, wobbling in and out of the light, in and out of focus.

The lights snapped back on and Mary squinted against them. There was definitely something wrong with Jane. A broad smile spread across her face, but her eyes were wide, terrified. She held one hand out towards Ollie, and lifted one foot as though wanting to take a step forward, but otherwise didn't move. Just swayed, unsteady, and stared into Mary's eyes in fear. "We're all so tired of fighting."

"Jane . . . what?" Mary asked, and edged between the librarian and her son. Just in case.

A weird shadow-rat with too many legs was attached to Jane's neck. It flickered, strangely, in and out of sight and was almost impossible to focus on. Every time Mary tried to get a better look at it, her gaze seemed to slip away, off to the side, out of her control.

Mary knew she should run. The power was back on, the doors would be open. Dimly, she could hear scuffing on the floor behind her, the other patrons obviously doing the sensible thing and getting the hell out. She owed it to Ollie to pick him up, and do the same. But go where? Home held no safety for either of them. And Jane had always been so kind.

"Who have you lost?" Jane asked. Her voice sounded gentle, even reasonable. And yet absolutely nothing like her. "Brothers? Husbands? Sons?" Her eyes darted from side to side. She shook her head, but her mouth kept on moving. "Don't you think it's time to bring them home?" Meaningless, robotic words. They didn't make sense.

Then Ollie wailed. Mary spun. That bulbous *thing* was on the table again, skittering towards him.

Mary leapt for the table, knocking Ollie out of the way. He landed with a thud and a cry, and a great smack of guilt in Mary's stomach. No time for that now. She grabbed the top of the hurricane lamp, twisted the glass free. Heat bit into her fingers and surged up her arm, but she sucked in a sharp breath and ignored the pain. The shadow seemed to surge towards her, but she was fast, adrenaline beating through her, her heart too loud in her ears. She brought the glass down, and trapped it.

Ollie was crying. Mary, starting to shake, held the lamp as steady as she could and stared through the glass. The strangest mechanical concoction struggled against it, snapping in and out of visibility like flipping a switch. It looked like someone had pulled the guts out of a VR helmet, sewn on tiny cameras, needles, and given it life.

Before Jason, before Ollie, Mary had been studying things that looked a lot like this. She'd loved it, been damned good at it to, but never managed to finalise her qualifications. Ollie hadn't been, well, planned, and she'd married Jason in too big a hurry and now, there was no way he'd let her go back. Even if they could afford the tuition, which they couldn't, not with the docks bombed out, and the burns Jason suffered when they hit, and the grog he needed, the only thing that could numb the pain. Her role was at home, caring for her husband and her child, even if she spent so much of it at the library now.

Still, she had a vague idea what the thing was doing. It was remotely accessing her visual cortex, trying to disguise itself. Not doing a great job, but the fact that it was doing it at all—

"Why do you keep struggling?" Jane asked, and finally teetered forward onto her upraised foot. A single step. Slowly, she lifted another. "Wouldn't it be better if we all just . . . all just . . . " Her voice trailed off. She froze to the spot, all but her eyes, which stared down at Mary pleading desperately, silently.

Why do we keep struggling? Mary shook her head. She'd asked herself the same question, over and over again. In the face of horror, from the docks to the barbed wire on the beaches, the food shortages, the air raids, the thousands of young men and women conscripted to their death. Why did they bother?

From the house that was once a home, but was now a prison. From the man who used to love her, but now glared down at her in hatred and contempt. But the war was raging and it wasn't his fault, and what were her small battles compared to so many bigger ones?

"Why indeed?" she breathed the words, as she peered down at the creature trapped beneath hot glass.

The device was gradually losing its disguise. There were sections she recognised. A circuitry cortex of almost artistic intricacy, exposed to the world. Its 'skin' was a mesh of mirrors, receivers, and transmitters, and pierced in all places by the tips of countless tiny needles. It moved around on limbs that reminded her of an octopus, though there were only three of them, elastic, curling against the glass, riddled with jutting gears.

Ollie, still crying, hauled himself to his hands and knees and crawled to her side. She resisted an urge to push him away. The noise wasn't making this any easier.

She could see what the exterior of the device was for. Camouflage and manoeuvrability. But what was with all the needles?

"*Please?*" Jane gurgled a strangled word. Mary looked back over her shoulder. The older woman's face was contorted, her whole body wracked and struggling. "*I can't . . . control . . .* " She shuddered, dropped to her knees. "*It's not . . . real . . .* "

Mary's gaze flicked between the machine beneath glass, the thing on Jane's neck, the needles, and the woman's desperately contorted mouth. Could it be? It was hacking her visual cortex remotely, but for a more complicated job it would need direct access to her systems. It could change only a little bit of what she was seeing, but if it wanted to mess with thoughts, plant words, influence deeds . . .

Ollie's crying grew louder. He clutched at her arm and she tried to shake him off without lifting the glass. "Shh, darling. Shh." She had to concentrate.

"Why not just surrender?" Jane asked, suddenly bright again, tone artificially chirpy even as tears ran down her cheeks. "That way, no one else has to die."

"Surrender?" Mary whispered in reply.

Then Jane pitched forward, face slamming into the floor. She arched back, hands scrambling at the thing on her neck, and released a terrible, gurgling scream.

* * *

The street suppressors interfere with Oliver's internal systems as he approaches the library, sending a jarring feedback loop through his brain. Whispers, fears, urges that don't belong all instantly generated and dashed to pieces inside his own head. Anyone else might have trouble coping, but Oliver has years of practice. He ignores them, and activates the implants in his eyes. They're wired into the half dozen or so hamstrung pulses shoved into the pockets of his jacket, his baselevel output. Not strictly legal for civilian use, but he's gone to a considerable amount of effort to cultivate his homeless-old-man smell and a strategic layer of grime, and so far that's been enough to dissuade any enthusiastic security guards from searching him. His vision focuses. He can see every weakness in the black steel bars, every fleck of rust and poorly maintained weld. He zeroes in on a particular fault-line in the welding, wraps his hands around the bars, and pushes. But nothing happens.

He leans back. "Frankie old mate," he calls, low and soft. "Give me a hand here, would you?"

Frankie is a waver in the air and a weight on his shoulder. He's decided to keep himself invisible, but that doesn't make any difference. Already, the remaining systems in Oliver's body have started to react, as Frankie closes the circuit.

Pulses were originally designed for propaganda, created to hack into the brains of an entire city and convince it to surrender, but they didn't stay that way for long. Almost as soon as they were deployed, they began to misbehave. Oliver believes that's because they aren't just scurrying hallucinogenic machines. They observe the world around them, and change accordingly. They make decisions, assess and choose their targets rather than attack at random. They seem to be able to judge how a person will react even before they latch on. And you can never tell when a pulse will change its mind, and just stop cooperating. So Oliver insists on testing all his implants on himself first, with Frankie as his failsafe.

Oliver calls it sentience. The investors at pulse Repositioning did not like the term, or appreciate his warnings. Which is why he's taken his skills . . . elsewhere.

The feedback worsens as the stronger pulses implanted beneath his skin and sewn into his clothing kick in. Under Frankie's strict supervision they begin activating the nano-threading within his arms, and injecting him with a complex cocktail of hormones and pain suppressants. Muscle growth takes a lot of energy, and is bloody painful too. Images flash through his mind as he grips the bars. Memories of the woman who raised him, and the pulse shelter where he grew up. He doesn't fight them. They will pass.

He pulls, and the steel bars buckle, then snap. He opens a gap just big enough to squeeze through. The steel has left splinters in his palms, so he switches on his immune response boost, flooding his bloodstream to head off any developing infection.

Oliver slips into the library.

The corpses of countless, inactive pulses litter the floor, inches deep in places. They crinkle and break beneath his feet, all the delicate wiring, the complex circuitry, and the tiny polished mirrors reduced to junk.

What happened here? Suppressors can't deactivate pulses—just dull the influence of their cloaking transmitters and scramble their sensors. Beside him, Frankie is suddenly completely visible. Definitely interference, but coming from what?

The rest of the interior is remarkably intact. Sagging couches, mouldy, but otherwise unharmed. A desk in the corner, near the doors. Rows of ancient readers—old-school technology, with screens instead of implants. They haven't been touched. The walls are clear of graffiti.

That's unusual for a neglected public building.

There's only one empty space, in the very centre of the library, and in it lays a body. A skeleton, to be exact, still dressed in the torn remains of grey slacks and a pale blue shirt. Frankie, on his shoulder, peers down as Oliver crouches beside it. His cameras are overactive, focusing and refocusing, snapping constant pictures, switching between infrared and night vision. More interference? Or excitement?

Oliver sucks air into his lungs, but it's not enough. His head is spinning. The bones are absolutely riddled with a mesh of fine neurological wires. It's messy stuff. The wires themselves have thickened so much that in places they resemble coral. Set a little apart, no longer connected to the skeleton itself, is a hand.

Something rustles behind him as Oliver picks up the hand. He glances over his shoulder. He can't shake a haunted feeling. It feels more like a cemetery than a library. Hallowed ground.

The bones have been fused with something he could only describe as a giant, mutated pulse. A spiders' web of needles, wires, and steel hooks connect bone to machine. The pulse itself has been changed, dramatically. It's more than one, all shoved together, badly fused, messily wired and—he almost drops it when a single bulb flashes somewhere inside that mess.

It's still active.

Dimly, it whirrs. Mirrors shimmer, a broken pattern shimmies across its surface—a poor attempt at cloaking. Its signals are weak, no match for Oliver's internal suppressors, and yet he can sense the faintest of touches. What's it doing? It's rough work. He's surprised its held this long. Whoever did this had skill, yes, but not the tools, and not the experience. It almost feels like it's being held together by sheer force of will alone. Like somewhere, in this fading electrical brain, some part of the programmer still remains.

Frankie winds his way down Oliver's arm, touches his nose to the altered pulse, and closes the circuit.

And a voice whispers in the nodes in his brain, nothing but electrical symbols, but still oh so familiar. Even though it's been so long since he last heard her.

Ollie?

* * *

The old woman doesn't recognise us, but that means nothing. I used to bring her offcuts from the aviary before I escaped, pigeon feet and sparrow feathers. Eden collected skink tails and indiscriminate bones from the train tracks, but no one ever forced him to. No factory hands to beat him, no impossible debts to pay one dead bird at a time. Eden did as he pleased. That's what drew me to him in the first place.

Why would she remember us? So many kids bring her things, for the crims, for the factories and the butchers, some even for the council.

She peers at us through cracked glass lenses. Her eyes are a sunken, pale blue. Her red and green stained hands shake as she stirs something blubbing over little gas-powered flames. A generator rattles and hisses in the roof above her, sending fumes into the tightly packed room that make my head spin.

I feel small, as we weave our way through her shop of potions and artefacts and dried-up dead things. Like I've gone back in time.

She ignores *us*, but Georgie catches her eye immediately. She heaves herself off a precarious stool and waddles around the table. Grips his head, turns it one way, the other. Looks into his mouth, the undersides of his eyelids. Peels bandages away. Shoves a pale, smooth stone under his armpit then brings it to her lips.

"Nasty bites," she says, finally. "None too clean." She looks up at Eden, then across to me. Her purple painted lips are smiling, but her eyes are grim. "Infected. Won't last long."

"We know that," Eden snaps. "What can you do for him?"

She chuckles to herself. "Take more than pigeon feet and flat lizards to sort out this one." I shudder, sounds like she remembers us after all.

"What can you do?" Eden says, his voice low. He keeps his anger tight, goes cold, not hot. But he's dangerous, like that. Seen it at work.

The old woman eyes him for a moment. I think she can see it too. When she licks her lips the paint doesn't wipe off. "Potions do you no good, won't lie. None of me meds either, and I gotta few. But you won't leave empty handed. Don't do that to my customers. Don't like to let good product go to waste neither." She shuffles to a curtain behind her desk, waves at us to follow.

There's a nutcase in the room on the other side.

We all stop in the doorway and stare at her, not sure what to do at first. She's fresh but she's calm, just lying with her back against the wall, not much of a dress on her and her hair cut rough and short. Two pulses are latched onto her skin, one on her chest, the other on her outstretched leg.

Pulses aren't supposed to work inside town, and I wonder how the old woman's messing with the suppressors. And why. "Mummy," the nutcase hums when she speaks, almost like singing. "I love you, mummy." She's not seeing the real world like it is, that's for sure, but she's not too far gone that she's lost in one of her own.

The old woman ignores her, and removes the pulse from her leg. It comes off easy, never seen one do that, and it's got this dangly thing all attached to it, long and bloody and sparkly. "She were a trader," she says. "Before a pulse got her. One day, she came back real hurt and looking like that fool boy of yours. But not dead. Got help, she did. Got this thing here. Watched it with my own eyes, as her red faded and her heat cooled and the gash that sliced right down to her bone well sealed itself. She don't need it no more, so I trade you for this. Only chance you got."

The old woman gives nothing for free. We all have to pay. She takes a chunky lock of my hair, and a swab from the inside of my mouth. Asks a lot more from Eden though. Hair and nails and something he has to do behind the curtain, something that leaves him red and silent. She even takes parts from Georgie. A dollop of his puss, a cloth damp with his sweat, and a small glass bowl of blood. At least it's payment we can make.

"Gonna need to turn it on," the old woman gives me the pulse with the dangly attachment, but she's watching Eden. "Think you're a trader, boy. Think you can find what she found. Someone gave her this, set it up on her leg, turned it on. Someone with no name, somewhere too dangerous to tread. Place all the traders know. Think you know where."

"The library," Eden hisses.

"The library will help you. If you're lucky."

* * *

Propaganda.

The word played over and over in Mary's head as she stared at Jane, thrashing on the floor. She remembered her history lessons, from so long ago. Leaflets dropped on cities, radio broadcasts, network hacks. A war of thought and ideas, and now? The thing on Jane's neck. The thing trapped beneath glass.

"What's happening?" a quiet, warbling voice asked, close to her ear. It surprised Mary so much she jumped. The old homeless woman, small and wrapped in layers of clothes matted with dirt, stood beside her. Eyes wide in her filthy face, almost hidden beneath dreadlocked hair.

Mary didn't stop to think. "Hold this!" She grabbed the old woman's hand and slammed it on top of the glass cage. "Don't let it get out!" Then she hurried over to Jane. Ollie followed her with his tear-stained face.

Jane slammed her head against the carpet, arched her back, twisted her neck. Mary had to get that thing off her. She'd worked so hard to forget most of what she'd learned, trying to put the future she'd wanted out of her mind, the image of herself as a wealthy VR technician, in control of her own money, her own life. Because it wasn't Ollie's fault.

Now, she was fighting to remember. Mary glanced around. The VR stacks. Mary narrowed her eyes. Yes, that might do it. Overload the feeds, send a shock through Jane and into the device.

"Stay there!" she cried to both Ollie and the homeless woman. Both watched her, near identical expressions of confusion, disbelief. May pushed down the guilt that rose in her belly as she darted away from Jane to the VR stacks. She should be seeing to her child. Calming him, reassuring him. Wasn't that what mothers did?

Instead she grabbed the closest VR set, plugged it in and turned it on. She lined up as many random feeds as she could, slammed the switch so they flooded into the set. Then she returned to Jane, VR held out in front of her like it was alive and wiggling.

She edged around Jane, focusing on the machine on her neck. Almost as though it knew Mary was there and could guess what she was doing, the device began to fade. Mary rubbed at her eyes with her free hand. She had to remember, that wasn't real. It was an extremely powerful transmitter, messing with the signals in her optical nerve. A sudden shiver passed through her, a flash of fear. Sweat broke out on her forehead and for the briefest of moments she believed with absolute certainty that Jason was standing behind her. Pissed out of his mind, furious and bored from a fruitless day searching for work. Ollie in his hands, so small, so vulnerable.

Mary spun, gasping. Ollie still sat close to the homeless woman, and instantly, the sensation passed.

"What's wrong?" the homeless woman asked.

Swallowing hard, Mary shook her head, turned back to Jane. She'd just been remotely accessed.

Fear of Jason still floated somewhere in the background of her mind, ready to be triggered. And it wasn't just him she feared, she realised, as she crept closer. It was the life she'd lost to his fists. No, the life she'd allowed herself to lose. The capable young student looked down on the battered housewife with incredible self-loathing. It was paralysing. It was sickening. It was her.

"Not any longer," she whispered to herself.

Because she could do this.

Mary threw herself on Jane. She pinned one arm above her head, couldn't reach the other. Something slammed into her gut and knocked the breath from her lungs, but Mary didn't let up. She used her body to hold the woman down and jammed the VR over Jane's head.

The thrashing stopped, and Jane went suddenly stiff. The thing on her neck snapped into clear relief. Mary took a gamble, released her hold, grabbed the device instead and tore it free.

It was lighter than had appeared, warm, and vibrating. How many more of them were there? They could be anywhere, creeping through the library, invisible, sharp and beaming their signals into her brain. Or *Ollie's*. And they wouldn't even know.

The device turned itself slowly, like a baby waking from sleep, to rest cradled in her hand. Its needle tips shivered, before slipping into her palm, one by one. Calm settled over her. Wonderful, numbing, entirely false. So easy to give into, such a blissful way to be.

See how it can be a voice in her head, not quite like her own. *See how nice, when you just stop fighting.*

"Just stop . . . " slipped from her lips like someone else had spoken them. "So nice."

Ollie was crying, far, far away. And there was Jane, in the fog too, her face so fearful. Couldn't they feel the calm? "Mary?" she was calling. Mary could hear it, see it, and some part of her knew it was real but . . . but the library was changing.

Another room settled across her vision like a slide lowered gently into place, not quite hiding the library from view, just altering it. She remembered this room. Rows of benches, drawers with soldering tools, VR screens, shallow dishes growing cells. So many people, all her friends, a buzz of energy around her as they worked and talked and learned. She smiled, drew a deep breath, and something eased within her, all the doubt and the fear and the deep, deep regret. It wasn't Ollie's fault. She tried so hard to be a good mother to him, and never let her resentment show. But she didn't have to do that anymore. He hadn't even been born here.

Don't you want to stay like this? Wouldn't it be nice?

"Oh yes," Mary breathed.

"Mary?"

She turned, and the room spun a little too far, everything suddenly unsteady. Her old lecturer, Dr. Carol, holding papers, all nodding and proud and—no, wait, no. It was Jane. One hand gripped her shoulder, the other pressed against her bleeding neck, face so close to hers. "Don't give in to it!" she cried. "It's a lie! Nothing but lies!"

A lie, yes. The device was accessing her memories to lower her defences while it tried to take control of her functions. Jane had fought it. Mary could too. But . . . would that really help?

"Well done, Mary. Top marks, as always. You have a bright future ahead of you. A bright future indeed."

Don't you just want to stay here?

"Yes." Mary smiled.

But somewhere, she could hear him crying. Ollie. Her son.

For a moment, her mind cleared. She'd never been very good at looking after him. Jane, who hardly knew him, did such a better job. Wouldn't it be easy, just to stay here, and let the librarian take over? Yes, he would be happy with her. But somewhere in the library were more of those things. Maybe outside, too? She'd have to do something about that. She wouldn't let him be taken. He had his whole future ahead of him. Such a bright future.

So she turned to Dr. Carol. "I want to stay here. I do. But there's just one problem." Moving like she was pushing through water, Mary approached one of the work benches. The library servers flickered beneath it. "I never finished my final project." She knelt and opened the drawer in her mind, sliding open the server casing in the real world. Wires and circuits in both. "So that's what I have to do. My final project. With this." She lifted her hand, brought it close to her face. Such an amazing machine. Dr. Carol had been such an inspiration to her. Dr. Carol could teach her how it worked. How to change it, to suit her purpose.

She glanced over her shoulder. Jane, Ollie, and the homeless woman all switched in and out of erratic focus. Soon, she'd probably not be able to see them at all. "You should go," Mary told them. "While the doors are open. Take him away from here. But not to his father. I'm giving him to you. Make him happy, please. I know you can." They were almost gone. "I couldn't keep him safe from Jason, but I will keep him safe from these things. Tell him, I'm sorry. Tell him, I have to do my best. Maybe, one day, he'll understand."

Dr. Carol sat beside her, and began instructing Mary on things she thought she'd long forgotten, like how to rewire the device attached to her hand so she could get inside it, and change its programming. Instead of using its transmitters to hack into the minds of the people around it, those transmitters could be taught to search for other devices like it. Maybe, even, deactivate them.

"That's a complex project," Dr. Carol sounded unsure.

"I can do it," Mary said. "For my son." The best gift she could give him.

* * *

He's been here before.

Oliver sits on the sagging couch, Frankie in his lap, the messy array of pulses and bones in his hands. All his implants are uncertain. They worry at the edges of his mind.

I'm sorry, Ollie.

His memories are hazy, and unclear, but he knows that voice.

Above him, a pulse crawls in through a gap in the wall and drops to the ground, rattling.

"You're calling them here," he says, finally, because it's easier to talk about pulses. "You reprogrammed the transmitter to latch onto their own signal, instead of the electrical discharge of the human brain, then override the basic imperatives. You've convinced them to come here and die."

I shouldn't have left you all alone.

Oliver closes his eyes. He doesn't want to think about that. "That's a remarkable achievement. Working with whatever equipment you could find. And, it seems, you even co-opted some of the pulses that came here to bolster your original. Impressive, Mu— ah— impressive."

My final project. I had to do it right.

With his free hand, Oliver rearranges the deactivated pulses on the couch. Groups of three, like the petals of sparse flowers. It keeps him calm, and makes Frankie happy. "But now what?"

Aren't you proud of me?

"Your signal is fading. This—" he hefts the device "—is dying. Running out of juice." He hunches over to rest his forehead against the fragmented mirrors, and a tiny spark jumps between them. Frankie makes a disgruntled growl and shakes, but doesn't break the circuit. "Once it's gone, you will be too." Again.

You used to draw kitties. When Jane gave you the crayons. Always a kitty.

Jane. Oliver presses his forehead harder against the pulse. His guardian. He remembers her as an old woman with a hearty laugh. She'd remind him, over and over, that she wasn't his real mother. What details she could give him were sketchy, and that was so long ago now that Oliver isn't sure he remembers them right. His mother's name . . . No, he can't remember that. But Jane always told him that she'd tried so hard. And he shouldn't be angry at her. And one day, maybe, he'd understand. Was this what she meant?

My final project. Aren't you proud?

He used to dream of her, as a boy, and in his dreams she was always crying. But Oliver doesn't know his mother. And she doesn't know him. And now, there is hardly anything left of her. What small parts of her personality can have survived amalgamation with the pulse? Just enough, he thinks, to keep it working, to give it that drive. Just an obsessive shadow of sentience.

"Very proud, Mum." His lips tremble with the word.

I'm sorry, Ollie.

"You shouldn't be." Oliver straightens, glances around the library. "Look at what you did. Every one of these pulses is a person who didn't get caught."

I had to do it right.

She is little more than a series of routines, set phrases, basic imperatives.

"What now?" Oliver whispers, as he wraps a gentle hand around Frankie's middle, lifts him just an inch, and breaks the connection. "What should I do?"

He stands with a grunt, places Frankie on the floor at his feet, and carries his mother around the room. He tidies, as he thinks things through. That always helps. He starts sorting the deactivated pulses into piles—there is a range of generations here, some from as long ago as the first deployment, others showing traces of recent mutations. The most up to date have developed increased battery life and a tendency towards psychosis. Not all of the new ones are completely inactive, it seems they are better able to fight his mother's influence than the older models.

"How long will this keep working?" Oliver mutters to himself, as he pushes a small table over against the couch to clear up more floor space. "She's already fading, and they're getting too strong for her. Without help, this will end."

Frankie leaps up on the table and pins Oliver with his camera-eyes. They whirr and focus on him, and he gets the strangest sensation that the cat can see more than Oliver had ever programmed him to. Something deeper.

"We should go." Oliver crouches to his level. "Keep moving, quarter to quarter. If we stay here, they might find us." But does that really matter, any more?

Oliver sits back on his heels, and surveys his neatly arranged piles. So many tools to work with, to finish what his mother had started.

It feels right, somehow, that he should be the one.

Frankie balances on his shoulders, steel-tipped claws digging into his coat, as Oliver ties his mother's pulse device to his own neck. That way, they can keep the circuit open, even as Oliver continues to sort through the library. He tells her about growing up in the shelter. Jane's kindness. The friends he made. Then his years working up through pulse Repositioning, the skills he gained, the friends he lost. Maybe she knows what that's like, the connection he always felt to the machines. His difficulty trusting people.

"Maybe I got that from you, Mum," he whispers, pausing in his work to rub Frankie behind the ears. It's nice to have the cat visible, like this.

I'm sorry, Ollie. But I had to do it right.

* * *

There're two big roads across from the library. They used to be safe once, Eden says, with shops and lights of their own. But not any more.

We huddle behind the wall of an apartment on the other side of these two big streets, staring out the window, as hidden as we can be. Eden, coiled and tight next to me, and Georgie sagging, breathing ragged, but forcing himself to stay on his feet. He's got to look good in front of Edes, after all. Idiot boys.

No one goes to the library.

There're too many pulses here, and they're different. They litter the street, cling to the walls, and you never quite know which ones are active. Nutcases are weird too. They've each got two or more pulses latched on. Get too close, and you'll never know what they'll do. Sometimes a trader can walk right in and come out with the most amazing stuff, like books and electronics, that fetch a real high price. Stuff like the dangling thing I'm holding in my hand. But I've never seen one of these at the stalls before.

But that's only sometimes. Most people come here and never leave again.

"Leave it to me," Eden breathes. "I'll get in. Believe me. I can do it."

I shake my head and grab his arm. "We all go," I hiss.

We stay close to the ground as long as we can. It's hard on Georgie, who's sweating and swaying, legs not quite doing what they're told. But for Eden, he'll do his best. There's a crumbled down stairwell, used to be a walkway across the streets. We duck in there, catch our breath, and run.

Eden loves it. I can see it on the smile he can't hide, the strong length of his limbs. Most of the nutcases don't even notice us, but one spins, shrieks, lunges forward. Eden shoulders into her, knocks her down, pins her there until we can get past.

We scramble down the halfway mark—patch of scrub and dry dust that might once have been a garden between the streets—and things get dicey. Not just nutcases now, but pulses too, squirming in the dirt, lashing out with coiling limbs and sharp needles. Eden's got the strongest boots, capped with steel, so he runs in circles around us, kicks them away.

I'm watching the ground too hard and run straight into the back of some big guy, pulse stretched taught across half his face, another clinging to his arm. He turns slowly. His face is all a mess of sores, and a he stinks terrible. He swipes at us, the fear in his eyes probably because there're two pulses sending conflicting dreams into his brain, and even now some part of him refuses to believe.

No time to rely on Eden. Holding Georgie firmly with one hand, I grab my saucepan with the other. I brace myself, swing with all my strength, and catch the guy on the chin. It's not much of a blow, glancing, inaccurate, but it's enough. He roars in pain, clutches at his wounds, and I drag Georgie away.

Eden catches up, and grins at us. I can't help but smile in return. Lord help me if I'm starting to understand why he enjoys this.

When we get to the gates, they're chained shut.

"No." I shake the bars, devastated. But Eden's a trader, they all talk about the library, and he knows what to do. Further around, there's a weakness, somewhere the bars have been bent. They unscrew, make a little gap. We all slip through.

Never thought I'd find myself in here.

Feels strange. Dark inside, not much light coming in. Sounds strange too, a deep and constant hum.

There're pulses all around us, tangled together to form shapes. They hang from the ceiling, looking vaguely human. I realise, with a shudder, that's because there're nutcases bound up in them too. I can't tell if they're alive. Nothing moves, the whole bizarre structure just hums and flickers. More pulse than person.

"Are you sure about this?" Eden whispers. It's unsettling, to see him uncertain.

Most people who enter the library don't leave it.

I clutch the pulse the old woman gave us tighter to my chest. Guess it's my turn to be strong, then. "I am." I pull him forward. "Georgie's ours, whether we asked for it or not. We need to do what we can, to help him."

But I stop, a second later, when one of the bodies, thick with pulses, begins to shudder. Georgie's whimpering, pressed against me. Eden moves to stand in front of me, protect us both. But isn't it my turn to be strong? So I pull him back, hiss at him not to be stupid, just this once, when a creature emerges.

We stare down at it in shock. Got some pulse in it, definitely, but also fur, a dusty and faded gray. Eyes are bright, big and round in its face. Two sharply-pointed ears. It takes delicate, precise steps towards us, and sits. A crooked tail wraps around dainty feet.

"What is it?" Georgie whispers.

I swallow hard. "Cat."

Eden frowns at me from over his shoulder. "Ain't no more cats."

"I know." All I can do is shrug at him. "But I've seen pictures, back in town. That's a cat."

More delicate steps, and the cat sniffs at Georgie. I help him kneel. Eden steadies his shoulders. Small paws on his knees—they're capped in metal, I notice, rusty and worn—and the creature stretches its long body to get closer to Georgie's wounds. He watches the whole thing wide eyed, and shivers, constantly.

Finally, the cat releases him, takes another steady look at all three of us, but stares longest at the pulse in my hand. I'm not sure what else to do, but I have to be strong here, take the risks this time. So I hold it out.

"We—" I cough to clear my throat. "We were given this, told to bring it here. For Georgie— for him. The lady that had it, she doesn't need it anymore. Please. Can you help us?"

The cat's eyes are moving fast, they're shiny and reflecting the few points of light in the room. I wonder if it can understand me.

"Please?" I whisper, again. "He's . . . family."

The cat turns, takes a few steps, looks over its shoulder and waits for us. Desperate not to lose it, I drag Georgie and Eden behind me, and follow.

The cat leads us to an old man, sitting on a couch, in a clear patch in the middle of the library. We slow at the sight of him. Big, filthy jacket. Long, tangled beard. He's holding something in his lap, but I can't quite make it out. His skin is sunken, gray like the cat. Is he just another dead nutcase, waiting to be hung?

The cat jumps up on his knees, takes one last look at us, and leans into the dead man's hands.

And the whole library seems to breathe.

It starts in whatever the old man is holding. It shakes, little blue lights shine within it, then spread. Down cables I hadn't even noticed, tracing patterns across the floor, up the walls, and into every pulse-riddled nutcase hanging from the ceiling. A flush of light, a whisper of air. Warmth rolls up from the floor.

Eden takes a shaking step back. I grip his hand, force him to be still, but I understand why. We're surrounded. For Georgie, I hold the device she gave me out in front of me, and step toward the couch.

"Well, Frankie. What have you brought us?"

The voice doesn't come from the old man. He still looks dead, and hasn't moved. Instead, the library itself is talking. I glance around, all the strings of lights are hazy, like there's something in my eye, making my vision blur.

"Dammit," Eden hisses. He's gone pale, and gritting his teeth. Georgie looks around in wonder. And that's when I work it out. No one's talking to us, not in the real world. It's all in our heads.

Some pulse is creating this voice, and shoving it into my brain. Maybe more than one. Maybe all of them. Takes a lot of juice to make three people all hear the same thing.

I'm not sure what to do. Feels wrong to talk, somehow. Like this place is all magical, like we don't belong here, like its dangerous and wonderful too. But I know I have to do it.

"Excuse me." I'm not sure where to look, so I stay focused on the old man and the cat. "Um, we were told to come here. With this." I shake the old woman's device. "To help him." And point at Georgie.

For a moment, there're no other noises but the constant hum, and the rattle of dangling pulses in the warm rising breeze. I try not to think about nutcases, or ghosts, or the feeling of this place, the way all the lights are blurring into each other, and just hold my ground.

"What is your name, child?" the library asks, finally.

I take a deep breath. "I'm Abigail." *Abi* wouldn't sound right. "This here's Eden." He flashes me a furious look, like hiding his name could protect him. "Little one's Georgie. And he needs helping."

Another pause. What does a library have to think about? Is it wondering whether to help us, or eat us? "Bring the child closer, Abigail. Let Frankie have a look at him."

I guess it means the cat, and push Georgie forward. The cat's still stretched out on the old man's lap, but it lifts its head and stares intently at Georgie. Those too-big eyes widen, narrow, flash and click.

"Careful," Eden hisses. "Be ready to run."

But I shake my head. "Shush," I snap. "This time, you're doing what I say."

He looks a little shocked at that. But entering the library was never part of our arrangement. Neither was saving the life of a boy who came to us, unasked for.

"Poor boy." The voice of the library changes. Sounded like a bloke, at first, but now it's definitely a woman. Sounds sad. "I'm so sorry." A short pause, and when it keeps talking the library's a man again. "I think I see why Frankie led you here. Big softy."

Why do I get the feeling there's this conversation going on that I can't even hear? Like the cat and the voices are talking in deeper ways than we can understand.

"You have my immune boosters. That's good. He's pretty far gone, child. But hopefully, it should help. Won't be easy though. Will hurt him, and you'll need to insert them properly or they'll do more harm than good. Are you still willing?"

I straighten my shoulders. Don't like the idea of Georgie hurting, but it's better than dying. And the kid's tough. He's a survivor. "We have to try."

And in the end, it really is up to me. Because even though he's way different than birds, I'm the one that's used to slicing into things, that knows the feel of skin and muscle and bone. Got a rough idea of where all the important stuff is, too. I've still got my skinning knife, and I use it, following library's instructions. I'm used to cutting like I'm told to, and I don't worry about the blood.

Eden holds him down, and thankfully the poor kid's passed out pretty quickly, so he doesn't feel much. The booster don't go in his leg like it did for the nutcase, but up on his back, close to the bites on his neck. I slice shallow patterns into his skin and thread them with wires. When that's all done, the pulse part sits on his shoulder. Won't work on its own. Gotta lift him, careful, and carry him over to Frankie, the cat. A touch of his paw, ever so gentle, and it turns on. Slips needles into Georgie's skin, flashes little lights to the same beat as the library.

"You did well," the library tells me, when it's finished. "Have to do it right." Two different voices, both together.

I wish I could wash the blood from my hands. Georgie doesn't stink the way the birds always did, but I don't like the memories it's bringing back. The aviary, and the council blokes who ran it.

Eden wraps one arm around my middle and stops me rubbing my fingers raw. "Shush," he whispers in my ear. "That's all gone now." He knows, he remembers too.

"Idiot," I breathe the word, but lean back, against him, and let him make me feel safe. Boys are idiots. But so am I.

The library doesn't want us to leave until Georgie wakes up. When he does, there's some part of me convinced he'll be a nutcase, pulse on his shoulder like that. But he's not. He's Georgie, through and through. He groans and he sits up, he looks at us all offended, at first, aching and betrayed that we would hurt him so. But then his face turns to wonder, and he pokes around at his neck, and at the pulse.

"Don't hurt," he whispers. "Don't hurt no more."

And everything falls out of me, all at once. Tears down my cheeks—you don't dare cry in suburbia, or the town either, so I can't remember the last time I bawled like a stupid little child like this.

"Painkillers taking effect," the library says. "Make sure you keep his fluids up, and feed him too. Cell repair needs a lot of energy."

"Starving," Georgie says, as Eden picks him up. Kid can't walk on his own yet.

"And don't leave him all alone," the library whispers. "Never again."

The cat leads us back outside, as the library fades into darkness around us. It stops at the door, sits all neat, its big eyes looking up at us and flashing, clicking. The dusk is heavy with smoke from the ever-fires. The nutcases on the street seem quiet. They don't even look our way.

I crouch, as close to Frankie as I dare. "Please thank them for me," I say. "The library voices. We will look after him now."

Frankie's ear twitches. It stands, and disappears into the library.

"*Starving*," Georgie says again, a petulance in his voice I'm so relieved to hear.

Eden, watching me, nods. Georgie is part of the arrangement now, that's for sure.

And together, we run.

❋

BEAUTIFUL

JULIET MARILLIER

THERE WERE NO MIRRORS IN OUR house. My mother would not allow them.

"What need have you for a mirror, Hulde?" she asked. "You are beautiful."

"To fasten my gown . . . plait my hair . . . " My hair was fair as summer wheat, thick and coarse. Loose, it reached down to my knees. The harder I tried to keep it tidy, the clumsier my fingers became.

"Why do you imagine we have servants, stupid girl?"

True, we had a small army of them: cooks, cleaners, scullions, gardeners, washerwomen, guards. Maids to dress me in the morning and undress me at night. Maids to brush and braid my hair, when I let them. It was a lengthy and painful process, and often I dismissed them with the job half done.

I did not ask the servants if I was beautiful. There was no point, since they were allowed to speak only the words essential to doing their duty, such as *Yes, my lady.* Those who erred were punished, and my mother had a heavy hand with the whip. So I was careful what I asked them. I hardly ever heard the servants speak, even to one another.

Our servants did not look like my mother. Their hands, though work-roughened, were finer and daintier than both hers and mine. The skin of their faces was softer. Although each had two eyes, two ears, a nose and a mouth in more or less the same position as those I saw on my mother's face, their features were different from hers. The servants were all of a kind, and that kind was not ours. It made me wonder.

"As for beauty," Mother said, "have you forgotten that when you are sixteen, you will marry the Prince of the Far Isles? He is the most beautiful man in all the world. He would hardly have chosen you, Hulde, if you could not match him." Her eyes were gimlet-sharp, examining my face. "Have you been gazing into bowls of water again? Seeking your reflection in a bronze plate or silver ewer? I have told you how those images distort the truth. They would make of the most fine-featured woman a monster. Turn your thoughts elsewhere, Daughter. Vanity does not become you."

I did not tell her how often I glanced at myself in the castle pond; how, when Marit or Lina brought me a bowl of water for washing, I looked with something like hunger into my reflected eyes. I did not tell her what I felt as I thrust my hand into the bowl and erased that girl who was a younger version of my mother.

I had never met the man I was to marry. The Far Isles were a great distance away. To reach our castle, the prince faced a long and arduous journey, across the sea and over wild lands full of unspeakable perils. Our home lay east of the sun and west of the moon, atop a mountain of glass. No wonder he did not come to visit. Nobody came.

On fine days I would watch the geese cross the sky and imagine myself as a crippled bird, left behind when the flock moved on to warmer climes. Though that was wrong. I never had a flock. I had no brothers or sisters. I had no friends. My father died when I was a babe, killed in a conflict my mother refused to talk about. From that great sorrow arose one blessing: she secured as my future husband a man who was not only beautiful, but wealthy beyond measure. How she had done this, she did not say; but she never let me forget the debt I owed her.

A child thinks little about marriage and what it means. My sixteenth birthday seemed as far away as those isles where my future husband lived. Time stretched out in an endless parade of empty days. I had no duties to carry out. The servants were afraid of me; they tended to my needs only because they had no choice. My mother was always busy, and I did not want her company anyway. I feared my mother's displeasure above all things.

On the matter of visitors to the glass mountain, there was one exception. At midwinter a horde of folk who resembled my mother would come all at once, and there would be a great fire, and whole pigs and sheep roasting on a spit. There would be shouting and singing and things smashing. On those nights I would hide away in my bedchamber with my head under a pillow and my heart pounding. The next day, they would be gone.

"Who are they?" I asked my mother.

"Kinsfolk," she said. "From the Realm Beneath. Be glad we need tolerate them only once a year."

I told myself those wild, loud folk with their grinning mouths and mad red eyes could not be the same kind as me. I tried to convince myself that I would never, ever be like them.

The year I turned seven Rune came, and my whole life changed. He climbed up the glass mountain with no trouble at all, using his claws. Rune was a bear. I was at my high window when he came, and as I watched him climb steadily onward, I felt my heart turn over with wonder. If anything in the world was beautiful, he was. His eyes were the blue of a summer sky. His fur was long and soft, with every shade in it from shadow grey to dazzling white. His ears were the shape of flower petals, and his smile . . . Could a bear smile? It seemed to me that this one could, and although his smile was full of sharp teeth, it, too, was beautiful. There was a sadness in it that went deep down.

There were many grand chambers in our castle; too many to count. Some held only scuttling spiders. Some were furnished with huge ancient beds like squatting monsters and dark hangings that moved strangely in the draughts. When I peered in, I saw ghosts in the shadowy corners, monstrous shapes concealed in the tapestries, awaiting the moment when I should take one step too close. I liked exploring the castle; in the long, lonely hours I had discovered secret passages and hidden stairways, deep cellars and high perches. But I was afraid of those echoing rooms.

I had thought Mother might house Rune there. Instead, she put him in a disused storeroom set underground, with steps linking it to an old walled garden. At the far end of the garden there was a locked gate, where two guards stood at all times. Perhaps my mother thought Rune would turn wild. Perhaps she only wanted to keep him safe.

The walled garden was planted with hardy, small-leaved herbs. Their tiny flowers hid half-under the leaves as if afraid to show their faces. Lichens crusted the walls, clinging hard against the mountain winds. There were two spindly trees. Each winter they bowed down lower.

At first, when Rune came, I was both shy and fascinated. I peered through the bars of the gate, and there he was, looking right back at me. My mother had ordered the guards not to let anyone in.

Perhaps I should have feared the bear, but I was too ignorant to be frightened. I did not even know that in the outside world, bears do not speak as men and women do. I had my own secret route into the garden, behind a row of thorn bushes that grew hard against the wall, then up and through a gap where two stones had fallen away. From within, the hole was concealed by the creepers; from outside, the thorns covered it.

I climbed through, then sidled across the garden and sat down on a bench, in a corner where the guards could not see me. Rune approached me little by little. He settled near me, without a word, and began playing a game with pebbles and sticks. Dexterous with his long claws, he would hop a pebble, roll a stick, glance at me over his shoulder, then go on playing. And almost before I knew it, I was squatting beside him, using a twig to sweep his stones away as the two of us laughed together. When my clumsy fingers knocked something over, he did not snarl or slap me as my mother would have done. He did not scold me when my too-long nails scratched him. He was a bear, and understood such things.

After that I came every day, and if the guards saw me, they made nothing of it. Rune never told me to go away. He never said he was busy or that I was wasting his time. But every day when dusk fell, he retired to the storeroom and closed the door. He told me I was not to visit him by night. I never questioned that. I understood, somehow, that to want more would be to risk losing what I had.

My mother did not come to the garden. Sometimes she called for Rune. The guards took him to the house while I waited alone. Sometimes I heard an argument, my mother's voice shrill, Rune growling. He would return sombre and silent.

Apart from that, between sunup and sundown he was mine. When I had learned all his games we invented new ones. The guards brought food and the two of us ate it together, enjoying the quiet, watching the birds fly over. I learned to smile. And if I did not quite learn to trust, not so quickly, one thing was certain. Before that first summer was half over, I had given him my heart.

Rune had brought a leather bag with him, slung around his neck. In it he had gifts for me: a wax tablet and a stylus. The tablet was set in a hinged wooden cover, and was small enough for me to hold comfortably. Rune showed me how to write on it, and he showed me that the writing could be erased, the wax smoothed so that the tablet could be used over and over. That summer, he taught me my letters and began to show me how they fitted together to make sounds and words. He said that when I had learned some more, I would discover that those words opened up a whole world of tales. Tales of wonder. Tales of princesses and ogres and giants. Tales of humans turned into creatures and creatures turned into men and women. Tales of quests and adventures and far-away places. If I practised hard, Rune said, then next time he came he would teach me to read. With his claw, he scratched a whole alphabet on the storeroom wall. Then he asked me which words I wanted to learn first. I told him: *Kitten. Sky. Free. Bird. Magic. Far. Sea. Beautiful.* After he had written all of these, and made pictures of them—for *beautiful*, he drew a flower—he wrote his name at the bottom.

He left on the last day of summer. When he was gone, I sat huddled on the storeroom floor, filling my tablet with crooked letters. *Rune*, I wrote. *Rune. Rune.* Tears ran down my face and splashed onto the wax surface. My mother would have called it foolishness. But I hid the tablet, and I hid the stylus, and she never saw the markings on the wall.

"He'll be back in three years," Mother said the next morning. "That is the agreement. You'll be ten next time. Then thirteen, and a woman. Then sixteen, and ready to be wed."

If I had been ten, or thirteen, or sixteen, I would have known not to ask the question. "Why can't Rune come back every summer? Why can't he be here all the time?"

"Don't be a fool, Hulde. Rune has his own castle, his own lands, his own responsibilities. You are lucky that he spares any time for you." Her tone told me she could not imagine why anyone would want to do so.

Rune had said nothing about a castle, but I saw it in my mind straightaway. It would be all gardens and greenery, and the rooms would have big windows through which light would pour in. It would be by the sea. I hardly knew what the sea was, only that it sounded like a true adventure. I wished I could marry Rune instead of the Prince of the Far Isles. But Rune was a bear.

"Nothing to say for yourself?"

When Mother used that voice my insides shrivelled up into a tight ball, and I lost all my words. I shook my head, staring down. The black and white floor tiles blurred into grey. I must not cry. She hated it when I cried.

"You've grown attached," she said. I could not tell if she thought this a good thing or a bad one.

"Rune is kind." That seemed safe enough.

"Kind!" Mother spat the word out as if it were spoiled food. "What use is kindness? Strength, resolve, an iron will, those are the qualities a leader requires. More pity that your father died when you were a babe in swaddling, Hulde. Now *he* was a fine example of a man. A true leader."

I did not understand. If my father had been a true leader, how was it that he had lost a battle and been killed? "Is there a picture of my father?"

"What a foolish question! If such a portrait existed, do you not think it would hang in pride of place here in my reception hall? Off with you, Daughter! You're wasting my time."

As I walked out, she spoke to my back. "Tears are for the weak, Hulde. There is a softness in you that does not bode well for the future. Let me not see you with reddened eyes again or, believe me, I will give you something worth crying about."

The years between were hard to bear. I had nothing to do but wait. My mother considered household duties beneath me. She saw no reason for me to have lessons, and besides, there was nobody to teach me. Our servants did not have children; that was not allowed. I asked, once, if I could have a puppy or kitten, and Mother said I would only kill it with my clumsy hands. I spent my days in my chamber, or in the walled garden, now empty. The storeroom was locked, but I knew where the key was hidden, in a crack between the stones. I touched the markings on the wall—*free, far, beautiful*—and wished him back. But he did not come until the summer I turned ten. He was more beautiful than ever, and he seemed even sadder, though he greeted my mother courteously and found a smile for me. Suddenly shy—it had been a long time—I looked down at my feet, and my mother reprimanded me.

"You are a king's daughter, Hulde! Stand up proudly!"

It shamed me to be scolded in front of Rune. I squared my shoulders, set my jaw, blinked back tears. "Welcome," I whispered.

"It's good to see you, Hulde," said Rune. "You are much taller." He did not ask me about my writing; it was our secret.

I *was* taller. It was no longer so easy to squeeze through the gap in the wall. But I managed.

Rune had brought me a book. The pictures were in rich colours, with here and there a touch of gold. There was magic in every one of them. The stories on the pages opposite were written in big clear letters, and because I had been practising hard, I could read a word here and there and guess at others. I wondered if Rune made the book himself, but I did not ask him. I practising my reading all day and late into the night, devouring the book over and over by candlelight.

Rune asked me which was my favourite picture. There was the princess in the tower, her long golden hair drifting in the breeze, and a little bird perched on her graceful hand. There was another I loved, with a handsome young man and a lovely young woman riding a black horse together, laughing, a dog running along behind. There was a strange picture of a half-woman, half-fish, seated on rocks with wild water crashing all around her. I did not choose any of those.

"This one," I said, showing him a picture of a girl in a grey hooded cloak. She was making her way through dense woodland. Her hands were scratched by briars, her skirt was torn, her bare feet were bruised and bloody. She was not as lovely as the golden-haired princess, or as happy as the laughing woman on the horse, or as magical as the woman with a fish's tail. What I liked was the look on her face. Her eyes blazed with courage. Her mouth was set firm. Even if I had not read the tale, I would have known this girl could do anything. "If I could be a person in a story, I would be her." Her tale was called *Faithful Solvej.*

"You are a person in a story, Hulde," said Rune. "We all are. You can shape that story any way you choose. Don't forget that when I'm gone."

He was wrong. While I lived here on the mountain, my story was shaped entirely by my mother. The only part that belonged to me was my precious time with Rune.

In my thirteenth year, my mind was full of doubts. The weight of them kept me awake at night and fearful by day. Mother said moodiness was common in young women of my age and made me drink a foul-smelling tonic. I longed for someone to confide in, someone to talk to, anyone who was not her. Two men came sometimes with deliveries on a cart. Their oxen breathed painfully after the long haul up the mountain. The men spoke one to the other, mostly things like "Over here," or "Easy now." They did not linger. They drew up the cart and unloaded their cargo, one of our servants gave them a little bag of silver, and they were on their way again with the beasts still exhausted. I sat on a wall and watched them, just to hear their voices. Sometimes I came close to thinking that the outside world was only a dream; that even Rune was only my imagining. Those men and their shaggy creatures helped me to be strong.

And there was the book; the precious book. Although I'd been careful, the cover was showing signs of wear, rubbed patches, little nicks where my nails had caught the cloth. One of the pages was torn. I had wept over that. I did not know how to mend it, and there was nobody I could ask. I wanted to copy the stories, to keep them safe. But my wax tablet could not hold so many words. I practised saying them over, without the book. I hid them away in my mind.

That summer, Rune brought me powders to make ink. He brought me quills and a knife and parchment. He showed me how to scrub and dry a sheet so I could use it more than once. He brought me a little book of beasts, and a book about the stars, and a book of maps. One of the maps showed the glass mountain, with the north wind puffing his cheeks out. Tucked away in a corner were the Far Isles.

"Oh! It is such a long way," I said. "How will I get there, when I marry the prince?"

Rune went very still; so still it was as if he had frozen where he sat. "I don't . . . " he said, and stopped. "That is not . . . "

There was a long silence. I felt my heart beating. Somewhere within the house my mother was shouting at the servants.

"What has your mother told you about that, Hulde?" Rune asked.

Something was wrong. I heard it in his voice. "She said that once I turn sixteen, in three years' time, I'm to marry the Prince of the Far Isles. Long ago an agreement was made that it should be so. I don't mind going away from the mountain." When he said nothing, I went on. "But . . . I am a little afraid. The prince is a stranger. What if he is not a kind man?" My mind shrank from that possibility. I might escape my mother only to find that he was even worse. It was all very well for her to say the prince had chosen me. But how could he choose, when he had never seen me?

Rune was silent for a long time. Then he said, "You should ask your mother to tell you the truth, Hulde. Ask her about your father. About what happened."

My father? What had he to do with this? I was afraid to ask my mother; afraid of her sour tongue and her quick, sharp-nailed hand. "Why can't you tell me?"

"You must ask her." Oh, he sounded weary; as weary as those oxen after they had laboured up the mountain. I crept away without another word.

Later, I gathered myself and went to my mother. She was hanging her smallest whip back on its hook.

"Wretched woman," she muttered. "One would think that after fifteen years in my service, she would know how to fold a gown without creasing it."

It was not the best of times to ask a question, but if I did not ask now, I would lose my courage. I wanted the truth, good or bad.

"Mother, it is only three years now until I'm to be married."

She looked me up and down, brows raised. I saw in her eyes that she thought me still a child, and a tiresome one at that. "So?"

"Will you explain what the agreement was with the Prince of the Far Isles? How did it come about?"

"Have you been deaf all these years, Hulde? When you turn sixteen, you wed the prince. That is the agreement. There is no more to be said about it." In defiance of her own words, she went on. "Remember one thing only: your intended is wealthy beyond imagining. We will be able to restore this place to its original grandeur. Think, Daughter! Farewell forever to leaking roofs and holes in the walls! The treasure room once again awash with gold!"

What could she mean? "But . . . will I not be living in the Far Isles once I am wed?"

"Are you so desperate to run away? Who will be Queen of the Mountain after me, if not my own flesh and blood?" A darkness entered her eyes; her hand reached out toward the coiled whip.

I had words ready, but they dried up in my mouth. Faithful Solvej would have stood strong and asked the questions that should be asked. It seemed I was not as brave as I'd thought.

Still later, when I was in my chamber alone, I heard her and Rune arguing. She was shouting, stamping about, thumping her fist on something. His answers were quieter; I could not hear what he was saying. I caught a few of Mother's words: . . . *owe me . . . gave your word . . . don't think you can get out of this* . . . I could make no sense of it, so I held my pillow over my head to block out the sound, and thought instead about what she had said earlier. Had she really meant that the Prince of the Far Isles would move here when we married? That I would stay on the glass mountain my whole life? Surely not. Why would anyone want to come and live here, trapped with the silent servants and Mother's rages and my clumsiness? And where did Rune fit in?

Nobody to ask. Nobody to explain. Soon enough, Rune was gone and three more years of waiting began. I studied the books he had brought me, in particular the book of maps. Some of the maps had tracks marked on them, paths I thought might lead to the bright and wondrous places spoken of in the stories. Birch forests inhabited by slender fey folk. Broad rivers on which barges floated up and down, visiting settlements where as many languages were spoken as there were stars in the sky. Lakes and rivers. Valleys and grazing fields. The sea. If a person could keep walking long enough she could reach all of those. I looked again at the Far Isles on the map. Why would the prince come to live here if he could be there? Who would look after his castle and his people?

By my sixteenth year I was growing desperate for answers. Though she had never admitted it, I knew that my mother was capable of working magic. Not grand, powerful magic of the kind that conjures dragons and makes whole cities fall. Hers was a small, cruel kind of spellcraft. She used it sometimes to punish the servants. One of the women might find her nose lengthened threefold for a day, or her feet turned into a horse's hooves, or her garments rendered transparent. Sometimes Mother grew so angry that magic seemed to burst out of her. I had seen her hurl a chair the full distance of the reception chamber. When it hit the wall it shattered, not into splinters of wood as I might have expected, but into a cloud of tiny buzzing insects that flew madly about until she waved a hand and they dropped dead onto the floor tiles. She made her maid gather them up one by one. I did not think I possessed the same gift, if gift it could be called. I was surely too clumsy to work even the simplest of spells. But I went searching for mirrors again, no longer frightened of the shadows in the empty chambers. It was easy enough to avoid Mother's notice. Between tormenting the servants and counting our store of gold coins over and over, she was occupied all day. She had never shown much interest in how I occupied myself, and that had not changed now I was older. I wondered how she expected me to be the next Queen of the Mountain, if she never taught me what a queen should do. Perhaps she believed she would live forever.

I made a plan, as Faithful Solvej might do, and set about carrying it out. I ordered my maidservants to stay out of my sight all day; they backed away, looking relieved. I began a search of the empty bedchambers. I left no corner unvisited, no mouse-hole untouched. My hair was veiled in cobwebs; my gown turned grey with dust.

As a child, I'd wanted a mirror so I could see what I was not. I'd hoped its reflective surface would show me someone beautiful; a girl who could match up to the Prince of the Far Isles. At fifteen and a half, I knew I was no such girl. I knew I was my mother's daughter, and no amount of wishing could change that. But Rune had said I could make my story any way I chose. There was a story in my mind about a girl who found a magic mirror: a mirror that could change the future. A mirror that would give her choices. Who was to say I could not make that story come true?

So I hunted until my hands were raw and my back ached and my nose streamed. I hunted for days and days, as the season passed and my sixteenth birthday drew closer and closer. I hunted on the day Rune should have arrived for his summer visit; the day when he did not come. I searched on the days that followed, hoping the magic mirror, when I found it, would offer an explanation for his absence. Would he not want to be at my wedding? A gown was being sewn, a feast was being planned, though I could not imagine whom we would invite other than Rune and our quarrelsome kinsfolk from the Realm Beneath. But maybe the Prince of the Far Isles would bring a whole retinue of courtiers. His family. His own mother. How would they get up the mountain?

With thirty days left until midsummer, I found it. It was not in any of the echoing bedchambers, but in Rune's empty storeroom. I was looking for somewhere safer to hide away my books, and when I stuck my hand into a crack between the stones, there was the mirror. It was small enough to fit on my palm, and simple, with a tarnished metal frame and a surface that reflected the chamber dimly, as if through a mist. The moment I touched it I knew it was the one I needed. I made the mirror vanish into my pocket. Then I went straight to my own quarters and closed the door. Mother was busy overseeing the wedding preparations. Too busy, I hoped, to bother with me. My gown was ready, a stiff, awkward thing encrusted with gems. It hung on my bedchamber wall, mocking me.

I drew the little mirror out and held it before me as carefully as if it were a new-laid egg. My heart was doing its best to escape from my body.

"Show me," I whispered. "Show me the story." And it seemed to me the spiders in the corners and the scuttling things in the walls and even the creaking boards under my feet echoed my words back to me. There was magic everywhere.

I gazed into the polished metal, and there in the depths I saw a girl. Not me; a girl of the same kind as our servants, only she did not have their worn-out, beaten-down look. This was a fierce, determined face, the face of someone who was quite sure where she was going. For a moment I thought it was Faithful Solvej, but no—this girl had hair the colour of autumn leaves, and eyes as green as grass, and a scattering of freckles across her face. Her gown was tattered and dirty; her shoes had holes in them; hers were not a fine lady's soft hands, but a working woman's, worn and reddened. She had a pack on her back and a sturdy knife in her belt. The girl was crossing wild country pitted with great stones and grown over with thorn trees. Above her in the sky, heavy clouds massed, threatening storms. She came steadily on.

"Where are you going?" I whispered, but she could not hear me. And I wanted to ask, *Can I come with you?* but I did not. Because in the mirror, in the far distance, rising up above the expanse of wild country, there rose a great mountain of glass. The girl was coming here.

Soon enough the mirror turned back to mist and shadows, and no matter how hard I pleaded, it would reveal no more. The story must wait until another time.

Against my expectations, the house filled up. There were not only the wild folk from the Realm Beneath, but folk like the ones in Rune's book of tales, only not so beautiful. They brought their own guards and maids and serving men with them. I had captured the mirror only just in time, for Mother had ordered the servants to scrub and clean every corner of the castle, including the outbuildings, before our guests moved in. I, so long starved of company, now found that company scared me. All I wanted was to be alone with the mirror and my imaginings. I longed for Rune. But Rune did not come.

The wild kinsfolk cared nothing for formal dining, or walks in the garden, or admiring the view. They made their own amusements, mostly by night, and slept off their revels next day. The other folk, whom I assumed to be connections of my future husband, were housed in a different part of the castle, and I saw little of them. The summer advanced and there was still no sign of Rune. I did not go into the walled garden. I was too big to squeeze through the secret entry now, and my mother had said nobody was to be let in the gates.

The mirror yielded up its story at its own pace. As the days went by, I caught a glimpse of the green-eyed girl talking to an old woman beside a swift-flowing river—I knew rivers from Rune's books. I could not tell what they were saying, but the crone seemed to be pointing the way forward. Before the girl rowed herself over, using a boat so rickety I thought the story would end with her drowning before my eyes, the old woman gave her something small and black, and the girl tucked it away in her pack. She crossed, and walked on, and the mirror-mist swallowed her.

One day I saw her traversing a bog, leaping across the sucking expanses of mud on nimble feet. Another day there was nothing at all, and I wondered if she was sleeping, or had given up her quest and gone home. Why would anyone make such a journey? Why would anyone want to visit us? I found myself hoping, day by day, that she would succeed. I thought she and I might be friends; she would be a companion, like Rune, someone I could talk to and play with. Then I remembered that I was to be married at midsummer, and that I must live here, and that I had not even seen my future bridegroom. I remembered what I was, and how the servants shrank from me. A friend? The green-eyed girl would likelier befriend a warty toad.

I endured the fitting of a wedding veil. I squeezed my feet into narrow shoes with silver rosettes on the toes. Hobbling along in them, I felt as if knives were piercing my feet.

"Your bridegroom will love you in this," said Mother, tweaking the delicate folds of the veil. "How could he not?"

"If he does not get here soon, he may miss his chance." Even as I spoke I regretted it. She would surely strike me for such words.

But no; her face wore an indulgent smile. It was the smile of someone who has been keeping a delightful secret. "Oh, but the prince is here, Hulde," she said. "He has been for some time."

I stared at her, dumbfounded. I could not think what question to ask first.

"Go," my mother said to the seamstress, who fled without a word. When the woman was gone, Mother said, "Hulde, there is something you must understand." She began to pull out the pins that held my veil, not bothering to be gentle. "A bridegroom must not catch sight of his bride for the last turning of the moon before the wedding day. To do so would bring down all manner of bad luck on the marriage, and we wouldn't want that, would we, Daughter? The Prince of the Far Isles will remain in his quarters and you will remain in yours, and all will be well. Think, only ten days left! Ten days, and then your whole life will be transformed. Be grateful, Hulde, and do not ask questions. You are the luckiest girl in the whole world." She wrenched out the last of the pins, making me gasp with pain. I heard the fabric rip. "Now look what you've made me do! Stupid!"

"But, Mother . . . How could the prince have travelled here without my knowing? When did he come? Where are his servants? His courtiers? His family?"

"Are you deaf, Hulde?" Her gaze passed over me, cold as hoarfrost. "I have told you all you need to know. He is here. You will marry him. You will be Queen of the Mountain after me. Now go! You are to remain within this part of the house, understand? No running about in the garden. No sticking your nose where it is not wanted."

Foolish me. I could not hold back the question. "Is Rune not coming to my wedding?"

Mother did not hit me. She did not rake my face with her claws. Instead, she laughed. "Oh, Hulde! Nearly sixteen, and still such a baby! Off with you now!"

As I fled, I heard her bellowing for her maids, then berating them over the torn veil. There was the slash of the whip, and a cry. I stuck my fingers in my ears.

In the mirror, the green-eyed girl climbed through a dark forest, just like Faithful Solvej in the picture. A fierce storm came over, and her fiery hair was plastered to her pale cheeks. She shivered, hugging her cloak around her, but kept on until she reached a tumbledown cottage, where another old woman gave her shelter. In the morning the sky was clear and she set off again. Before she left, the crone gave her something small and white, which she tucked into her pack. The glass mountain looked closer now. Would she be here by midsummer?

I disobeyed my mother's command. How could I bear to stay within the confines of my own quarters? How could I survive without looking at the sky, and watching the birds fly over, and hoping beyond hope that Rune would come? Or, if not him, the green-eyed girl? I knew it was foolish. She was a stranger. If she was like other folk, she would be scared of me; too scared to speak. But I needed to imagine it. I needed to believe that Rune was right, and that I could make my own story.

There was no going into the walled garden, though I longed to sit there and dream of how things had been. I could have scared the guards into opening the gate. But that would have been to bring down Mother's anger on them and on myself. I found a sheltered spot high on a ledge, a good vantage point for watching the pathway up the mountain. With luck, Mother would not think of looking for me in such an out-of-the-way place.

The sun was shining; the day was almost warm. I could see a long way before the landscape vanished into a mist of brown and grey and purple. How far had the green-eyed girl come? Would she be here today? Tomorrow? If she came after midsummer it would be too late. I would be married, and trapped here forever.

Stupid, I told myself. *She cannot save you. You have to save yourself.* But how? If I refused to wed the prince, my mother would kill me. When she got into a rage, she hardly knew what she was doing. I could not simply pack a bag and walk away down the mountain. She would send guards after me. She would find me.

What was that? A flash of blue inside the walled garden; from this perch I could see over the wall. Someone was there. I stood up, wobbling on my ledge, my body tight with longing, though I knew it could not be Rune. Rune would not have come here without telling me. He was my dearest friend.

Ah. Only a serving man in a blue shirt. He came up the steps carrying a bucket, tipped its contents out on the garden, then went back down. Down into the storeroom where Rune had lived when he came to the castle. Down into the chamber with the letters scratched on the wall. The empty chamber.

Rune had taught me puzzles and how to solve them step by step. This one did not make much sense. Perhaps our servants' quarters could not hold the additional maids and men, and some had been housed in the storeroom. So perhaps what I had seen was nothing more than it seemed: a fellow emptying a chamber pot.

But then, if only serving folk were using the storeroom, why were there so many guards on duty at the gate, far more than before? Why had my mother forbidden entry to the walled garden, even to her own daughter?

There was someone in that storeroom that she didn't want me to see. The most obvious choice was my future husband, banned from my sight for thirty days before the wedding. But it couldn't be him. The storeroom was all very well for a bear, but my mother would never have put the Prince of the Far Isles in such modest accommodation. To ensure he and I did not meet before the wedding, all she'd needed to do was house him in a distant wing of the castle and order me not to wander about. Which was what she had done, as far as I knew.

I waited and waited, but there was no more activity in the walled garden. So I went back to my own quarters and fished out the mirror. This time I sat by the open window, so I could keep one eye on the track up the mountain. I did not expect the mirror to cooperate. But no sooner was I settled than the face of the green-eyed girl showed clear as clear. And for the first time I heard her voice. *I'm coming to fetch you*, she said. *Hold on. I'm coming to save you.*

It was true! Rune was right, I *could* make the story come out the way I wanted! "Hurry," I whispered. "You need to get here before midsummer, and it's only a few days away."

The girl in the mirror showed no sign of hearing me. She pulled her pack higher on her back and kept on walking. But she understood. I was sure she did. I watched as she climbed a rocky hillside, traversed a deep valley, then made her way across a desolate plain where the grasses grew no taller than one joint of my little finger. The north wind whipped her hair into a brave red banner. *I'm coming to save you.* Those words thrilled me deep inside.

She stopped for the night in a little hut by a frozen pond. The hut had icicles hanging from its eaves: winter in summer. I guessed she had reached the foot of the glass mountain, where it was always cold, and my heart raced. Night fell in the mirror, and dawn came rosy bright. The girl and an old woman stood outside the hut, and the old woman pointed the way. She gave the girl something small and golden, and the girl slipped it into her pack. Before the mirror misted over, she turned her forthright green eyes straight on me. *Wait for me*, she said.

"I will, I will!" I whispered. "But hurry!" It was a long, hard climb up the mountain. Unless you were a bear.

Seven days until the wedding. Mother made me put on all my finery and practise walking up and down with my head held high and a smile on my face. When I was not straight enough to satisfy her she corrected me with a long stick.

"You will be on show, Hulde. The future Queen of the Mountain. You must shine. What is the matter with you? You are all a-tremble, and your smile is a death's-head grimace. Even a simpleton would not be convinced by it."

"It feels odd to be marrying a man I have never met, Mother. And . . . I am sad that Rune cannot be here."

"You'll be happy soon enough, when the fellow's bedded you."

Not being quite sure what she meant, I said nothing.

"As for Rune, that puzzle will resolve itself with no need for your interference, Daughter. After your wedding you will never see the bear again."

I endured the rest of my deportment lesson with my heart near-breaking. My wedding was only a few days away, and Rune was not here. He would never be here again. How could I live without him?

I waited for the green-eyed girl to come. Or for a miracle to bring Rune up the glass mountain. Or for myself to turn into a beautiful princess like the ones in the stories, and for the Prince of the Far Isles to decide he and I would ride away to live in his castle after all. There were six days left. Then five. Then only four. What would Rune advise me to do?

Don't wait for other folk to solve your problems, I thought. *Take hold of your story. Shape it the way you want. Don't be afraid.*

But I was afraid of my mother; scared almost to death. Too scared to ask questions. So scared I had accepted half-truths and tales that made no sense. What if there was no old superstition about it being bad luck for a man to see his bride in the thirty days before the wedding? What if the real reason she was keeping me away from the prince was that, once he saw me, he would no longer want to marry me? What if Rune had stayed away because . . . because . . . But no. A woman could not wed a bear.

In the mirror, something strange happened. It was as if a different story was beginning, in a different time and place. But not entirely different, because the green-eyed girl was in it, with a man so beautiful to look on that he must surely be the Prince of the Far Isles. His features were noble, his nose straight and strong. His hair was dark and glossy as a crow's wing, his skin pale and unblemished. I saw him fast asleep, lying on a bed hung with rich red cloth. The girl was in a nightrobe. She had a candle in her hand. She leaned over the man, looking down at him with her face all soft with love. Oh, I had never seen such a tender look! Three drops of wax fell from the candle onto his shirt, and instantly he was awake, springing up so fast the girl shrank back in terror. The candle wobbled in her hand, making strange shadows dance around the chamber.

Oh, Wife, the man said, taking the candle in its holder and setting it safely on a chest. *What have you done?* His words sent a shiver through me.

I'm sorry, dear heart. My mother made me do it . . . I'm so sorry. The green-eyed girl was shivering; she put her hands over her face.

I must leave you now. You have broken your vow, and I cannot stay. A long journey lies before me, a journey from which there is no returning. He enfolded her in his arms; she wept on his shoulder. *Goodbye, Beloved. I must go.*

Wait! she cried, stepping back from him. *Oh, Husband, please wait a little longer! Let me come with you!*

I must travel alone.

I love you! the girl said. *I would do anything to break this curse! Is there no way out?*

A long silence. Oh, how they gazed at each other! My hand was hurting. I had been gripping the mirror almost to breaking point.

Then the man said, *There is a way. It is long. It will tax you hard.*

Tell me! the girl pleaded. *Whatever it is, however long it takes, I will save you. I promise.*

The mirror misted over, leaving only grey.

I was troubled. It seemed the green-eyed girl might be coming not to my rescue but to her husband's. And if she was climbing the glass mountain, that meant the beautiful man was here. Here, but under a curse only she could break. If he was the Prince of the Far Isles, how could he marry me? He had called the green-eyed girl *Wife.*

I thought again about the storeroom, the guards outside the walled garden, my mother's orders that I was not to stray. I thought about the blue-clad servant. I remembered the other way in, through the cellars and along a narrow passageway. The green-eyed girl was not here and time was running short. *Be brave, Hulde*, I told myself, shivering. As I made my way to the cellars, what frightened me most was not the prospect of my mother's wrath. It was the knowledge that to get to the heart of this, I would have to do what I had spent my whole life trying not to do. I would have to act as she would. I would have to be what I had most feared to see in the mirror: my mother's daughter.

Outside, it was close to dusk. Down in the maze of passageways and chambers that ran into the heart of the mountain, lamps hung along the walls to light the way. Here and there servants perched on ladders to trim wicks and top up the oil. I tried not to remember the time my mother had lost her temper and kicked out a ladder from under a boy. She had escaped unhurt; he had not. I could still see him burning.

The entry to the storeroom ran off a guard post. In this small chamber three men were sitting over a jug of ale, but they leaped to their feet when I appeared. I did not need to do anything to make folk frightened. And yet, I had never spoken an unkind word to them. I had hardly spoken any word at all.

"I understand . . . " That voice would not do; it was too soft, too hesitant, not the sort of voice the green-eyed girl would use. "I understand you have someone staying in that storeroom." That was better; a poor imitation of Mother's imperious tone, but firm and strong nonetheless. I pointed to the narrow way that led to the storeroom door.

The men exchanged nervous glances. No doubt Mother had given them orders that I was not to be let in; not to be told anything. There was an assortment of bottles, large and small, and the remains of some bread and cheese on the table. I wondered if they had broken a rule and were expecting me to punish them.

"Yes, my lady," said the oldest of them.

"That is an odd place to house a guest," I said.

"The queen's orders, my lady." The man shifted his feet.

"Who is it?"

They looked at each other again; looked at the floor.

"Answer me!" I took a step toward them and saw them cringe, though I had no whip in my hand. I had not even clenched my fists. I realised I was as tall now as the tallest of the guards, and as strongly built. I was almost as tall as my mother. "Speak up!" My belly churned; I wanted to be sick. I hated this Hulde, the one who could make folk shrink back in terror. I wished she had never been born.

"A nobleman, my lady. A visitor."

"Has this nobleman a name?"

"It's the prince," one of the others blurted out, earning himself a scowl from his superior. "The Prince of the Far Isles."

"The chamber has been comfortably fitted out, my lady." The head guard was pale. "This was . . . it was the prince's choice."

I was not as surprised as I might have been, having seen the green-eyed girl weeping over the man she called her husband. How could there be two such beautiful men in the world? I wanted to order the storeroom door opened, so I could confront the prince with the fact that he was already married. But perhaps the story in the mirror had been all my own imagining. And if it turned out the tale about ill luck and thirty days was true, charging in to confront the prince might set my whole future in jeopardy.

I thought could hear someone moving about in the storeroom, pacing to and fro with an odd, dragging kind of step. I wondered if my mother, in furnishing the place to befit my future husband, had ordered Rune's drawings to be scratched off the wall. That was *his* room. It was *my* room. Within its stone walls I had wept long for him. I did not want anyone else in there. I did not want anyone touching what he had made for me.

"I imagine the prince is not confined there night and day," I said, turning what I hoped was a fearsome glare on the head guard. "Yet

I have not seen him at the supper table or in the garden. Does he receive visitors?"

"No visitors, my lady. We're under orders to leave him alone during the day. We take in a breakfast tray before dawn and a supper tray in the evening, goblet of wine and all. Cooks send the food down."

"The prince did not travel with his own servants?"

"No, my lady."

"I thought I saw someone in the walled garden. A man in a blue shirt."

That glance again, as if they were weighing up my mother's anger against mine. "There's a fellow," the head guard said. "A mute. Does the dirty jobs. He goes in there to clean up sometimes."

"A mute? What is that?" I had never heard the word.

"Fellow's got no tongue, my lady. Can't talk." I thought he was going to say something more, but he thought better of it.

"I see." What I saw was another part of Mother's plan to keep the truth from me. Perhaps my future husband was already married. Perhaps he would think me so appalling to look upon that he would turn tail and flee at first sight—that would be why she was making me wear the wretched veil. Perhaps *he* was appalling to look upon, though I would not mind that very much, provided he was kind. Especially if he took me away from the glass mountain. Would he be strong enough to stand up to Mother? Was anyone?

"Thank you," I said, and made my way back up to ground level. What now? Three days and three nights left, and I had no idea what to do.

The mirror had no answers. Its surface had turned to a sullen, flat grey with not the least sign of an image. Where was the green-eyed girl? Had she fallen to her doom half way up the mountain? Or was she still climbing? I wanted to rip the poxy bridal gown to shreds. I wanted to hurl the silver shoes out the window. I wanted to scream.

And then, when I had dismissed my maids after supper and was attempting to tidy my hair, there came a tap at my bedchamber door.

"I told you to go away!" I snarled as the comb caught in a tangle.

"My lady."

The voice was not that of Marit or Lina. It was not my mother's voice. It was . . . I did not dare turn around, for fear I should be only imagining her. I held up the mirror to show the doorway behind me, and there she was, looking right at me.

I wanted to leap up, to throw my arms around her, to confide my whole story. I wanted to ask every question at once. I had so longed for her to come, a friend, a companion, a confidante . . . But the look on her face halted me. That look told me what courage she had had to find in order to come near me. It told me how scared she was. Of me. Even *she* found me loathsome, though she was working hard to stay calm.

"Lady Hulde?" she said. "I am but newly arrived in this house. A maidservant. I have something here, a gift for you. I . . . I heard that you liked kittens."

A kitten! I had longed for one since I was three years old. My hands ached to hold it. But I was no longer a child; I would soon be married. "I can't have a pet," I said. "I would kill it with my clumsy hands."

"Oh, no!" the girl said, breaking all my mother's rules by coming right into my bedchamber. She had a little bag with her, and now she set it down and lifted out something small and black. "You would not kill this kitten; it is very sturdy. If you wind up this little handle here, it runs about and chases a ball, and if you touch this little button here, it mews so sweetly. Its fur is very soft, and you can pet it all you like. When you are tired of it, just put it away somewhere. Let me show you."

I was entranced. I could have played with the kitten all night. It was a gift to equal the precious things Rune had given me. As I sat on the floor watching the little one run about, I asked the girl, "What is your name? And why would you bring this for me?"

"My name is Laerke," she said. "I thought you might be lonely, Lady Hulde."

It did not seem to matter that she was breaking more rules every time she spoke. This was different. She was the girl from the mirror, and ordinary rules did not apply. Laerke. What a wonderful name. I wished I was named after a bird.

"The gift is given freely," she said. "But I do have a favour to ask."

I waited.

"I understand you are soon to be married," Laerke said, glancing at the bridal gown on the wall.

"In three days."

"I need to . . . I want to . . . This is difficult, Lady Hulde. I don't know how to say it." She looked at me as a friend might, eyes wide, mouth half-smiling.

"Tell me," I said.

"I cannot explain why, but . . . the man you are to marry . . . he is a friend, familiar to me, and . . . and I need to speak with him alone. At night. That sounds odd, I know. But I hope very much you will grant my request. To . . . to spend the night in his chamber . . . "

"If my mother knew you had asked such a thing, she would have you killed. She would kill you herself."

"Yes, I . . . I have heard that the Queen of the Mountain is somewhat fierce. Hulde—may I call you that?—if I promise you that he and I will do nothing more than talk . . . If I promise that I will not touch him . . . Please?"

Nobody had ever spoken to me so sweetly. Apart from Rune, and Rune was gone.

"My mother gets very angry," I said. "Angrier than you could imagine. If she found out, we would all be punished. You, me, the guards, everyone. Her punishments are . . . rather harsh."

"Then she must not find out." Laerke's eyes were ablaze with courage; it was an invitation to be as brave as she was. "Help me, Hulde. Please."

She was sweeping the story forwards, and I could not resist her. "Very well," I said. "I'll do my best."

I did not tell her about the mirror. I did not tell her I knew—suspected—that she and my bridegroom were married. Should my mother learn that, she would see a simple solution. If Laerke met with a fatal accident, the prince would be free to marry again.

I told Laerke that the prince was locked away on his own, because of the need not to be seen by me before the wedding. I told her where she would find him, and how she could get into the walled garden. I was too big to fit through the gap in the wall, but Laerke was slender; she could do it. I explained where the storeroom key was hidden. I took her to my window and showed her where the garden was.

"You could go now," I said. "It's getting dark, but not too dark to see the way. There will be guards at the gate. In the morning, make sure you come out before it's light or they'll see you. I'm not sure you know what a great risk you're taking. If you're caught, I won't be able to help."

"I do know," she said. "Thank you, Hulde. I had heard that you were a kind person, and I see it is true."

Who could possibly have told her that? "Good luck. You'd best go. Come back in the morning and tell me what happened."

That night, I did not see Laerke in the mirror. I did not see the Prince of the Far Isles. But I did see a white bear running through a forest, his pelt catching the moonlight. "Rune," I breathed, wondering if he was on his way to the mountain of glass; hoping beyond hope that he would be here before the wedding and that everything would be made right. I knew it was foolish. What could he do? But I wept, and hoped, and held my black kitten close to my breast.

Laerke was back in the morning, after my maids had cleared away my breakfast tray. She had her red hair tied up in a kerchief, and was carrying a bucket and mop.

"Come in," I whispered, glancing up and down the hallway. I bundled her into my chamber and bolted the door. "What happened?" I saw, then, that her eyes were red.

"I couldn't wake him. I tried and tried. All night. I think he'd been given a sleeping draught. But who would do that?"

Why was she looking at me that way? Could she be thinking *I* had drugged my bridegroom? My heart clenched tight; I had thought we were friends. "My mother has a store of such potions," I said. "She might have ordered it done. I don't know why." I could not stop myself from adding, "I couldn't have done it, Laerke. There wasn't time. Besides, why would I help you see him, then prevent you from talking to him? That doesn't make sense."

"I'm sorry," she said, with a sweet smile. "I'm worried, that's all. Could we try again tonight?"

"I'll think about it." Only two days until the wedding. If Rune was on the way here, it might be better to wait until he arrived before taking such a risk. Maybe Laerke would uncover the truth, whatever it was. Maybe she would cause a disaster with her meddling. "Hadn't you better go and do your cleaning, so nobody gets suspicious?"

When she came back later, she had her little bag with her. I was on the floor playing with my kitten, but when she took out a snow-white puppy and made him run and jump and let out little wuffing sounds, I could not wait to play with him.

"Oh, how precious! What wonderful things you have!"

"For you, if you would like it. It's a gift, yours even if you say no to my request. We are friends, aren't we?" She put her hand on my shoulder. It was an offence that would have earned her a whipping if Mother had seen, but it filled me with warmth.

"We're friends," I said. "Try again tonight if you wish."

"Could you . . . is there a way to find out about the sleeping draught? Perhaps to be sure he does not take it?"

"Without alerting my mother? Almost impossible. I've already been down to the guard room once, asking questions about who was in that chamber. I don't see how I can do it."

She turned her eyes on me; laid both hands on mine. It was like a picture in a book of tales: *Faithful Laerke pleads with the Queen's Daughter.* "Please, Hulde."

"Why is it so important that you speak to him?" I made myself ask, though I was not sure I wanted an answer.

"I cannot tell you. I promised. If I tell, I will bring down a curse."

A curse! This really was like a tale of wonder and magic. And I was part of it. I must not be the part that prevented the happy ending. "I will try to find out about the sleeping draught," I said. "But I can't promise anything. This is very dangerous, Laerke. I don't think you can understand how dangerous."

I meant to do as I'd promised. I meant to go down to the cellars and find out if anyone was drugging the prince's wine. But my mother called me to her quarters and made me spend all day there learning a dance she said everyone would be performing at the wedding, a swaying, turning, tripping thing that made me dizzy. When I said I felt unwell, she made me lie down on her bed to rest. When I said I was hungry, she had her servants bring a tray of delicacies. By the time I escaped, it was dark outside and Laerke was nowhere to be seen.

I was tired and sad. I felt defeated. I had tried to be a hero, like Laerke, but I was no hero. I was clumsy and stupid. I had thought there might be friends for me. But Rune was gone, and Laerke would go, and I would be all alone again. Except for a prince who, I suspected, did not really want to marry me. And my mother.

I tucked my kitten and my little dog in my bed, as if they were real. I did not feel like playing with them. I took out the mirror. I did not feel like looking in it, but something in me, a spark that was not quite extinguished, made me look anyway.

The storeroom was almost in darkness. One lamp burned in a corner, throwing soft light over the sleeping form of the most beautiful man in the world, and the figure of Laerke bending over him, just as she had before when she had held out a candle to illuminate his face, and had startled him with drops of hot wax.

But it was not the same. Then, she had been trying not to wake him. Now she was pleading for him to wake. But the drug held him immobile, his chest barely rising and falling. Oh, he was indeed a beautiful man. Noble, strong and good. I need not hear him speak to know that. I need not look in his eyes. I knew it in my heart. Such a man would never, ever have chosen to marry me.

I watched a long time as Laerke wept and begged, and the prince lay deathly still. Finally, exhausted, she laid her head down on the bed and fell asleep. That was when I saw the shirt. It was draped over a chest, and even in the deceptive surface of the mirror I could tell it was the same one he had been wearing before. I knew that somewhere on that shirt there would be a mark from hot wax. I thought I remembered, in one of Rune's tales, that hot wax could be used in a magical charm. Laerke had said the prince was under a curse. And as soon as the wax drops had touched his clothing, he had told her he must leave her. Why would he bring that stained shirt all the way to the glass mountain, when he was wealthy enough to own as many shirts as he wanted?

I was afraid Laerke might sleep late and be discovered when the servant took in the prince's breakfast, but when I looked out my window in the morning there was no sign of a disturbance in the walled garden. The guards stood at the gate as usual; otherwise the place looked deserted.

One day until my wedding. One day and one night to shape the story the way I wanted. But what did I want? I did not want to be married on the strength of a lie or a curse, even if the bridegroom was beautiful and rich and my mother's choice. If I refused to marry him, Mother would be so furious she would probably kill me before she realised what she was doing. If I told her he was already married, she would hunt out Laerke and kill her. That was my mother's way.

Laerke came to my chamber in mid-morning, carrying her mop and bucket. She was sickly pale and her eyes looked bruised. She didn't say anything, only shook her head.

"I've made a plan," I said when we were both safely inside with the door bolted. "I couldn't do what you wanted yesterday, but I may have better luck tonight."

"Really, Hulde?" Her voice was trembling.

I wanted her to be brave. I needed her to be brave. Today, I had to lie to my mother. "I'll do my best," I said. "Be ready at nightfall, and don't alert the guards."

My plan depended on three things. Firstly, that my mother did not think it odd that I sought out her company for the day. Secondly, that I had guessed right about the sleeping draught—where it came from, and how it was being used. Lastly, that I could steal a small bottle from my mother's chamber and get it down to the guard room. *It's a quest*, I told myself. *An adventure.* I had not realised how terrifying a real adventure could be.

"Mother?"

"What do you want, Hulde? Can't you see how busy I am?"

"I was hoping . . . I need to practise the dance again. And walking up and down in my wedding gown. Could I do that here? I will keep out of your way. If you happened to have a moment or two free you could help me to get it right. To tell you the truth, I am a little nervous about being married. I would be happier if I could spend some time with you."

She hardly listened; she was sorting out the contents of a jewel box, perhaps deciding which of her adornments she would wear tomorrow. "Of course, if you wish," she said without bothering to look at me.

I had brought the gown, the silver shoes, the veil. I changed in and out of them. I practised dancing. I practised walking like a princess. I perfected my curtsy. I spent a great deal of time brushing my hair. When a maidservant brought refreshments on a tray I sat down with my mother to share them. The day passed, and I waited for my opportunity.

It came when a serving man knocked on the door, and told my mother the banqueting table was set up and ready for her to check. She rose with a sigh.

"How tiresome! These folk cannot be trusted to get anything right. I won't be long, Hulde. Perhaps you should come with me. One day, this sort of thing will be your responsibility."

"My feet are hurting." This was true. "I'd best go back to my own quarters. Thank you for helping with my dancing." She had been almost kind; the kindest I had ever seen her. If she knew what I was planning her mood would change in a flash.

"Very well. Make sure your maid irons that gown again and steams out the veil—there must be not the slightest crease. I can hardly believe it: my little Hulde, about to wed the most beautiful man in the whole world. Our lives will be transformed."

She swept out of the chamber, leaving me alone. I moved fast, bolting the door, then going to the special cupboard where she kept her draughts and potions. She used the sleeping draught every night. It did not fell her as it had the prince. I had seen that in order to sleep, she needed more of it now than she once had. She had the household apothecary make it up in small bottles, each a single dose. There were ten of them lined up on the shelf. I hoped she had not counted them.

With one bottle tucked under my sash, I closed the cupboard, collected my belongings, unbolted the door and returned to my own chamber. I tipped the sleeping draught out the window and refilled the bottle from my water jug. So far, so good.

Something flew past, whistling, and I ducked in fright. It flew by again, then landed on the window sill. A bird. A golden bird. Laerke had left me another gift. It was curiously made, its many interlocking parts fashioned of fine metal, though the feathers were soft to the touch. Its voice was high and clear. I could not hear it without imagining an open sky. "Oh, you are beautiful," I said, holding out my finger for the little one to perch on. It tilted its head to the side and examined me with eyes so bright and clever that I wondered if there was magic in the making of it. Over on the bed, the black kitten and the white puppy were sitting up, aquiver with excitement as they watched the newcomer. I did not remember turning any handles or pushing any buttons.

However this works out, I thought, *when it is all over at least I will have them. No matter that they are not truly alive. They are almost as good as real ones. And I will still have more friends than I had before.*

Later, I sent Marit with a message to my mother saying I would have my supper on a tray in my bedchamber. That seemed not unreasonable on my wedding eve. The kinsfolk from the Realm Beneath were celebrating for me, with a lot of shouting. There were flaming torches and folk running about outside. That scared me. What if Laerke was caught as she climbed through the garden wall?

I sent Marit early for the tray, then dismissed her. Most of the household was heading in for supper. I waited in a shadowy corner until no more guards came up from the cellars, then I went down. If I was wrong about the sleeping draught, this would be useless.

There was only one man in the guard room. When I came in he leapt to his feet.

"Only one?" I bellowed in my best imitation of Mother.

"Supper time—change of shift —"

The guard had turned grey with terror. It disgusted me that I could do this so easily. "Has the tray come down for the prince yet?"

"No, my lady. Should be here any moment."

"Go and check. Now. And keep your mouth shut, you understand, or you will pay for it."

"Yes, my lady." He fled, leaving the storeroom door unguarded. This was not as lax as it seemed, since heavy iron bolts were drawn across it. If I had so chosen, I could have pulled them open and marched right in. I could have confronted my future husband and made him tell me the truth. But that was not what I had promised Laerke; Laerke who had brought me my three little friends; Laerke who had crossed a wilderness and forded a river and climbed a mountain to get here. Laerke who stuck to her mission even when she was sad and lonely and scared half out of her wits.

That's what being brave is, Hulde, I told myself. *Not doing great deeds. Just keeping on going, whatever happens.*

No time to waste. I searched the cluttered table, hoping I was right about what I'd seen there the first time. Where was it? Ah! Here in a clutter of wine bottles. I snatched it and slipped it into my pocket, then brought out the other, identical container I had taken from my mother's cupboard. Provided this was where the prince's nightly wine was doctored, my plan would work. If the sleeping potion was already in the cup when the tray left the kitchen, Laerke would have another wasted night, and the wedding would go ahead as planned. I might be a little brave, but I was not brave enough to tell my mother outright that I refused to marry the prince. If I did, she would force the reason from me, and Laerke would die. I knew it in my bones.

The manservant was back. He set the laden tray down on the table, then stood waiting. Waiting for me to leave.

"Go ahead, take his supper in," I said. "Don't mind me."

Still he stood there, awkward, not quite prepared to speak.

"Shall I help you with that?" It was foolish, perhaps; but it would protect me from Mother's wrath if she found out. I stepped forward, picked up the little bottle, took out the cork and poured the contents into the goblet that stood on the tray beside the prince's covered platter. "There."

"You know about this, my lady?"

"Did I ask you to comment?"

"No, my lady."

"Then hold your tongue. Take the prince's supper in and, if you know what is good for you, stay silent on this matter."

There was a narrow escape on the way back to my bedchamber, as Mother came along a hallway and I was forced to shrink into an alcove, holding my breath. She passed, not seeing me. I fled. In my chamber, my three friends were waiting, the kitten and puppy now on the floor rolling about—most certainly, I had not wound them up—the golden bird perched on the peg that held my wedding gown. Curse it! I would have to call Marit or Lina to press the wretched thing.

I hid the three friends away in my storage chest, murmuring an apology. I called my maids and ordered them to take gown and veil away, get every crease out, and not bring them back until tomorrow. I closed and bolted the door after them. My supper tray was waiting on the small table, but I was not hungry. Outside, the light had faded into the long summer dusk. Soon Laerke would make her dangerous trip across the walled garden and into the storeroom. I let the little ones out, setting the kitten and puppy on the bed and letting the bird stretch its wings.

Time for the mirror. *You can do it, Laerke,* I thought. *Make the story brave and true. If he's yours, take him and be happy.* Because a good story always had a happy ending, didn't it?

In the mirror, the Prince of the Far Isles lay on his bed in the storeroom, the strong planes of his face turned to gold by the lamplight. His supper tray stood on a chest, the goblet empty. His eyes were closed, the dark lashes soft against his cheeks.

The outer door creaked open. He started, sitting up abruptly.

There was Laerke on the threshold, in her serving woman's clothes, with her red hair loose over her shoulders. She closed the door and turned to face him.

"Oh, gods!" she said, her eyes alive with joy. "She did it! You're awake!"

"Laerke!" The prince was on his feet. He opened his arms wide. "My love, my dearest, you're here!"

She ran into his embrace, weeping against his shoulder. He stroked her hair; she nestled against him as if he were her home, her heart, her safety from the storm. It was just like something from a grand old story, and it made me cry, but I did not know if I shed tears of happiness that he and she had found each other, or of sorrow that nobody would ever look at me like that, hold me like that, love me like that. I was clumsy and stupid. I had achieved this for Laerke only by doing bad things: lying, stealing, frightening people.

Laerke and the prince held each other for a long time, whispering words I could not hear. They touched each other in ways that were strange and new to me. At length they sat down side by side on the bed, hand in hand.

"Tomorrow," the prince said. "After sunset, since the queen will not let me out until I am in this form again. The key is the shirt, Laerke. Wash the shirt clean and you will win me my freedom. I will be a man forever, and we can go home."

"The queen will be furious," said Laerke. "When she's angry she kills people. She rips them apart with her bare hands. One of the serving women told me."

"Nonetheless," said the prince, putting his arm around her, "a curse follows rules, like any other form of magic. Once it's lifted, it's lifted entirely and forever. I will no longer be forced to switch between human and animal form; no longer required to come here every third summer; no longer bound to this marriage. She must let us go. We will be free to live our lives and to shape our own story."

I couldn't breathe. My heart hurt. A flood of tears waited to fall, somewhere behind my eyes.

"This is all my fault," Laerke said, hanging her head. "If I had not been curious . . . if I had done as you bid me, and not tried to look at you by night . . . "

"It is not your fault."

I wondered, now, that I had not recognised his voice, so deep and soft, so gentle and sweet. How could I not have known?

"We could not have gone on that way forever. It would have destroyed us. Now we have the chance to make things right, Laerke. That is thanks to you. I don't know how you did it. How you travelled all this way to find me."

"Could you not see me in your little mirror?"

"I lost the mirror," he said. "I thought you might not come. But you're here, my brave one."

"I do not deserve you," she said. "You are too good for me, dearest Rune."

"Nonsense." He kissed her on the lips. "You are precious beyond any treasure, my love. You'd best go now. Tomorrow, perform your usual duties all day and try to avoid notice. Just make sure that when the ceremony is about to begin, you are there, concealed in the crowd. Leave the rest to me."

"Rune?"

"Yes, my dearest?"

"What about Hulde? What will happen to her?"

The most beautiful man in the world smiled as he thought of me. It was not the sort of smile he bestowed on Laerke. It was the smile of a friend; the smile a kindly man might give to a child. "I have tried to help her," he said. "To give her the means to help herself. But I cannot do more. She must make her own life."

"I am a woman," I whispered. "And I love you. You are the sun, moon and stars. Don't leave me, Rune!"

But Rune could not hear. The mirror misted over and turned to grey.

For a heartbeat I was cold stone. Then the bird flew past me, trilling merrily. I snatched her in her flight and hurled her against the wall, where she smashed into a thousand tinkling pieces.

I wept until I was sick. I wept until there was not one tear left in me. For a little, I must have fallen asleep, for I woke to find the kitten pressed against my neck and the puppy curled by my side. *They forgive everything*, I thought. *Even the most terrible of rages, the most violent of acts, they forgive.*

It was possible, then, to get up from the bed. I poured water from the jug, washed my face, cleaned up as best I could. I knelt down and gathered every fragment of the bird, every last golden cog and wheel, every last tiny glittering feather. She was broken; she would never fly again. I wrapped her pieces in a silken kerchief and held her in my hands. She weighed almost nothing.

When someone dies, there are supposed to be words spoken. I could not think what they might be. "I'm never going to do that again," I whispered. "I'm never going to let anger get the better of me. I'm not going to scare people into doing what I want. I'm not going to let people scare me into doing what I know is wrong. I'm sorry. You were so beautiful." After all, there did seem to be more tears. When I had shed them, I tucked the silken kerchief into my secret hiding place, alongside my books and my wax tablet.

Then I had to face it, the wonderful thing, the terrible thing. I could marry Rune. If I went to my mother now and told her the truth, it could still happen. I loved him. Maybe he didn't love me, not the way he loved Laerke, but he was fond of me. Mother could dispose of Laerke; nobody in the household would even know she had existed. The wedding could go ahead as planned. If I told Rune how scared I was on the glass mountain, if I begged him to take me away, surely he would do it. Hadn't he said I should make my own life? Wasn't this the life I had longed for through all those lonely years of waiting? It was within my grasp. If I wanted it, I could have it.

I lay down on the bed with my kitten on one side and my puppy on the other, and told them my plan.

Midsummer, and my sixteenth birthday. The wedding was set for dusk; if the guests thought it odd that the bridegroom did not appear earlier, they made no comment. The folk from the Realm Beneath had been quaffing ale all day and were in high spirits. When the time came to gather, the other guests clustered together at one end of the reception hall. Lamps hung from the walls; in the chamber next door, a long table was set with cups and platters I had never seen in my life before. They looked as if they were made of real gold. "My grandmother's," Mother had said. "Not used since I married your father. One day you'll be bringing them out for your own daughter's wedding, Hulde. That gives me great pride. Great pride."

Now here I was, standing beside her in my stiff wedding gown, with my feet squeezed into the too-small shoes and my face covered by the veil, waiting. I was good at waiting; I'd had a lot of practice. But this was different. It was all I could manage not to collapse from sheer terror. My heart was juddering in my chest and my body was all cold sweat. It was just as well nobody could see my face.

There were musicians. Where Mother had got them from I had no idea, but now they struck up a fanfare, and into the hall came Rune, quite alone. He was clad in snowy white, the colour of the beautiful bear he had been, the bear I had loved with all my heart. He walked the length of the hall toward us, and I saw that the man had the same blue eyes as the bear, eyes as lovely as a summer sky. I began to understand why Laerke had broken the rules and looked at him, that night of the spilled wax.

He was very solemn. He looked more like a man attending a burial than his own wedding. At the foot of the raised platform where Mother and I stood, he stopped and bowed. "My ladies."

Mother dropped into a curtsy. "My lord prince," she said.

I bobbed my own awkward curtsy, but said nothing, lest my voice come out as a squeak of terror.

"Come up beside us, Prince Rune," Mother said. "Take my daughter's hand in yours."

"Ah," said Rune.

The crowd stirred. People craned their necks to see.

"There's something I must tell you," Rune said, half-turning so everyone could hear him. "I am bound by a solemn vow; a magical vow that I cannot break for fear of my life. I can marry only the woman who can wash this shirt clean." He brought out the shirt from the pouch at his waist; though rather crumpled, it did not look soiled. "There are three drops of wax here, near the right sleeve. She who can wash them out is my true bride. She and no other."

Mother was quivering with fury. Still, she managed to keep her voice in check. There was a whole hall full of people watching and listening. "I do not understand, Prince Rune," she said. "We have an agreement. You have promised to wed my daughter, and here she is, waiting. Would you break your word?"

Rune smiled. "If your daughter can wash the shirt clean, then I will marry her."

Mother cursed under her breath. She could not defy him. A magical vow had to be respected. "Very well," she snapped, then waved a hand at the household steward. "Fetch a bowl of warm water, soft soap, a brush. Now!"

The crowd was loving this. They edged closer, not wanting to miss a moment. The hall was abuzz with excited voices, though, knowing my mother, most kept their comments to an undertone.

I stood there like a forgotten statue as the materials for washing were brought in and set on a small table, up on the raised area where folk could see. Rune had not moved; he was at the foot of the steps, grave and silent.

"Now," Mother said grandly, "let us proceed, though I do find this all rather ridiculous. Daughter, push back your veil or you'll get it wet."

I lifted the veil and threw it back over my hair. Took a long look at Rune, with his glossy black hair and his summer-blue eyes and his fine man's body. Looked back at my mother. Straight into her eyes. "I won't do it," I said.

For a moment she stood stunned, unable to believe it. Then she went white. Then an angry red appeared in her cheeks, and her veins stood out, and her eyes looked about to pop from her head. Despite myself, I took a step backward.

"*What did you say?*" She spoke so quietly most of the crowd would not have heard. Her tone turned my blood to ice.

"I said, I won't do it. I won't wash the shirt." I willed myself not to faint, not to weep, not to lose control of myself in any way at all. "If that means I can't marry the prince, then so be it." I held my back straight and my head high, as she had taught me.

She lifted her hand to strike me. I did not flinch, though I knew what damage those long nails could do. Rune took a step forward, began to say something, perhaps, *No!* And Mother, maybe deciding she did not want her daughter to be married with a set of bleeding scars across her cheek, withdrew her hand. "Give me the shirt!" she snarled.

Rune handed her the garment and she plunged it into the water. She pummelled and wrung and twisted and scrubbed. She scratched at the stain with her nails. She rubbed it against the bowl. She spat on it and cursed it and, in the end, took the sodden garment from the water and held it up. What had been a tiny blemish, a mere three drops, now spread across the entire front of the shirt. The more she had washed it, the worse the stain had become.

"Sorcery!" Mother shouted. "Evil enchantments! Foul trickery! There's no woman in the world who could get this wretched thing clean!"

Rune glanced sideways; gave the smallest nod of his head.

"I can," said Laerke, stepping out of the crowd. She was in a gown and apron of plain grey, and her red hair was demurely plaited down her back. Her eyes were all courage. *Brave Laerke confronts the Wicked Queen.*

"Fetch clean water," said Rune. "Let us make this quite fair."

Mother was seething. She was simmering like a pot on the fire. I clutched my hands together, wondering if I would see Laerke torn apart before my eyes, and perhaps Rune too. If Mother killed them it would be my fault.

The steward brought clean water. When all was ready Laerke stepped forward, rolling up her sleeves. Rune handed her the dripping shirt; they were avoiding each other's eyes. Laerke moved up to the bowl and dipped in the shirt. She soaped it gently. She swirled it around. She touched the stain with her hand, then lifted the garment out.

It was snowy white. It was as white as the most beautiful bear in all the world. It was a garment fit for a prince. "There," Laerke said, holding it up.

The folk standing close nodded and pointed and exclaimed how perfectly clean it was. There was no way Mother could pretend otherwise. There was no way out.

"This is my true bride," Rune said quietly, and he took Laerke's hand in his. "I'm sorry, Hulde. I honour and respect you, but I cannot marry you. It could never have been. A man cannot wed a troll."

A troll. I had barely time to take the word in when my mother let out an unearthly shriek. The sound made the whole hall rattle and shake. The torches flared; the benches wobbled; folk gasped and clutched on to one another.

She screamed again and the floor shuddered. There were words in her cry, ugly, terrible words, some for Rune, some for Laerke, and some for me. Things I had never thought I would hear, even from her. Things I wished I could un-hear. If I had ever thought my mother loved me, even the tiniest bit, I knew now that for her I was only a means to an end, a commodity she could use to gain herself a fortune. Vile things tumbled and gushed and spewed out of her. Even the folk from the Realm Beneath blocked their ears. Rune had his arm around Laerke; they had backed away from the platform. I wanted to run. I wanted to hide. I wanted to be anywhere but here. Instead I stood motionless as the foul wave of insults crashed over me.

The third scream was her undoing. She filled her lungs, tipped her head back and gave a mighty bellow. There was a popping sound, a change in the air, and suddenly I was teetering on the brink of a great hole in the floor, a hole so deep it seemed to have no bottom. I threw myself backwards and fell sprawling on the tiles.

She was gone. My mother, the Queen of the Mountain, was gone. Her anger had destroyed her. I sucked in a breath. Staggered to my feet. Shucked off my silver shoes. Now I was queen, and there could be no running away.

I held up my hands. The crowd fell silent.

"Please leave the hall," I said. "There will be no wedding."

Things happened. I made them happen. Rune and Laerke helped me. There was a search for what remained of my mother, conducted by the wild kinsfolk, who were good at doing things underground. They found very little. I asked them, in passing, if there were others of our kind living elsewhere, and they said there were, though they could be hard to find. Everywhere there were mountains, there were trolls, they said. Everywhere there were bridges, there were trolls. Some friendly, some not so friendly. Troll was a name other folk gave them; they preferred to be known as hill folk. It was a good idea to take gifts, they said. They drew me a map, with likely spots marked on it. Then they left.

I despatched the other guests homeward. They went all too gladly.

Rune and Laerke offered to take me with them. Or, at least, he did. I was not so sure Laerke liked the idea, though she smiled and agreed when he said it.

"Thank you, but no," I said. "I wish you a happy life."

So they left, and I watched them go from my window, with my kitten in my arms and my puppy at my feet. My friends needed no winding up now; they were just like real ones. I watched until the most beautiful man in the world and the brave girl from the story vanished down the mountain on their long journey to the Far Isles and that lovely, light-filled castle I had once dreamed might be mine. I wondered for a little if I had been stupid to say no. But not for long.

I made a count of what was in the treasure room. I gave the servants three silver pieces each and told them they could stay or go, whatever they chose. The steward said he would stay. I put him in charge of the castle.

I packed a bag with a few clothes and all my treasures: the wax tablet and stylus, the books, the silken kerchief with the remains of my bird. Maybe, somewhere in the world, there was someone clever enough to mend her. I took a small bag of silver. I took some bread and cheese wrapped up in a red and white cloth, because that was what folk did in stories. I told the steward I would be back some time.

Then I set out, with my kitten on my shoulder and my puppy at my heels, to make my own story.

❋

OUR BACKERS

ICONDEROGA PUBLICATIONS PARTLY funded this amazing anthology via crowdfunding. The following list are our incredible supporters, those who made *Aurum* possible. Thank you sincerely for your generosity, support, and patience.

Adrian Smith
Alan Baxter
Alethea Peterson
Amanda Nixon
Anthony Ferguson
Anthony Panegyres
Ashley DeGroot
Ashley Knight
Brittany Shaw Nichols
Carly
Carol Ryles
Catriona Mills
Chad Bowden
Damien Warman and
Juliette Woods
Dave Versace
David Lars Chamberlain
Devin Jeyathurai
Dominic Quach
Elizabeth Fitzgerald
Finbarr Farragher
Garth Nix
Gavran
Geoff White
Gwenhael Le Moine
Helen Binks
Helen Stubbs
J. J. Irwin
Jason Nahrung
Joey Shoji
Jules Jones
Karen Elphick
Kate Tonkin
Kathleen T. Hanrahan
Kelda Knipe
Kristobelle
Lara Hopkins
LynC
Marie Hodgkinson
Mark Catalfano
Nathan Burrage
Pat McNamara
Pia Van Ravestein
R. L. Floyd
Rick D
Robert N Stephenson
Roger Silverstein
Roman
Rowland Rowlands
Simo Muinonen
Stefanie Weiss
Stuart Dunstan
SwordFire
Tarron Wheeler
Tasha Turner
The Morley family
Thomas Bull
Tom Dullemond
Tsana Dolichva
Zoe

ABOUT THE AUTHORS

Joanne Anderton writes speculative fiction for anyone who likes their worlds a little different. She sprinkles a pinch of science fiction to spice up her fantasy, and thinks horror adds flavour to everything. She has won the Aurealis, Ditmar and Australian Shadows awards.

Stephanie Gunn is an Aurealis- and Ditmar-nominated writer of speculative fiction. In another life she was a scientist, but now spends her time surrounded by words instead of test tubes, splitting her time between writing, reading and reviewing. Her work has appeared in various anthologies, including the Aurealis Award nominated *Bloodstones*, *Kisses by Clockwork* (which contains "Escapement", set in the same world as "Pinion"), *Hear Me Roar* and *Defying Doomsday*, and the Aurealis Award winning *Bloodlines*. Her fiction has won multiple Tin Duck awards, for the best short stories published in Western Australia. She lives in Perth with her family, including the requisite cat who cares not a jot for words, but thinks that books are fantastic to knock onto the floor and that warm laptops are great for sleeping on. She is currently at work on several novellas and novels. She can be found online at stephaniegunn.com.

New Zealand born, Australian resident **Juliet Marillier** writes historical fantasy novels and short stories, mostly for adult readers. Among her works are the Blackthorn & Grim series, the Sevenwaters series and the Shadowfell series. Juliet's books are published internationally and have won numerous awards. Her lifelong love of folklore, fairy tales and mythology is a major influence on her writing. Juliet's other passion is rescuing and rehabilitating old or sick dogs. She is a member of the Order of Bards, Ovates and Druids (OBOD). Juliet's website: www.julietmarillier.com

Angela (Angie) Rega is a belly dancing Librarian and language teacher with a passion for folklore, fairy tales and furry creatures. She was raised in a multi-lingual household where nobody finished a sentence in the same language and still struggles with syntax. Her short stories have appeared in publications including *The Year's Best Australian Fantasy and Horror*, *Crossed Genres*, BellaDonna Publishing, PS Publications and World Weaver Press. She keeps a small website here: angierega.webs.com

Cat Sparks is a multi-award-winning Australian author, editor and artist. A former fiction editor of *Cosmos Magazine*, she also worked as a media monitor, political and archaeological photographer, graphic designer and manager of Agog! Press. Cat directed two speculative fiction festivals at the NSW Writers' Centre and was a speaker at literary events including NSWWC's Quantum Words, Sydney Writers' Festival, Write Around the Murray, Thirroul Readers and Writers Festival, ANU Student Research Conference, Melbourne University's ThoughtLab, SLQ's Our Digital Future and Worldcon 75 Helsinki. Cat's debut novel, *Lotus Blue* (Skyhorse 2017) was shortlisted for the Compton Crook, Aurealis and Ditmar Awards. Her collection, *The Bride Price* was published in 2013. Seventy of her short stories have been published since 2000 and her 22 awards include the Peter McNamara Conveners Award for services to Australia's speculative fiction industry. She recently completed a Doctorate of Philosophy—Media, Creative Arts and Social Inquiry through Curtin University.

Lucy Sussex was born in Christchurch, New Zealand. She has abiding interests in women's lives, Australiana, and crime fiction. Her award-winning fiction includes the novel, *The Scarlet Rider* (1996, reprint Ticonderoga 2015). She has five short story collections. Her *Women Writers and Detectives in the Nineteenth Century* (2012) examines the mothers of the mystery genre. *Blockbuster: Fergus Hume and The Mystery of a Hansom Cab* (Text), won the 2015 Victorian Community History Award and was shortlisted for the Ngaio Marsh Award. She is currently a Creative Fellow at the State Library of Victoria.

Susan Wardle is a Wollongong-based writer and graduate of Clarion South. Her short stories have appeared in a range of small press publications and anthologies including Ticonderoga Publications, *Overland*, *Fables and Reflections*, *Antipodean SF*, *Shadowed Realms* and *Lady Churchill's Rosebud Wristlet*. Susan works full time, writes far less time and reads way too late. In between all this she is attempting to raise two small boys and a rambunctious dog.

ACKNOWLEDGMENTS

All stories are original to this anthology.

AVAILABLE FROM TICONDEROGA PUBLICATIONS

978-0-9586856-6-5 Troy BY Simon Brown
978-0-9586856-7-2 The Workers' Paradise EDS Farr & Evans
978-0-9586856-8-9 Fantastic Wonder Stories ED Russell B. Farr
978-0-9803531-0-5 Love in Vain BY Lewis Shiner
978-0-9803531-2-9 Belong ED Russell B. Farr
978-0-9803531-4-3 Ghost Seas BY Steven Utley
978-0-9803531-6-7 Magic Dirt: the best of Sean Williams
978-0-9803531-8-1 The Lady of Situations BY Stephen Dedman
978-0-9806288-2-1 Basic Black BY Terry Dowling
978-0-9806288-3-8 Make Believe BY Terry Dowling
978-0-9806288-4-5 Scary Kisses ED Liz Grzyb
978-0-9806288-6-9 Dead Sea Fruit BY Kaaron Warren
978-0-9806288-8-3 The Girl With No Hands BY Angela Slatter
978-0-9807813-1-1 Dead Red Heart ED Russell B. Farr
978-0-9807813-2-8 More Scary Kisses ED Liz Grzyb
978-0-9807813-4-2 Heliotrope BY Justina Robson
978-0-9807813-7-3 Matilda Told Such Dreadful Lies BY Lucy Sussex
978-1-921857-01-0 Bluegrass Symphony BY Lisa L. Hannett
978-1-921857-06-5 The Hall of Lost Footsteps BY Sara Douglass
978-1-921857-03-4 Damnation and Dames EDS Liz Grzyb & Amanda Pillar
978-1-921857-08-9 Bread and Circuses BY Felicity Dowker
978-1-921857-17-1 The 400-Million-Year Itch BY Steven Utley
978-1-921857-22-5 The Scarlet Rider BY Lucy Sussex
978-1-921857-24-9 Wild Chrome BY Greg Mellor
978-1-921857-27-0 Bloodstones ED Amanda Pillar
978-1-921857-30-0 Midnight and Moonshine BY Lisa L. Hannett & Angela Slatter
978-1-921857-65-2 Mage Heart BY Jane Routley
978-1-921857-66-9 Fire Angels BY Jane Routley
978-1-921857-67-6 Aramaya BY Jane Routley
978-1-921857-86-7 Magic Dirt: the best of Sean Williams (hc)
978-1-921857-35-5 Dreaming of Djinn ED Liz Grzyb
978-1-921857-38-6 Prickle Moon BY Juliet Marillier
978-1-921857-43-0 The Bride Price BY Cat Sparks
978-1-921857-46-1 The Year of Ancient Ghosts BY Kim Wilkins
978-1-921857-33-1 Invisible Kingdoms BY Steven Utley
978-1-921857-70-6 Havenstar BY Glenda Larke
978-1-921857-59-1 Everything is a Graveyard BY Jason Fischer
978-1-921857-63-8 The Assassin of Nara BY R.J. Ashby
978-1-921857-77-5 Death at the Blue Elephant BY Janeen Webb
978-1-921857-81-2 The Emerald Key BY Christine Daigle & Stewart Sternberg
978-1-921857-89-8 Kisses by Clockwork ED Liz Grzyb
978-1-925212-05-1 Angel Dust ED Liz Grzyb
978-1-925212-16-7 The Finest Ass in the Universe BY Anna Tambour
978-1-925212-36-5 Hear Me Roar ED Liz Grzyb
978-1-921857-56-0 Bloodlines ED Amanda Pillar
978-1-925212-45-7 Crow Shine BY Alan Baxter
978-1-925212-54-9 Ecopunk! EDS Liz Grzyb & Cat Sparks

LIMITED HARDCOVER EDITIONS

978-0-9806288-1-4 The Infernal BY Kim Wilkins
978-1-921857-54-6 Black-Winged Angels BY Angela Slatter

EBOOKS

978-0-9803531-5-0 Ghost Seas BY Steven Utley
978-1-921857-93-5 The Girl With No Hands BY Angela Slatter
978-1-921857-99-7 Dead RED Heart ED Russell B. Farr
978-1-921857-94-2 More Scary Kisses ED Liz Grzyb
978-0-9807813-5-9 Heliotrope BY Justina Robson
978-1-921857-36-2 Dreaming of Djinn ED Liz Grzyb
978-1-921857-40-9 Prickle Moon BY Juliet Marillier
978-1-921857-92-8 The Year of Ancient Ghosts BY Kim Wilkins
978-1-921857-28-7 Bloodstones ED Amanda Pillar
978-1-921857-04-1 Damnation and Dames ED Liz Grzyb & Amanda Pillar
978-1-921857-31-7 Midnight and Moonshine BY Lisa L. Hannett & Angela Slatter
978-1-921857-44-7 The Bride Price BY Cat Sparks
978-1-921857-60-7 Everything is a Graveyard BY Jason Fischer
978-1-921857-64-5 The Assassin of Nara BY R.J. Ashby
978-1-921857-78-2 Death at the Blue Elephant BY Janeen Webb
978-1-921857-82-9 The Emerald Key BY Christine Daigle & Stewart Sternberg
978-1-921857-57-7 Kisses by Clockwork ED Liz Grzyb
978-1-925212-06-8 Angel Dust BY Ian McHugh
978-1-925212-17-4 The Finest Ass in the Universe BY Anna Tambour
978-1-925212-37-2 Hear Me Roar ED Liz Grzyb
978-1-921857-38-9 Bloodlines ED Amanda Pillar
978-1-925212-37-2 Crow Shine BY Alan Baxter
978-1-925212-37-2 Ecopunk! EDS Liz Grzyb & Cat Sparks

THE YEAR'S BEST AUSTRALIAN FANTASY & HORROR SERIES EDITED BY LIZ GRZYB & TALIE HELENE

978-0-9807813-8-0 Year's Best Australian Fantasy & Horror 2010 (hc)
978-0-9807813-9-7 Year's Best Australian Fantasy & Horror 2010 (tpb)
978-0-921057-98-0 Year's Best Australian Fantasy & Horror 2010 (ebook)
978-0-921057-13-3 Year's Best Australian Fantasy & Horror 2011 (hc)
978-0-921057-14-0 Year's Best Australian Fantasy & Horror 2011 (tpb)
978-0-921057-15-7 Year's Best Australian Fantasy & Horror 2011 (ebook)
978-0-921057-48-5 Year's Best Australian Fantasy & Horror 2012 (hc)
978-0-921057-49-2 Year's Best Australian Fantasy & Horror 2012 (tpb)
978-0-921057-50-8 Year's Best Australian Fantasy & Horror 2012 (ebook)
978-0-921057-72-0 Year's Best Australian Fantasy & Horror 2013 (hc)
978-0-921057-73-7 Year's Best Australian Fantasy & Horror 2013 (tpb)
978-0-921057-74-4 Year's Best Australian Fantasy & Horror 2013 (ebook)
978-0-925212-18-1 Year's Best Australian Fantasy & Horror 2014 (hc)
978-0-925212-19-8 Year's Best Australian Fantasy & Horror 2014 (tpb)
978-0-925212-20-4 Year's Best Australian Fantasy & Horror 2014 (ebook)
978-0-925212-47-1 Year's Best Australian Fantasy & Horror 2015 (hc)
978-0-925212-48-8 Year's Best Australian Fantasy & Horror 2015 (tpb)
978-0-925212-49-5 Year's Best Australian Fantasy & Horror 2015 (ebook)

THANK YOU

The publisher would sincerely like to thank

Joanne Anderton, Lucy Sussex, Stephanie Gunn, Cat Sparks, Juliet Marillier, Angela Rega, Susan Wardle, Liz Grzyb, Donna Maree Hanson, Pete Kempshall, Karen Brooks, Jeremy G. Byrne, Marianne de Pierres, Jonathan Strahan, Peter McNamara, Ellen Datlow, Grant Stone, Sean Williams, Simon Brown, David Cake, Simon Oxwell, Grant Watson, Sue Manning, Steven Utley, Lewis Shiner, Bill Congreve, Janeen Webb, Jack Dann, Amanda Pillar, Angela Slatter, Kim Wilkins, Kate Forsyth, Garth Nix, Anthony Phillips, Anna Tambour, Alan Baxter, Deborah Biancotti, Stephen Dedman, Jason Fischer, Dirk Flinthart, Kim Gaal, Kathleen Jennings, Lisa L. Hannett, Robert Hood, Jane Routley, Martin Livings, Rivqa Rafael, Kirstyn McDermott, Jason Nahrung, Kaaron Warren, the Mt Lawley Mafia, the Nedlands Yakuza, Shane Jiraiya Cummings, Angela Challis, Kate Williams, Andrew Williams, Talie Helene, Kathryn Linge, Al Chan, Brian Clarke, Alisa and Tehani, Mel & Phil, Jennifer Sudbury, Paul Pryztula, Helen Grzyb, Debbie Lee, Hayley Lane, Georgina Walpole, Rushelle Lister, Nerida Fearnley-Gill, everyone we've missed . . .

. . . and you.

IN MEMORY OF

Eve Johnson

Sara Douglass

Steven Utley

Brian Clarke

www.ingramcontent.com/pod-product-compliance
Lightning Source LLC
Chambersburg PA
CBHW030825310726
48980CB00006B/643/J
9781925212334